THE VIS REMAINING TRILOGY

HAVOC
OF
WOLVES

H. E. SALIAN

Havoc of Wolves by H. E. SALIAN

ISBN: 978-1-7348004-3-2

For my family.

CHAPTER 1

Stori watched in a trance as Bry slumped at his desk while working. He blinked and frowned before turning to catch her eye, and Stori realized she had been staring. She offered a smile back, not even pretending she was focusing on her own work.

Bry's lip curled in a teasing smile. He raised his eyebrow and glanced between her and the desk covered in paperwork.

Stori smiled back with a shrug.

"You kids want me to leave?" The voice snapped Stori out of her thoughts with a flush. She turned a shy smile toward the far corner of Bry's study where Lawr sat at his desk, staring with bemusement and an arched eyebrow.

"No, of course not. We have work to do." Stori tried not to trip over her words as she quickly focused her attention on her own makeshift desk and the paperwork flooding it.

She glanced back to Lawr. His expression remained a perfect picture of unconvinced. He hummed as his gaze shifted lazily toward Bry.

Bry coughed. "We're working."

Lawr grumbled to himself at that. Stori watched a variety of emotions flit across his face in a rare expression of uncertainty.

"All the same," Lawr finally started again, standing up to stretch, "I'll take a break and grab lunch. You two want anything?"

Stori frowned suspiciously when the older man glanced at her. She hadn't known him to once take a break for himself. She watched him try to subtly sneak his AaD under his jacket and guessed this wasn't going to be the first.

"No thanks," Bry answered.

Stori's frown deepened.

"Actually, if you could bring some soup, I would greatly appreciate it."

Lawr turned an irritated gaze back to her as he paused at the door.

Stori couldn't help the smirk that twitched about her lips.

Now you do have to take a break and get lunch.

"If you don't mind," she said with her sweetest smile as Lawr's expression turned all kinds of sour.

"Fine," Lawr finally lamented, opening the door, "I'll get some for Bry too."

"I'm good, actual—"

Bry was cut off as Lawr closed the door just shy of slamming it.

A questioning gaze turned back to Stori.

She shrugged.

"It's good for him to actually take a break."

Bry stared at her with the same level of belief Lawr had shown for the soup request.

Stori ignored him and stared at the papers on her desk. The same paperwork she had been making zero progress on all morning. She sighed dramatically, turning her attention back to Bry.

"Are you all right?" Bry asked, her expression suddenly filled with concern.

Stori tried not to stiffen with the guilt of having made him worry. For the last several days, he'd been constantly concerned for her health. Ever since her birthday. She blushed at the thought.

"I am perfectly all right. As I keep telling you." Stori smiled at him.

"Yeah? Good." He returned to frowning at his own desk covered in documents and never-ending work.

Stori watched as Bry started distractedly rubbing at the scar on his face. She looked away, and her stomach sank. She could guess where his mind had wandered. But the subject of his father was never up for discussion.

Stori turned her frown toward her own work, though her thoughts didn't follow.

He has enough to worry about with his half-sister coming. That alone is stressful.

Stori stroked her hair in place as the thought held her attention.

What will she be like? Caelyn?

Stori's mind snapped straight to Loreda, but she shook her head to quickly dispel that notion. At just fourteen years old, Caelyn was still so young. Of course, she wouldn't have Loreda's calloused nature.

Stori shook her head to clear her mind of the dancing musings. She hoped the transition from tax laws to civil disputes was a step up since she had been inadvertently stuck with it.

She had, after all, only briefly asked about it after realizing how easy it had been for Loreda to use the public's discontent to her advantage. Chesler unfortunately seemed to have taken her interest as a curiosity to study every civil action raised since Bry's coronation. There were many.

Reading through reports of so many people dissatisfied was disheartening. Even if the majority were from right after his coronation, before they had a chance to know what kind of king he would be.

Stori worked to calm her anxiety about how quickly people had decided to hate Bry. Especially when they were planning on announcing what they had discovered about Oracaede as soon as Lawr fixed the AaD network.

I hope it takes Lawr a long time to fix.

The thought snuck into and registered in her mind before the guilt could chase it out.

The door opened, distracting Stori from both the thought and the guilt.

Lawr returned with a tray stacked high with bowls of food and a smug look.

"If I have to take a break to eat, so do you," he stated, setting the tray on Stori's desk and grabbing two snugly wrapped sandwiches off the top. He tossed one to Bry before returning to his own seat.

Lawr paused before sitting down, his smug smirk returning.

"Or did you still want me to eat out so you two can 'work?'"

"Lawr!" Bry chucked a random piece of junk from his desk at the older man as Stori hid a blush behind her new pile of food.

"We are working," she reiterated.

"I know." Lawr continued grinning.

CHAPTER 2

"H id!" The exuberant voice was, as always, an unwelcome intrusion into Hid's sleep-addled brain. He rolled over in his sleeping blanket to distance himself from the voice as it called his name several more times.

"Hidalgo, come on. Wake up!" The voice continued in the same jolly tone.

Hid muttered a threat that came out half in Spanish and all asleep.

"Dolly!"

Hid's eyes snapped open, and he grabbed the first solid object in sight, a boot, and chucked it toward the offending voice. A stream of Spanish cusses rolled off his tongue as he sat up to glare at Aike.

"I told you never to call me that, *gringo*," Hid snapped.

Aike's goofy grin was already in place and did not falter.

"Morning, sunshine!" Aike chirped in response.

Hid's return growl was cut short by an uncontrolled yawn. He gave up on sleeping and telling Aike off in favor of shrugging on his jacket and boots.

A boot. Singular.

He blinked and tried forcing his brain into cooperation to search for the other boot. It appeared in front of him, dangling from Aike's hand.

"Throwing stuff at your team leader is bad form, ya know," Aike said with an accent that twisted every word sideways.

Hid snatched his boot back and yanked it on as Aike stood and moved on to his next victim.

Stretching the kink out of his back, Hid noted that Aike had already started the fire before he moved off into the forest to relieve himself and gather an armful of more firewood.

He wandered back into camp just as Aike succeeded in waking Sa'dia up.

Sa'dia awoke, slinging enough curses in Arabic and English to wake the rest of the team.

Aike laughed as his attention returned to Hid. "Somewhere between the two of you, I can always count on waking everyone up."

Hid ignored him as he stalked into the camp and took notice of the direction the rest of the team headed. They each wandered off into the wooded area.

His worry spiked as soon as his team was out of sight, but he gulped a breath of air and told himself it was just the residual fear from his Shade encounter.

Dropping his bundle of firewood, Hid moved on to watch Aike balance on his toes by the fire, humming a too-cheerful tone as he set up the cooking pot full of water.

"You're that nervous about seeing the chief, huh?" Hid blinked, pausing his search through a nearby pack for breakfast oats.

It's my job to be stressed, hermano. Stay in your own lane.

Aike hummed an affirmative note as he continued staring into the fire.

"If it's another job, so soon, Idir's injury won't be healed," Hid stated with a frown. The Aynur chief, Erasyl, was usually lenient about giving them a rest between jobs. His wife, Reb, however, never was.

Hid shifted anxiously as he looked at the dark circles under Aike's eyes.

"No one on the team's completely caught up on all their missing sleep from the Shade attacks." Hid stated.

Aike only hummed and rubbed his eyes.

"At least everyone is sleeping through the night now," Hid started again, new worry pouring through his mind, "but we're all still pretty ragged."

"We'll handle it when we meet the chief," Aike returned, nodding to himself as the rest of the team started trickling back into camp.

"While a simple-minded cat could grasp the concept, I wouldn't expect you—" Bary's remark was cut short by an equally insulting and vapid comment from Sa'dia as the two entered the camp already amid their first argument of the day.

Idir and Caesar Apollo were the next to return, each with a handful of berry vines, though Idir only used his good arm, while his other remained stationary in a sling. Caesar Apollo also carried a huge armful of firewood, enough to last a day.

The two behemoth-sized men approached Aike and handed over the berries before Caesar Apollo dropped the firewood too. He nodded in Idir's direction while pointing at the berries.

"Thanks, Idir." Aike hummed with a smile as he examined the berries. "Where did ya find them?"

The dark man pointed out a direction with a grunt. "Short walk by the boulders."

"They'll be great with breakfast." Aike cooed as he turned and held the vines out in the air.

Xiulan's fair hand wrapped around the stocks as she passed by on her way back to her sleeping spot. She sat in a graceful motion and started picking the berries, separating them into eight little piles.

Hid gave Caesar Apollo a nod of thanks, mostly for making sure Idir didn't aggravate his injury by trying to carry everything.

Caesar Apollo nodded, understanding as he and Idir both moved to sit and watch the fire.

"Retha!" Aike called over his shoulder at the forest. "Ya gonna stop tormenting whatever small animal you caught and bring it here for breakfast?"

Hid cast an eye toward the forest when he caught a glimpse of a small shadow bouncing in their direction.

"Make sure it's dead!" Hid called and watched the shadow pause before emerging into the clearing.

Retha bounded over, swinging two small rabbits by their ears.

"Of course they're dead." The small dark girl chirped as she dropped down on a log, already starting to field dress the dead animals. "And I only even broke their legs. My snares are perfect."

Retha held up the half-skinned rabbit in a flaunting gesture while making a face at Hid.

Hid grunted a 'good job' while Aike complimented her on her restrain as he leaned over and pulled a twig from her wild, kinky curls. Retha batted the hand away with a bloody knife.

"My restraint is excellent. I've been working on it," she said, puffing her chest out with a glance at Xiulan.

Xiulan tucked a lock of inky black hair behind her own ear as she returned a soft smile to the younger girl.

Sa'dia scoffed and grumbled as she turned her attention away from an argument with Bary long enough to take in what was around her. Her attention froze when it reached Xiulan and the berries.

"I told you they were edible!" she snapped at Bary, ready for a whole new quarrel.

"Never said they weren't, just that it was improbable," Bary said with a smirk as he gave a handful of berries from his pocket to Xiulan.

Sa'dia held Bary's smirking gaze before lunging for him.

"I was going to pick them!" she yelled.

Hid watched with growing nerves as the two weaved in an animated fashion around the campsite.

"Now, Sa'dia," Aike distracted as he raised his attention from the cooking pot where he had been ignoring them. "I know you love a good run in the morning, but is this the best space?"

Bary suddenly dropped down next to Retha on the log gasping for breath.

"Bary? Did you take your medicine this morning?" Aike asked with a sharp tone that immediately stopped Sa'dia's chase.

Hid's anxiety pinched at the mere question, and he leaned closer for the answer.

Bary shook his head between gasps as he held his chest.

Sa'dia wasted no time grabbing his pack and riffling through it until she held up a vial labeled 'Bary.' She hastened to give it to her bickering partner.

Taking sips between gasps, Bary worked to complete his daily dose before he could catch his breath.

The whole camp waited in frozen silence until Bary could control his breathing and talk again.

"I had another pocketful for you Xiulan. It's Sa'dia's share." Bary grinned and gave Hid a quick glance as a plea to move the conversation along.

Hid cleared his throat and extended a hand toward Sa'dia for the vial. The tanned girl glared at Bary before handing it over.

"You're gonna need to get some more today," she directed Hid as she gave Bary a little shove before standing and moving back to her spot on the ground.

"*Sí*," Hid agreed.

His fear of Bary someday running out was amplified when he gave the small, mostly empty vial a little shake. Only one more dose was left.

He handed it back to Bary with a promise, "We'll get more in our meeting."

Aike took the cue and stood up. All attention snapped to him.

"The meeting today is likely a mission from Reb, so don't count on any rest between jobs."

A round of groans sounded at the mention of a job from the chief's wife and second-in-command.

"Focus." Hid barely needed to mutter before the grumbling was silenced and the team's attention returned to Aike.

"We'll just play this easy," Aike started again with a nod to Hid. "We'll go in and get the job without the chief or any of the ranking Avare leaders noticing the extent of Idir's injury or the wallop we all took from the Shade's mind tricks."

He turned to Caesar Apollo, "Stay on guard." Toward the girls and Bary, "Run interference and distractions as needed."

Hid watched each of his teammates nod back understanding to Aike in turn. Aike waited for a nod from Hid before he melted back into his normal jocular attitude for the remainder of breakfast.

After the meal was finished and they began packing up camp, Hid made rounds again. Talking with each teammate to make sure they were all mentally well for their trip to the Aynur market.

Even if Aike did not worry about the lingering effects of their encounters with the Shade, Hid was.

All the team members insisted they were fine so Hid returned to gathering the last of his own gear before they all headed out. He matched pace with Aike as they led the way through the grayed-out forest to the next doorway.

A short wait was all they had before Aike could open the doorway into the Empty, and the hike continued.

Hid was relieved distance in the Empty between the sphaeres of Eidola and Glacius Tesca was short this time of year compared to the usual two-day trek.

Small mercies.

Hid nodded to himself as he continued to ignore Aike's incessant prattle in favor of worrying about their meeting with the chief.

Once they reached the desert sphaere, Aike fell back to help Idir out of his sling and to situate the big man's injured arm comfortably and inconspicuously at his side.

Hid adjusted his stride once he saw Aike finish and take his place at the rear of their little precession.

The rest of the walk was silent other than the growing noise from the marketplace. Through the dust-covered tents and stalls, Hid weaved a careful path to the chief's tent. He came to a halt just outside the circle of tents that made up the chief's camp.

Hearing Aike's short whistle, Hid sensed the team scatter without having to look back. He turned to check on Idir. The dark man melted into the shadows of one of the tents. Caesar Apollo stood directly in front of the injured man with the chiseled look of a Roman statue. His silent, towering presence dictated to anyone with a functioning sense of self-preservation to steer clear.

A presence at his side brought Hid's attention back to Aike. The freckled man gave him a smirk and a wink before straightening out his expression. Hid watched the normally goofy features drain of life and energy, settling into a blank mask, before Aike stepped toward the chief's tent.

Hid followed. Schooling his own features to reflect perfect apathy resulted in less of a change than it did in Aike, but he still made the effort.

The tent was poorly lit with a campfire rather than Aequorian torches. Setting the glow of the fabric interior to a shade of orange rather than soft blue.

Aike greeted the chief and the chief's psychotic wife, Reb, with a small bow before he and Hid knelt. Aike launched into a toned-down report of their mission in Eidola, covering all details as quickly as possible for the sake of their knees on the rocky ground.

Hid spoke even more cautiously, adding information if necessary and ensuring their stories matched perfectly.

Most of their lies pertained to the team's mental health and Idir's injury, which had already healed significantly, but they made it out to be even more minor to avoid Reb's unpredictable wrath.

At the end of the report, they both waited in silence for either their next mission or some petty grievance about their last.

Erasyl made a few short and stopping remarks, but nothing Hid considered of consequence. The tent's silence grew more unsettling as Hid fought against glancing over at Reb. The air's stillness suggested she was angry over something, but she always was so it was hard to tell what she had found irritable in their report this time.

"Is fool's injury going to affect his performance on next mission?" Reb snarled the question.

"No," Aike answered, "The injury is only minor and—"

"Shut up, glib rat," Reb snapped. "Wasn't asking a liar."

Her eyes seared holes through him.

"The injury is not severe," Hid answered, making sure to enunciate the words and hide his accent, which had been what set Reb off the last mission report.

A growl from Reb's direction drew Hid's attention again as she turned back to Aike.

"New mission." She spoke in choppy sentences, switching between languages unimpeded. "Devlet Orospu needs more Avare strength for their mission to succeed."

Reb paused to snarl an insult in Erasyl's direction. The chief yawned and ignored it.

Hid's stomach twisted at the mention of the organization. He used the chief's pause to glance at Aike. His long blink suggested they shared the same thought.

Devlet Orospu. Oracaede—Let the bloodbaths begin.

Reb continued. "Stir up trouble in Sentre. Need city in unrest and ready for uprise."

Erasyl shifted forward, pulling all attention toward him. "Their dogs require a meeting with the chiefs in Oroitz, Medius. We go," he said, jerking a quick motion between Reb and himself, then paused to frown.

"They mean change work requirements," Reb snarled.

Erasyl nodded, followed by a grunt.

"Yes, changes. So, keep an AaD open to receive our call when we find an agreement."

Reb snapped curses in three languages before addressing the Wolves again. "Now. You do no more than current orders. We not give Devlet Orospu free work."

"Understood," Aike and Hid said in unison.

Hid did not dare to breathe as he waited. He stayed stressed and hoped Reb would clarify their scope of work.

"Mission starts now," Reb said, throwing a dismissive wave in their direction. "Leave."

But... We need more information.

Hid did not dare question Reb either.

"Chief," Aike started, earning an immediate glower from Reb.

She shifted as though preparing to lunge at him.

"Bary is out of medicine." Aike continued, "He needs more before the mission."

Hid glanced between the chiefs and Aike, hoping for clue as to what his move should be.

"Weak link has all he needs." Reb leveled a challenging gaze at Aike.

"The last mission ran longer and involved more stressors than we anticipated." Aike returned the challenge, though Hid was glad he at least managed to duck his head at the end.

Challenging Reb on any matter is never a solid plan, hermano.

"This next mission will likely be long and taxing as well," Hid added, desperate to pull Reb's enraged gaze toward himself, away from Aike.

Out of the corner of his eye, Hid saw Aike shoot him a thankful but concerned glance.

Both remained still and waited, watching Erasyl for a reaction as Reb continued growling insults at them.

"Reb," Erasyl said, catching Reb's glare with lazy indifference. He jerked his head toward the back of the tent.

Hid dared breathe when Reb started moving. She moved to the back of the tent and rummaged around in a large chest before returning to her seat. She chucked a small object at Aike's face with the clear intention of shattering it.

Luckily, Aike had long since become used to Reb's irrational hatred of him and snatched the vial easily before it struck him.

Reb scoffed. "Now leave."

Hid nodded and hastily moved to leave with Aike a step behind.

Once outside, Hid threw an anxious glance to the shadow of the tent where Idir had been. The dark man was out of sight, but Hid breathed again when he caught a glimpse of Caesar Apollo's shoulder further around the corner. Idir would be there.

"At 3 o'clock and 11."

Hid turned his attention in the directions Aike specified. Ahead and to the left were Sa'dia and Bary. They appeared to be arguing, but it was far too sweet and friendly between them to be anything except an act. Not that the three ranking tribe members would be able to tell as they joined in the discussion.

Hid caught the hint of a shadow he recognized as Retha. The small dark girl darted passed one of the arguing tribe members, no doubt relieving the woman of a few valuables before disappearing through the tents.

With a casual glance to his right, Hid watched the small scene Xiulan had created. The dark-haired beauty stood poised next to a stall with a mess of fruit spilling out on the ground around her. Hid could hear the silken tone of her sweet voice as she again apologized to the merchant and military leader, who were picking up fruit. Xiulan made an entire show of fanning herself and holding her blouse open just enough to keep the militant man's full attention as he aimlessly fumbled at the mess of fruit on the ground.

Hid shock his head at the scene. He couldn't fathom how anyone could have thought Xiulan's graceful, perfectly calculated movements would have been clumsy enough to cause the mess in the first place.

That is the beauty of her spell.

Hid sighed as Retha popped out near Xiulan and again moved to the two distracted men working on the fruit with nimble hands.

"Ah, right where we left them," Aike noted with his token goofy grin back in place. He handed the vial of medicine over to Hid before he started walking a few steps and calling back, "Round them up, eh."

Hid pinched his fingers in his mouth and gave a pitched whistle that was barely heard over the din as he followed after Aike. Within moments, every team member fell in step in the space between them. Hid gave a second, short whistle to let Aike know everyone was accounted for.

Hid stayed in the rear. He was glad for the chance to watch over his teammates and make sure there was no trouble until they reached the edge of the marketplace. Only when they reach that level of safety did he switch his focus to his AaD tablet.

He passed through the rest of the team, handing Bary his medicine, before reaching Aike and changing their direction of travel toward the quickest route to the nearest doorway.

Only after they were safely in the Empty did Hid turn his focus to their mission.

Aike was thinking hard. Hid could tell because he was humming and groaning excessively, which were always tell-tale signs.

"I assume 'stir up trouble' means *civil* unrest in Sentre?" Hid started.

"But 'ready for an uprising' could mean we need to rile the city up more aggressively. Riots, murder, and the like," Aike challenged with a hum that turned into a groan.

"Not giving Oracaede any free work is going to be impossible with those vague instructions." Hid tried not to groan himself. He had a small, vain hope that Aike might have teased more definite instructions out of Reb's words than he had.

"Hey," Aike shoved Hid a step to the side to gain his attention before he laced his hands behind his head, "at least it couldn't be any worse than our last job."

"*Hermano*, every time you say that you jinx us."

"Really?" Aike tipped his head back in thought. "Oh, you're right."

Of course, I'm right.

"In that case, this will definitely be so much more difficult than our last job." Aike's grin took on a shark-like appearance. "Catching a Shade for Oracaede will have been so easy by comparison."

"Aike, shut up."

CHAPTER 3

S verre kicked at a remnant of a sword that hadn't burned with the bodies of the Oroitz battlefield. The multiple pyres had done their job to erase the multitude of bodies, but they didn't burn hot enough to melt the odd pieces of metal here and there on the bodies. As such, the former combat zone was strewn with metal bits over all the dried blood stains.

A sharp whistle snapped Sverre's attention to the distant treeline. Not a branch moved to give away Dain's position.

He turned to scan his surroundings for whatever had concerned the sniper. It wasn't the Nomad chief they were waiting to meet. Dain hadn't used the right signal.

A movement to Sverre's right drew his attention as he relaxed. A familiar form took shape over the small hill. The initial relief faded as the man drew closer.

"Echo," Sverre greeted the silent messenger when the man came to a halt in front of him. "What does Atanas want?"

"Boss is angry. He anticipated the king's loss here," Echo stated in a monotone voice.

"King Brynte won on his own, nothing I can do now," Sverre lied without bothering to act convincing.

Echo hummed an unbelieving note but didn't break his training to reply.

"Atanas orders," Echo started, "Win the Aynur chief to Oracaede's side. Need the ally."

Sverre grumbled to himself.

"Atanas knows the Avare hate Oracaede as much as they hate anyone, right?" Sverre said.

He twisted to look back at the forest but stopped when his stitches from the sword wound he received from saving Brynte pulled uncomfortably.

The Nomads are late.

He made a quick gesture to Dain to make sure he hadn't missed the sniper's signal warning of the Nomad's arrival.

Dain whistled a short note that meant 'no.'

Echo didn't spare a glance in the sniper's direction as he continued his empty stare.

"Acknowledged," Sverre finally stated.

Echo bowed a nod before turning to leave. "And fix AaDs, Atanas can't call with messages."

Sverre scoffed. "He didn't *tell* you to say that."

Echo shrugged and gestured to the hill he had appeared over.

"Long walk."

Sverre nodded. This wasn't so much a message from Atanas as it was Echo annoyed at the situation.

Atanas's silent messenger may not have been allowed to speak freely, but he had found ways of repeating things other people said out of context to say what he was thinking. Only when he wasn't around Atanas or Duqa would he dare to do so though.

Echo shifted and started trudging over the hill, moving in the direction of the forest without waiting for a response.

Sverre watched the messenger until he disappeared into the trees to give Dain the same message. He turned over Atanas's exact wording of the orders in his mind, trying to find a loophole that would make the impossible request feasible.

The call of a bird not native to the area made Sverre groan. Dain had spotted the Nomads. Sverre lifted his hand to rub his head, signaling to Dain that he had heard and understood.

Within a couple of moments, a large group of raggedy-looking people shuffled over the horizon and continued the long walk toward Sverre. The Nomads never had the impressive appearance of Sentrians, the Merii, or any other factions Sverre dealt with, but they could bring numbers like no other. Far too many to fight easily.

Sverre ran an unconscious hand from his still-aching ribs from his last unfortunate encounter with Duqa to the stitched laceration in his side.

Too many to fight, period.

He fought the urge to glance back toward Dain.

Echo, don't distract Dain, now.

Sverre had to keep his eye roll in check and hoped his partner was focusing.

The Nomads stopped moving when they were close. Not striking range close, but enough that they could land a hit with a sword before Sverre could draw his gun. He again fought his sense of self-preservation to back up to give himself more maneuverability.

Win over the Aynur chief.

He repeated his orders though he still hadn't found a good way of carrying them out.

"What does Devlet Orospu's dog want?" Rebkka, the chief's wife, spat while the chief only grunted as a greeting.

Sverre nodded a polite greeting. He turned his attention to Erasyl and hoped he could ignore Reb for the entire conversation. He wasn't fond of any Nomads, but Reb always found it necessary to call him a dog anytime they met.

"Come to change agreement, eh," Erasyl stated before Sverre could say anything.

Sverre grimaced. Maybe if making friends wasn't possible, Atanas would accept workable enemies.

"Oracaede requires an equal trade of work for the benefits it offers," Sverre said the line as though it were true. Anyone who heard it could believe it rather than see it for the complete lie it was.

Both husband and wife scoffed with bitter anger at the lie.

"Already equal trade, ghost dog," Reb snapped in the Glasic Tongue before switching to Turkish. "Tribe completing last request now. Then done work for Devlet Orospu."

"Yes, however—"

Erasyl stepped forward, shrinking the distance between them with a growl. "Tribe completing request. If Devlet Orospu adds another request, they pay a separate fee."

"Atanas requires all the tribes led by Aynur to move against the Median king," Sverre stated, ignoring Erasyl's interruption and the fact the man was nearly within striking range. He remained still to avoid them noticing the injuries he hid.

Reb didn't notice him at all as she swore in more languages than Sverre could understand. Erasyl remained silent though Sverre could still see him seething.

"Four tribes were already lost against the Medians," Erasyl finally snarled.

"Oracaede requires more," Sverre answered without thinking, using the exact words Atanas had said every day of his training. He blinked.

Oops.

"What?!" The two leaders exclaimed, each in a different language.

Sverre kept still and silent, watching both their reactions.

Win over the chief? How about walking away alive?

Sverre's doubt of the last one even being possible grew as the husband and wife snarled to each other in a language he wasn't fluent in. He guessed they were arguing about the best method for gutting a dog. If only he wasn't the one they always called 'dog.'

That'd be nice on its own.

Erasyl stepped closer—too close—gesturing angrily and snapping at Sverre in every language the Avare used.

Sverre steeled himself not to step back as he jerked a quick signal to Dain to hold his fire. If he was concerned about the chief's aggression, he could only imagine Dain was reaching twitchy-trigger-finger level of concern.

"The sniper and I will assist your Wolves in Sentre to complete this task to Oracaede's standards," Sverre said, fighting to keep his voice from sounding rushed. He hoped the mention of Dain scoping them would at least shock the pair toward calming down.

A feral growl tore out of Erasyl as he lumbered closer, readying a fist.

"Then do work yourself!" he snapped, swinging a fist of brass knuckles.

Sverre jumped sideways to dodge, and his stitched side immediately notified him it was a poor move.

He ignored it to stop Reb's dagger from the opposite side. Behind him, he could sense Erasyl swinging again.

He jerked out of the way again. Too slow.

The metal-encased fist caught his injured side, throwing him back a step.

Sverre doubled over, clutching at his side and trying to force his lungs to breathe again.

Above him, he saw Erasyl swinging a brass-knuckle fist toward his face.

A sharp crack echoed through the field, interrupting the swing. For a moment, Erasyl's eyes remained wide open, and his body threatened to bash a hole through Sverre's head.

For a moment, Sverre thought he would. That the man could somehow ignore the bloody bullet hole through the center of his head.

The moment passed. Erasyl's body dropped in a heap on the ground. His eyes remained open and unseeing as blood pooled at his head.

Sverre sucked in a breath and staggered back a step, forcing his body upright again despite the shooting pain lighting up his side.

He signaled to Dain to hold his fire again as he watched for Reb's reaction.

So much for winning them over.

Reb stared at her husband's body with a stricken, wide-eyed look.

Sverre scanned the rest of the Nomads. They were quicker to overcome the shock of their leader's death and turned toward Reb for instructions.

"This was not the intended outcome of this meeting, Reb, but the result of hasty actions." Sverre started in as gentle a tone as he could manage while still trying to steady his breathing and hide that his stitches were bleeding again.

Reb's wild eyes snapped to him at the sound of her name.

Sverre studied every emotion flickering across the woman's face with growing concern. He kept one hand behind his back to signal Dain which of their dozens of tactics might work.

Reb dove at him sloppily with a knife in hand. He easily dodged. A sharp kick sent her sprawling and caused another stab of pain through his side.

He made a quick signal not to shoot Reb.

We need at least one leader alive, remember that Dain.

Sverre willed his partner to be cautious while he continued to watch Reb. She pushed herself up from the ground, slicing at the hands of the tribe member who had tried to help her.

At least Erasyl was reasonable.

Sverre shook his head at the thought.

There's no value in lamenting dead people.

Reb snarled at him from where she stood but stopped moving to attack him. Instead, she turned to one of the tribe members and snapped a quick order.

Sverre recognized the words 'kill' and 'dog' as three Nomads stepped toward him, drawing weapons.

Plan S, for Screw This, it is.

Sverre signaled to Dain. Three loud cracks rang out as the men dropped to the ground dead.

"Attempting to kill me will be a waste of your men," Sverre stated, emphasizing the 'your' and drawing her focus away from scanning the treeline, where she searched for the sniper.

Reb only snarled at him as she repeated the same order and gestured two more men forward.

The two men exchanged a nervous glance from each other to Sverre as they hesitantly stepped forward, not even bothering to draw their weapons.

Sverre signaled for injuries, not kill shots.

Two more loud cracks and both men lay screaming on the ground holding their legs.

The screams did wonders for morale. The rest of the Nomads inched backward, throwing wild eyes from Reb to Sverre, the trees, and back.

Even Reb seemed to break from her stupor of rage as she stared at the bleeding men.

Her gaze slowly settled back on Sverre with a cold, controlled loathing.

"I will dismember you." The words were not said with the tone of a threat, but a statement of fact. A promise.

Sverre nodded in acknowledgment.

The moment dragged on in silence until Reb shouted an order to withdraw. A few Nomads shuffled forward with hands held out in surrender and scared glances to the treeline until they reached their injured and dead companions and dragged them back.

Reb leveled one last hate-filled glare at Sverre before turning to follow her men. She pushed one of the men carrying her husband out of the way to take his place as they continued walking.

Only after they were out of sight over a distant hill did Sverre turn to start walking back to the forest. He quickly signaled Dain to wait for him there rather than come out to meet him.

Sverre worked to stanch the bleeding at his side as he moved. He was nearly to the trees when he looked up again to see Dain waiting for him. Echo stood next to him.

Sverre paused a step; he had thought Echo would already be gone.

He held in a groan as he moved closer.

There goes having time to create a good argument for why this was necessary before it's reported back to Atanas.

"How'd it go?" Dain asked as he paused from wiping mud, dirt, and sticks from his clothes. The casualness of the question didn't distract from his quick glances to Sverre's injured side, another question reflected in his concerned eyes.

Sverre nodded that he was fine, though Dain would never believe that statement even when it wasn't a lie.

"You saw," he answered the spoken question for Echo's benefit.

Echo's empty, dead-eyed fish expression never changed.

"That went to hell fast," the messenger stated.

Dain elbowed the man. "Don't use things I just said."

Echo's gaze skewered Dain a moment before turning back to Sverre. "Message?"

Sverre sighed and moved to rub his head, but the pain in his side stopped him. He glanced at Echo, but if the messenger noticed, he did not show it.

"Due to unavoidable circumstances, Erasyl had to be dealt with and was." Dain filled the silence with a quick message.

"Reb will still complete the mission as leader of the Aynur tribe," Sverre added.

"Really?" Dain blinked. "She actually agreed?"

Sverre tightened his jaw. "More or less."

Echo hummed.

"Less, but she will still follow through," Sverre corrected.

Echo nodded and spoke again. Slowly, searching for each word of things that had been said to him.

"Atanas will hear. Reb will complete the mission."

Echo paused, opening his mouth a few times but never finding the words for what he meant to say.

"Thanks, Echo." Dain stepped up to the messenger again and gave him a pat on the back. "What is your name?"

Sverre rolled his eyes. Dain asked that question every time he talked to the messenger, but Echo could never overcome his conditioning enough to answer.

"Let's see, Mason? Arovik? Terren? Bob? Sten—"

Sverre interrupted Dain's attempt to guess Echo's real name randomly.

"If you could start your report with Reb's compliance, we would appreciate it."

Echo hummed again as he made a quick motion for payment.

"Oh, yeah, sure." Dain jumped at the chance, "What do you want? An insult?"

Echo nodded again.

"Hmm." Dain tapped his chin and made a show of pacing.

Sverre used his partner's distraction to check his wound while Echo's back was turned. It had stopped bleeding. He motioned such to Dain as the man suddenly found a good insult for Echo's payment.

"I offer you the term 'blundering blowfish' for a general idiot," Dain said with a bow.

Echo raised an eyebrow and glanced around to Sverre, motioning for a proper response.

"Weak." Sverre booed Dain.

Echo nodded and repeated, "Weak."

"Weaker than a sunburned snowflake, but that's what you get for asking me." Dain shrugged as their attention turned to Sverre.

Sverre frowned a moment as he worked to recall and translate one of the insults the Nomads had just said to him.

"'You're a dog's dog, without the intelligence needed to speak.'"

That can't be the right translation.

Echo sighed, rubbing the heel of his hand into his forehead in exasperation.

Dain shrugged again.

"You want insults, you really shouldn't be asking us."

"Blundering blowfish." Echo scowled at them before turning to leave.

They watched as the messenger disappeared into the valley, over the hills.

"Need new stitches?" Dain gave Sverre a sidelong look.

Sverre nodded. "Just a few."

Dain hummed a doubtful note as he took his AaD out and plotted a quick course.

"Doorway's this way," he stated, moving back toward the forest. "Through the damned trees."

Sverre scanned the battlefield one last time.

Atanas will be so pissed.

He shook his head and turned back to Dain, who was scowling at the forest as though it being there was a personal insult to him.

"You'll survive."

CHAPTER 4

Caelyn stared up at the outer walls of Sentre as the pit in her stomach grew. The crystal gray walls reflected the world around her. Reflected how tiny she and her loud peacock hat were in it.

Mom, why didn't you take me into exile with you?

She bit her lip at the question. Loreda's explanation that she wanted Caelyn to have a proper life as royalty still sounded hollow.

Caelyn wasn't sure what else, if anything, her mother wanted her to do while she was in the capital.

She looked up at the walls again as they passed through the gate.

"Into that killer's domain," Caelyn said, in dramatic fashion, glowering toward the castle. A memory of her father, Jeshua Harailt, flitted through her mind with sorrow and a growing bitterness toward Brynte. She shrunk her exaggerated reactions back into herself. They could no longer make her father laugh or her mother roll her eyes.

Now her father was dead, and her mother was sending her to live with the person who killed him.

Caelyn sniffed at the thought and swallowed her fear and irritation.

"There is no use being a sad sap, Caelyn. Pull yourself together," she ordered out loud, ignoring the strange looks the guards riding next to her gave.

She had already received plenty of concerned looks from them. Some from her audacious taste in clothes, and some for her insistence on riding her own horse for the journey rather than in the gold-encrusted carriage the king had sent. As though she would accept anything from the king and not ride the horse that was the last gift from her father.

Her horse, Mygic, started sideways, jerking Caelyn's thoughts back to reality as she settled the startled animal.

"Easy, girl, it's okay." Caelyn stroked the creature's mane and glanced around for what had scared the horse.

Caelyn gulped at the sudden throng of people. The moments she was distracted by her thoughts, they had passed into one of the marketplaces of Sentre.

"It's okay, girl." Caelyn returned to stroking the horse, now as a means to calm herself. "It's just a few people."

More than either of us have ever seen, but don't mind that.

Every cramped stall and filthy alleyway was teaming with individuals yelling and shoving over their little corner of the city.

"It's dismal now," the bodyguard on Caelyn's left commented.

Caelyn pulled her attention from the bustling city long enough to look questioningly at the female guard.

The guard extended her hand toward the crowded space. "There used to be twice as much."

"I couldn't imagine it being any busier than this," Caelyn chirped. She ignored the sweet smile the woman gave at her naivety.

Caelyn returned to watching the people in the streets as they continued through the city in silence.

Only once they reached the castle courtyard did the silence disintegrate. The guards chattered amongst themselves until the castle doors opened and a trio stepped out, followed by an entourage of servants and guards,

Caelyn studied the three as she dismounted from Mygic.

The redhead was ugly, with a distracting scar eating up one side of his face.

That's my half-brother, right, Mom? The king.

Caelyn flinched back with disgust and turned her attention to the other two following the king down the steps.

She had never seen a wraith before, but Caelyn guessed that was what the thing to the left of the king was.

I didn't know their skin moved like that. It looks like a Shade.

The thing was grinning like an airhead. Caelyn frowned.

She shook her head and turned toward the young woman of the trio. The queen, Istoria, only looked a couple of years older than herself but moved with such grace, Caelyn could only stare in envy.

Caelyn scowled and gritted her teeth with guilt at her reverent notion of the queen.

If she hadn't interfered with Mom's plan...

Caelyn cut herself off from the useless thought. She was here, and her mom was gone. Forever.

No need to dwell on ifs now.

"I wish someone could have stabbed him earlier," she grumbled with a glare toward the king as he approached.

"Afraid I can't stab him," the same bodyguard whispered from beside Caelyn. "I could try to trip him, though."

Caelyn gave the guard a double take.

The woman winked before bowing to the king with the other guards.

Caelyn used the time to notice the woman for the first time. The guard's skin was a few shades deeper than suntanned, and her thick, wavy dark hair, which was tied high in a ponytail, perfectly matched her dark eyes.

"You're dismissed. Thank you."

Caelyn turned back to the king as he waved the guards away with a crooked smile.

A pang of loneliness struck as she watched the female guard give a sad shrug before following the other guards from the courtyard.

"Hello. It's Caelyn, right?" Brynte started speaking before Caelyn could decide to ignore him. "Am I pronouncing that correct?"

Caelyn scoffed and avoided his gaze.

Manners, young lady. Her mother's voice echoed in her mind.

"Yes, Brynte." She mispronounced his name while giving him as withering a look as she could manage.

Sorry, Mom.

Brynte smiled a lopsided look. It had to be to move around the thick scar tissue that hampered his expressions just enough for Caelyn to notice.

"You can call me Bry. Love the hat."

"You're ugly enough, I could call you Scarface and get away with it," Caelyn snapped on instinct, tipping her head back to bounce the hat's feathers. She bit her lip and recoiled at her own harsh tone. She mumbled an apology too low for anyone to hear.

She ignored the surprised looks of the entourage and the now hesitant grin on the king.

"True, true. You really could," the wraith said as he moved next to her and patted her shoulder. He was back in the spot next to the king with a laugh, moving much too quickly for Caelyn's comfort.

She puzzled over the wraith, odd thing that he was. Bry frowned at the wraith a moment too. The wraith returned the look with an unsure shrug before both men turned back to Caelyn.

"I'll try to make your stay here as comfortable as possible," Bry said, still smiling but looking more unsure.

Caelyn grimaced that he had completely ignored her remark.

If you wanted me to be comfortable, you could have let my mom stay too.

Caelyn bit her tongue to stop herself from voicing that thought. She would make the most of her time in the castle, if only because it was what her mother had told her to do. 'At least try' were Loreda's actual words.

"Speaking of comfort," the gentle voice caught Caelyn's attention and held it, "you must be tired from your long journey. Please come inside to rest."

Caelyn blinked at the unassuming smile Istoria was sending her way. She could only nod. The snippy remarks she had planned sizzled out of her mind under the queen's soft gaze.

"Right." Bry smiled at Istoria and latched his arm with hers to lead the way back into the castle.

The wraith stepped to her side as they walked toward the doors.

"I'm Shad, by the way." He winked and smiled. "It's a pleasure to meet you, princess."

Caelyn blinked and tried not to be mesmerized by his smile and the wisps of shadows wandering lazily across his face.

He's a friend of Bry's, don't be tricked.

Caelyn leaned away from the wraith at the remainder.

"The pleasure's all yours."

Shad laughed but continued walking a step further away. He attempted different bits of small talk, but Caelyn made sure to rebuff every attempt. She would have been content to walk in silence and just watch the shadows and the wraith. She'd never seen one before. However, Shad didn't seem to like the silence and changed his pace to walk next to Bry and Istoria, chattering continually.

After several hallways and flights of stairs worth of meaningless banter between the two men that Caelyn had been successfully ignoring, they stopped walking at a door.

"This room is yours," Bry said with a smile as he pushed the door open.

Caelyn gaped at the room as she shuffled inside. It was larger than her and her mom's bedrooms combined. She opened the door to an attached study that was even larger.

"It's good— huh, satisfactory, I hope." Bry's voice followed her into the room, breaking her from her moment of awe.

Caelyn squared her shoulders and contorted her face into a frown to hide any of the awe that might show through.

"It'll do."

"If you need anything, I'm—"

"If I need anything, I won't ask you," Caelyn snapped, leveling the best glare she could manage at the king. Bry looked less than affected by it, more tired than anything.

"All right, then." Bry smiled at her before he exchanged a look with Shad as he backed out of the doorway.

Istoria remained at the door a moment longer.

"If you need anything." She paused and held Caelyn's gaze long enough to make the younger girl nervous about her rejection. "All our rooms are just nearby. Come see any of us."

Caelyn shuffled her feet and mumbled understanding as she couldn't keep her own gaze level with the queen.

Manners. You are a princess.

Loreda's voice chastised in her head. Caelyn jerked her head up with a clear statement of understanding on her tongue, but the door was already closed.

"I understand, but I don't need anything from you people," Caelyn stated to the empty space. Her lip trembled.

Caelyn looked around the room again, this time taking in what a big vacant space it was. Furnishings aside, she was all alone.

Again.

Caelyn fought against the pull of loneliness by walking around her new space. She talked aloud to herself, designating areas for all her clothes, hats, and most importantly, all the odds and ends she collected to make new flamboyant outfits.

CHAPTER 5

B ry frowned at the closed door.
That went well.
He shook his head at the thought before turning to Stori and Shad as they started walking away.

"I don't think she likes us," Shad stated with a look that he had just discovered a profound idea.

"Whatever gave you that idea." Bry rolled his eyes.

"Intuition."

He ignored Shad and focused on Stori as she collected her thoughts.

"This is a big change for her. It does not help that we are the ones who took both of her parents away from her."

Stori finished her thought with a small smile to Bry. He smiled back.

Shad hummed in disinterested annoyance, lacing his hands behind his head.

"Probably doesn't help she has only heard 'bout you two from Loreda. But why would she dislike me?" he mused aloud, turning down a side hallway.

Bry recognized the new direction as their back-alley way of reaching Klaas and Eleanora and turned to follow without pausing. He took Stori's arm with a wink when she floundered at the unfamiliar direction.

Another smile passed between them as they followed Shad in silence until reaching the healer's chambers.

Shad knocked a short, obnoxious beat before entering and further announcing their presence.

An unintelligible reply came from the kitchen as the trio already started picking their way across the messy living room.

Shad shouted a triumphant noise as he entered the kitchen.

Bry rounded the corner to see Lawr pausing mid-bite through a biscuit with a tormented look.

"So this is where you've been hiding."

The older man swallowed his remaining mouthful of biscuit in a gulp before answering.

"I'm not hiding. Just working in peace," he leveled his gaze at Bry, then Stori, "and quiet." He turned toward Shad at that.

Both Bry and Stori nodded with varying levels of chagrin. Shad just made a mocking sputtering noise as he waved off the comment.

"Sounds like hiding to me." Shad remained unrelenting as he turned to hug Eleanora before taking a seat between Klaas and Lawr.

Bry moved to greet Eleanora with a kiss on the cheek and a pang of guilt for not having visited recently.

Eleanora smiled and patted his arm before moving to hug Stori.

"I was starting lunch, but I'll make some more for everyone. The whole family hasn't visited me all at once recently."

"I have some work I need to finish." Lawr stood with a vague wave upwards. The slight smile on the usually indifferent face was Bry's only clue that the older man was lying and maybe uncomfortable.

Stori acted before Bry could even move.

"Family means you too." Stori was at Lawr's side, patting his arm with enough directive that he returned to his chair.

"Of course, it does, Lawr. What you're thinking, I never understand." Eleanora admonished.

Bry saw Lawr take a quick moment to check the people in the room for disagreement. Bry gave him a smile when he finally caught his eye.

Lawr relented and settled back into his seat.

"By the way, Bry," Lawr started again, his business decorum returned in a moment, "I made progress with the AaD issue," he snuck a cautious glance at Eleanora as he leaned closer to Bry, "you know, the FCKing Mess."

Bry nodded as he also flicked a glance between the two women of the group. Stori remained smiling politely, and Eleanora continued pretending not to hear. Bry guessed that meant it was as good a time as any to continue the discussion, but Klaas interrupted.

"Before that," Klaas held up two fingers, "your sister and lunch."

Bry tried not to groan. "Right, Caelyn."

"She doesn't like us," Shad said in the pause Bry had left open. "Any of us, if you can believe that."

"I can." Klaas nodded.

Two pairs of frowns stared back at him. Stori just laughed quietly into her napkin.

Klaas shrugged. "You two are a lot to handle. And I'm sure she didn't really dislike Stori."

"True." Bry, Shad, and Lawr agreed.

Bry and Shad smiled at Stori, but Lawr looked as though he agreed with the entire statement rather than just the last sentence, as they were.

Stori smiled in a cute, bashful way before she tried arguing. "I did not feel she actually disliked either of you two, but as I said, it is quite a large change for her."

"Whether she likes us or not, I promised to take care of her, and I will." Bry nodded to himself. The memory of promising anything to Loreda made him scowl. He hid the look with a smile that seemed to do nothing to convince the others as they changed topics.

The conversation meandered through lunch and several more topics before curving back around to Lawr and the FCKing Mess.

"'Sorta almost' has progressed to 'I think I can fix it, but it'll take time.'"

Bry nodded along. "That's great to hear."

He waited for Shad and Stori's congratulating to die down for Lawr to get to the bad news.

There always has to be bad news.

Lawr's expression was already turning sour before he spoke again with a frown for everyone at the table.

"Like I said, though, it'll be time-consuming. I'm anticipating a couple of months for the full network of Medius to be back to full capacity, but Sentre itself will still be a few weeks minimum."

"Months?!" Shad blinked and paused at a glare from Lawr and started rubbing his head in thought. "Could you use some help?"

"Yes, actually." Lawr rolled his eyes. "If you know anyone *trustworthy* who is versed in data structuring and algorithms, send them my way."

Shad held Lawr's glare for a moment before smiling. "Will if I find anyone."

"Is there anything we can do, though?" It was Klaas's turn to receive a level glare.

Lawr grumbled thinking about it but relented anyway. "No. Not right now, anyway." He rubbed his head in a frustrated motion. "I have to figure out a practical way to get this done first. Once I have a better idea, then maybe, yeah."

Klaas nodded, satisfied with the answer. Bry exchanged a glance with Shad, marveling at how easily he had worked a straight answer, especially one regarding helping, out of Lawr.

Lawr's sharp gaze pierced through Bry as the conversation settled.

"You should still start preparing to tell your people about Oracaede for when I get it fixed."

Bry groaned at the change of topic. The one problem he was hoping to ignore for a little longer.

Why is it always me who gets stuck with this kind of problem?

He heard a laugh stifled from Stori at his side. Bry turned a questioning look toward her.

"Sorry." Stori smiled at him. "I am only happy I am not the one who has to make a speech this time."

Bry rolled his eyes. "Thanks."

"No sarcasm in your speech, Bry," Eleanora chastised.

"Yes, ma'am." Bry forgot he still didn't speak as well as he thought. Certainly not what the people expected from their king.

Why couldn't Oracaede at least give me a chance to work on this one issue before they wreck everything else?

He frowned again at the thought.

"We need to use what Lawr decoded from the Lucianca data as proof about Oracaede. Anything that shows they're still in operation."

"I can—" Lawr started, but Bry raised his hand quickly, cutting him off.

"No, I want you to focus on the AaD problem. Give all the info-information you found to Chesler. He can make a convincing case out of it. I can work with him to be convincing."

"Info-formation."

Bry ignored Shad's mocking as he turned to Stori. "I know you're still working on those tax laws, Stori, but if you could spend some time checking in on Caelyn, I'd appreciated it. We can all work on making her feel comfortable here, but you were the one she was least hostile toward."

Stori nodded, smiling her sweet smile.

"Bring her here, Stori, darling," Eleanora said as she returned to shuffling about the kitchen. "Whenever you are able, we'd love to meet her."

"What 'bout me, boss?" Shad turned his thousand-watt, gray and blue grin toward him.

Bry fought his sarcastic comments.

Kingly, Bry, kingly. Don't let him mess with you.

"So now I'm the boss, eh, Shad?" Bry grinned at Shad with enough teeth his friend would know the insults he was holding back.

Shad's smile widened more than what should be possible as he pretended not to have seen Bry's look.

Bry returned to thinking about what else they needed.

What don't we need to cover? Bry rolled his eyes.

"The Nomads." Bry decided finally. "We should expect them to retaliate for the tribes they lost in Oroitz. Shad, you know people, see if you can't find someone with information on what they're up to."

Shad scowled at his tasking for a moment. "Of course, *I* have to deal with the Nomads."

"The boss says so." Bry grinned again.

Shad scoffed, but his expression turned from mocking to thoughtful as he considered his task.

"Oh, good, now that everyone has their jobs, dessert." Eleanora returned to the table just as Bry was about to stand with Lawr, shifting to do the same.

"We were—" Bry tried.

"Dessert. Eat." Eleanora held his gaze with a sharp look as she held a bowl of some cream, berries, and pudding.

Bry returned to his seat without trying to argue more. Eleanora was not one to have her food wasted.

CHAPTER 6

Hid and Aike bounced ideas and insults between themselves while they walked through the Empty. Aike had mentioned the gist of the mission to the rest of the team, and occasionally, one of the other Wolves would toss forward an idea to them.

By the time they exited the Empty into Medius, Hid might almost consider the snippets of multiple ideas to be a good beginning for a plan.

That is, he might if he was feeling generous and unstressed. Those feelings rarely ever applied to him and this moment, for this mission, was not the exception.

Hid still needed to figure out how to keep them, and particularly Aike, from running afoul of Reb's vague orders.

"Hello!"

Hid sighed and turned toward Aike. The man still held his hands cupped around his mouth, making greeting noises to the empty space in Medius. Hid recognized the noises as Gaelic, but only just.

"Yep. No one here." Aike dropped his hands and turned expectantly toward Hid. "Where we at?"

Hid scanned the hilly plane around them, which showed no signs of life. He pulled out their AaD, ignoring the ping of a new message waiting and Aikes' incessant noisiness. He looked at their coordinates and tracked a route to Sentre.

"Come on. What do ya say? Rapid-o? Rapio?"

Hid raised his attention from the AaD to level a glare at Aike. The freckled man was still twisting his face up, trying to make sense of the foreign word.

"It's '*rápido*,' *hermano*," Hid corrected, "and shut up. I'm working on it."

Hid returned to ignoring Aike, repeating the word with a growing distortion from his own Irish accent.

"12 met-reaches from the city," Hid stated with a directional wave when he finished calculating the distance. He turned toward the waiting message. It was from Reb.

He frowned.

"Aike." Hid moved a few paces away from the group, Aike following. "From Reb." He pointed at the voice message.

Aike's expression soured, and he hummed, "Play it."

Hid started the message, which immediately began with Reb snarling out information, apparently having started talking before the message began recording.

"Those *Devlet Orospu* dogs think they will join you for Sentre mission. Aike, bastard, kill them. If they live, you fail, you die." Reb trailed off into a tangent of curses and threats.

"Oracaede's sending someone?" Hid exchanged a nervous glance with Aike's collected one, "To help?"

"Who does she expect us to kill?" Aike was still frowning at the device and listening when the recorded curses veered back toward actual useful information.

"I send Tromix Wolves to kill them, but if they fail and damned Ghost joins you, kill him. Him and whoever that damned sniper is…They're dead." Hid paused the message as Reb spiraled back into curses.

Aike's face drained of blood so fast, Hid stepped closer to catch his friend if he passed out.

"The Ghost!?" Aike overcame some of his shock while he continued staring at the AaD. "She expects us to kill the Ghost. Is she crazy?"

Aike kept his voice low as he rambled out his own curses and confusion. His accent twisted the words too much for Hid to even understand what he was saying.

Hid glanced from Aike to the rest of their group. The Wolves all stood waiting and watching them with growing frowns of confusion and concern.

"She plans to have one of the other tribe's Wolves try to kill them first? She knows they are going to fail, doesn't she?" Hid shook his head. He pitied the Wolves that had been absorbed into the Aynur tribe.

A deep sigh snapped Hid's attention back to Aike as the man had gone quiet, glaring daggers at the AaD.

"Play the rest of it," he finally said.

Hid nodded, remaining mute as he played the rest of the message, the majority of which was Reb cycling through every Avare language for curses until the end.

"Bastards will pay for killing Erasyl. You will make them pay." The message ended.

"Wait. What?" Hid blinked at the device and replayed the last moment again.

"Erasyl is dead," Aike repeated the information with a resigned look.

Hid only shook his head. New scenarios played through his head of how every meeting with the chief would go if it was only Reb. His stomach twisted at the notion.

Couldn't they have killed Reb instead?

Erasyl was not a pinnacle of greatness as far as Hid and the other Wolves were concerned, but at least he kept Reb's psychotic nature in check.

"Shit," Aike said, ever succinct in describing their situation.

Hid nodded. "*Mierda.*"

"How could she even have found him?" Aike grumbled aloud as he turned to watch their team pretend they weren't trying to listen in.

"Reb wants something done, she finds a way. Especially if he was in Glacius Tesca. She has spies everywhere reporting to her."

Hid frowned after he answered with another glance toward Aike. The man was not actually listening, he had just asked to give himself another moment to think.

"The Ghost and a sniper, huh," Aike continued mumbling to himself more than attempting to communicate with Hid.

"She said they were going to…help us?" Hid asked, waiting for Aike to correct him if his understanding of Reb's jumps between languages was off.

Aike nodded, chewing his lip as he thought. A smirk fought its way to his lips.

"At least they'll be close."

Hid scoffed at him. "Stupid optimist."

Aike shrugged and headed back toward the others.

"What's the news?" Sa'dia pushed Bary back a step to be the first to ask.

Aike hummed as he tipped from his toes to heels a few times with his face screwed up in duck-faced contemplation before answering.

"Well, we're about to be a mite buggered."

The others groaned at Aike's expression.

"Listen," Hid said in a low voice.

Everyone's attention snapped back to Aike as he continued rocking on his feet.

"Has our mission become that much more difficult?" Xiulan asked next, her voice soft as rose petals and her timbre always finding a way to rhyme her words.

Aike nodded.

"Erasyl's dead."

The others each expressed their surprise and irritation.

Hid listened as the question 'Reb's in charge now?' was repeated at least twice.

"Oracaede killed him, and yes, Reb is in charge, and she is raging about it. She wants us to kill them on our current mission," Hid stated.

Aike took over before the others had a chance to say anything.

"She already sent a Wolf pack to try and kill them. Be thankful we at least have the time to plan. When they fail, our targets will be working with us in Sentre."

Silence settled for a long moment as the team thought over the information.

"The ones we have to kill, it's Oracaede's Ghost, isn't it?" Caesar Apollo finally asked in his shrill voice.

"Aye, aye, and a sniper, 'bout right." Aike held his reassuring cheerful expression and spoke again with force. "Ya'll stay out of worry. Hid and I will get us a plan together. We can work out the details as a team later."

"Until we meet up with Oracaede's people, the mission is the same," Hid added.

"Keep yourselves easy when we do meet them. We can't do a thing until we have a chance." Aike pitched in with over-jolly optimism.

A begrudging chorus of agreement answered, and Hid turned to double-check the direction of the city before walking in that direction. He paced his gait until Aike made his way to his side.

"This won't be good, no matter what we try," Hid stated. He swallowed and ignored that he was talking more to himself than his friend. "I can't see us getting out of this without losing some of our team."

H. E. Salian

Aike merely hummed in response.

"How can we do this, Aike? I mean, it's the Ghost. All the stories about him...The guy must be a psycho and a force of nature."

"Can't do anything for it now." Aike spoke with confidence that might trick Hid into believing he was actually sure of what he was saying. "Can't do a thing until they join us. Just focus on what we can."

Hid continued in silence as he turned the 'wait-and-see' idea over in his head. He didn't like it. But he didn't have any plan around it either.

"If we fail our mission in Sentre," Hid finally said, "Reb will still take your head for it."

"See, focusing on the positives is already helping." Aike's goofy grin returned, and Hid was certain his friend was just doing it to annoy him and distract his worrying.

"You're a stupid fool."

"What? No Spanish?"

"*Pendejo.*"

37

CHAPTER 7

S verre's hair looks nice grown out.

Ali surprised herself with the thought. The notion continued to occupy her brain despite her attempts to dislodge it.

It is true after all. It does look nice.

She relented and indulged the thought for a moment. On his recuperating hiatus, he had let his hair grow until it hung over his forehead. Of course, he had needed to cut it before he left on his last job. Oracaede regulation, military standards, and all.

He's very handsome.

She pulled back at the thought immediately. What was she thinking? Sverre was in another world on a dangerous mission, and she was thinking about his hair and how good he looked.

"Ali?" Leon's voice startled her, and she jumped, bumping her knees against the underside of the table.

Really? Doing that again? She thought back to the last time she had knocked her knees like that when Sverre had startled her. The thought annoyed her, but she pushed it down to focus on Leon.

"Yes?" she asked, hoping he hadn't already asked his question. The boy was pushing his workbook toward her with a confused frown.

"Right," Ali reached for the book, "let me check them."

"I'm not done," Leon pulled the notebook back a fraction, "I don't know what to do here."

Please be something I know, *Ali repeated to herself as she leaned close to see.*

Leon pointed to an example of grammar structure for the Glasic Tongue.

Why is it never something I know, she complained to herself while she pretended to think about the grammar.

"What do you think you would do here?" Ali crossed her fingers, hoping it would work.

Leon pursed his lips in thought before explaining some grammatical nonsense that sounded about right for the language.

Ali nodded, pretending she understood a word of his explanation.

"Okay, write that answer down."

Leon looked at her with sidelong suspicion that confirmed he saw what she was doing. Ali shrugged as he pulled his notebook back toward himself and wrote down his answer.

Sverre will have a lot of correcting to do when he returns.

Ali smiled with only a little chagrin at the extra work she was created for the albino.

As long as he does return.

She swallowed at the thought.

Before they had left, Sverre mentioned he was considering taking Ali and Leon to stay with Dain's wife, Ercilia, and their children. Ali had privately cried tears of joy when he decided against it.

Ali could only see it as being a preparation step. Preparation for the day Sverre would not come back.

One day he won't.

Ali balked at the thought, pulling away from it as fast as she could.

A ping from the kitchen counter notified them of a new message. Ali and Leon both leapt toward the device.

Leon reached it first and snatched it up. Ali read over his little shoulder as he opened the message. Four short words.

Back by dinner.

- Sverre

Ali couldn't contain the smile she shared with Leon. The world, their small little world, was going to be all right.

"They're coming back!" Leon screeched as he engulfed her in a hug.

Ali squeezed him back before he quickly and inevitably bounced away, already chattering out ideas.

"They'll be hungry, we have to make them dinner," he chirped with a glance out the window to the late afternoon sky. "'Cause Sverre'll be too tired to cook, and his ribs'll be sore. We should make something great!"

Leon continued rambling as he set the AaD down and scurried around the kitchen.

Ali nodded along to his plan then caught herself. She caught Leon too, after an effort to reach him.

"Oh, no. I'll start dinner, you have to finish your schoolwork."

Leon groaned and started protesting, but Ali ignored him as she pushed him back toward the kitchen table.

"The sooner you finish, the sooner you can come help," Ali reminded him. "You don't want to leave me alone in here for too long, do you?"

Ali's lack of cooking skills had improved from watching Sverre, but not enough that she couldn't still wield them as a threat against the boy.

The threat worked. Leon darted back to his schoolwork with new determination.

"Just don't burn the kitchen down before I'm done," he called back at her.

"Yeah, yeah." Ali waved him off as she started scouring the kitchen for ingredients.

Ali bustled about, preparing every food item she could find, and had just started cooking when Leon joined her. They switched places so she could grade his answers. Correct, incorrect, or question mark for the ones she wasn't sure about. Fewer question marks doted the page than when she had first started, but several still cropped up.

Returning to the kitchen, Ali and Leon worked until dark, making everything they could think of and had ingredients for. Looking over the pots and pans of food, Ali realized the feast they had prepared could last ten people for days.

It's only a little too much for Dain and Leon, then.

She smiled.

Noisy steps at the front door alerted Ali as she and Leon made another dash in that direction.

Ali reached the divide between the kitchen and the living room before she stopped short and grabbed Leon, clapping a hand over his mouth and pulling them back to the kitchen in one motion. A chill danced along her spine as she tried to figure out what exactly was wrong.

It's not them.

The quiet voice warned from the back of her mind, and she didn't doubt it.

The door handle jiggled but remained locked and unopened. When no one was even fumbling with keys on the other side, any doubt Ali had vanished. It was Sverre's rule to always keep the door locked.

Leon's confused grumbling and struggling in her grip snapped her attention toward him. She held a finger to her lips and gave a sharp warning glance as she released her grip on him.

He nodded and still looked confused as she grabbed his hand and tiptoed across the living room, down the opposite hallway.

A sharp crack sounded, and Ali dropped to the floor, pulling Leon down and hunching over him. She listened and waited, but no one came into the house. Another wood splintering crash and Ali leapt to her feet, still dragging Leon as she raced to her window and peered out.

A group of seven or eight people milled around the front door. The man closest to the door held something that glinted in the fading light as he used it to pry the wood door to pieces.

We have to leave. Ali fought to breathe through the panic that wracked every thought. *Sverre, where are you?*

She scanned the landscape out the window for any sign of white hair. The desert was empty.

A loud crack from the front porch startled Ali as she flinched back and squeezed her eyes closed.

They'll be inside in minutes.

The thought fueled her panic, as did every thought after.

"Ali," Leon whispered, grabbing a fist full of her sleeve and holding on.

She watched the terror in his eyes build. His fear snapped her into action.

I need a weapon.

The panic subsided enough for something useful to filter through. That lone thought permeated every move as she grabbed Leon's hand and crept across the hall to Sverre's room.

She knew he kept most of his weapons not on him out in the shed. But he was way too paranoid not to have a few in the house.

Leon pulled away from her and moved to the nightstand. He opened the top drawer and pulled out a handgun similar to the ones Sverre always carried. Leon's hands shook as he stared at the firearm before turning his moon-shaped eyes toward Ali.

Ali swallowed and took the weapon from Leon as another crack of wood from the front door made her jump.

"An AaD," Ali whispered to Leon. "Find and AaD and call Sverre."

The boy turned immediately to begin searching as Ali focused on the gun in her hands.

She closed her eyes, hoping to steady her breathing as she struggled to remember every scrap of firearm knowledge she had ever learned. Every snippet of information she could recall revolved around safety and *not* shooting someone.

Bullets.

A useful thought filtered through the white noise in her mind. She needed to load the gun.

Ali's breathing ran from her as she pressed every convex surface on the weapon trying to find the clip release.

A small hand settled over her shaking ones as Leon expertly handled the gun, pulling it back toward him and heaving the slide back after a momentary struggle. He tilted the firearm so she could see there were bullets in the clip, but none in the chamber yet.

He handed the weapon back with the same care and awareness of where the muzzle was pointed.

Ali tried swallowing passed the dryness in her throat as she took the weapon. It wasn't the first time she was aware of her lack of knowledge and experience with guns. But it was the first time she realized that lacking could mean the end of their lives.

"Y-you have to put a round in the chamber to load it," Leon whispered in a voice that trembled as much as Ali's hands did. "Pull the slide back and let go."

Ali nodded and gripped the slide. It was heavy. She tightened her grip and yanked it with all her might. The slide slammed back, and she released in jerky surprise.

"It's a Glock," Leon whispered. He continued when Ali only stared at him unsure of what he meant. "Safety's in the trigger. Just point and shoot."

Ali nodded as she caught Leon's frightened gaze and held it. "Stay here and call Sverre," she repeated.

"Just squeeze the trigger and don't mash the gun," Leon whispered back before moving off to look for an AaD.

Ali repeated his advice to herself as she tiptoed out toward the living room. Peeking around the hallway corner, she saw a hole in the solid wood door. Another crack and the blade of an axe buried itself in the wood, splintering the hole wider.

An unconscious, fearful noise rose from her throat as she raised the gun and pointed it toward the hole in the door.

Ali squeezed her eyes closed, hoping for some miracle.

That won't happen.

The jaded part of her conscious said. She clenched her hands around the gun.

It fired.

Ali jumped and barely kept from dropping the weapon. She swore.

As did the people outside. Curses erupted from the front door.

Ali grasped the gun more carefully before focusing again on the door. A small new hole had appeared in the wood, a full foot away from the large ax hole she was aiming at.

"Ghost!" a young man's accented voice called from the other side.

Ali flinched at the sound, nearly firing the gun again.

A ghost? They're looking for a dead person?! Ali's mind spun with some happy thought that this was just a misunderstanding.

No, Sverre. Ali sobered at once. *They're looking for Sverre.*

"Ghost!" the same voice called again. "Reb from the Aynur tribe has a death mark for you, and as the Wolves of the former Tromix tribe, we're here to collect."

Ali blinked. She recognized some of those words. *Wolves* and *Aynur* from when she was kidnapped, but Tromix? She frowned.

An image of Leon's slave brand and his words, '*Tromix brands everyone,*' jumped to the forefront of her mind.

She raised the gun again, keeping her eyes open this time. She aimed and tried to squeeze the trigger more gently this time.

Ali still jerked on reflex from the sound of the gun firing, but it didn't startle her as much. No new bullet hole appeared in the door, but the people outside also didn't sound injured as they continued to swear.

Another bang and a thud. This time, Ali did jump. That shot was louder than her gun, but she hadn't fired again. Two more shots rang out, followed by thuds and exclamations of panic.

Movement on the other side of the door preceded the sound of slashed flesh and screams of pain that lasted only a moment before all was silent.

A whine of fear escaped Ali as she retrained the sights of the handgun at the hole in the door.

"Leon? Ali?"

Ali could cry at the voice. "Sverre!?"

She ran to the door, still clutching the gun with both hands.

Sverre's face appeared as he peeked through the hole before reaching in and straining to unlock the door.

"Sverre, you're back. They just came to the door, and they were noisy, You're never noisy, and Dain is loud but not noisy. I knew it wasn't you. And I didn't..." Ali realized she was blabbering through tears but still couldn't stop herself.

Sverre stepped through the door, a bloody knife in each hand.

A sound behind Ali preceded Leon only by an instant. The boy crashed into Sverre with a hug and unnerving silence.

Sverre flicked his wrists, dropping both knives so they stabbed into the floor. He wrapped one arm around Leon and used the other to gently pry the gun out of Ali's hands and set it on the table near the door. He wrapped Ali in a hug with his now free arm.

As soon as the gun was out of her hands, whatever dam had been keeping her emotions at bay burst. She sobbed and hugged him back, still babbling without saying anything.

"I'm so sorry," Sverre said against her head. He repeated the words as the three stood motionless for a long moment.

"Sverre?" Dain's voice pulled Ali back to reality as the man appeared in the doorway, rifle in hand and breathing heavily.

Ali could feel Sverre turn his head to look at Dain, but she didn't bother looking herself.

"They're fine."

Sverre stepped back, a hand still on each of their cheeks.

He forced Leon to look up at him. "You are going to be fine." His gaze turned to Ali. "You both did so great."

Sverre held onto them a moment longer. "We need to leave."

CHAPTER 8

Ali sat motionless. She gripped Leon's hand, and they both sat on the living room couch, watching as Sverre and Dain moved through the house with clean efficiency to gather what they would need.

The front door was closed, but Ali watched the pool of blood that had formed under it. Her mind lazily turned over the idea of what would be on the other side. The thoughts were met with apathy, but her stomach instinctively rolled at the sight of blood.

She swallowed at the nausea and turned until her gaze drifted and settled on Leon. His eyes were cloudy as they remained fixed on the door and the red puddle. Ali couldn't fathom the idea of releasing his hand, so she instead twisted awkwardly to wrap her free arm around the boy and pull him into a weak hug.

Sverre returned to the room and paused as he passed them. Ali ignored his attempts to catch her eye.

"Leon?" Sverre sat on the coffee table in front of them.

Leon shifted in Ali's hold to look at Sverre. His attention stopped on the blood before reaching Sverre.

"Leon, I'm sorry this happened." Sverre's face was pinched in pain as he spoke. "Now that someone knows where this place is, we can't stay here. Do you understand?"

Ali watched Leon nod but remain mute.

"Where are we going?" Ali asked.

Sverre turned his attention to her. "You are going to stay at Dain's house with Erc and their kids. It's in Lux Aequor."

"And we'll be safe there?" Ali's newfound doubt sat heavy in her voice.

"Yes." Sverre was slow to answer.

"How?" Ali fought to keep her voice steady. "You aren't going to be there, are you? How will we be safe?"

Sverre's face stiffened to an unreadable mask as he held Ali's gaze for a moment longer before turning to Leon.

"Leon, I packed your things, but you should go check your room and grab anything else you want to carry." He paused and caught the boy's free hand. "We won't be coming back."

Leon sniffled at the last statement but stood up obediently and moved toward his room. Ali heard Dain's voice as he spoke softly to the boy.

"Ali," Sverre started with a halting tone, "you should grab whatever you want too. I packed you a bag, but..." He glanced around the room.

Ali nodded but remained where she was, staring into space and the door.

Has the pool of blood grown?

She couldn't tell and blinked as she forced herself to look away.

That would have been Leon or me.

"Ali..." Sverre's expression and voice were still unreadable while he continued watching her.

She frowned at him.

"This was supposed to be safe. Here." She gestured at the house as her attention fell back to the door. "It wasn't."

"I know. And I don't know how they found—"

"Then how could you know Dain's place is safe?" Ali snapped. She glared through him but hoped he would give her something. Anything she could trust. Some expression she could understand that would mean they would actually be safe.

He frowned.

"They came here looking for me. Not you, not Leon. Me." Sverre nodded as though he were convincing himself rather than Ali. "And these were Nomads, it wasn't Atanas."

Ali growled an unconscious noise of disagreement. She leaned forward until her face was only inches away from Sverre's.

"They would have killed us all the same."

Sverre was still. "I know."

New tears sprung to Ali's eyes as she thought aloud. "They would have killed Leon. And me. If you hadn't been here...If they had come yesterday."

Sverre pulled her into a tentative hug and stroked a hand through her hair.

Ali fought to collect her emotions, but they slipped away from her whenever she thought she was in control again. She envied Sverre's coolness. Or even Leon's apparent apathy, though his was just shock.

"They won't come looking again." Sverre's voice was warm next to her ear. "They wanted me, but for this mission, I'll be working next to them. Reb will not need to send anyone else to look."

Ali nodded against him.

"We're ready." Dain's voice startled Ali, and she jerked back to look as he entered the room with an arm around Leon's shoulders. Leon clutched his backpack tight to his chest.

"I just…still need my books," Leon muttered. He shifted a moment before running past them into the kitchen where his schoolwork remained strewn across the table.

Ali stood and moved passed Dain to her room. Her eyes flickered to the window with its view of the front door. She turned away immediately.

On the floor was an already packed duffle bag and an empty backpack next to it. Ali picked up the empty bag and wandered the room. Sverre had already packed most everything that was hers, but she looked anyway.

There was nothing else that belonged to her, so Ali grabbed a handful of books off the shelves and her house robe from where it had slipped behind the couch. She struggled until she heaved both bags onto her shoulders.

She returned to the living room. Leon was already there, mumbling to Sverre about dinner. Ali too remembered the long-forgotten feast they had made to celebrate.

Sverre noted her entrance to the room with a nod before turning to Dain. Ali watched a short conversation pass between them in silence before Sverre picked Leon up and Dain moved toward her.

"I can hold that for you." Dain eased the heavy duffle bag out of her grip and slung it over his shoulder alongside his rifle. He gave a small reassuring smile as he laced his arm through hers.

"Ali, keep your eyes closed. Dain will lead you out," Sverre said from where he stood next to the beaten door.

Leon's eyes were already screwed shut before he buried his head into Sverre's shoulder.

Ali nodded and closed her eyes. She heard the door opening and followed along as Dain started walking.

"Step over," Dain said from beside her as they reached the porch.

Ali stepped but kicked something when she did. Solid but yielding. A body. Her breath hitched, and her eyelids flickered to check her footing, but she squeezed them shut.

"It's okay." Dain's voice was at her ear.

Ali kept walking until they were down the steps and on the sand.

"You can open your eyes now, but don't look back," Dain said.

Ali squinted in the darkness, watching Sverre's white hair as he led the way along the side of the house to the lean-to. Leon's face was still hidden, and Ali could hear Sverre speaking softly to the boy. Leon would occasionally nod, but he never looked up.

Once in the attached shed, Sverre set Leon down with an order to prepare the lizard-horse creatures for travel.

Dain carried on a constant stream of a solo conversation as he helped them saddle the animals. Sverre darted around the shed, amassing more weapons to himself with every turn.

"Ready," Dain called out, dropping his singsong tone as soon as they were finished with the animals.

Sverre appeared next to Dain in an instant and handed him a bulging duffle bag that clinked with metal. Sverre carefully handed over a second smaller bag with something square and heavy. They both treated the second bag with reverent care as they fastened it securely to the creature's back.

"The parts for the second blocker are in here." Sverre patted one of his own smaller bags. His voice couldn't match the small smile he tried for. "Still missing everything crucial."

Dain nodded in rare silence before gripping Sverre by the back of his neck and giving him a quick kiss on the forehead.

"Thank you," Dain said without even a hint of jest.

Sverre nodded, moving away to one of the lizard creatures and strapping his own bag along with Leon's house bag onto its back.

"I want to ride with Dain," Leon said when Sverre moved to lift him onto the animal.

Sverre froze and a look of pain flitted across his face but was lost in an instant.

"All right." Sverre gestured Leon toward Dain. He turned to Ali. "You'll ride with me then." Rather than a statement, Ali heard the hint of a desperate question in his voice.

She nodded and traded places with Leon, giving the boy's shoulder a comforting squeeze as she passed him.

Sverre helped Ali onto the creature and climbed on after. Dain and Leon mounted and started out of the shed as Sverre followed.

They rode in silence until the first bluff, not far behind the house, when Sverre paused. He pulled a small device out of one of his many pockets.

Ali strained in the saddle until she was turned enough to watch him fidget with the device a short moment before pressing a button on the side.

The desert remained silent and still as Ali waited for something to happen.

Maybe it was broken.

She had just finished the thought when dancing light from the house caught her eye.

Ali sniffled in a breath. She could only stare at the fire, which was now dancing in the windows and eating its way up the outer walls of the shed. She could hear Leon crying quietly and saw Dain shifting to try and block the boy's view of their burning home.

Ali turned more to look up at Sverre as he watched the fire. The man's face was ever unreadable, but his eyes were bright, reflecting the fire.

"Sverre?" Ali wouldn't dare speak above a whisper.

"I just thought…maybe I could build something. A life away from…" Sverre's own whispered reply died out as he faced forward again with his jaw clenched painfully tight.

The creatures were walking again. Ali closed her eyes and tried to block out the sound of wood crackling and the smell of it burning. The only other thing she could listen to, however, was Leon trying not to cry.

CHAPTER 9

B ry paced up one hallway and down another before finding himself
in front of Caelyn's door again. He had reasoned it would be best
for Stori to talk to her, but he still hoped a conversation with his
half-sister might be possible.

He froze a moment when a nearby guard shifted. The armor clanked.
An easy, normal sound, but Bry's mind snapped to rattling helmets and a
blood-soaked battlefield.

He shut his eyes against the memory, but that only made it more vivid
in his mind. He forced his eyes open and continued pacing until the images
faded.

Bry stopped walking when he reached Caelyn's door again and
knocked. The solidity of his resolve weakened as the moment of silence from
within the room grew longer. Finally, footfalls came from within.

He straightened his back and waited.

The door was opened by a dark-haired, copper-toned woman in a guard
uniform. Bry blinked a moment before recognizing her as the bodyguard
assigned to Caelyn.

"Your Majesty," the woman greeted with a tone of cool indifference.

Bry nodded back before shifting his gaze passed her into the room.
Caelyn sat at her desk with an empty chair pulled up next to her. She was
wearing a flamboyant pair of matching neon green gloves and a scarf that
clashed with her bright blue dress.

"Hello, Caelyn. Mind if I come in?" Bry asked with an earnest smile
and waited at the door for her invitation.

Caelyn scowled at him and made no effort to hide her disdain. She finally shrugged, which Bry took as a positive.

Bry struggled to keep up a cheerful look as he passed the guard while listening to the younger girl's dismissive grumblings.

His foot caught on something, and he stumbled forward a step before catching his balance. He remained in a defensive stance as he pivoted back to the door and the guard, ready for any attack.

"My apologies, sir," the woman said with the hint of a Spanish accent and a stronger smile, looking beyond Bry.

It's not a fight. Don't be so jumpy, Bry chided himself as he forced his legs to straighten out of a fighting stance.

A snicker snapped his attention to Caelyn, who was making a poor attempt at hiding her amusement. He looked back at the guard in time to catch a wink to Caelyn before the woman left the room.

Bry worked harder to keep his smile friendly. Whatever joke Caelyn had with the guard, it had at least put her in a better mood.

"You're accustoming to castle life quickly then, I see," Bry said as he pulled a hand through his knotted hair and glanced at her outfit again. "Like the scarf."

Caelyn went straight back to frowning at him.

So much for a better mood, Bry sighed.

"There is nothing so special about living here," Caelyn stated, turning her attention to a book laid open on her desk. "If my mom wasn't so insistent that I live here, I would have much preferred to stay at the forest villa."

Bry hummed as he walked around the room before finally depositing himself on the empty chair he imagined the guard had vacated.

"Yeah, it did surprise me when *our* mother asked for you to come live here." Bry slipped the correction in as subtly as he could, but that didn't stop Caelyn from snapping her head up. Fire glowed in her green eyes.

Loreda's eyes. And mine. Bry blinked as he noticed the similarities. *They match the scarf though. A little...*

"*My* mother wanted something good for me," Caelyn spat. "*You* exiled her. If things went the way she wanted...you should be dead."

Bry stared dumbly at the blatant hatred in her voice. He had not expected that much pure loathing from his half-sister.

He opened his mouth to speak but found nothing to say. In the silence, he heard her mumbling under her breath.

"And *you* should have died. Not my dad." Her lip trembled only enough to be noticed for a scant moment before her mouth twisted into a grimace again.

Bry rubbed his head.

Should have let Stori handle this.

He leaned forward in the chair to catch her eye.

"I am sorry you lost your father. I am. But I can't apologize for protecting my kingdom or for living." He paused a moment as she turned her gaze of unshed tears toward him. "Your parents committed treason. I'm sorry you have to suffer for it, but that is what it is."

When her gaze turned from pain to anger, Bry realized he shouldn't have said the last part.

"I hope you die," Caelyn stated with a voice of ire.

Bry twitched. He continued anyway, hoping something to find the right words, the right explanation, for the girl to understand.

"Loreda wanted what was best for you when she asked for you to live here. I intend to honor that, for your sake, not her's."

Caelyn's jaw clenched shut, and her eyes burned with hatred.

Bry gave up after a moment of angry silence. He moved to the door, pausing again for her to say something but left when she remained silent.

The moment he closed the door, an object crashed against it.

"I hate you!" Caelyn screamed from inside.

Definitely should have let Stori handle it.

Bry shook his head sadly before turning to head to Klaas and Eleanora's.

CHAPTER 10

"So, the Vis."

Lawr rolled his eyes at Shad's feign of solidarity as he spoke around a mouthful of elderberry muffin.

He had come to Klaas to find answers and a quiet place to work, but Shat had found him within five minutes and disturbed all that.

Maybe he's practicing using his powers.

Lawr blinked at the idea. Since Shad had been back from Oroitz, he had lamented a few times that he had not been able to find Harailt before the battle.

Maybe that's why? Or maybe Shad was already on his way down here and I'm thinking too much.

Lawr shook his head.

"Yes, the Vis." He turned back to Klaas, hoping the man would continue his roundabout explanation without prompting.

Klaas slurped at his tea but remained otherwise stoic and silent.

"What about the Vis can't be questioned?" Lawr continued, waiting for a sign the older man would be answering anything. "Shad said it couldn't be talked about or something."

Shad started to pitch in a cheerful, mouthful-of-muffin retort, but Lawr silenced him with a glare.

Klaas remained quiet long enough for his audience to twist with eager frustration at his sloth-like pace.

"Shad isn't far wrong, actually," he said when he finally spoke.

Shad beamed at the praise.

Lawr waited.

"It isn't that you *can't* ponder about the Vis. It is just that you will never truly know what it is."

Lawr shifted with new questions, but Klaas cut him off with a raised hand and a question of his own.

"What happens when you shine a light on a shadow?" Klaas glanced between them for an answer.

"Nothing," Shad stated.

"The shadow recedes," Lawr said in unison.

Klaas nodded.

"No matter how much you try to light up a shadow, it can never be done. Vis is like a shadow." He frowned. "No, Vis is a shadow. Vis is everything that is not."

"Everything that is not," Shad and Lawr repeated the phrase with frowns.

"Yes, exactly. Think of everything that exists," Klaas continued, ignoring their confused faces. "Now think of everything that does not."

Excessive frowns.

"The more you chase a shadow, the more it flees. You cannot *know* the unknown. If something is known, it isn't Vis."

"I don't think my brain likes this," Shad stated, pinching the bridge of his nose and frowning at the two older men.

Lawr remained silent as he worked to remember and pull up old conversations to form new questions.

"How does Vis leave a world then? Terrae has less Vis. The air is certainly less heavy"—He frowned at his word choice—"less full. Lucianca is even more full."

Klaas nodded with a mischievous smirk.

"Many Terranians are afflicted by a terrible need-to-know. Always with questions." Klaas directed his smirk toward Lawr before turning somber again. "People chase the shadow. They light an entire room to find it. They do find explanations. Between gods, religion, and science, there are answers, but the shadow is gone to only the darkest corners. The things that are unknown, that *need* the unknown. They disappear too."

"Sounds dangerously close to 'ignorance is bliss,'" Lawr stated, cutting his sharp tone with a smile.

Klaas chuckled. "Ignorance is never true bliss, but neither should you confuse knowing with understanding."

Lawr hummed at the answer but remained in thought. The shadow analogy had thoroughly marred his idea for using an understanding of the Vis for the AaD network problem.

He stole a glance at Shad. The kid was stuffing his face with muffins, apparently content to ignore the rest of the conversation.

Shad can't stay in Terrae for long. Low Vis.

Lawr thought back to their conversations. He remembered Shad mentioning there used to be more. The word 'dragon' flickered through Lawr's mind and found a place on his tongue before he could stop it.

"Are there dragons here then?"

Shad turned a pair of confused glowing eyes toward Lawr. The kid wouldn't even need telepathy to tell Lawr he thought he was a bit crazy.

"Dragons?" Klaas gave the word a frown. "I will thank the loss of Vis in Medius that, no, there are not."

Still some in other sphaeres though. Shad's voice said in Lawr's head. He turned to the wraith, whose mouth was still overfull of food.

"Really? Which ones?"

"I believe there are a few in Lux Aequor, Sylva, and even Lucianca," Klaas answered.

Lawr darted a glance from Klaas to Shad. He didn't know Shad could telepathically talk to multiple people at once.

The sound of a knock followed by the door opening brought the discussion to a pause.

"Hey, Bry," Lawr called out while waiting for the king to make it into the kitchen.

Bry wandered around the corner, rubbing his head with an impressive look of woe about him.

"Hey Bry, long day?" Shad greeted with a smile and held out a muffin to the redhead who accepted and ate it in two bites.

Shad frowned a moment and turned to Lawr. "How'd you know it was him?"

"'Cause you were already here," Lawr answered.

Obviously, Shad, you're the only other person who would enter after knocking without waiting for someone to answer the door.

Lawr wasn't sure if Shad was listening or not, but he didn't think the question needed a verbal answer. Especially not when Bry was looking so worn out at mid-morning.

"Tried talking to Caelyn again," Bry explained, apparently answering Shad's first question. He leaned his elbows on the table and reached for another of the baked goods, eating it slower this time.

"Didn't go so well?" Shad asked, his trademark smile masking any emotions.

Bry grunted, picking at the crumbs in front of him before answering.

"Guess I wouldn't be the first king in history to have all my blood relations want me dead."

"That bad?" Klaas frowned.

Bry groaned to himself before shaking his head.

"Probably not. She just thinks of me as the person who killed her father and drove away her mother. No, she *does* definitely hate me. 100%."

"I'm sure she'll come around," Lawr offered, not really sure of anything.

Bry shrugged but looked unconvinced. He glanced around the room, ending with a small frown.

"Where's Eleanora?"

"Out doing her 'court healer' duties. Sorting out the nobility and stuffy sorts in the castle," Klaas answered, taking another muffin, tearing it in half, and placing half in front of Bry.

Bry ate, seeming to take no notice of where the half muffin had come from.

Lawr raised an eyebrow at that.

"My assistance was offered," Klaas continued without noting any oddity, "but apparently my humor doesn't impress those sorts."

"He's benched," Shad snickered.

Bry snorted and started cleaning the crumbs before another muffin appeared from Shad's hand.

"I'm good" Bry placed the baked good back on the plate, but another appeared.

"You're behind two," Shad stated with vague indifference as he started eating another one. "Going on three."

Bry scoffed and rolled his eyes, not taking the bait. After staring at the muffin for a moment longer, he relented.

"You're on."

Lawr was tempted to roll his eyes at the odd little competition but instead focused his observational skills on Bry.

He has lost weight.

Lawr blinked at the sudden realization. He wasn't sure when it happened, but the king was definitely slighter than when they had first met.

He may even be slimmer than he was when he left for Oroitz.

Oroitz.

Both Bry and Shad were always oddly out of sorts when the topic of Oroitz or that battle was being discussed.

Lawr shifted his attention to Shad. The wraith seemed to be eating fine, but his blue-gray skin was paler than usual and dark circles under his eyes were black-gray and deep.

I need to watch out for him too.

"So, what riveting conversation did I interrupt with my dull and gloom?" Bry's question interrupted Lawr's thoughts, but he was glad if his curiosities could still be answered.

"Vis and dragons," Shad offered.

Bry raised an eyebrow and turned toward Lawr. "Uh-huh."

Lawr shrugged. "They are good topics for a snack break. We were on dragons." He glanced between Shad and Klaas, "and I take it they're not well-liked."

"Oh, no, no, no." Shad waved his hands, beating what looked to be ardent disagreement from Bry.

"I'd say. Dragons are great," Bry stated. "As long as you have enough time to deal with them."

"Right, they're awesome." Shad nodded. "Just better from a distance. They usually house some twisted sorts of personalities."

"Wait, they are intelligent?" Lawr fought the smile clawing at his lips as his mind flickered back to all the dragon movies he had loved as a child.

Maybe Dragonheart was close.

"Intelligent?" Shad scoffed. "They're smart"—He cringed at the word as he said it—"but I don't know if I'd call them intelligent."

"They can be," Klaas added. "Though most I've heard of are more like a talking dog or a small child."

"I heard of one in Lucianca that was considered smart, even by the Lucians." Bry frowned. "Never met one myself, though."

Shad waved a finger in Klaas's direction, "Yeah, a child or talking dog. That's probably the best way to think of them. A 10-ton dog with a sense of humor and no idea what 'consequences' are."

"A *flying* 10-ton dog," Bry corrected. "Most can fly."

"Yeah, they're great and super entertaining." Shad nodded, focusing back on Lawr. "Just as long as they are nowhere near your house or anything you don't want potentially destroyed."

Lawr rubbed his brow, checking his eyebrows had not departed off the top of his head at the explanations.

Scratch Dragonheart, that movie is now dead to me.

"Noted," He conceded when he noticed the young pair staring and awaiting an answer. The pair nodded, content they had made their point.

A moment of blessed silence and thought passed before Bry interrupted it again.

"So, how's all the other work coming?" Bry's tone was as unassuming as possible, but Lawr still grimaced at the familiarity of status updates. No matter how useful and valuable they were, he still despised the waiting to tell of his lack of progress.

Shad exaggeratedly groaned and let his head fall against the table in his usual, dramatic fashion.

"Pitifully."

Bry nodded even though the wraith couldn't see it and waited.

"The friend of a friend said all the tribes are all riled up. Shocking, I know. As usual, each tribe's Wolves are nowhere to be found. The Aynur tribe seems to have become the de facto leader. It has absorbed all the stragglers from the four tribes we obliterated in Oroitz." Shad paused to hold up a finger. "And that includes their Wolves."

"The Aynur tribe now has five Wolf packs at their disposal?" Bry grimaced.

Lawr frowned as even Klaas looked perturbed by the news.

"Yeah, five." Shad sat up to look grim. "That's all I've been able to find out. Everything with the tribes is a mess, they're not organized to do anything yet, but they seem to be working on it."

Lawr held up a hand to gather their attention.

"What are Wolves? I assume you're not talking about the animals."

"They are the Nomad's stealth fighting squad." Bry used each descriptive term with air quotes and a frown.

"They are kids," Klaas added. "Nomads are slave traders, kids they take between five and eight years old, they train up to be Wolves. Packs are a group of kids that were trained together, usually six or eight kids in a Pack. Packs usually rotate every two to three years."

"Rotate?"

"As the members die off," Klaas frowned darkly, "Wolves have a very short life expectancy. I've never heard of one reaching even twenty."

"Of all the terrible things the Nomads do." Shad tapped against the table with an angry frown, "the things they do to their Wolves are the worst. They're just kids."

"But they are effective and well-trained," Bry added after the silence had sat for a moment. "Not to be underestimated."

Lawr ground his jaw, thinking about it.

They don't even live to twenty? All those kids live such short lives.

He thought of everything he had done since he had turned twenty, so many many years ago.

"So, Lawr?" Bry again interrupted Lawr's dejected thoughts.

"Yeah?" Lawr blinked as he couldn't remember what they had been discussing before.

"How's your work going?" Bry asked in a tone broaching on hopeful.

Lawr despised that hope since he was going to disappoint.

"Shuffled all the Oracaede intel I decoded off to Chesler. There are still portions with security in place that I've been picking at when I have a free moment." Lawr paused, thinking over his work on the FCKing Mess.

Not the physics definition of work. Lawr grimaced at the thought.

"For the FCKing Mess, I've hardly made any progress yet. I was able to connect one device to another in the same room, but that's it."

"One device to another." Bry repeated with a pained look.

"Abysmal, I know." Lawr growled, rubbing his scruffy whiskers with a hand. He still had no ideas for how to connect all the AaDs to the Vis again. He had hoped an understanding of Vis would help, but apparently not.

And we're right back to square one. Again.

"If it makes you feel better," Bry started with a sheepish but pained smile, "I haven't made any real progress with how I'm going to convince my people about Oracaede. So, I am actually glad for the extra time."

"No, that doesn't make me feel better, but thanks anyway."

They returned to picking at the muffins.

Lawr thought about the AaDs. He recalled the televised speech Stori had given when Bry was in Oroitz.

Maybe I could broadcast a signal to force the AaDs to connect?

Lawr paused mid-bite to think through that idea.

It might work. Worth a shot at least.

"You going to eat that Lawr, or wait for it to disintegrate?"

Shad's question pulled Lawr, irritably back to the present.

He gummed through the mush in his mouth before swallowing and frowning toward the wraith.

"Huh?"

"Nothing." Shad was back to focusing on his own muffin with a wink.

Lawr rolled his eyes and continued focusing on his idea.

This should work.

The relief at being useful and solving some problem was as tangible to him as the chair he sat on.

CHAPTER 11

Stori adjusted her posture again as she waited for Leha to return with their breakfast. She shifted her corset as much as possible to put less pressure on her sore chest.

She wondered if the discomfort stemmed from her previous night with Bry. The thought still pulled heat to her cheeks even after the several nights they spent together in the last few weeks.

She shook her head of the thoughts and shifted the corset again as she heard the latch of her door open.

"Leha?" She stood from her bed and moved to the study. "I was afraid you had been the one lost this time."

The smile and another tease drifted from Stori's face and mind when she saw her maidservant's red-rimmed eyes as Leha was struggling against tears while trying to push the breakfast cart into the room.

"Leha? What's wrong?" Stori rushed to her friend, pulling the car through the door and out of the way as she wrapped her shawl around Leha.

Leha was sniffling back sobs as Stori led her to the couch and guided her to sit.

"Can I get you anything?" Stori scanned the breakfast cart for anything of comfort. "Tea? Biscuits?"

Leha shook her head, drawing in heavy breaths.

"He's gone," she finally whispered. The words unleashed more tears flowing.

Stori wrapped her arms tighter around her friend. She furrowed her brows, trying to think of who Leha meant.

"They...they found his helmet from the battle," Leha continued.

Stori bit her lip. She had one idea for who Leha was talking about.

"Chess?" she whispered, hoping she was wrong.

"Who else?" Leha wailed.

Stori breathed and hugged her friend tighter.

"I'm sorry, Leha."

Stori tried thinking of what else she could say, but there was nothing. Nothing in her mind to console her friend in her loss.

They sat in silence instead until Leha's crying died back to barely audible. Stori leaned back into the couch and rubbed circles on Leha's back, waiting for the girl to decide to talk.

"He was a castle guard." Leha twisted her fingers together. "He should never have been in that battle."

Stori watched as her face grew darker.

"If His Majesty had handled the Nomads better…"

"Leha," Stori spoke instinctively to defend Bry, but she paused, trying to think how to comfort her friend. "Bry did everythin—"

"No, he didn't!" Leha snapped. Her glare burned through Stori as she clenched her fists. "He should have acted sooner. If he hadn't waited so long—"

"That isn't fair, Leha, and you know it."

"I don't care!"

Leha wrenched away from Stori to stand. She glared down at Stori a moment before the look turned tearful.

"You don't care. You got what you wanted, His Majesty came home."

"Leha." Stori stood, calming words on her tongue, but Leha spun abruptly and ran out the door, fresh tears rolling down her face.

"Leha!" Stori called after her but to no avail.

She slumped back to the couch and held her head as she tried to think about what she could do for her friend.

No immediate solution presented itself. Stori called an attendant to find what information they could on the man's funeral arrangements.

Stori ignored a severe stomach ache, hoping it was just from a lack of breakfast, as she grabbed a plate of food from the breakfast cart and moved to the passage to Bry's room.

Once at his door, Stori didn't even bother knocking as she entered. As she suspected, he was already in his study.

If he even left at all last night.

She sighed at the thought.

Bry's voice carried through to her from the study as a constant monolog, interrupted every so often with a stream of self-directed curses. Stori imagined his practice for giving the speech about Oracaede was only going as well as the short spaces between curses.

However, Stori was too focused on Leha's loss to listen as she entered the study with a light knock.

"Have you had breakfast?" Stori asked, setting the plate of food at his desk without waiting for him to say no. Lawr had mentioned the need to force Bry into eating, and every time Stori saw him, she agreed more.

"Was going to go for food in a little bit." Bry smiled as he returned from his pacing path to the desk.

Stori smiled and gave him a kiss. "No, you weren't."

Bry opened his mouth to speak but seemed to think better of it. His smile morphed into a concerned frown as he studied her.

"Is something wrong?"

Stori frowned and sat on the edge of the desk, fidgeting with the corners of some paperwork.

I shouldn't have brought this problem to him.

She thought as she studied her husband's bloodshot eyes and the permanent dark circles under them.

"I probably can't solve the problem right now, but I can listen to it," Bry offered with a raised eyebrow.

"It's Leha," Stori stated after offering a small smile at his joke. She explained about Chess and the conversation a moment ago.

Bry scowled for a moment at Leha blaming him but didn't comment on it.

"She knew him long enough to be so attached?" Bry asked, doubt held strong in his features.

Stori recoiled, ready to defend her friend.

"About as long as I've known you."

Sympathy returned in Bry's look. "I see."

He waited a breath. "Is there anything I can do for her?"

"No." Stori hurried the negative answer. The last thing she wanted was to create more problems for Bry to worry about.

"I'm thinking of what I can do to help her," Stori explained. "I was hoping to come upon a useful idea while talking to you, but I still can't think of anything."

Bry sat in his chair, leaning back in thought.

"Wouldn't keeping her company while she grieves be the best thing for her?" Bry glanced at her as he spoke. "Within reason, I know you are busy too."

"Yes, I can do that." Stori frowned. "But I don't want her blaming you for it."

Bry laughed humorlessly. "Don't worry about defending me. One more person hating me doesn't make that much of a difference."

"Bry." Stori glared. She didn't want anyone hating him, especially for something that wasn't his fault.

And especially not Leha.

Bry shrugged.

"I'm sure she doesn't really mean it anyway. She's upset and lashing out. Please don't take it personally on my account."

He patted her hand, and she pouted back at him.

"She's your friend and was your friend before I became your husband. See her through it, and seriously, don't worry about me." Bry smiled. "One more person thinking I'm a monster isn't going to be the end of me or Sentre."

"You're not a monster though," Stori stated firmly. The word 'monster' instantly pulled forward thoughts of Loreda. She hated the thought.

"You'll work something out," Bry reassured. "With her, Caelyn, and all the people who won't listen to me."

Bry smiled at some joke only he knew as Stori groaned at the mention of his half-sister.

I still haven't even spoken to Caelyn yet.

CHAPTER 12

Aike stepped up to the bar and ordered another drink while keeping a keen eye on the men he had been talking to. They were leaning close, discussing the 'news' he had brought to Sentre.

The influx of refugees after the Avare...

Nomads. Aike reminded himself. *To the rest of the worlds, they're Nomads, not Avare.*

Battle in Oroitz meant more new people in Sentre and an easier time for the Wolves to blend.

The added confusion of each refugee telling a different tale made it impossible to distinguish the lies Aike and the Wolves weaved in with facts. The Wolves' stories were far less flattering of Brynte than most others.

Aike's attention wandered to the corner of the tavern that Hid occupied. He highlighted his younger appearance by drinking coffee rather than a strong drink. Acting young worked in Hid's favor as he spoke with two overbearing-mother type of women about his woes in another village near Oroitz. His Hispanic appearance and accent worked perfectly for the region he was pretending to be from.

Oh, I hate you for that, Hid.

Aike slurped a sip of bitter beer and wished he had picked a cover identity closer to his actual age. Or at least one that didn't drink.

Hid snuck a nervous glance that turned condescending in Aike's direction. As though he could sense Aike's drinking-aged regret.

"Bastard," Aike grumbled and wandered back to his own table and audience. He tucked away his native accent as it didn't lend itself to the region he was supposed to be from.

He sat as the three men at the table glanced over their shoulders with extra caution before leaning in close.

"The king really did that?" One who chewed too much tobacco to ever leave the rancid smell behind asked.

"I'd heard da king could be ruthless, but..." The one still nursing bruises from his last bar fight trailed off.

The third man in Aike's audience was skinny and quiet, but he, too, frowned and mumbled something. The only word Aike could make out was 'Vlasis,' to which the others shared a nod and grimace.

"The bastard probably thought no one from my village would survive to tell," Aike growled through another sip of ale. He glanced around nervously, "And it'd be best that he don't be finding out."

"Da bastard thinks he'll sacrifice a whole village to stall the Nomads and get praised for it," Bar Fight growled, thudding his fist against the table and sloshing ale from Aike's mug.

Aike helped a bit more to tip out before withdrawing it from the table with a practiced, annoyed look.

"Of course, they didn't kill everyone. Greedy bastards." Aike continued, savoring how the three men leaned closer, caught on his every word. "Nomads always take slaves."

The men swore amongst themselves but stayed attentive when Aike opened his mouth again.

"My new wife, Kassia." Aike paused to gulp at his drink. He worked not to cough over the flavor but instead twisted his features from disgust to the proper level of sorrow.

"The bastards took her," he finished, letting his voice quiver, just sorrowful enough before turning to anger to finish the performance with clenched fists. "I came here for supplies and information before I go looking for her, but the bloody AaDa aren't working."

Tobacco grumbled, "Yeah, they've been out since the 'ol queen tried taking the thrown."

A fresh round of grumbling before Skinny added, "Just before the king came back, it was."

Aike watched the men's expressions a moment, carefully timing his comment, "Well, that's just convenient, ain't it."

Three pairs of eyes snapped back to Aike.

"Convenient, yeah." Bar Fight seemed to be turning the idea over in his head.

Aike glanced around again before leaning closer. "Mine can't be the only village he did this to, but with the AaD network down, who's to say? Could be a whole slew 'a villages that can't get the word out."

The men cussed anew at the thought.

Aike sat back, sipping his ale, watching the men's reactions.

From the corner of his eye, Aike noticed movement as Hid stood and made his way toward the exit. Hid drummed his fingers against his thigh in a manner easily mistook for a nervous tick that fit his nature. Every Wolf in their team knew better though and Aike acknowledged the tapped message of where Hid would be waiting for him outside.

Aike waited another span, letting the men draw their own conclusions before he excused himself. He stood on unsteady feet, sickened to the idea of walking, and worked to stop his stomach from rolling as he exited the tavern and turned down the next alley over. Halfway down the alley, hidden behind empty ale casks, Hid sat waiting with a bucket he handed to Aike in favor of a greeting.

Aike skipped a greeting just the same in favor of emptying his beer-laden guts in the bucket.

"Next time," Aike mumbled as he finished spitting out his insides, "you get to be the drinking-aged one."

"Why, *hermano*?" Hid shook his head. "My ladies perfectly bought me as a tender young soul. And apparently you didn't have any issues convincing even the barkeep that you should drink."

Aike grimaced and wiped his mouth on his sleeve as he stepped around the bucket to continue down the alley. Hid matched his step and was at his side in a moment.

"'Cause you're older than me, for one," Aike continued. He carried the conversation out into the street with his token grin and accent back in place. His mouth still tasted of rot and bile though.

"Can hardly fault me six months," Hid countered. "Besides, without the ale to grimace at, you'd be grinning too much. Nobody would trust a word you said."

"Gobshite jerk."

"*Cállate estúpido*."

Aike laughed out of habit as they turned down a side alley and started weaving a twisted path away from the main streets toward their inn. He watched the rooftops as he moved and noticed Hid watching the dark corners of each alley too.

Oracaede's Ghost and the sniper had yet to arrive in Sentre or, if they had arrived, had yet to contact the Wolves. The more time passed without word from their new targets, the more nervous Aike was about taking them out. The idea of having any of Oracaede's agents around was nerve-wracking enough, but at least with them in sight, Aike and Hid could plan a way to kill them.

If I have to explain to Reb they never showed up…

He shuttered at the thought. Reb would have him killed and probably shunt the assignment onto Hid and the others anyway."

"We need something big to get the public where we need them," Hid stated.

Aike's attention snapped back to the world of alleyways around him. He frowned and nodded at the statement.

"The king has given us plenty to work with already." He chewed on the thought a moment. "The AaDs being down is a huge benefit too."

"I used that in my story, too," Hid said.

"Too useful to leave out," Aike said to fill the silence. "But they'll have it fixed any time now."

"But for something big enough to cause the civil unrest Reb is looking for…" Hid paused and waited until Aike picked up the point.

"If we can use an existing issue without creating one, that may fit into the timetable."

"Especially once Reb moves it up as she always does." Hid sighed as they moved toward the lower section's marketplace for any new news.

"Surely we can find something useful." Aike gesticulated widely at nothing.

The walk was mute for a moment.

"The old queen, Loreda?" Aike threw it out, already knowing it wasn't good enough.

"Considered it." Hid chewed his lip. "Only thing we could say is that he was too soft with her sentencing."

Aike laced his hands behind his head.

"I don't know about you, but the king being too soft does go against my stories," he said rhetorically. The king being too brutal was their front-running plan.

They reached the marketplace plaza. A televised broadcast from the king was displayed against the wall building.

"Well, shit," Aike spat. "There goes our best weapon."

And I needed the AaDs to still be down for my stories to really—

Hid grabbed Aike's arm in a tight grip.

Aike glanced and frowned at the smile blooming as Hid remained fixated on the broadcast.

Aike focused on the broadcast too.

King Brynte was in the middle of a speech addressing the people of Sentre with an update on Oracaede.

The devil of an organization was still in operation.

Shocker.

Aike ignored the gasps and mumblings of the people around him. One interesting, interesting point caught his attention.

Brynte had known about Oracaede for some time and kept it secret.

"Well, well." Aike grinned as he heard the king say that.

"I believe that will do nicely for our unrest," Hid said as he pulled out a notepad and started scribbling notes from the speech.

CHAPTER 13

C aelyn stared with her mouth agape as she watched the speech from her personal AaD.

Oracaede.

The name tumbled around in her head. Even her mother was afraid of them.

Rhoeo, the bodyguard she was glad to have with her, stood at her side, staring at the screen with the same rapture.

"*For all the Vis above,*" Rhoeo whispered in Spanish.

"*Sí.*"

"He knew about this," Rhoeo stated as the broadcast ended. "You don't think he'd work with…" She trailed off without finishing the question.

Caelyn tensed at the idea.

"I don't know," she stated finally. "I have no idea what he might do."

Caelyn bit her lip to keep it from trembling.

Mom, I wish you were here.

She could cry at the thought. The homesickness overwhelmed her, but she swallowed it back before Rhoeo could see. Loreda wasn't there to help her. She never would be again with Brynte ruling.

"Do you think he'd tell you if you asked?" Rhoeo asked with a note of caution.

Caelyn recoiled at the thought. Just the idea of seeing him made her angry.

"I doubt he would tell me anything," she snapped, then immediately apologized to Rhoeo.

"I could try." Caelyn finally relented when Rhoeo stood waiting with an expectant look, for more than just an apology.

Rhoeo nodded. "Do you want me to come?"

Oh yes. For the love of all the Vis in the world, yes.

"Do what you want," Caelyn said instead in a tone just shy of flippant. She stood and walked to the door.

She smiled as she turned outside the door and Rhoeo was noiselessly following her.

Down the hallway, up a flight of stairs, and she stood before Brynte's study door. She floundered outside for a short moment as she tried hardening her nerves against seeing her half-brother again.

Just do it already.

Caelyn kicked at the door with her fuchsia-colored riding boots as a preferred alternative to knocking. She entered without waiting for an invite.

Inside, Brynte sat at his desk, surrounded by his wife, the wraith, and a lanky older man Caelyn didn't recognize.

"Brynte, I want to talk for a moment," Caelyn stated with a tone she had stolen straight from her mother when Loreda refused to be ignored.

The redhead blinked at her with an arched eyebrow that distorted his already ugly scar even further.

"Sure, Caelyn."

Caelyn twinged with something unfamiliar and painful as she watched the jovial group dissipate.

The older man already had the wraith's arm and was dragging him toward the door.

"We'll be leaving for lunch first then, Bry," he called back to the king. As he passed Caelyn, he nodded a polite gesture to Caelyn but never stopped frowning.

"See you later, Caelyn! Hope you've been well—" The wraith's attempt at conversation was cut short as the older man closed the door behind him.

Stori remained at Brynte's side a moment longer. She gave her husband's arm a light squeeze.

"I expect to see you down there, Bry. You shouldn't keep Eleanora waiting too long."

The queen's gentle smile turned to Caelyn before she moved to stand directly in front of her.

"It is good to see you again, Caelyn. I hope we could talk soon." Her smile shifted as she held out her hands to give Caelyn's a light squeeze.

"Would you care to join me for afternoon tea today?"

Any biting, rude remarks she had for Brynte sizzled out of Caelyn's mind as she faced the queen's soft smile.

"Maybe." She finally conceded when she could make her tongue say 'no' outright.

"Excellent." Stori smiled brighter and gave her hand a warm squeeze. "I will be looking forward to your company."

Caelyn watched until Stori left the room, taking all her goodwill with her.

"Is this about the broadcast just now?" Brynte asked as soon as the door was shut again.

Caelyn's agitation returned at the first sound of his voice.

"Yes, as a matter of fact." She marched the distance to his desk and slapped her hands against it, happily unsettling a few papers that drifted down to join the many on the floor.

"Are you working with them?" Caelyn timed her question to just cut off the king as soon as he opened his mouth.

Brynte's expression sunk to a frown before lightening again with a too-tight smile.

"I must not have done a good enough job with my speech if that was the impression it gave."

"Forgive me, Your Majesty," Rhoeo spoke with the briefest of respectful nods, "but it is a natural assumption. Especially given Vlasis's past connection."

The scowl was back.

"What Vlasis did as king has nothing to do with me," he snapped.

Brynte immediately pinched his brow as he squeezed his eyes closed a moment.

"I apologize, that was rude of me."

"It's a fair question," Caelyn snapped back with an urge to defend Rhoeo.

"I see it was a mistake to send Shad out," Brynte mumbled just loud enough to be heard as he glanced back and forth between them.

"Your father was the first Median king to work with Oracaede. Naturally, people would be suspicious," Caelyn stated. She felt exactly how petty it was to emphasize that Vlasis was only Brynte's father, not hers, but she ignored the guilt.

Bry sighed as he rested his elbows on the desk, weaved his fingers together, and propped his chin on top of them.

"Vlasis has nothing to do with my rule," he repeated more forcefully. "I did know about Oracaede for a time, but I have been working to overthrow them since finding out."

Caelyn rolled her eyes as the verbiage he had used in his speech made its way into the conversation.

"Yeah, we know. We heard the speech," she chided.

"And publicly stating you're against them means nothing in this room," Rhoeo added with a sharp edge.

Brynte narrowed his eyes as he regarded Rhoeo. He unlaced his pinkies and pointed them toward her.

"Who are you again?"

"My bodyguard." Caelyn shifted her weight until she moved back into Brynte's line of sight. "And she makes another fair point."

He gazed at Rhoeo with a frown a moment longer before turning his attention back to Caelyn with a softer look.

"Caelyn," Brynte's gaze stared straight through her, "I know you aren't going to believe anything I say, so you will have to watch what I do and make up your own mind. I am against Oracaede."

She scoffed and glanced away.

How dare he glare at me like that with Mom's eyes.

"We'll see what's true about that."

Brynte sighed and jerked a hand through tangled red hair.

"Yeah, we'll see."

His attention had returned to Rhoeo with a suspicious frown.

"You look familiar," he stated in an offhand manner.

"She should," Caelyn jumped in. Somehow his attention toward Rhoeo unsettled her. "She's been with me since I arrived."

"No, that's not it," Brynte mumbled before shaking his head.

Caelyn wanted to argue the point, but Rhoeo caught her arm and gestured toward the door.

Of course, Rhoeo doesn't like his distrust either.

Caelyn started toward the door without saying goodbye even as she heard Brynte wishing her a good day.

Retracing her route back to her rooms, Caelyn slumped back into the chair she had vacated. Her mother's voice in the back of her mind reminded her to sit up straight, which she begrudgingly did.

Rhoeo was beside her, chewing a thumbnail with unusual anxiety as she poured herself a glass of water and, after a moment, poured one for Caelyn too.

"What do you think?" Caelyn asked as she took the cup.

She disliked Brynte as much as ever but couldn't imagine him actually working with Oracaede.

Rhoeo's sharp eyes regarded her for a long moment before she answered, "I think he wasn't very convincing."

Caelyn swallowed at the answer. She wondered what Rhoeo had seen that she hadn't, but decided to ask later.

Caelyn mumbled an okay as she turned over the terrifying idea in her head.

What would I do if he is?

The question scared her as she again wished for her mother's reassuring presence.

CHAPTER 14

Ali walked through the Empty, annoyed that they had to leave the lizard-horse creatures in Glacius Tesca. Sverre and Dain both said the creatures stood out too much in Lux Aequor and wouldn't be of much use anyway since boats were the most common mode of travel.

Time was hard to track after they entered the Empty, but the last day and a half of traveling through the desert had been exhausting enough before they started walking.

Ali stifled any of her own complaints about the trip as she watched the men carrying their heavy loads.

Dain still carried his rifle, which was now pulled around front, but he had been carrying Leon too since they had entered the Empty and the boy was asleep standing up.

Sverre kept a steady pace, though he carried both the weapon-laden duffle bags without a word of dissension.

Ali shrugged her and Leon's backpacks, trying to keep the straps from digging into her shoulders.

They walked in silence except for a few solo conversations Dain held with a forcibly cheerful tone.

Sverre was quiet beyond his normal.

Though, Ali reminded herself, *that could relate to how tired he has to be, carrying all that.*

Leon worried her. He had remained quiet since they left the house and only wanted to ride with Dain.

"…glad you get to eat Erc's cooking again?"

Ali caught the tail end of a question Dain asked and answered himself without waiting for Sverre to comment.

The mention of Dain's wife Ercilia brought new questions and curiosities to the forefront of Ali's mind again. Though Dain talked incessantly about her and the kids, Ali wasn't sure she actually knew anything more about the woman she was going to live with.

Still more than you knew about Sverre and Leon, Ali reminded herself.

She had wanted to know more about the water world of Lux Aequor too, but Dain confessed he had never been to the island his family had only recently moved to.

Sverre hadn't added anything except saying the area was beautiful and words didn't capture that. Neither Ali nor Dain pushed him into talking about Erc's home so soon after losing his own.

Erc...

"What's she like?" Ali finally asked. "Ercilia?"

"Well," Dain started immediately, but he paused just as quickly, a smile flickering over his scarred face.

Sverre just shook his head, but Ali was glad he at least responded.

If he would interact a little, I'm sure it will help.

Ali crossed her fingers, ready to carry on a conversation on her own until she could get Sverre to speak.

"You know how, on Terrae, someone might call a person a *spitfire?*" Dain finally continued with a mischievous glint in his eyes and a grin toward Sverre.

Ali nodded.

"Well, only someone who doesn't know Erc well would call her that." Dain paused long enough to give Ali a wink before turning his attention to Sverre. "A more apt description is...what was it you called her, Sverre?"

Ali smiled as she noted Dain seemed to have the same idea about drawing Sverre out of his unnaturally quiet shell.

She watched Sverre frown and grumble something about 'should have kept my mouth shut.'

"Come on," Dain encouraged.

"I just said 'hellfire' was a better description than spitfire. And I said that as a compliment after a week locked up with her," Sverre defended.

Ali clenched her jaw to keep her face stony and blank. She didn't know Sverre had spent any length of time 'locked up' with Dain's wife. She wasn't sure how much more she wanted to know on the matter.

Dain just laughed.

"That's your own fault. If you can't stand the company, don't kidnap people."

Ali balked at that.

"You kidnapped his wife?!"

How are you two even friends?

Ali could not even guess at the answer. The more she learned about the two, the less she understood them.

Dain's grin only widened at her question as he sauntered his gait to match Sverre. Even Ali could guess he wasn't going to stop teasing Sverre now that he had softened his mood.

"Well, to be fair, he kidnapped me too. Forced me to join Oracaede."

Ali frowned at Sverre who was now stubbornly silent, but his posture was more relaxed even under the weight of the bags.

"Oh, yeah," Dain continued smiling broadly as he started a juggling act of supporting Leon and his rifle with one arm so he could wrap his other around the albino's shoulders.

"I hated this little punk so much at the time." Dain nodded to himself with a quick glance around at Ali. "There was a long time there when I would have killed him on the spot if I had the chance."

Ali blinked at the statement. Dain was now watching her, seemingly waiting for her reaction. She waited, sneaking glances at Sverre to see if this was a topic he wanted to avoid. The last thing she wanted was to threaten him back into his silent shell.

Sverre, however, had relaxed at Dain's half hug even as he attempted to extricate himself.

Well, if Sverre isn't bothered.

Ali ventured.

"What changed?"

"Who says anything has?" Dain chirped back and received an elbow to the gut, careful to avoid Leon's sleeping form, from Sverre in response.

"Stop teasing Ali," Sverre said, blocking a light return jab.

Ali frowned.

Is Dain teasing about all this?

She wasn't sure. It sounded like him, but she still couldn't tell when he was being honest or not.

She began to ask, but Dain was already beating her to an answer.

"I was only joking about the last statement," he continued, smirking.

"I really did want to kill Sverre for…a long time."

Dain opened and closed his mouth with a smile and a frown ready a few times before he decided on a tone.

"You have to understand," he continued with a serious disposition not exaggerated in any way like his normal conversational tone. "I thought he was holding my family hostage for some nefarious purpose that was even too much for Oracaede to agree to."

Ali waited for him to continue, but Dain just frowned a painful look into the darkness in front of them without answering.

"Anyway, when did it all change?" Dain continued to answer the question Ali had forgotten she had asked.

He walked on, pondering.

"Probably after my first official assignment for Oracaede." Dain's smile slipped, and Ali watched him fight to keep it up.

He bounced back without continuing the sentiment. Ali pretended not to notice.

"About the same time, I found out Sverre was only seventeen." Dain was back to smiles.

"I don't know why Erc had to tell you that. It wasn't important." Sverre gripped.

"Now, now." Dain managed to loop his arm around Sverre's shoulders again as he practiced condescension. "She just wanted to remind me how cute you were."

Sverre scoffed.

"I wasn't cute."

Ali smiled at the disgust in his voice that matched the blush.

The same warm smile Dain sported whenever he was talking about his family adorned his lips. He gave Sverre a squeeze of a hug before Sverre could shrug him off.

Ali smiled at that too. She could see Dain thought of Sverre as a little brother more than a friend or co-worker.

Even she wasn't sure when Sverre had gone from captor to protector. Protector to a friend. And from a friend to…whatever he was now.

Ali still wasn't sure about that, but her cheeks warmed at the mere thought.

She listened to Dain ribbing Sverre about how cute he had been. She hadn't thought before about how young he had started for Oracaede, but even among the teasing, she could tell it still bothered Dain too.

"Check the AaD," Sverre finally said, distracting the sniper from his jokes.

Dain commenced the balancing act again as he pulled out the AaD that was already queued with the address.

"Almost missed it." Dain hummed and made a face. "But not quite."

Dain continued trying to work while he walked, but Sverre managed to grab the device away with a quick 'don't drop Leon.'

A huge doorway opened onto an empty hilltop of a world already asleep for the night.

"Lady and gent," Dain hastened out of the Empty, taking in a deep breath, "welcome to Lux Aequor."

Ali followed Sverre out into the darkness of the world. The weight of the air in her first step made her pause to focus on breathing.

Vis. Wow, it's heavy here.

Ali marveled at just how *heavy* the Vis made the air.

"We're there?" Leon's sleepy voice startled Ali after he had been quiet so long. The boy rubbed his eyes with a slow glance around, but Ali could see he was still more asleep than not.

"We just arrived in Lux Aequor." Sverre was quick to stand close to Leon and rub his back. "Still a ways from Erc's house. Go back to sleep."

"It's too heavy. The Vis," Leon grumbled, though he was already resting his head against Dain's shoulder again with a yawn.

Ali watched with a sad smile as Leon was already back asleep.

She finally glanced around to where they were. For a water world, as Leon had often described it, there seemed to be a surprising lack of water. But the vegetation around them was thick, tropical, and obscuring the view.

She did have to blink at the three moons hovering in the sky overhead.

Ali turned to take in the panoramic view but stopped at the strange loop of elegant machinery behind her, where they had just come through a doorway.

Tracing the curve with her eyes, Ali saw it pinched at the top before gracefully sloping another loop toward the ground some 100 feet away. The whole shape looked like a figure-eight folded over in a curve at the midpoint.

"Sverre?" Ali questioned in a light voice so as not to didn't disturb Leon. She glanced at him. Sverre and Dain were already staring down a pathway.

Sverre stepped back beside her. He followed her gaze up at the loops.

"It's a gaet," he said. "The Aequorians make them to channel where a doorway can open.

"Like the AaDs?" Ali questioned with a frown. She had heard gaets mentioned in passing before, but never really understood what they did.

Sverre shook his head.

"No, the AaDs predict where a doorway will be and help open it. The gaets force doorways to open at a specific location." He used his restricted mobility to gesture. "Here."

"They aren't used often, cause of how they affect the Vis," Dain said as he stepped up to the edge loop of the gaet and gave it a soft kick. The sound echoed through the whole structure with the pitch of a bell. "But in a world like Lux..."

"It's the only way to guarantee you won't be opening a doorway in the middle of an ocean," Sverre continued where Dain had stopped.

"Does Earth, Terrae, have gaets? It's mostly water, too," Ali asked as she looked over the elegant loops again. She would have thought it was an attempt at modern art if it hadn't been for the doorway.

"No—"

"Not like this at least," Dain interrupted as his face scrunched into a thinking frown. "There are a lot of *old* things in Terrae, I believe. I don't know if they were gaets, but when there was more Vis in Terrae, they might have done something. No Aequorian gaets, though, for sure."

"Wow," Ali breathed. She thought of the old architectures of the world, her world, and wondered what they might have done when there was enough Vis to operate them.

"Now, in Terrae," Sverre continued after he watched Dain a moment to make sure he was done, "there is too little Vis to operate one of these. And Terrae does have much more land than Lux Aequor anyway."

"No one from the united sphaeres really travels to Terrae either." Dain frowned at the thought before adding in a quiet voice, "Except *us*."

The 'us' Dain emphasized must mean Oracaede rather than them two specifically with how he said it.

Ali nodded, ignoring the *us*. There was so much to her new life away from Earth that she didn't know about. Too much, without even involving Oracaede.

"The Aequorians made the gaets anyway, and they are the only ones that use them." Dain returned to a conversation as they all started toward the path. "There are only a few here anyway. Five. They're illegal to have elsewhere."

"That's interesting," Ali said when she didn't know what else to say.

There is so much I still have to learn about this place.

"There's a village on the coast," Sverre said, leading their group down the path. "We can rent a boat to get to Erc's…your"—he nodded toward Dain with a smile—"island. It's still a solid day's travel though."

"I hope you and Erc picked out a good island," Dain said with a beaming smile that didn't dissipate during the walk.

"I had less than nothing to do with it," Sverre stated in a grumble about Erc. "Woman just does as she pleases."

Dain scoffed.

"That's my darling." He winked at Ali. "Can even bully Sverre."

CHAPTER 15

A week after Bry's speech and he was certain the whole thing had been a terrible idea.

Should have never said anything. Or let Chesler write the whole thing. Or…

"Or nothing," Bry interrupted his own thought with an irritated growl.

Chesler paused his long-winded report over how everything was a complete mess and settled a cold glare at Bry.

"Sir?" he asked with the rise of an annoyed eyebrow.

"It's nothing, keep going," Bry muttered as he tipped his head back to rest against the top of his chair.

Chesler mumbled an acknowledgment before continuing again with the depressing news.

Bry continued half-listening. Everything was negative. Some rumors were circulating about his committing war crimes in his fight against the Nomads. Those rumors weren't helped by others about his working with Oracaede. Everyone seemed to be questioning his decision not to tell his people sooner.

Not that that would have worked either when all I had was an AaD message.

Bry contented to grumble to himself until Chesler was finished and excused himself. Bry watched the man leave before tipping his head forward and burying it in his crossed arms on the desk.

"It's a bloody mess." He sighed to the mercifully empty room.

"Bry?"

Not empty enough.

Bry groaned and lifted his head.

Shad grinned at him as he stepped into the room.

"Just let me die in peace." Bry dropped his head again.

"No can do, pal."

Bry felt the desk shift as Shad sat on it.

"Klaas and Eleanora are having a little dinner party. Just us friendlies. No one to bite your head off."

"I have work to do, Shad," Bry lamented, taking in the heaps of paperwork he still needed to finish, strewn across every surface within arm's reach.

"You're not going to eat lunch *or* dinner today?" Shad raised a brow as he made a small gesture to the untouched lunch cart.

Oops.

Bry had forgotten the servant had not come to hide the evidence yet.

"I was saving that for later," Bry tried lamely.

"It's after dinner time now."

"I'll get around to it." Bry made the empty promise with only the smallest of guilt about lying.

Sorry, Shad.

"I do have to get this work done," he insisted.

Shad was ignoring him as he watched the smokey shadows swirling across his hand.

"I've been getting better at this since Oroitz." Shad finally stated, talking mostly to the swirling shadows. He shifted his fiercely glowing blue eyes to catch Bry's. "See."

Get off your ass and go eat!

Shad's voice shouted in Bry's head, followed by an unnatural but insatiable compulsion to find food.

"Shad," Bry growled even as he stood obediently, eyeing the lunch cart with new desire. "You don't get to do this."

"No?" Shad's voice lost any degree of friendly pleasantries. "Well, as your friend, I don't get to sit around and let you starve yourself either."

Shad intercepted Bry's move toward the lunch cart to drag him to the hallway and through the back corridors toward the healer's chambers.

"Stop dragging me, Shad, I'm fine." Bry twisted to escape Shad's grip, but all his attempts were in vain.

This is ridiculous, Bry.

"Shad!"

Shad paused his trek to flash Bry his most irritated smile. "If you were fine, I wouldn't be able to drag you, now would I?"

Bry continued to struggle, but he sobered with the realization that even when he was trying his best, he could not break Shad's grip on him.

"All right, fine! But let me go," Bry relented when they were nearing their destination.

Shad obligingly released him but remained watchful as though he thought Bry would waste precious energy trying to run away.

They continued until they reached the hallway to the healer's chambers. The door was open, and Klaas casually leaned against the door frame, regarding Bry.

"You didn't have to drag him?" Was his remark when they drew near.

Shad waved a hand to dismiss the idea. "Not at all."

Bry was grateful for the small lie until Shad held out an open palm to Klaas. Klaas grumbled but dropped a few coins into the shadowy hand anyway.

"You had a bet?" Bry glared at his friend as Klaas disappeared into the room.

Shad winked and patted him on the back. "I can always trust you to be a stubborn ass."

He tossed the coins in the air before they disappeared into his pocket.

"Jerk," Bry grumbled as he followed Shad into the room. In the kitchen, true to Shad's word, only their little family of friends was there.

"Hello, Bry." Stori smiled at him sweetly, "I'm glad Shad didn't have to be forceful."

"Oh, for the love of Vis," Bry threw his hands up, "who else had a bet?"

Lawr was actively not discreet in handing money to Shad.

Bry gave his friend a shove before taking his seat between Shad and Stori.

They began passing food around the table, with every person at the table commenting on Bry's portions and Shad being cheerful in adding more to Bry's plate at their behest.

By the time they were ready to eat, Bry had a pile of food no healthy, sane person could eat in two sittings together.

And there is going to be hell if I don't finish all this either. Bry grimaced as he resigned to do his best impression of a squirrel with winter nuts.

His best attempt happened to be the entire serving plus another helping of meat. For the second time since being dragged to dinner, Bry was chagrined at his own failing when it came to his wellbeing.

Have to be babied by everyone...

The thought trailed off as he glanced around his little family.

Now if only we could get Caelyn to consider joining.

He turned to Stori at that musing thought.

"Have you been able to connect with Caelyn at all?"

Stori set her glass of flavored water down and patted her lips with a napkin before answering.

"I did have tea with her last week and again two days ago. I could not say that her feelings toward you have changed, but she seems more amiable toward company now."

She paused with an apologetic smile toward Bry. "I have been spending most of my time comforting Leha. I'm afraid I haven't made much progress with either of them."

"No, don't worry about it, that's perfectly..." Bry cut off the beginnings of his ramble.

He had forgotten Stori's maidservant had her own heartbreak and tragedy.

"Your friend requires your attention too. More than Caelyn. And I should be trying to spend more time with her myself."

Stori nodded with a look of gratitude that made Bry feel guilty for putting this extra burden on her at all.

"How is poor Leha?" Eleanora asked.

Stori shook her head with a sad look.

"Still as upset as when she first learned the news."

"Of course, the poor dear." Eleanora nodded. "Is she still angry at Bry?"

Bry sensed the point of the question. Eleanora had been taking the ugly rumors that had been surfacing the last few weeks about Bry in a personal way.

"I don't know. If she is, she wouldn't mention it to me again," Stori stated.

"She just needs time to grieve freely." Bry jumped in before Eleanora could add anything cutting.

Stori smiled a small smile that radiated love. She opened her hand as an invitation to hold it. Bry reached and gave her hand a kiss and a squeeze.

"I don't think she'd do anything to harm Stori," Shad said. "And since Bry is an extension of Stori"—He elbowed Bry playfully in the gut—"that may keep him insulated from her anger."

Bry rolled his eyes and elbowed Shad back without letting go of Stori with his other hand.

"One can only hope," he stated as he turned back to stare into Stori's shy smile and brilliant silver eyes. He kissed her hand again.

"So...do we all have to leave now, or what?" Lawr's voice snapped Bry back to the reality that they weren't alone.

Bry coughed and elbowed Shad again for laughing but kept ahold of Stori's hand anyway.

CHAPTER 16

Hid stood between Sa'dia and Bary with the primary goal of preventing them from bickering as they entered yet another tavern. For their new plan of putting the king's speech to full effect, it was now better for them to be seen in groups when they were canvasing people.

Hid hoped Aike was having good luck with Caesar Apollo and Xiulan on the more unruly side of town. Or if they weren't lucky, at least he hoped they would stay safe.

They all agreed to leave the militants of the city to Idir. Leaving out only Retha. Dear, sweet, psychotic Retha, who, on her best day, with Xiulan's best makeup, could not hope to pass for a day older than 16.

He held in a sigh for whatever mess their youngest member was likely making of their inn rooms at the time. As long as she did not burn the place down, he would have to be content.

Hid wandered over to the barkeep while keeping a watchful eye on the inhabitants of the room. Most of the bar patrons were castle workers of some capacity enjoying a midday drink after their morning shifts.

"Ya still don't be lookin' old enough to be here, boy," the barkeep, a grizzled-looking, middle-aged woman noted as she eyed Hid with constant suspicion.

Why doesn't anyone ever say that to Aike?

"And yet," Hid held up a castle guard's insignia on a silk ribbon, making sure not to smile since that too would make him look his actual age, "I still am."

Castle guards needed at least five years of military experience to even be considered. Added to the age he would have had to be to enlist and the metal insignia was better than any other identification card for proving his age and employment.

And it's so much easier to steal. The king really should upscale his security, this is just too easy.

The barkeep nodded a begrudging nod, but her gaze remained just as dubious.

"Beers. Three." Hid threw a few coins on the counter as he returned to scanning the room.

The barkeep raised an eyebrow at the few coins. Hid cut her off before she could ask for more.

"Cut them with water until this covers it."

Anything to make this trip less nauseating than our last.

With a tap at his left shoulder, he leaned toward Bary.

"One o'clock. Far corner," Bary said softly.

"'Ere at ten o'clock, too." Sa'dia also whispered.

Hid observed the tables they pointed out.

In the far corner, a young lady sat nursing what appeared to be her third ale with a tear-stained face. Hid recognized her from their research into the castle staff as being the queen's personal handmaid.

Damned lucky.

He turned toward the old man at the ten o'clock table. He could not help the smirk that twisted at his lips.

Aike'll owe me some fair coin. His luck is never this good.

"Sa'dia, the girl."

Sa'dia groaned. "You're just assigning her to me because we're both women. Rather go for—"

Hid caught her gaze with a sharp glare. She tensed immediately.

"She's upset and three drinks into the afternoon. Emotional problems. Do you think she's open to talking to a strange man in her state?"

"No," Sa'dia answered with a quick duck of her head.

"Such a whining spirit. I have to talk to a man." Bary was fast to pick an argument. "Think I wouldn't rather talk to the pretty drunk lady."

Hid was just as fast in grabbing their ales and shoving Bary toward their target. He had to be quick before Sa'dia could snap back and bring the potential argument to fruition.

"Mind if we join you?" Bary returned to his cordial manners as they stood before the ten o'clock table.

The heavy-set man's frown gave him a practiced look that could melt iron. They both smiled and waited for him to decide.

The man growled and, either from being tired of craning his neck or not thinking it worth his time to get rid of them, waved his hand in the laziest possible motion, inviting them to sit.

"Much obliged." Bary smiled as he slid over the thick wood bench, making room for Hid to sit across for the man.

"Can I buy you a drink?" Hid offered, already raising his hand to flag the barkeep when the man interrupted with a curt gesture.

"I ain'd drinking," the man stated as he rested his arm around his plate, cradling his food away from them.

"Commendable, even if I could not settle much a hearty meal without a little drink." Bary continued smiling as he took a sip of the bitter ale. Hid knew Bary hated the drink as much as Aike and had an even weaker stomach.

Hid hated having to make Bary drink at all. They never knew what might aggravate his condition, but he needed at least three people in his group for safety and appearances.

"It's General Jair, isn't it?" Hid waited until the grimacing, cautious face turned back toward himself before continuing. "I know we are late in extending our thanks and congratulations for your efforts in Oroitz against the Nomads, but we had to, anyway."

"We are just recently to town, you understand," Bary added in a clear attempt to displace some of the suspicion in the general's features. "Lost our homes on those bastards' account."

Jair paused from taking a bite of his dwindling meal to eye them again.

"Sorry 'o hear. Wish you luck in finding a place here," he said earnestly.

"Thanks. It's been quite a mess here since we arrived in the city," Hid continued.

Jair only grunted at that.

Hid waited a space, taking a sip of the ale he loathed to have to partake of.

Really, all the Wolves are too young for it, why is this always necessary for a job?

He suffered another sip before trying to continue.

"We've been in town long enough to see some reruns of the king's speech on Oracaede." He pulled an appropriately disgusted face at the name, as did Jair. "Nasty business."

"A few people we had spoken with had some interesting thoughts on King Brynte's involvement with them," Bary tried. Jair's turned immediately into a guarded frown.

"We're just trying to understand the real situation," Hid quickly added, hoping to placate the general's distrust. "Find out who to trust while we are settled here."

"You can 'drus'd Bryn'e's doing all he can for 'da si'uation," Jair countered immediately.

"Of course." Bary nodded, though Hid noted him chewing around his next statement. "It just makes one concerned about the secrets the king may still be keeping about those tyrants."

Jair drew back with a discerning frown.

Shit. Too quick.

"Not that we would ever doubt the king's intentions, it's just passing concern," Hid added, observing the old general's expression.

Jair's frown turned darker, but small fidgeting movements with his plate showed his indecision.

Hid opened his mouth to take advantage of the pause, but Jair already made the decision he had been concerned with. He stood up.

"'Dis isn'd a conversation for me. Good day." He left his tray and moved toward the door.

Hid paused before making a quick decision.

"Fine, fine. But next time we'll buy you an ale for your trouble," he called after the man with his best smile.

Jair half-turned back to him with a confused frown but continued out of the tavern without stopping.

Bary shoved his drink away.

"Sorry, Hid. I lost him. And he would have been helpful too."

"Keep drinking, *muchacho*. Drinking, chatting, and most importantly, smiling." Hid took another sip, twisting his lips up passed a grimace, and kept his voice low. "He may still be useful."

Bary forced a solid grin in place and reached to grab his mug and cradle it again.

"You want people thinking he's with us anyway?"

"The people we have already spoken with here know we're up to something about the king. Let them think his most trusted general is against him too."

"Anyone ever tell you, you're a devious bastard?" Bary's grin turned real as he also watched the bar's occupants, giving a few nods to the said people already friendly to their plans.

"Aike does. Everyday."

They shared a grin as they continued sipping on their drinks and casting occasional glances toward Sa'dia when they could.

Half their ales were gone, and Bary already looked queasy for it by the time they saw Sa'dia move to join their table.

"Well, fellows, I see your target left early." She sneered at Bary as she plopped into the empty seat and dropped her empty mug down for show. "Want me to finish that for you, Bary? Lightweight."

She moved to grab his mug.

"As if I need your help," Bary growled back, jerking the mug away and chugging the rest of his drink.

He thudded the empty mug on the table with an expression that he might have to return the entire drink to its container in a hurry.

Luckily the moment passed, and he settled further into his seat, sneering at Sa'dia with a green tint to his face.

"Ours may still be useful," Hid informed Sa'dia, once he was sure he didn't need to evacuate Bary to an alleyway with a bucket. "How was yours?"

Sa'dia glanced back around at the girl and smiled. "She will be of some great help, s'long as nothin' is involving her mistress, Queen Istoria. But for the king, she was very open to the notions I suggested."

Hid nodded as he continued sampling his drink.

If only I could make it disappear without using Bary's method.

"One and a half, then. Better than we've done the last few days."

He spared a concerned glance toward Bary as he spoke. The green, queasy look had only grown.

Hid stood and helped Bary up to make a strategic escape before the curly-haired man lost his battle with nausea.

Once outside and around the corner to a dark alley, Hid paused to reevaluate.

"How you doing, Bary?"

"Yeah, Bary, how you doing?" Sa'dia grinned, though she was less stable on her feet than she had been sitting down.

Bary groaned.

"Think I will need to put all that beer back where it belongs. In the dirt." Bary was already bending over with his hands on his knees and leaning against Hid for support.

"Take your time." Hid patted his back and tried positioning himself to keep Bary on his feet without getting anything on the sole pair of shoes he owned.

"After that, I'm going to need my medicine."

That comment shut down Sa'dia's jeering quicker than anything. She grabbed his vial of medicine from his jacket pocket and measured out a dose.

"It's ready whenever you are." She handed the dose and vial to Hid, "I'll go buy some bread you can eat with it to settle your stomach."

Hid nodded and watched her dart out of the alley on steadier feet now that she had a job to accomplish.

Hid waited until Bary was done being sick and Sa'dia had returned before giving him his medicine. After Bary was more stable, they all trudged back to their inn.

CHAPTER 17

"What happened?" Hid growled, jumping up from their inn room's one couch.

His group had only just settled into their inn room. Bary rested on the floor with Retha holding ice to his head and Sa'dia fanning him with the book she wasn't reading when Aike's group arrived, each looking worse than the last.

Apart from a busted lip, Caesar Apollo hardly looked injured. That is unless one knew him well enough to note the cautious way he walked and how he was protecting his ribs.

Xiulan came in next. Hid froze at the sight of her. A red, hand-shaped welt was beginning to rise on her cheek. She held her shredded silk skirt together with one hand and used the other to hold a large rip in her matching silk blouse.

Lastly, Aike trailed in. His whole face was bleeding, along with his nose, which he was pinching and holding his head back. His shirt was torn and streaked with blood.

"Sa'dia." Hid didn't have to say more as the tanned woman was already disappearing into the girls' room.

"I'll get the kit," Bary said without prompting as he forced his way to his feet and moved to grab their medical kit.

Sa'dia returned in a moment with Xiulan's long bathrobe, which she draped over Xiulan's shaking shoulders.

Hid grabbed a clean towel from the kitchen and stepped toward Aike. He carefully padded the blood on his face. Hid scowled at the bits of glass sticking out of Aike's skin.

"You jump through a window, *hermano?*" Hid asked, hoping for an explanation as much as just hearing Aike talk would help quell some of his own anxiety.

He spared a glance toward Xiulan as Sa'dia and Retha surrounded her and guided her toward the girl's room.

Caesar Apollo carefully sat on the couch with Bary assisting as much as he could.

"Not quite. Ow." Aike flinched.

Their knock code sounded at the door before Idir entered. The dark man froze in the entryway.

"What?" Was all he managed before he moved to help Bary get Caesar Apollo's shirt off to assess the damage to his ribs.

The girls reappeared then with Xiulan dressed in another matching silk outfit, though she still clutched the robe hanging around her shoulders.

"What happened?" Hid asked again, fixing his gaze on Aike.

"Twas a small misunderstanding is what it was." Aike used his favorite expression to say they had a fight. Though his grin never faltered, Hid could see the total want of humor behind it.

"Ruffians, in the lower city." Caesar Apollo said, his high-pitched voice bouncing off the walls as his anger wasn't even close to settled. "They mistook Xiulan's appearance to be a prostitute and attempted to force their misunderstanding."

Hid glanced at Xiulan. Her expression remained serene and gave nothing away, but she had wrapped her arms around herself in a tight self-hug.

Retha followed suit with a crushing hug that her short stature wouldn't suggest possible. She held Xiulan in a comforting manner.

"Want me to hurt them?" Retha asked, looking up at Xiulan with a sweet smile.

Aike laughed.

"You are helpful as always, Retha. But Cae and I already ground some manner into them. They won't be able to feed themselves for a month as is. Would hardly any fun for you, would it?"

"Doesn't need to be fun for me," Retha snapped back, looking around Xiulan to Aike. "It would be purely for Xiulan's comfort."

Hid paused his ministrations to Aike to turn to Xiulan as well.

"She's right. Every one of us who hasn't had a turn at them yet would be more than glad to see them further dissuaded from any such similar conduct."

Xiulan nodded. She stood a moment, stroking Retha's head, disturbing the fuzzy black curls that stood a full handspan from the top of her head, before reaching a decision.

"It is all right, love," she said, addressing Retha with a fair smile until the younger girl nodded.

She turned her kind gaze to Hid. Just her soft look was enough to calm his fear for her emotional state.

"As Aike said, if they learn any more 'manners,' it would be on the way to a graveyard."

"I could live with that," Sa'dia interjected quickly. Bary nodded too, and for once they agreed.

"But I will not condone it," Xiulan stated in a firm voice with an elegantly arched eyebrow.

She stood in quiet thought a moment before speaking again with careful consideration.

"In truth, my wardrobe for that section of town was ill thought out and could naturally give rise to such notions from the lowbred amassed there."

The entire room was poised to disagree, but Xiulan held her hand up and spoke first.

"I will take greater care to be cautious on future outings. Now the matter is closed."

She looked to Aike for assistance while the others grumbled in disagreement.

Aike held her gaze for an assessing moment before nodding and addressing the room.

"She has the say. Matter's closed," Aike stated without leaving room for dissension, "I expect ya'll to follow Xiulan's lead on this."

The others nodded, however begrudgingly.

"Now," Aike continued with his goofy grin firmly in place now that his nose was no longer dripping blood. "We'll be needing more bandages for Caesar Apollo. Ya took a good ol' beating to those ribs."

"For your face too," Caesar Apollo added immediately. "That one bastard with glass knuckles clawed you up good."

Hid clenched his jaw. "Glass knuckles, Aike?"

Glass knuckles were common in Avare markets. If one was caught stealing from one of the more unforgiving merchants, one's face was rearranged. The steel plate across the knuckles could break bones, but they had just enough fabric wrapped in front that could be stuffed with glass shards.

Hid didn't know they had become popular in Sentre too. But he should have considered it with all the new refugees bringing in new weapons and ideas for using them.

"Aike, you're getting treated first."

"What?" Aike stepped back with an appalled look at the idea. "But Caesar Apollo...? His ribs?"

Hid gave Caesar Apollo an apologetic nod, which the large man waved off.

"Him first, watching him squirm is painkiller enough," he stated.

Hid turned back to Aike as the freckled man stepped backward.

"But—"

"But every moment you waste fussing is making Caesar Apollo wait in suffering," Hid stated in a tone as dry as he could make it.

He motioned toward the free section of the couch.

"Sit down, Aike."

Aike glanced between Caesar Apollo, Bary, and Idir for help but received none. Finally, he yielded and moved to sit.

"You play dirty."

"*Sí.*"

Hid sat on the coffee table across from Aike and gathered the tweezers and gauze he needed to dig out glass bits.

"You're not gonna ask for your coin of luck?" Aike asked as he irritably dodged away from Hid's attempts to treat his injuries. "Maybe you weren't so lucky either?"

Hid recognized Aike's easy style of asking for a mission report. He ignored it long enough to catch a handful of Aike's hair. He made use of his new leverage point to finally work on removing the glass.

"Well, you're the leprechaun, aren't coins yours to give out as you please?" Hid asked as he continued his rough treatment, pulling Aike's head to one side or the other as needed. "We had excellent luck. One fully willing to help and one whose name we could use to our advantage."

Aike hummed appreciation.

"And no injuries, save what beer inflicted," Hid added.

"You do have me beat there," Aike relented.

A pat at Hid's shirt pocket was tell enough that Aike had slipped him his duly won coin from their bet.

After the long half of the afternoon was spent treating the most unwilling patient, Hid could finally move on to Caesar Apollo. The big man sat like a bronze statue. A picture of the most perfect patience, Hid wished Aike would learn.

A small shadow moving around caught his attention.

"Retha."

The shadow stopped.

"Listen to Aike and Xiulan. The issue is closed." Hid didn't look away from Caesar Apollo as he spoke. "Whatever you're planning on sneaking off to do. Don't."

"On that matter," Aike spoke without missing a beat, "the low side of town is off-limits for now. If anyone must go there, it'll be Hid, Bary, and Idir. Together. The girls aren't going there. And Caesar Apollo and I can't go back."

Aike leveled a humorless grin between Sa'dia and Retha as the two grumbled a few moments beyond what was necessary.

"What was that?" Hid asked in a voice just above a growl.

"Understood," Six voices said in unison.

CHAPTER 18

"Has your time been enjoyable since coming to Sentre?" Stori asked taking a sip of tea and ignoring the pain of a stomach ache and nausea plaguing her since the morning. She had thought it was just her time of the month, except it had been a near-constant discomfort the last two weeks.

Whatever strange indigestion she was suffering, Stori took extra care it didn't show on her face. She raised an interested eyebrow to hear the answer to her question.

"It's taken some getting used to," Caelyn said as she spent more time fidgeting with her teacup than drinking from it.

Stori smiled at the younger girl's informal language. It reminded her so much of Bry when they first met. She wondered if Caelyn would appreciate the similarity.

I do need to try something.

"Yes, it took me a while to accustom myself to life here as well. And Bry too. When he first returned from exile and I was first introduced to him."

Caelyn's features tensed at the mention of her half-brother. She only grumbled something unintelligible.

Stori quickly transitioned away, talking of castle life in general and asking what was most jarring for the younger girl.

"Umm." Caelyn scrunched her face up in thought.

Stori bit her lip, not commenting on the cute expression.

"Being so far away from my horse, maybe," Caelyn said finally. She glanced at Stori for...

Approval..?

Stori could not quite decide what.

"A fine creature, indeed. I saw it only briefly when you arrived," Stori said with a smile, hoping Caelyn would continue.

"Thanks," Caelyn said with a blush and a smile. "She—Mygic's her name—she was a birthday gift from my fa—" her speech stumbled as her face fell into a frown, "From my father."

Stori's smile faded at the mention, but she was determined not to let the first real conversation thread of tea time be lost.

"I see. She is a very fine horse. I am fond of animals myself. Fenrir was a wedding gift."

She almost said 'from Bry' but decided not to chance the conversation halting over a mention of her husband again.

Stori held her hand out and whistled for the Pyxis, who had so far only been interested in pestering Caelyn's bodyguard, Rhoeo.

Fenrir doesn't like Rhoeo.

The thought was strange to Stori. Fenrir had liked or tolerated everyone he had met so far, but he refused to let the guard out of his sight the entire afternoon.

Fenrir, having caught his name and Stori's signal, came bounding back to the table with the lumbering footfalls of a giant. He stooped his head low enough to rest on Stori's lap as she petted him.

Stori turned her head from stroking her pet to observe Caelyn. She was pleased to see a smile bloom across the girl's face as she shifted her chair closer to the Pyxis.

"Fen, go say hi." Stori pointed toward Caelyn.

The happy creature immediately obeyed, pivoting his huge body until he could rest his torso-sized head on Caelyn's lap. Stori could only hope he was not drooling on the young girl's bright green dress.

Caelyn grunted under the weight but laughed before Stori could say a word about her pet's rudeness. Caelyn stroked Fenrir's head and baby-talked compliments at him.

"I apologize. He doesn't know how large he is," Stori said with a smile as she watched them for a few moments.

She spoke again when Fenrir also tried putting his dinner-plate-sized paw on Caelyn's lap.

"Careful, he will attempt to sit in your lap if he thinks he can get away with it."

Stori stood and gave the creature's collar a light tug. He turned around toward her at once.

Fenrir sniffed at her midsection before raising his head to rest against her chest as he let out a low whine.

"Yes, yes, go play now." Stori shooed him away as she used a napkin to pat off any drool he had left on her clothes. "And stop pestering Miss Rhoeo."

"He's such a sweetheart." Caelyn smiled as she watched him bound away before returning her attention to Stori. "I've never seen a Pyxis before. Will he get any bigger?"

Stori laughed as she took her seat again.

"I hope not."

Her stomach pain sounded again, and she tried not to flinch at it. Or at least hide her response from Caelyn. A glance at the younger girl showed she was still too focused on Fenrir to notice.

Caelyn's attention returned to her too quickly for Stori's comfort.

"It is hot out today." Stori cringed at her own bland attempt to keep Caelyn's attention away.

"Really?" Caelyn frowned at her. "I was deciding if I should grab a shawl or not."

"Oh? Do you run cold?" Stori couldn't think of anything else to say. She just wished she had a fan.

"Not really." Caelyn was still frowning with her full attention and vivid golden-green eyes focused on Stori. "Are you all right?"

"I am fine." Stori flushed that Caelyn should notice her unfortunate discomfort.

Her reddening face didn't seem to do anything to convince Caelyn of her health. The girl stood and moved toward Stori to rest the back of her hand against Stori's forehead.

"Are you ill? You don't feel hot." Caelyn started chewing her nail as concern showed through her features. "Should I call someone? Of do you want to go see the court healer?"

"No, no. It is nothing…" Stori paused. She didn't think Caelyn had met Eleanora and Klaas yet.

Meeting them can only improve her opinion of Bry.

"Actually, it may be a good idea to go visit Eleanora, the court healer," she ceded, hoping for all the Vis that Bry or Shad would not be there to scare Caelyn out of any comfort she might otherwise feel.

Stori stood slowly, conscious not to grab her stomach as she did. Rather than see a healer, she would have preferred to lie down for the next several weeks.

They made their slow way to Klaas and Eleanora's' chambers with Rhoeo and Fenrir following behind.

"Stori, my dear!" Eleanora exclaimed the moment they entered her chambers. "And who is this? Caelyn, I presume. You must be with this bright gown, very vibrant. And with those pink boots, I love it."

The older woman was beaming as she engulfed them both in a strong hug.

Caelyn was left sputtering in confusion as Eleanora pulled back.

Stori had to laugh at the girl's confused face.

Is that what I looked like when I met Eleanora too?

"Eleanora and her husband, Klaas, Bry's former tutor, were with him in exile. They are closer to him than either of his parents ever were," Stori explained the pertinent details as quickly as she could and hoped Caelyn wouldn't withdraw at the mention of Bry.

"Oh, and who is this?" Eleanora was all smiles as her attention turned to Rhoeo as the guard entered the room, still under close watch by Fenrir.

"I was Miss Caelyn's bodyguard during her travel, and I'm here as her friend now," Rhoeo stated with curt efficiency and an unsure smile. "I hope I'm not intruding, ma'am."

"Of course not." Eleanora batted away the idea as she hugged Rhoeo as well. "Klaas is out at the marketplace looking for some specific book, I don't know, but he likely won't be back for a time. So it's just us girls. Except Fenny."

Eleanora paused her ramble to nod at the creature. He snorted back happily.

"Are you here for a late meal?" Eleanora continued as she led the way into the kitchen. "I always have leftovers saved for when family drops by, you know."

"Actually, umm, Stori wasn't feeling well outside. And she thought it was hot out," Caelyn tried as she nervously glanced around to Stori for confirmation.

"I was in a bit of discomfort during tea," Stori stated for Caelyn's sake. "But I am feeling better now that I'm out of the sun."

Stori tried not to flush at the embarrassment of having worried Caelyn over such a little thing. Even though she still felt as ill as she had outside.

"Nonsense," Eleanora said as she led Stori by the hand to one of the back rooms.

Eleanora waved to the others before closing the door, "Make yourselves comfortable. There are cookies on the table."

Stori obligingly sat on the tall, firm couch Eleanora directed her to while still trying to tell the woman she was fine.

"Then this will be quick, dear, but I have a duty to ensure you are healthy," Eleanora stated as she shifted a tall stool in front of Stori and perched easily on top.

"So, what is the trouble?" Eleanora smiled easily.

"It is nothing. My time of the month, I think. I was just trying to get Caelyn to come visit you." Stori wanted to disappear at that moment, but with Eleanora still waiting expectantly for her to tell everything, she hurried on. "I have just been having cramps for a couple of weeks now, but I'm sure it's nothing. I was only feeling a bit nauseous and hot earlier."

Eleanora nodded with quiet confidence and not even a touch of embarrassment for the subject matter.

"A few weeks you say? That sounds like more than nothing. Is that normal for you?"

Stori answered a negative.

Eleanora continued with more questions as Stori's desire to melt away increased, but so did her concern. Hearing herself list though all the discomforts she had been experiencing for the past several weeks grew a new fear there was something wrong with her.

If something happened to me, how would Bry recover? Or Leha?

The thought of even worrying those two was painful.

"Is something wrong with me?" Stori finally asked after Eleanora's questions had ceased. She hated the fear that crept into her voice.

Though, maybe she shouldn't be afraid.

Eleanora was smiling. At the question, her smile grew even brighter.

"Wrong? Surely not. Just a little different." She reached forward to squeeze Stori's hand. "Though I will need to do some tests to be positive."

"Test? For what?"

Eleanora squeezed tighter as she moved her other hand to rest on Stori's midsection. "For a new member of the family."

Stori's jaw dropped. "A baby?!"

Eleanora nodded and reached to pull her into a hug.

"I'll have some tests to be sure, but from what you've told me, yes."

"We're having a baby," Stori breathed as the idea fixed in her mind.

Eleanora stood up and kissed her forehead.

"I have to tell Bry." Stori leapt up with sudden excitement and sprang toward the door. She stopped before opening it and returned to hug Eleanora again. "Thank you."

Through the kitchen, Stori flew past Caelyn and Rhoeo but stopped and returned to hug Caelyn.

"Thank you, Caelyn, I would have ignored it instead of coming here, but you insisted..." She kissed both of Caelyn's cheeks, ignoring the girl's confusion. "I have to tell Bry."

She darted from the room and ran through the halls, up the stairs with breathless vigor until she reached Bry's door.

Stori threw the door open immediately, without a thought that she was panting and so out of breath she couldn't speak.

Bry wasn't alone in the room as he and Chesler both turned to stare at her with confusion and greater concern.

"Stori, are you all right? What's wrong?" Bry jumped up from his desk and ran to her side in a moment, guiding her to sit on the sofa.

"Here is some water." Chesler grabbed a glass from the food cart and held it toward her. "Should I call someone for you? The healer?"

"No, I was just there. I'm well. I just needed to speak to Bry," Stori said panting between sentences. She gratefully took the glass and drank, hoping to catch her breath enough to explain.

"Very well. I'll come back later them." Chesler nodded to Bry and headed for the door Stori had left open. He glanced back with concern until he closed the door behind himself.

"What's wrong?" Bry asked again, moving from the spot where he had been kneeling to sit at her side.

Stori couldn't contain her smile even as she tried composing her features.

"It's just wonderful," she stated, finally having enough air to speak.

Bry continued staring at her with a countenance full of doubt.

"It is." She gripped his hand tightly. "I was having tea with Caelyn, you know I have been trying to win her over, and she loves animals too, you know. And I thought it was hot outside, but she didn't. And my stomach had been hurting, which I was trying to ignore, but she—"

"Stori," Bry's firm voice interrupted her pointless ramble, "are you all right?"

Stori's smile broadened. She pulled his hand to rest over her belly.

"Eleanora said she would run tests to be sure, but…Bry, we…" Stori couldn't finish as tears of joy started falling.

Bry blinked, confused at her, and glanced at the hand she held a few times before realization dawned.

"Pregnant?" He stared wide-eyed at her.

Stori could only nod.

"We're having a baby!" He squeezed her into a hug and kissed her lips. Bry jumped up and paced the room before returning to her side and giving her another kiss.

He was on his feet again with a smile that rivaled her own as he seemed too overjoyed to remain still.

"We're having a baby," he repeated to himself. "Eleanora knows, of course. Klaas? Anyone else?"

Stori shook her head.

"Klaas was out. But Caelyn and her friend, Rhoeo, were there. I didn't tell them, but Eleanora probably had to explain why I ran out on them."

Stori ducked her head at the memory of abandoning poor Caelyn, but she still would have acted the same if it meant being able to tell Bry immediately.

"Of course, Caelyn." Bry stopped mid-pace. "Shad! We have to tell Shad. Where is he?"

He ran to the door and threw it open. He shouted for his friend, then, thinking better of it, told the guard stationed at his door to find Shad.

Bry was back at her side with a loving hand on her belly as he kissed her cheek and whispered kind words to her.

Stori relaxed and leaned against him in complete comfort.

The moment was interrupted by Shad's loud and cheerful entrance.

"Bry, if you only call me for bad news now, I'm going to assume you don't—Oh, hi, Stori! Have you been crying? Bry, what did you do?"

Stori nodded a greeting, unable to hold back her smile any more than Bry. Though Bry was much more apt at teasing.

"Shad, you're loud. And what were you saying? 'Assuming I don't what?'"

"Assuming you don't appreciate my good company." Shad smiled at some joke he had found, but Bry interrupted before he could verbalize it.

"Good company? You?" Bry scoffed, though he was still grinning from ear to lopsided-around-the-scar ear. "Of course, uncles are meant to be the bad influence, so I guess that's right."

Bry leaned back now that he had told his joke and informed Shad at the same time.

"While uncles are supposed to be a bad influence, you certainly wouldn't be. But I'm not that bad, anyway. And kids are just so cute with their chubby little fingers and cheeks."—Shad smiled as he pinched imaginary cheeks—"And best of all, at the end of the day, I can just give the back to the parents to—"

Shad had his arms out, thrusting back said imaginary child to imaginary parents when he froze. He blinked a moment and tilted his head toward Bry and Stori.

"Parents?"

They both nodded.

Shad let out a screeching chirp and jumped toward them. He gave each a tight hug before sitting at Stori's free side. He never stopped spewing forth congratulations, name ideas, and questions.

"Klaas and Eleanora know?" he finally asked a sensible question and paused long enough to hear an answer.

"Of course, Eleanora knows." Bry rolled his eyes. "How do you think we know?"

"I don't know, womanly intuition?" Shad shrugged.

"Afraid not. I was completely surprised by the news."

"We were going to head down there now. Klaas was out when Stori found out, so we still need to tell him."

Bry stood and carefully helped Stori up.

"And it's not completely certain," Stori felt compelled to add. "Just from my symptoms Eleanora said, but…"

Stori trailed off as they headed toward the healer's chambers again. She didn't know why she thought it was needed to say.

If it turns out I'm not…

The thought was suddenly terrifying. At that moment, she wanted the baby more than anything.

"Ellie knows best on these things. If she says so, you can be sure." Shad reassured as he walked beside her.

Both Shad and Bry laced their arms in hers whenever the wider passages allowed.

When they reach Klaas and Eleanora's chambers, they found Caelyn and Rhoeo had already left, but Eleanora had called Klaas and Lawr. She had even managed to get Leha to join them for an early dinner.

Stori was momentarily saddened that Caelyn had left.

This would have been the perfect time to convince her how good Bry is.

She lamented the loss only for a short while before the overwhelming joy of the time with their family and friends filled her mind.

CHAPTER 19

A li watched the world pass by from the small, oddly motorized boat Sverre had rented. The motor was some Aequorian technology. In Lux Aequor, everything more advanced than the wheel was Aequorian technology, according to Dain.

The world was, as promised, a vast ocean. Though the corner they occupied had hundreds, perhaps thousands, of small islands dotting the landscape. The islands were covered in exotic plants, had white sandy beaches, crystal clear turquoise water, and fit every vision she had of a tropical paradise from magazines and advertisements on Earth. Except these islands had the added benefit of privacy, or so she was told.

Dain had been ecstatic since the start of their boat ride. He talked incessantly about the islands, the Merii, and of course, his family. He had hundreds of questions for Sverre about his family's home. Though Sverre's slower pace of speaking only managed to answer every third or fourth question.

When Sverre had stated they were getting close, Dain had stopped with the questions and steered the boat in the direction Sverre said. All of his considerable energy was now focused on coaxing every last bit of speed from the engine as he steadily watched the horizon.

In the otherwise quiet final stretch of the ride, Sverre made every attempt to carry on the solo conversation in Dain's absence of mind. He pointed out this or that in frequent attempts to rouse Leon's attention or occasionally to direct advice toward Ali.

"As I mentioned, the Merii are particular about etiquette," Sverre stated with a nod to Ali.

She could not recall his mentioning that, but figured he must have. She watched as he fidgeted with his grip on the side of the boat. The most nerves he had shown in some time.

"Erc will have a book you could read up on," he continued, tapping Leon's side to include him in the suggestion.

Leon nodded but didn't answer.

"I'm not that bad," Ali protested.

She straightened her posture and gave him a teasing smile.

"I can be rather proper when I wish."

Sverre raised an eyebrow as he shifted further under the shade of the small awning, out of the sun.

The interference the awning caused to their speed was negated by the fact their dear albino couldn't last the sunny boat ride without changing a dozen shades of burn.

"It's not about 'that bad' or 'rather.' The Merii expect perfect mannerisms when you communicate with them. I brush up on the subject whenever I visit the islands."

Ali frowned.

"Fine, I'll review."

Sverre nodded.

"Erc has several boats. When you are bored of exploring their island— it is small—you could venture further. But be careful. There are a lot of creatures and beasts inhabiting the islands. Not all are friendly."

"I'll be careful," Ali assured him. Sverre's twitchy fidgeting showed his concern more than words would ever do him justice.

"Was that a Merii?!" Leon's jumped up in the boat, forgetting his sorrow in a moment of excitement.

Sverre peered overboard. "I didn't see it. Did it look like one?"

"It looked somewhat like a person, but I couldn't see anything past the waist." Leon frowned as he stared intently at the water.

The boy didn't notice how elated everyone else in the boat was with him talking again.

Sverre shifted out from under the shade to sit closer to Leon.

"It probably was then. Merii's can camouflage their tails." Sverre frowned at the statement. "All their scales actually, including the ones on their upper body. You could stare right at one and never see it."

He turned a smile toward Ali,

"Of course, they would consider that very rude, so they rarely camouflage their upper half. Except…?"

Sverre nudged Leon for the exception.

"Except when they're hunting."

"Right." Sverre acknowledged, tousling Leon's hair. The boy was too busy trying to spot another Merii to even protest.

"Hunting?" Ali raised an eyebrow as she also scanned the water. "I assumed people so advanced to create the AaDs and all this"—She motioned toward the motor at Dain's feet, but thought of the gaet—"wouldn't need to hunt."

Sverre nodded and smiled.

"It's for sport more than necessity. What culture, advanced or not, doesn't enjoy a little bloodlust?"

Ali pursed her lips as if she wanted to say hers didn't.

Apart from football, boxing, and all the movies and video games.

"That's true, I guess."

Other than Sverre calling out directions for the twists and turns around islands, silence settled between them. They left one cluster of islands behind and headed for the next when Sverre spoke again.

"There it is, Dain." He pointed to one of the islands with a dock. "That's your island."

Dain was beaming as he headed for the dock.

Ali leaned forward to observe. The island wasn't large, but big enough to have one jungle-covered hill standing tall above the ocean. She saw no house or other structure apart from the dock, which had several dinghies and a larger boat tied up.

An immediate concern jumped to the forefront of her mind that they wouldn't be living in a house so much as on the boat. It couldn't have been large enough for a family of three, much less two extra people.

She glanced at Sverre, hoping not to have to verbalize her question and risk insulting either him or Dain, but Sverre's attention was caught between Leon and the island.

Not that there is any choice in the matter anyway.

She swallowed at the reminder. This was where Sverre thought they would be safest, so she would make do.

As they pulled alongside the dock, Sverre jumped out with a small flinch as he favored his side. He tied the boat up and helped Leon out before turning to Ali.

"Is your side okay? Is it your ribs?" Ali whispered her concern, hoping Leon wouldn't notice.

Sverre looked surprised, as usual with any concern, but then he smiled. "I'm sorry you noticed. I'm fine."

Ali wanted to shake him.

He stopped and seemed to notice his use of the clear lie without her reminding him.

"I have a couple more stitches since last time, but they are healing nicely and are only sore. My ribs are healing well too."

She frowned at him, but he met her gaze without hesitation.

"All right." Ali gripped his arm and squeezed it. "Just be careful. Please."

"I will."

Ali watched him turn to help Dain with the boat before she glanced around the dock. She was ecstatic to see a path cut into the jungle, leading up the island, that had been hidden from the boat's view.

Hope for a house yet.

Dain hopped out of the boat as soon as it was secured to the dock, leaving their supplies and bags in the boat for now as he hastily ushered everyone up the pathway.

The hike through the jungle was as miserable as Ali would have suspected in the humidity. She was quickly covered in a sheen of sweat, and her thighs ached with a special hatred of hills.

I need more exercise.

She grimaced as she noticed she was the only one in the group so struggling.

Her only consolation was the lack of bugs. However, that consolation was short-lived when she saw a bee the size of an orange buzzing around a flower.

Ali gulped and moved away from the insect to the other side of Sverre.

"Just don't aggravate them," Sverre offered when he noticed her stare.

"So long as they don't come near me," Ali said as she started noticing more bees and other oversized insects. The island started to seem less like a paradise and more akin to some exotic hellscape.

"You'll be fine," Sverre assured.

Around a turn in the jungle, the pathway led to an engineered cutaway in the hillside. The path continued into the ground until the walls on either side were taller than a person and the path curved out of view, where she assumed some entryway was hidden.

They paused before the cut in and Sverre drew Ali and Dain's attention upwards.

Ali's jaw dropped as she saw that the jungle ahead had disappeared into a cleverly camouflaged building. The structure was made of jungle material and climbed at least three stories high.

Ali and Dain both whistled.

MUCH better than a boat.

Dain wrapped one arm around Sverre's shoulders and squeezed him in a tight hug.

"You did great on the house," Dain stated as he released the albino.

They proceeded forward on the path but stopped short at the sound of a gunshot.

Sverre had dragged Leon and Ali off the path before Ali could even blink. Dain crouched next to them, already gripping a handgun and staring toward the house with wide-eyed dread.

Before any of them could move, a shout erupted from around the corner of the path.

"Come and get it, you little bastards. I've got enough rock salt to whup ya'll asses back to your mammas."

The relief was tangible on Dain's face but only lasted a second before it was replaced with a look as close to a frown as pure joy could render it.

"Damn it, woman. What are you giving us warning shots for? If you're gonna shot at someone, they should be dead!"

He stood and moved back to the path.

Ali glanced to Sverre for direction or an explanation. Sverre was shaking his head with an expression of why-do-I-do-this before he followed Dain's lead. Leon and Ali followed last as a woman stepped out from behind the curve of the pathway from the house.

"Dain?" She stared with her mouth open as she clumsily leaned a shotgun against the wall.

The shock only lasted a moment before she screeched and ran to Dain. She jumped on him and wrapped her arms and legs around him in a full-bodied hug.

Ali fidgeted at the idea she was an outsider as she watched the two remain engulfed in each other with a shower of kisses and a never-ending hug.

She took the moment to observe the woman while Dain was holding her up and twirling around. Her skin tone was a few shades darker than Dain's, the purest ebony. She had tightly kinked, shoulder-length hair tied back in an artless fashion with spare strips of cloth.

She's gorgeous.

More screeches of joy filled the air as two children darted from the house and collided with Dain. He had only just set Erc down and braced himself, the only reason the assault didn't knock him flat.

Ali shuffled back a step to give the two kids room to hug and climb up their father.

The girl looked about twelve and was the spitting image of her mother. The boy was about Leon's age. He, too, looked like their mother, but he had the mischievous grin that so often adorned Dain.

Erc stepped away from her husband long enough to hug Leon before the boy could squeeze away to greet the other children. Erc moved toward Sverre.

"You sweet-hearted little punk brought my husband back to me again." She gave him a tight hug.

"And almost lost him right at your door."

Erc made a sharp sound of dismissal and waved the idea away with a hand.

"Thought I heard the geckos out whistling. They've been stealing my honey fruit. It wasn't loaded with anything to kill, anyways."

Sverre hummed a strong note of doubt but didn't say anything. He turned to Ali and gestured her forward as Erc's attention immediately turned to her.

"This is Ali. She's been staying with Leon and me for a while. She was unfortunately caught up in a mess I created."

"Ahh." Erc grabbed Ali's forearm in greeting, with enough strength to completely break Ali's grip.

Definitely with the exercise.

Ali chastised herself.

"You and your messes." Erc was shaking her head as she glanced between Ali and Sverre for a moment before reaching a conclusion.

"So, is she your girlfriend now, or did you just kidnap her too?"

Sverre reddened at the question but tried passing it off as being from the sun's heat. "Closer to the second. Similar to Leon actu—"

"You bought her!?" Erc exclaimed, staring at Sverre. She swung her arm around Ali's shoulders and pulled her along toward the house as she walked.

"Of all the dastardly...man doesn't know how to get a girlfriend."

She paused to poke Ali in the chest.

"And you shouldn't be lettin' him get away with this."

Ali tried uselessly to rebut Erc's indignation. Or to correct her on the idea that she was Sverre's girlfriend.

I mean, I'm not, right? Or...maybe?

She glanced back to see Sverre sigh and shake his head as he followed them into the house.

Ali was dragged into the living room and promptly deposited on the sofa, while Erc berated both her and Sverre.

"Erc, woman," Dain interrupted his wife's tirade, "it was either Sverre or Duqa. You know Sverre is as honorable as can be if he takes someone under his roof."

Erc waved him off.

"I know, handsome, but if I don't tease him about it, who will?"

She turned to Ali again. Erc grabbed a bowl of fruit and set it on the coffee table in front of her.

"Duqa, eh? Anyone'd be better than that monstrosity, but Sverre's the best sort of person you could've hoped for, I reckon."

"I realize that." Ali smiled as she glanced at Sverre.

Erc turned toward the albino again.

"And you. I am serious, you have to stop kidnapping or buying people. You gotta learn how to actually make friends."

Sverre opened his mouth, but Erc cut in.

"Dain doesn't count. Using us as hostages negated that."

"Yes, ma'am."

Erc made a contented sort of snort as she looked around the room. Dain hadn't made it passed the entryway where he stood, an arm around each of his children, talking to the girl, while the boy traded animated stories with Leon.

"Come and sit yourselves down." Erc motioned sharply as she had noticed Ali was still the only one sitting.

"Sit, sit, sit. I'll make lunch."

She hastened toward the kitchen.

"I can help if you want." Sverre offered, though he hesitated to move in any direction.

Erc turned back to him for a short moment to fix him with a glare before she pointed to the couch.

"Eat some fruit, you look like shit. And that had better not be blood." She pointed to his sleeves but turned and walked back to the kitchen before Sverre could say anything.

"Yes, ma'am."

Sverre sat next to Ali and rolled the sleeves of his shirt up to hide the blood stains that had been there since the attack at the house. He picked up two kiwis and handed one to Ali before he leaned back.

Ali leaned closer.

"Hellfire, eh?"

Sverre smiled back at her.

"Manners are important in this house too."

CHAPTER 20

Ali sat at the dining table and marveled at what would be her new living companions while she watched Erc mercilessly tease Sverre. She would have fawned over him more to see his flustered reaction to it. In Erc's mind, it seemed, he was less an assassin and more some wayward troublemaker who needed good motherly—tough—love.

Sverre made frequent attempts to pass off her attention to Leon or Ali, but Erc always found her way back to teasing him.

After many attempts, Ali managed to pull Dain's attention momentarily away from his kids to ask if it was always like that when Sverre came to visit.

Dain nodded and raised his voice to make sure everyone heard.

"I'm thinking Erc is still trying to get back at Sverre for the whole kidnapping thing."

Erc scoffed but didn't respond as she had been in the middle of a tease.

Ali smirked at Sverre's expense before focusing on her meal. She bit into a vegetable that looked like a giant stick of celery, had been roasted like a squash, and tasted like pineapple chicken.

The food on the island was going to take some getting used to, but it was delicious.

"Your cooking is excellent, Erc," Ali complimented, drawing the woman's attention briefly away from Sverre.

"Good to hear," Erc said with a new smile twisting her lips. "So, who's better? Me or Sverre?"

Ali drew back, full of 'um's and surprise as she tried to think of what was tactful to say.

"Don't answer that." Sverre shook his head, though the same smile that had taken up residence with him since the beginning of lunch didn't falter.

"I've been eating a lot of Sverre's food lately, and I've got to say, it's good." Dain stated in good nature, having decided to play with fire.

"Ohh! The student has overtaken the master, eh?" Erc said, grinning at Dain now with a look that spoke of payback.

"Your food is great, too, Mrs. Erc," Leon pitched in helpfully.

"Thanks, Leon." Erc smiled in earnest while reaching to clean his face of excess sauce.

Ali saw her chance for escaping the question and took it.

"You taught Sverre how to cook?"

"Of course. Who else would have? Atanas? The clown?" Erc stabbed at her food with a sudden, vehement hatred. "It's not exactly in Oracaede's handbook of necessary skills for their child soldiers."

"I hadn't thought about that before, but that makes sense." Ali nodded. The 'child soldiers' part hurt as she glanced at Sverre.

"That's right. I said...do you remember what I said?" Erc bumped Sverre.

"It was something along the lines of, if I was going to take care of Leon, I'd better learn how to cook. The phrase 'too damned skinny' was weaponized and thrown around many, many times, as I recall."

"For both of you. You were too damned skinny too."

"Yes, ma'am, I know. Much too skinny. You have made me aware of it. Repeatedly."

"You could still stand to eat more," Erc noted, eyeing him.

"If I eat anymore, I'll burst. Honest, I was full two servings ago." Sverre pushed his plate away to further his point.

He and Erc held a silent stare down.

Ali pushed down a twinge of jealousy while she watched them.

I wish I could tease him like that. Erc can be so playful with him.

She wondered if Dain could be jealous of his wife's attitude toward Sverre.

Dain continued paying them next to zero attention as he sported with his children and Leon.

Definitely not jealous then.

She supposed Erc's attention to Sverre was more motherly than anything else.

Not exactly what I want.

Erc broke their stalemate first. "You want dessert?" she asked.

Sverre shifted in his seat as though trying to readjust the contents of his stomach.

"What do you have?"

"Honey cakes."

"Yes, please. Thank you, ma'am."

"That's why you're my favorite albino." Erc squeezed his shoulder as she stood to get the dessert.

"I'd be flattered if you knew any others."

"Insolent punk."

Sverre smiled and turned his attention to Ali as he immediately switched roles.

"You have enough to eat? There's more."

Ali shook her head.

"I'm stuffed, but I want to try those honey cakes."

Sverre nodded, content with the answer.

"Leon," Ali pulled the boy's attention away from Dain, "are you full? You haven't finished your plate."

Oh my gosh, it's a cycle.

Sverre laughed, looking at the expression on Ali's face.

"Rubs off on you, doesn't she?"

Ali ignored him as she started moving plates out of the way.

"What are you doing?" Erc was back, scolding Ali this time. "I'll take care of that. You're a guest."

Ali paused, plate in hand, suddenly full of doubt.

"I should help since I'm going to be staying here..."

"Yes, and you will. Tomorrow." Erc returned to Sverre's side of the table as she set down a cover dish. "Today, you are our guest. Now put that down."

Ali complied. The girl picked the plates up immediately and began carrying them to the kitchen.

"Incara, grab some fresh dessert plates too. Charlton, the silverware." Erc directed.

Charlton dashed to the kitchen ahead of his sister and Leon sprinted after him.

The boys returned in a short moment, arguing over a hand of silverware.

"Boys, quiet down," Sverre ordered.

The two were perfectly quiet until they reached the table.

"Ma, did you want spoons or forks?" Charlton asked, trying to jerk the utensils away from Leon, who held on just as tight. "I think forks, but Leon said—"

"Put them both down and everyone can choose." Erc ended the bickering.

The boys did as instructed as Incara returned.

"Dain, honey, would you cut the cake? I'm going to make tea." Erc disappeared back to the kitchen.

Dain hopped up to oblige, pushing Sverre, who had started removing the cover, out of the way.

"What do you think?" Dain turned his beaming grin toward Ali. "Ready to spend some time in paradise?"

Ali laughed as she glanced around the room but rested her attention on the table and the people around it.

"I wish you two were staying."

The words slipped out before Ali could stop them.

"Hell, we do too." Dain chuckled.

"And we'll be back before you know it," Sverre added, holding her gaze.

"When do you have to leave?" Leon's unusually somber voice asked, reminding Ali that all three children were listening.

Sverre and Dain exchanged glances.

"After lunch," Sverre answered.

"So soon?" Ali gaped. She thought they would be staying at least a few days.

The men exchanged glances again.

"We're already well overdue," Dain said.

"The sooner we're gone, the safer you'll be," Sverre added just as Erc came back into the room.

"Ma, they're leaving after lunch," Incara cried, turning her big golden-light eyes to her mother with an imploring look for Erc to change the fact.

Erc's jaw slackened a moment as she paused and stared at Dain. Her gaze shifted to Sverre before she started walking again, setting a tray of steaming mugs on the table.

"Of course, they are, honey. They have work to do." She gave her daughter a side hug before setting mugs out for everyone.

Ali thought she saw Erc's eyes glisten with unshed tears, but they were wiped away in a moment before Erc returned to serving everyone dessert and teasing Sverre.

CHAPTER 21

Bry paced the length of his office, shuffled the items on either his desk or bookshelf without improving the organization of either, then paced back. He watched Chesler do the same, minus the faux organizing.

The new report that had arrived while Chesler delivered his old one shocked them both. They were both impatient for an answer, Chesler perhaps even more than Bry.

Heavy footsteps from the hall alerted them to Jair's approach long before he thudded at the door and was bid enter.

Bry observed the big man carefully, trying not to let his considerable bias cloud his judgment.

"Wha'ds da problem?" Jair's frown turned thoughtful as he watched both Bry and Chesler, but his question and confusion were directed toward his friend.

"Jair, we received a troubling report while I was updating Bry," Chesler started.

Bry assumed he meant that if he hadn't been in Bry's presence, he would have discussed it with Jair in private first. Bry couldn't fault him for that; Jair was a friend, after all.

"The unhappy and unsettled people of Sentre seem to think you're united with them against me, was the gist of the report," Bry stated when Chesler had remained paused for too long.

He really shouldn't pause for so long if he doesn't want people to jump in.

Bry shrugged when Chesler threw him an irritated glance, then immediately checked himself.

Jair continued staring expectantly as though waiting for the punchline.

"Wha'd?" He growled when it didn't come.

"Obviously, some mistake has been made," Chesler stated, staring at Jair, seemingly to will the man into finding a suitable explanation.

"Do you have any idea why someone would arrive at such a conclusion?" Bry asked. He, too, would be thankful for some innocent misunderstanding.

Jair was still his only useful general. Especially with all the rumors and stories coming out about Oroitz, he needed someone who had been there to be on his side for the current fallout from the gossip.

"I have no idea," Jair growled before he also started pacing.

"Has anyone spoken to you recently about Oroitz or a general dislike of the king?" Chesler questioned. "Anything useful?"

Jair scoffed and shook his head but paused as his already furrowed brow frowned more.

"Since you men'tion id' several people have been speaking 'o me abou'd Oroi'dz and da king." He glanced between Chesler and Bry before landing on Bry. "I 'dough'd id' was because I was 'dere wi'd you and I 'dried correc'ding 'deir false ideas, bu'd 'dey didn'd seem 'o like 'dose answers."

"So they believe the rumors and expect you to confirm everything." Bry nodded as he raked his hand through his hair in agitation.

"Seemed 'da'a way. I made repor'd of everyone who was concerning," Jair offered.

"I'll look into them." Chesler made a note of it on his AaD.

"They already think you're disloyal too. Wonder where that rumor started…" Bry tapped his chin as he thought.

"Jair, when was the first time someone talked to you about anything related to Oroitz or dissension with king Brynte?"

Jair scrunched up his face and shook his head.

"Don'd remember."

"Think harder."

Jair scowled but returned to scrunched face concentration as he paced.

"Maybe a couple of weeks ago," he answered finally. "'Dwo young fellows came up 'o me during a meal, wan'd 'o chad' abou' 'da king."

"Can you remember any specifics about them?" Chesler asked, poised with the AaD ready for notes.

"Were bloody young 'o be drinking and 'draveling. Said 'ey were refugees, bu'd 'dey were clean and organized for anyone new 'o Sen'dre."

"Remember what they said?" Bry tried.

Jair was shaking his head.

"No'd specifically. No'ding concerning a'd 'da 'dime. I lef'd when 'dey was saying you were making a mess of 'dings and migh'd be lying abou'd Oracaede."

"Thanks for that, at least." Bry groaned as he returned to his desk. He glanced to Chesler when he didn't have any forthcoming ideas of his own to stop the rumors.

"Any thoughts?"

Chesler was quiet a moment longer. When he finally did speak, he directed it to Jair.

"First thing to do is dispel this notion that you're disloyal to the king. Jair, you should address the soldiers in the castle first. And if anyone comes up to you talking discontent about Bry like before, have them arrested. I want to talk to them and find out who started these rumors."

"Think you'll be able to find them?" Bry asked.

Chesler was slow to answer again but shook his head.

"Not from Jair's description, there are a lot of new refugees in Sentre. But they may have talked to other castle staff. I'll conduct interviews to see what I can find."

"Great." Bry stood again and moved to extend his arm to Jair.

The man gripped it firmly.

"Thanks, Jair. You don't know how glad I am that this was a misunderstanding."

Jair eyed him a moment.

"I 'dink I can guess. By 'da way, I hear congra'dulations are in order."

Bry couldn't help the beaming smile that overtook his face.

"Yep, and thanks."

Jair nodded with a cheerful look instead of his usually solemn expression.

"Right, congratulation." Chesler sputtered with a failing attempt at friendliness, "Good thing you declined working with Oracaede when they sent someone, otherwise I'd be saying condolences."

Bry gave the fidgeting man a crooked look of skepticism. "And why is that?"

Chesler drew back and glanced nervously toward Jair.

"I hadn'd mentioned id' ye'd." Jair scowled.

Bry blinked between the two of them.

Jair cleared his throat, "I had decided 'dere was no poin'd in keeping a secre'd of da disagreemen'd I had wi'd Vlasis. I had planned on 'ledding' you know, now 'da'd you have a child on da way."

Bry frowned and waited. He could not guess what the event which had led to Jair being shunned from military service had to do with Bry having a child, but he remained quiet for the explanation.

"Id is Oracaede's rule, 'o insure loyal'dy." Jair shifted in a rare show of discomfort. "'Dey ordered Vlasis 'o give 'dem his firs'born child."

Bry drew back.

"What?" He breathed the question, glancing toward Chesler for confirmation or preferably denial.

Chesler only nodded, "I couldn't believe it either. I looked through all the records from the time Vlasis started working with Oracaede. Queen Loreda did give birth to a child, but it was reported to be stillborn."

"Da child was alive." Jair stated, "I never saw id', da nurse gave id' 'o someone from Oracaede immedia'dely. I 'dink 'dere was some'ding wrong wid' 'd because Vlasis was glad 'da baby wasn'd his heir anymore."

Bry slumped against his desk. He took a few breaths to calm the sudden panic twisting in his gut for Stori and the baby.

After a moment, he swallowed and stood up to pace. He paused and turned toward Jair.

"So, I may have an older brother or sister? That's what you're saying?"

Jair hummed doubtfully and frowned.

"Not necessarily." Chesler answered, "There's no reason to think they even kept the child or kept it alive. It was a test of loyalty, I don't think they have any means to raise a baby."

Bry nodded to himself at the information.

"Did Loreda know?" The thought suddenly came to him.

Jair shook his head, "She was 'dold id' was s'dillborn 'oo."

Bry returned to slumping against his desk. He took the moment of silence they all instinctively shared for the child to collect his thoughts.

"Thank you for telling me this, Jair." Bry stated, moving to grasp Jair's arm again, "I appreciate knowing."

Jair nodded and returned the gesture.

A light knock interrupted them. Bry recognized the knock as Stori's and called for her to enter. He sucked in a quick breath, steadied his face to a pleasant expression, and stuffed any lingering thoughts about what Jair had said into a back corner of his mind.

"Sorry." Stori half stepped in with Shad peeking around the door behind her. "Am I interrupted a top-secret war meeting?

Stori's eyes sparkled, Bry groaned, and Shad snickered.

"Stori, don't talk to Shad, he's a bad influence."

"Of course." Stori smiled sweetly.

Chesler cleared his throat.

"We have what we need to start working."

He nodded to Bry and Stori as he passed her. Jair grunted a goodbye to Bry but paused as he passed Stori to congratulate her before he also left the room.

Bry focused on his wife and best friend.

"Well, I can always expect trouble when you two are together."

Shad scoffed with a perfect show of indignation as they both took up residence on the couch and waited for Bry to join them.

"We were thinking of baby names." Stori smiled the most brilliant smile Bry had ever seen. "Eleanora did her tests. It's for sure."

For sure.

The words meant so much. Bry hugged Stori again and held her tight for a long moment.

"So, baby names," Shad said after waiting for them to part.

"I had not thought that far ahead," Bry admitted with chagrin. He was still so relieved that he had declined Oracaede's offer of help when they had asked. The idea of losing this child as soon as the baby was born was a weight he did not want to think about.

"That's okay, we've been thinking for you," Shad said, giving Bry a sideways look, a question of what was the matter.

"All right," Bry shook his head that he was fine, "what do you have?"

Shad held his gaze intently before he nodded and moved his attention fully back to the topic of baby names.

"I was thinking Shadric for a boy." Shad stroked his chin in a deep, reverent pondering.

"Vetoed."

"And Shadia for a girl."

"Double veto."

"Actually," Stori interrupted what was sure to be an epic comeback from Shad, "we were thinking either Alina or Jassmira for a girl. And Hazael for a boy."

She paused at each name to savor the sound of it. Eventually, she turned back to Bry.

"What do you think of those?"

Bry furrowed his brow in thought. They all sounded nice.

How do you go about naming a whole new person, though?

"See," Shad was leaning to talk to Stori and smirked at Bry at the same time, "I told you he'd have nothing."

"Shut up."

Bry glanced back to Stori.

"Honestly, they all sound so lovely."

Stori nodded and continued staring into space with a light frown that showed she was thinking hard.

"They should definitely have Bry's hair, don't ya think," Shad said, clearly thinking less hard.

"Yes, that would be lovely," Stori said with a dreamy voice.

"But hopefully Stori's eyes." Shad squinted at Bry's for a moment. "Yep, definitely, Stori's would be better."

"Shut up."

"What?!" Shad threw his hands up. "Aren't you excited? I'm excited."

"Of course, I'm excited." Bry rolled his eyes. "I'd be bouncing off the walls if you weren't taking all the space."

Shad scoffed but immediately returned to thought.

"Stori's eyes would be so cute with red hair."

"Yes, I know," Bry said, focusing on his wife's eyes as she blushed under his gaze.

"I like Hazael, but what if there's twins." Shad entered deep contemplation at the idea.

"Twins." Stori sighed with love in her starry eyes.

"Let's start with the idea of just one for now." Bry tried but failed to reason with either of them.

CHAPTER 22

In the bathroom mirror, Aike tentatively examined Hid's stitching on his face. The careful, neat stitches to minimize scaring held together the small, scabbed cuts.

Gotta be healed enough by now.

He scratched at the little scabs and stitches, wondering if he could pull them out. Or rather, if he could remove them without Hid pitching a fit at him for doing so.

Nope, definitely not.

Aike grumbled as he resigned to leave them alone, at least for a little longer.

He exited the bathroom and quietly padded around the dark, silent apartment. It would still be hours before the others woke up.

Aike moved to sit on the couch, grabbing Hid's notepad off the coffee table as he did. The pad of scribbled paper held the notes Hid faithfully made on each mission, including the plans they had been considering the night before.

Aike squinted in the dark beneath the window. He added a few notes as he thought of them and set the notepad back down again.

He stood, shuffled around the room again, and picked up a random book. He scanned a few pages, though it was much too dark to read and set it back down again before he returned to the couch with a yawn.

Aike curled up on his side, thinking again of everything he needed to do the next day.

Later this morning? Yep, that's it.

He yawned again as his eyes drifted closed.

Aike started at a sound near him, but he immediately relaxed his body to appear still asleep as he listened. He genuinely relaxed when he recognized the sounds of Idir's movements.

"Morning, Idir." Aike smiled as he sat up and watched the man fix coffee. "Can I get some too?"

Idir raised an expectant eyebrow.

"Pretty please."

Idir breathed a scoff from his nose as he nodded.

"Thanks." Aike yawned again, closed his eyes, and waited. A cup of coffee was suddenly in front of him, and the strong smell was relaxing as he reached for it. He slurped gingerly at it, his eyes still closed.

"Mmm, you make the best coffee, Idir, I say it every time."

"I know," Idir said in his low voice Aike would have missed if he had not been listening for it.

Aike continued an aimless ramble for the sound of some noise.

"You never burn it, it's just thick enough. Hid always makes it too thick. Have to eat it with a spoon—"

"Not sleep?" Idir asked without any note taken that Aike had been talking.

Aike quieted and continued sipping his coffee.

"Not really. Thinking about the plan."

Idir nodded and remained ever quiet. They sat drinking the thickened coffee in silence before Aike spoke again.

"It'll work, I'm sure. I just…the details are so fuzzy to plan around."

"Details are Hid's job."

Aike grinned.

"I know, right? I'm terrible at getting all those little pieces of a plan in place, aren't I?"

It wasn't a question. Aike was awful at realizing the smaller elements of a plan. And Hid always lost sight of the big picture.

Schemers who can't work by ourselves, that's what we are, Hid.

Idir nodded.

"Leave details to him. Miserable when you worry."

"I am, aren't I?" Aike grinned and continued prattling on while Idir returned to completely ignoring him.

The comfortable early morning was interrupted by an AaD chiming. Idir picked it up and passed it to Aike without a glance at who was calling so early.

Only one person is so unconscientious.

"Mornin', Reb," Aike answered with only a glance at the screen. "How are you this fine morni-"

"Shut up," Reb snapped predictably. "You're late for update."

"I am?" Aike's voice was the same light unconcerned tone, but he frowned. He wasn't late.

"Give update in person. Alone."

"Reb did somethi—"

"Now!"

Aike flinched away from the AaD at the yell.

"Certainly, Chief," Aike said as he heard her hang up.

Idir watched him with a calm gaze.

"Want I should wake Hid?"

Aike forced a light laugh.

"What, you think I'm that cruel? I wouldn't make you wake the beast." Aike set his mug on the table and stood with a stretch. "If you wanted, making some coffee for him would probably help."

Idir nodded and stood to do so.

Aike walked into the bedroom he and Hid shared and paused at Hid's bed. He shook Hid's sleeping form, then jumped back.

"Hid, wake up."

Not a stir.

He shook him again.

"Hidalgo."

Desperate times, as usual.

"Dolly? Wake up!"

Aike maintained a safe—if there was such a thing when Hid's most hated nickname was used—distance.

An incoherent stream of Spanish flowed from Hid proceeding a short-bladed knife thrown in Aike's general direction. The handle of the knife bounced off the wall, leaving a small dent before it clattered to the floor.

"You're paying the innkeeper for that, and it's not coming out of team funds, I hope you know."

More Spanish was lost on Aike, though he recognized Hid's favorite swear words.

"We don't have the time for this." Aike rolled his eyes. "Dolly, wakey, wakey."

Hid flew upright with a snarl, clutching his pillow.

"*Lo juro, gringo,* if you call me 'Dolly' one more time, I'll take this pillow and shove it *por tu culo!*"

Aike held his hands up in surrender and smiled as the morning beast finally awoke, though not enough to stick to one language.

"Mornin' sunshine!" Aike chirped his usual greeting.

Hid continued to growl at him in Spanish, as was his usual prerogative.

"You know, you're gonna have a morning every day of your life. No need to make an enemy out of it."

Hid spat some insult Aike couldn't understand before stretching and yawning as he glanced around the room. His eyes fixed on the closed curtains around the window. The window which usually streamed light in the morning.

He swung his gaze around to bore holes through Aike.

"Aike, it's not even light not. Where's this 'morning' you speak of?"

"Idir thinks it's morning," Aike stated with a grin.

Hid snarled and lunged at Aike but remained helplessly tangled in blankets. Aike maintained a healthy distance.

"Get over here so I can strangle you, *pendejo.*"

"Hey, hey, hey. Okay, I didn't wake you up for no reason this time."

Aike took another step back as his humor was lost on the struggling Hid, still intent on throttling him.

"Reb called," Aike stated simply.

Hid quit his struggles immediately.

"Wants a chit-chat. I'm leaving now."

Hid drew back and rubbed his already messy hair as he continued staring at Aike with a thoughtful, slightly less murderous, frown. The frown turned to a worried, pinched look as it always did.

"I'll get my boots."

"No."

Aike clapped his hands together, trying to channel every bit of Reb's snarling tone.

"Alone," he repeated.

Hid's worried look darkened further.

"I don't like it."

"Neither do I," Aike shrugged as he gathered a few supplies for the walk, "but such is our lot in life."

CHAPTER 23

A ike departed the city in record time as he headed toward the nearest doorway. It was still an extensive hike before he reached it.

He passed the time and exhaustion by talking to himself and practicing his report to Reb. Even in his head, he rarely made it through the entire report before Reb flew into a rage over some small infraction.

"This never goes well for me," he complained to himself as he opened the doorway and shuffled into the Empty.

That's what you say, but this could be the change.

"After all, you've never given a report without Erasyl around."

Well, that'll just make it worse.

"Shut up." Aike rolled his eyes at his pessimistic conversation.

Space and time passed immeasurable in the Empty before he arrived at a doorway in Glacius Tesca before the sun reached its full height.

He paused on arriving to check his AaD and wrap a thin scarf around his head and face to protect his delicate, freckled skin from the brutal sun and winds in the long walk.

Aike continued to gripe to himself as he trekked across the expansive desert toward the Aynur marketplace. He reached it as the sun dipped into the horizon.

He navigated the tent city, stopping to eat and guzzle water before heading to the chief's tent.

Reb was still snarling orders to several tired clan leaders as Aike entered. She ignored him as she continued laying out plans for the leaders to begrudgingly follow.

Aike waited off to the side, practicing remaining stone-faced and devoid of thoughts and feelings. He maintained the look from practice but still fought back grins and snark whenever Reb asked for something clearly unreasonable.

He listened keenly to everything said as he tried piecing together Reb's plan or, at least, her thought process.

An invasion force was what he understood her grand plan to be.

Why the hell did we have to do all that stealth work if you were just going to invade anyway, Reb?

Aike just stopped from rolling his eyes as Reb's attention shifted to him.

"Wolf. What progress you make?" Reb growled the question from grimacing lips as she dismissed the clan leaders with a disrespectful wave.

Aike bowed and started with his practiced report, summarizing what they had accomplished. He made an effort to highlight Idir's work in case Reb remembered his injury and held doubts as to his ability to operate.

Reb listened with a snarl until Aike mentioned the Ghost hadn't shown up.

"You haven't killed him!?" Reb lurched from her seated position, snarling at Aike like some feral beast.

"He hasn't arrived yet. If you wish us to change our priorities to hunt him—"

Aike flinched and barely avoided a water vase hurled at him.

"Don't presume my orders! And don't move," Reb yelled, grabbing another clay pot and heaving it at him.

Aike bit his tongue against his instincts to duck as he let the pottery shatter against his shoulder. The hit stung, but a quick twitch and roll of his shoulder revealed it hadn't done any damage other than a future bruise.

Reb continued to scowl at him.

"I apologize," Aike said, though he couldn't guess what Reb expected him to apologize for.

Even Reb's not usually this crazy.

He frowned and mentally berated the Ghost and the sniper for not killing Reb instead.

Who knows how enraged and crazy Erasyl would have been at that, though.

"As soon as those bastards arrive in Sentre, you kill them, or I'll have your head. And," Reb stepped closer and grabbed Aike's jaw, forcing him to look at her, "I'll have the heads of every one of your Wolves."

Reb continued holding his jaw with crushing pressure as Aike choked out a "Yes, Chief."

"My orders stay the same," Reb snarled, shoving Aike away. "I need the city rank against its ruler. I bring a force to fight. They must not unite to fight back."

"Yes, Chief," Aike repeated, rubbing his aching jaw.

"You have a few weeks now."

Aike gapped at her.

"A few weeks?" he mumbled half to himself.

"We need weeks just to get everything in position, causing this much chaos takes tim—"

"I said a few weeks!" Reb snapped again. "Less if these lazy useless scum clans move their asses on time."

Aike gulped at air as he scanned over their plans in his head.

We are so screwed.

"Yes, Chief," he answered instead.

Reb jerked a rough hand motion for him to get out as she called in the next group of clan leaders from the former Ea tribe.

Aike dodged passed the leaders and pushed outside as he heard Reb start again with unfeasible requests.

He rubbed his jaw again and rolled his shoulder.

Bitch.

Aike meandered through the market in the growing darkness as he thought over what she had said.

"As if disrupting a kingdom in a few weeks isn't impossible enough." He grumbled to himself.

He repeated to himself Reb's threat against his team if they failed to kill the Oracaede operatives.

She wouldn't consider anything about our mission a success if we don't deliver one of the deadliest assassins in the Caelepta at her feet.

"Cause that's perfectly reasonable."

Aike groaned and rolled his eyes again as he weaved through the market, buying anything the team had requested from the closing merchants.

He pulled out his AaD and plotted the way back to Sentre.

Thank the Vis it isn't as long as getting here.

It would still be a long walk. Aike headed in the direction of the doorway and entered the Empty before deciding he needed to sleep that day. He set an alarm on his AaD for when the Empty would start shifting and nodded off within a moment of sitting down.

His nap was of short duration before his AaD beeped, and he hurried to arrive at the next doorway.

By the time he arrived in Sentre, it was midday, though Aike wasn't sure if one day had passed in Medius since he had left or two.

He set a straight route for the inn with every intent on sleeping until the middle of the next day.

Retha was suddenly at his side a block from the inn.

"Back so soon. And in one piece?"

Aike didn't start at her surprise appearance since that was how she usually appeared, but he did raise an eyebrow at her chattiness."

"You've cost me a coin in the bet," she was saying.

"You bet against my returning healthy? Rude!" Aike swayed into her, pushing her away a step. She bounced back, trying to push him without any success before she relented and fell in step beside him.

"It was most logical. Bary said so."

"Oh, and did he bet too?"

"Of course not. He's Bary." She frowned at him with concern, as though he was the one waving at insanity from a short distance.

""Course not," Aike repeated as they neared the inn.

Retha pitched up to walk on her tip-toes as she leaned closer to whisper in his ear.

"Targets are here. Just arrived late this morning. Hid's talkin 'em through the plan."

"Shit," Aike grumbled.

There goes talking to Hid about the change to the timeline in private.

He sighed.

And there goes my nap.

Retha nodded.

"And so far, not a single opening to kill either of them."

Aike struggled to keep smiling but wrapped an arm around Retha's shoulders as they entered the inn and headed up to their rooms.

"We'll figure something out."

We bloody well have to.

Aike unwrapped himself from Retha when they reached their door. He tapped their quick knock code before unlocking the door.

Hid glanced up as Aike entered. Aike caught his friend's questioning concern and nodded that he was all right.

Next to Hid sat the Ghost. His blood-red eyes watched Aike's every move. Every instinct Aike had carefully honed in his life screamed at him to run. To grab his friends and put as much distance between himself and this man as possible.

Aike swallowed the instinct, twisted every tensed muscle in his face to smile, and stepped into the room.

The sharp attention in the red eyes shifted back to the notepad in front of him as Hid started speaking in a low voice.

Bloody hell, Reb. How do you expect we'll be able to kill this monster?

Aike's attention moved to the sniper, who was in the middle of an animated story-argument with Sa'dia and Bary. The story used Idir's walking staff as the storyteller swung it around, pretending it was the rifle still strapped to his back.

"So now we're hanging off the side of this wall, Sverre's tied up in the rope with a broken arm, he can't do anything. I'm hanging there upside-down, watching out target ride away and trying to brace against Sverre to get a clean shot."

The sniper tried to show the precariousness of the situation by laying over the back of the couch and resting the staff atop the albino's shoulder. The Ghost didn't even spare a glance at the other's antics.

Bary interrupted the story with a criticism of the logic of the situation. Sa'dia started arguing the opposite. The sniper, jumping up from the couch and returning Idir's staff in one graceful motion, argued and answered a completely different point that immediately turned the bickering pair against him.

"Imma scout around."

Aike heard Retha mumble from the doorway before she disappeared. He guessed her animal instincts to flee were even stronger than his. He couldn't fault her for that and was glad at least one of his Wolves wasn't in the room with the assassins.

Aike moved to the couch, forcing his smile that had slipped.

"Alo pal, I'm Aike."

Red eyes fixed on him with a cool intensity that struck at something nauseating in Aike.

"Sverre." The albino motioned to himself, then the sniper, "that's Dain."

The sniper seemed too focused on his argument to even notice the introduction, much less add anything. But Aike guessed he was actually listening as much as talking.

"It's good you're here. Our timetable has just been moved up substantially, per Reb."

Hid stared at him and quickly tapped out a question, asking whether he was playing the assassins.

Aike noticed Sverre's glance as Hid tapped. He was a little annoyed the assassin was so quick to catch their signals, but it didn't matter since their tap code was a unique pattern they had created and no one outside the team knew.

"Reb's planning an invasion in a few short weeks, and she needs the people of Sentre riled up enough to rebel before following the king in battle."

Aike tapped back to Hid as he spoke.

No, Reb is serious. And crazy.

Hid sighed and focused a frown on his notebook.

"Well, Sverre, that will substantially change our plans here."

"Yes, it will," Sverre said quietly to rival Idir's tonality. He stood in a fluid motion, and every Wolf snapped their attention toward him.

Dain was at his side in a moment with a greeting to Aike by name.

Knew he was listening.

Aike frowned but quickly rebounded with a smile.

"Dain and I need to see the state of the city ourselves. We'll leave you for the evening to review your plans."

Oh, thank the Vis, they're leaving.

Aike almost sighed in relief but caught himself.

When the two assassins closed the door behind themselves, the room's tension dropped like a marionette without a handler.

Bary collapsed on the couch at the same time Sa'dia did, only they didn't even turn to argue some ridiculous point.

"Tell me I'm not the only one who thinks we are way out of our league trying to assassinate those guys?" Bary asked the room while holding his head in his hands.

Aike swallowed as he heard Reb's threat against him and the rest of his Wolves echo around in his skull.

Shit. We are so dead.

CHAPTER 24

Caelyn shifted in unease as Rhoeo paced the room.

"And now I heard a rumor that Brynte abandoned an entire village to be taken by the Nomads just to buy time." Rhoeo turned again at the far side of the room, a concerned frown eating up her pretty face.

"That was near Oroitz. My village is close to there, and I haven't been able to contact any of my family with the AaDs still only half working."

Caelyn's stomach twisted in further despair. There had been nothing but bad news since she arrived, especially after Bry's speech, but...

How does everything just keep getting worse?

"If you need to return home, I guess I could spare you for a time." Caelyn tried to appear unconcerned as she spoke, but her fingers twisted knots in her shawl regardless of how she tried to settle them.

She has to go, it's only right.

Caelyn hated the thought of losing the only friend she had in the city.

Rhoeo had paused and stared at her. The worry in the guard's features melted into a gentle smile.

"I couldn't leave you all alone here either, now, could I?"

She stepped closer to Caelyn and squeezed one of the hands still tangled in the shawl.

Caelyn released a shaky breath and glanced up at her bodyguard. The only person left who hadn't abandoned her.

"Thank you." She mumbled, uncertain how to show how truly grateful she was.

Rhoeo squeezed her hand again before releasing it and returning to the chair she had repeatedly left for pacing.

"Your brother, though," she started with a shake of her head.

"Half," Caelyn muttered the correction.

"He is making a fine mess of this kingdom. Loreda did some good in her time ruling at least."

Caelyn remained quiet at the mention of her mother.

What would you do, Mom, if it was you here?

She recalled a brief snippet of conversation with Stori where the queen had mentioned more of Loreda's plans the Caelyn had known. Hearing her mother's callous plan to kill Bry scared her. She had never thought her mother would do something like that.

Even I can't hate him that much.

For another moment, she considered whether her mother had been in the right. Or if Bry was right to exile her. She despised thinking of it, but she couldn't wholly agree with her mother now.

Mom, why did you leave me?

"Loreda could have done a better job with the Nomads, at least," Rhoeo tested, sending a cautious glance at Caelyn. "Though anyone could have done better in that than Brynte has."

Caelyn shrugged as she tried not to show her growing discomfort with the conversation topic. She sensed Rhoeo was waiting for her response. To agree.

"I don't know what anyone would have done differently." Caelyn tried to meet Rhoeo's eyes as she spoke. Tried to sound more confident than the confusion she felt on the subject.

She didn't.

"It doesn't matter," she continued in a mumble, "he's the one ruling."

Rhoeo sighed and stretched like a cat, arching her back as she glanced lazily around the room. "He won't rule forever though."

Caelyn's attention snapped toward her at that.

Rhoeo shrugged and held up her hands in a soothing gesture.

"I don't mean anything by it, it's just a fact. No one lives forever, and at some point, someone else is going to rule and clean up this mess."

Caelyn only relaxed a little at the clarification.

"With the way he's not fighting the Nomads, it'll probably be sooner than not," Rhoeo added under her breath, just loud enough for Caelyn to hear.

"I don't think that…" Caelyn lost her words as she tried to think what to say without angering Rhoeo at all. "Stori would rule next, and then their child."

She decided to just correct the point rather than confront her friend.

Rhoeo held her gaze a moment before smiling. "Yes, you're correct. And Stori is a great queen already, don't you think? And you two get along well. Friends, perhaps?"

Caelyn was relieved at the change in topic.

"Yes, we get along, I guess."

She frowned. She did like Stori, but they weren't friends or anything so close. Stori was so far ahead of her. So grown up and sure of herself.

Caelyn envied that and hoped she could be as confident as Stori one day.

"Although, one problem with being queen," Rhoeo started with a mischievous glint in her eyes as she bounced out of her seat, "you can't go out much. No exploring."

Caelyn lit up at the thought of getting out of the castle.

"Where did you have in mind?"

Rhoeo shrugged.

"You're the princess, Your Highness." She bowed with a teasing grin. "You tell me."

Caelyn grimaced playfully at her guards' teasing.

"Though, I've heard the Lower Market is a riot, not a place for royalty," Rhoeo said offhandedly and winked. She absently thumbed through one of Caelyn's many organized wardrobes of brightly colored clothes until she found some of Caelyn's old riding clothes. They had once been a brilliant shade of red until she started riding. She quickly realized she did not have any natural skill on a horse. She eventually learned to be a proficient rider, but the clothes had seen so much mud and dirt, they were permanently stained a dull brown.

"These are the only things here that might pass for commoner clothes." Rhoeo held them up doubtfully.

Caelyn grinned back as she grabbed the clothes away.

"Rhoeo, I could use a walk. We'll go explore the Lower Market, I think."

"Very good, Your Highness." Rhoeo bowed again, her face holding an expression of dignified seriousness, but her eyes still glinted.

Caelyn giggled as she quickly changed out of her large flowing dress into loose trousers and a long shirt with a stiff vest. Rhoeo helped her take the ornaments out of her hair before she tied the long auburn locks into a ponytail.

Rhoeo led the way out of the room and down the servant's corridors. They descended several winding staircases before reaching a side door that exited into a small courtyard. Several servants milled around, washing clothes and attending to other chores without paying any mind to the pair as they went.

Caelyn was ecstatic to be able to blend in again. It had been so long since she could move around freely without attracting so much undue attention as a princess.

"This way." Rhoeo led them out of the courtyard, down a cobblestone lane that twisted and turned until it dropped them out in the city below.

They wound their way through city streets that grew progressively dirtier as they traveled lower, further from the castle.

Rhoeo pointed out a few of her favorite places and stopped a couple of times before reaching the Lower Market.

Caelyn stared at everything she passed with unabashed awe. The awe at everything new turned overwhelming.

There were new sights, sounds, and, most especially, smells strong enough to taste. The strength of the place's character leaked out of every crevasse.

Rhoeo continued the tour of the market without noticing Caelyn's growing discomfort.

Caelyn forced herself to smile and keep moving, hoping she could ignore the growing panic that she was lost anytime Rhoeo was more than a couple steps ahead or turned a corner before her. She nearly clung to Rhoeo's cloak as the tanned woman moved on with a quick pace.

There's nothing to be scared of. Just keep up.

'Don't slow Rhoeo down' became Caelyn's mantra as she followed the guard's path through the streets, weaving through alleys and back again.

She strained to maintain a feign of interest whenever Rhoeo spoke while agonizing over how to ask her friend to slow down without showing how overwhelmed she was.

Rhoeo touted a tavern they would get a good meal at as she turned down one more shaded, dirty alley. Caelyn agreed, eager for any chance to rest.

A shadow moved in their path.

Rhoeo stopped, and Caelyn walked right into her before bouncing off and staggering back a step. She glanced around to see what was wrong.

Blocking their way stood a large man casually flipping a knife over in his hand.

"Hey there ladies. Where might you dolls to going in such a hurry?" He smiled easily as he spoke, addressing Rhoeo.

Rhoeo shifted to stand squarely in front of Caelyn, motioning her back with one hand while gripping the hilt of her guard's sword in the other.

"We are going where we will. Move out of the way," she ordered in a firm tone.

Caelyn peeked around Rhoeo to watch the man, who was still grinning, He made a threatening gesture toward her with the knife.

"Sure thing, ma'am. Why don't you leave your coin purses here, though? It's a rough neighborhood, wouldn't want them to cause you any trouble."

Rhoeo remained silent for a moment. Finally, she moved to unclasp her coin purse and motioned Caelyn to do the same.

"I suppose we'll have to oblige you." Her voice was just above a growl, but Caelyn thought she heard a smile in it as Rhoeo took both their purses and walked slowly to the man. She held the leather pouches out, a cautious distance, as she stood before him.

"Indeed, indeed. Much obliged." The man smirked as he reached for them.

Caelyn blinked and the whole scene changed. The man was on the ground at Rhoeo's feet, clutching his stomach as his skin turned a sickly shade and his lips blue.

"Spathacea," Rhoeo said with a sweet smile splayed across her lips that made Caelyn pause. The woman carefully tucked away a small dagger hidden in the palm of her hand. "Poisonous and at this concentration, deadly."

"Dead—" The man was choking as he fought to breathe. "Wasn't part of—"

Rhoeo's sword stabbed through the man's neck.

Caelyn yelped when Rhoeo jerked the sword out; blood rushed in a hurry to soak the ground. Only a few shreds of flesh attached the man's head to his body.

Caelyn turned away as fast as she could, emptying her already empty stomach on the ground as she did. She coughed, spat, and squeezed her eyes closed, but the image of the man, the blood, everything, stood out as clearly in front of her mind as when she had been looking.

"It would have been a slow miserable death. He's grateful, I'm sure."

Rhoeo's voice was next to her, speaking in the same cool tone Caelyn heard her talk about her meals or daily life.

"Rhoeo?" Caelyn opened her eyes and turned, the body drawing her attention even when she tried to look away. "Di-did you h-have to kill him?"

Caelyn trembled as the sight of the man threatened the inside of her stomach with a reappearance.

Rhoeo slid in front of her view, blocking the man's body from her sight. The guard spoke in a sweet, calming manner she led Caelyn back the way they had come, out of the alley.

"I'll send some guards for him after we return to the castle," Rhoeo said once they were back on the street.

Caelyn glanced back toward the alleyway, but Rhoeo caught her chin and forced her attention forward.

"It's all right, Caelyn. I will do whatever is necessary to protect you." Rhoeo was still speaking, though Caelyn wasn't listening to half of what she said.

Her attention focused instead on the hand laced through her arm. The poisoned blade was completely hidden, with not even a splotch of blood to give it away.

Caelyn walked through the muted world, replaying what had transpired over again in her mind.

"What if you stabbed yourself with it?" she finally asked when she thought of a question not about the dead man.

Rhoeo regarded her for a moment.

"I've built up an immunity to the poisons I work with."

"Oh," Caelyn continued, staring at the sleeve.

"Caelyn, it's my job to keep you safe."

Caelyn nodded out of habit.

Could have just given him our purses.

She bit her lip but didn't say anything.

They continued. Rhoeo pointed out a few landmarks, but Caelyn didn't pay attention.

Did he have a family?

She shook her head. He had held them up with a knife. Surely, he deserved...

The image of the nearly decapitated head bounced again to the forefront of her mind.

"Oh, here." Rhoeo held out the leather purse. "This one's yours."

Caelyn took it and held it gingerly. The weight of it was suddenly disgusting to her.

A life traded for this?

The need to be rid of the pouch struck Caelyn. She coiled her arm to throw it, but the purse was gone.

"Maybe it's better I hold on to it until we've reached the castle again."

Rhoeo was tucking it away again.

"How about we return to the castle now?"

Rhoeo had already started retracing old ground to return before she asked.

Caelyn only nodded.

"Being out like this is, maybe, a bit too much for a sweet girl like you," Rhoeo continued in a bored, detached tone. "Perhaps it would be better for you to only go out with a few more guards."

"No, I can try again," Caelyn mumbled. She hated the thought of Rhoeo passing her off to other guards.

Don't slow her down.

The mantra from before floated through her head again. She had slowed Rhoeo down.

"Brynte should be appraised next time, with the added guards. You could go out with his permission. I'm sure he would ensure you only go to the safe areas."

Caelyn balked at the idea.

"I don't need his permission. And I don't want to only go to safe places. I want to explore."

Caelyn glared, hoping Rhoeo would believe her more than she believed herself.

Rhoeo hummed, a cool grin slipping across her face.

"All right then. We could try again in a few days if you're sure you wouldn't prefer relying on Brynte."

"I'm sure."

She was sure she didn't want to lose a friend or any of Brynte's help, but not of anything else.

CHAPTER 25

Ali's discomfort grew as she watched Incara scale higher into the tree. The young girl nimbly reached a cluster of fruit and started throwing them down to the sheet Ali and Erc held loose.

In a neighboring tree, Charlton and Leon tussled one another as they raced to each fruit cluster with reckless abandon. They called arbitrary victories before scampering on with enough speed, sure-footed or not, to make Ali's stomach flip with worry.

She bit her tongue to keep from telling them to slow down, her passed warnings had not been heeded and she hated the voice in her head saying she was just nagging.

"Incara, there's more on your right, hon!" Erc called up as she weaved her side of the sheet to catch some poorly aimed fruit.

"Boys! Watch what you're doing. Don't make me come up there."

Ali had no doubts that, even in an ankle-length wrap skirt, Erc would make good on her threat if needed.

Apparently, the boys believed her too.

"Yes, ma'am!" they both called down.

The day lazily progressed from gathering fruit to peeling and chopping them and finally cooking them in a huge pot. The result looked like chunky pink applesauce. The whole batch, aside from a few bowls of taste testing, was sealed in jars.

"We'll bring these to the storage island on our way to the village," Erc announced to the room when they had finished, Ali guessed she was really only talking to her.

Ali nodded and followed after Erc as they loaded up the boat.

She was still learning all the chores and the rhythms they stuck to on the island. Every few days, they'd boat over to a nearby village where Erc would trade fruit preserves and wood carvings for essentials.

The kids would use the time to play with the other kids and visit what Ali assumed was a loose form of a school run by the other parents. The kids turned in projects they had finished since the last visit and received a new one with some books.

Ali was impressed and proud that Leon was actually ahead of most of the other students, and they all gathered around him and listened whenever he explained a topic or just told stories.

The island's peace was almost enough for Ali to relax and forget about the troubles of the worlds.

Almost.

Every quiet moment always turned dim as she worried about Sverre.

"You keep frettin' like that," Erc's strong voice made Ali jump as the woman appeared behind her, "you'll have a host of worry lines before he gets back."

Ali's face betrayed her even as she tried smoothing out her features into a smile.

Erc wasn't paying any attention as she held out a basket of supplies for Ali to tuck away in the small boat.

Ali hurried to take the basket and the next one before precariously balancing them on her way to set them down and move them out of the way.

"You be watching yourself out there, you hear Erc." An unfamiliar voice said.

Ali spun to see the newcomer. An older man, one of the locals, with the weathered skin of someone who spent all his long years at sea under the scorching sun.

"Always do, Märsik." Erc gave the man's shoulder a rough but friendly pat. "You best watch yourself 'round here. You know them weaving grannies will jump you at once they see you talking to another gal."

"This a serious matter now," Märsik retorted, drawing rickety fingers through a scraggy beard and keeping one eye shut as he spoke.

"There's be thieving and wrecking around these waters. Something hungry."

Erc sobered and gave the man a hard stare as she continued handing the last of the supplies to Ali.

"Hungry for human flesh?" she asked with a tone as hard set as her eyes. Her gaze snapped around to find the children.

Märsik waved off the question.

"Nah. It ain't be killing no one. I'd have haunting parties out if it was." He gestured toward the boat they had just finished loading. "It's big and comes from the water. Been sinking boats and eating the supplies."

Erc cocked an eyebrow.

"It's sinking boats, but not killing anyone?"

"Nah. It seems careful not 'a kill."

"It's 'ntelligent?"

Märsik nodded. "Still destructive, though."

He shifted his posture and turned a searching gaze across the bay before landing on Ali. He nodded a greeting and crocked a smile.

"I be worried about you five out there by yourselves. May be easy pickin's for it."

Erc snorted and lifted the rifle that was always by her side, setting it in the boat as she stepped in.

"It may try, but we ain't gonna be easy."

Märsik turned his one open eye to her with a smile.

"Now, how did that boy Dain, who's never around, end up with such a treasure."

He shook his head, gave them a farewell nod, and turned to leave.

Erc watched him walk away for a moment.

"Kids! Round up, we're leavin,'" she hollered in the direction of the village.

Erc shifted some of the boat's contents until she found what she was looking for. She held up a shotgun.

"You know how to use one of these?" Erc asked.

Ali tried swallowing the desert out of her throat. The memory of Sverre's house, the splintering door, the pool of blood.

The blood...

"A little," she said, though her head shook 'no' on reflex.

"Humph." Erc propped the shotgun next to Incara's seat. "Ain't been around Sverre or my man long enough then."

Ali ducked her head and stared at her fingers, twisting the fabric of her skirt. She wasn't sure if Erc meant it as a chastisement, but the feeling of helplessness from that night with the Wolves returned with nauseating strength.

"Hey." Erc's sharp voice drew Ali's attention.

"We can fix that when our men get back. In the meantime, I'll teach you what I know."

The gentle smile on Erc's lips was fleeting but as warm as any. Ali smiled back at the idea.

"Thanks," she mumbled, even as she couldn't quite ignore the quiet, scared little voice in her head that spoke only fearful things.

The boys, clearly racing, ran full speed into the boat, toppling over each other to avoid falling out the other side. They bickered at who was the winner as they settled into their seats.

Incara was slower as she waved goodbye to a couple of the girls in the village before taking her seat. She frowned at the shotgun a moment, but picked it up, checked the weapon, and with a nod from Erc, held it in loose readiness and her eyes trained over the water.

Erc wordlessly traded places with Ali, taking up a position at the stern with her rifle.

Ali gulped at being left to control the boat as the motor. She squashed at her fears as quickly as she could, started the engine, and guided them out of the harbor the same way she had seen Erc do, albeit slower.

She breathed a shaky sigh as they cleared the bay and she stared down the vastness of the island-speckled ocean beyond.

Leon gave her a broad smile as he turned a map on the boat floor around to face Ali. He traced their route around the islands and then pointed out the same islands on the horizon ahead of them.

"Thanks, Leon," Ali breathed, squeezing the boy's shoulder.

She had half the route memorized but appreciated the confirmation that she was on the right course.

The ride back to their island was blissfully uneventful apart from Charlton sending Leon overboard in a moment of roughhousing.

Ali had walked the path to the house enough times she could reach the top without being winded, though still sweaty. She marveled with a twinge of jealousy as the boys raced up and down the path three times before she reached the house once.

Their endless energy was the saving grace that prevented her from making the trek twice though. They had all the supplies unloaded by the time Ali and Erc reached the house.

Ali longed to collapse on the couch for a nap. Still, Erc had instructions for putting everything away that required attention. Ali pushed through her exhaustion to complete the chores to Erc's standards before she fell bodily onto the couch.

"Aunt Ali, want to come fishing with us?" Charlton appeared before her, startling Ali from what would have been a lovely afternoon nap.

Ali's aching legs clamped up at the idea of treading the long way down to the water again, but she smiled.

"Thanks, but I'll pass this time."

"Okay, have a good nap."

Charlton and his mischievous grin were gone in an instant.

Ali guessed the boy had found time to practice Sverre's tricks with how good he was at stealth. Though that only applied when he was not around Leon.

"Have a good fishing trip," Ali called to the empty air.

"Boys, be careful by the water," Erc said from the pantry.

"We will!" A pair of young voices called back, already a distance away outside.

CHAPTER 26

S verre overlooked the castle courtyard from his position in the shadows
of a buttress high above.

He watched the queen enjoying tea. Or trying to. Between
consoling her maidservant and the young princess, Sverre guessed she was
less excited about her afternoon break than she might have been on other
days.

Sverre continued circling the castle grounds until he was satisfied with
the state of disorder inside. He returned to the city and wandered the streets
in his cloaked disguise until he found Dain.

The rifleman, sans the rifle he had loathed to leave in hiding, was
quietly conversing with some of the rough elements of the city. His
conversation was focused on a tanned man with an eyepatch and uglier scars
than Dain's.

Sverre maintained an inconspicuous distance as the conversation
concluded, and Eyepatch drifted away with the other less descriptive men.

Sverre moved toward Dain, but a curt signal from the sniper waved him
off. He changed course to peruse the shops and explore the back alleys more
thoroughly until another group of people, still led by Eyepatch, approached
Dain.

The interaction was of short duration before they moved on, taking
Dain with them. He quickly signaled to Sverre that he was fine and to wait.

Sverre acknowledged and continued circling the area as night set in. He
shrank further into the shadows as the growing darkness drew out more of
the unruly types who had any chance of recognizing who he was.

Finally, Dain was back.

Sverre sensed his partner before he ever saw him and relaxed when the man manifested next to him, already starting in the middle of an empty conversation for appearance's sake as they fell in step, heading toward their lodgings.

As soon as they were inside their private room, the pretense of conversation dropped.

Dain cleared a small space through the mess on his side of the room, just enough to collapse on the couch. Sverre moved to the kitchen to start a pot of coffee before anything else.

"Those kids are good." Dain groaned. "Too good."

Sverre returned to the living room, pausing a moment at the lack of any sitting furniture Dain wasn't draped over before settling on the coffee table.

"The castle is in chaos too." He tapped the table as he thought. "Thacea is already set up there."

Dain stiffened, glancing at Sverre with a grumble, "That woman...I didn't know Atanas sent her."

"Me neither, but we will need to avoid her. If Atanas didn't say anything about it, then our jobs don't conflate."

"Avoiding her is always the best idea." Dain relaxed back into the couch cushions.

The silence settled over the room. Sverre watched Dain frown, chewing his lip, and started grieving the inevitable loss of the quiet as he waited for Dain to find what he wanted to say.

"Reb is gonna use those kids, you know," Dain finally said.

Sverre nodded even though Dain wasn't looking at him.

He already guessed Reb would use the Wolves to try to kill him and Dain as revenge for killing Erasyl. He pitied them for having been given such a task.

The Wolves at your house were the same.

Sverre clenched his jaw.

He would still feel worse about killing the Wolves he had already met than the ones Reb had sent to his house.

The faces of those kids flickered across his mind for the umpteenth time since that night.

"Any chance to get them out of Reb's control?" Sverre asked, shaking his head free of the image.

Dain nodded before he continued explaining the results of his research.

Of how much damage the Wolves had already done to the stability of the city.

"You have to admit," Dain sighed, "they are good at their jobs. Everyone in the city now distrusts the king to some degree."

Sverre nodded again from habit.

"What do you want to do?" Dain asked as he continued frowning at the ceiling.

Sverre remained silent as the thought.

"Castle folks can't know we're here," he stated.

"You ever gonna tell…Well, never mind telling Brynte the whole truth, what about telling them our allegiances?"

Dain propped his head up to stare Sverre down with the question.

How am I ever going to be able to tell him everything?

He groaned at the thought but cleared it from his head quickly to focus on the present problems again.

"With all the Wolves have done, we will have to wait for this to settle just to have an idea of who to trust."

Dain nodded as he dropped his head again.

"Can't risk saying anything with Thacea in the castle anyway."

Sverre frowned at the mention of the woman but ignored it as he went to the kitchen to pour them both a mug of coffee.

Still lots of work to do tonight.

"You want to complete Atanas's side quest now or tomorrow night?"

Dain asked with a yawn as he sat up enough to take the mug Sverre handed to him.

"Tonight," Sverre stated, ignoring his annoyance that Dain had already guessed what he had been thinking.

"Right, we'll have our hands full with those Wolf kids tomorrow," Dain agreed.

They drank their coffee, sparing a few words for a plan, but not much speaking was needed.

When they finished, Sverre exchanged his black cloak for Dain's brown one and settled a mask and hat over his most distinct features as Dain did less to cover his.

They left their little apartment through Dain's window, which faced an empty alleyway, and snuck through the still wide-awake city to the castle.

Breaking in was concerning for how easy it was.

Brynte, you need to work on your security.

Sverre smiled at the thought since it made their work easier.

They moved down to the lowest levels of the castle, where the computer mainframe for the AaDs stood, running with a constant hum.

They incapacitated the guards without any trouble. Sverre moved to keep watch as Dain moved to the computer with the technology skills Sverre could only envy.

"Ohh, someone's put some updated security on this thing." Dain purred, clearly enjoying the challenge.

Sverre ignored him as he paced the surrounding halls and the path to their way out.

His third time around the loop, and two more incapacitated guards later, he stopped in to see how Dain was faring.

The darker man smiled and continually mumbled to himself as he worked.

Sverre walked the halls another two times before Dain was finished.

"All right, all the files from Lucianca they backed up are destroyed. There are another two AaD copies."

Dain handed over a torn piece of paper to the owner of one of the AaDs, Lawrence Dara, and the AaD number.

"The other's with the castle manager." Dain smiled and patted Sverre on the back. "I assume you wanted to go steal that from Ali's uncle to say hi anyway."

They parted on an upper floor as Dain headed further into the castle and Sverre headed to a nearby window.

Sverre traced his way around the outside of the castle until he found the window to the king's study he had used before.

He peeked inside.

Just his poor luck, the king was still there. It was his better luck, though, that Brynte looked asleep and alone.

Sverre opened the window, careful to be silent, and stepped inside without causing Brynte to stir. He observed the room's stillness and only moved toward an organized little desk when he was sure the stillness wasn't disturbed.

He cautiously picked through the items in the drawers until he found an AaD with a matching serial number to the paper Dain had given him. He tucked it into his cloak to be destroyed later.

Brynte shifted in his sleep.

Sverre froze and waited until the redhead was settled back to sleep before crossing the room again.

He paused before leaving to glance back at Brynte. The king still held a pen in his hand that was leaking ink onto a piece of paper.

Sverre took the pen and set it on the desk before glancing at the paper. It contained a list of names in three sets of handwriting. The header read, 'Think of some baby names, Bry. If I have to name your kid, I'm calling them Shadric/a'

Sverre blinked at the paper as he glanced over the names. Three of them were underlined with smiley faces next to them.

The queen's having a baby?

He smiled at the sleeping form before picking up the pen and adding a name himself.

Ara.

Sverre walked to the couch and grabbed a blanket to settle over the redhead's shoulders.

If you're having a kid, you need to learn to take care of yourself so you can teach them that.

Sverre hurried out the window as he heard a ruckus in the hallway. He watched a moment to see a troop of guards burst through the door, startling Brynte awake. The king was up, staggering with his sword half drawn before he could recognize his own guards.

Sleeping is taking care of yourself too.

Sverre shook his head at just how exhausted Brynte looked while awake before turning to leave.

CHAPTER 27

B ry knocked on Stori's door and entered before she could respond. "Are you all right?" he asked as he closed the distance to her and enveloped her in a hug.

"Bry, what's wrong? Are you well?" Stori sputtered out in surprise.

Bry scanned the room instead of answering. It was empty of human inhabitants. The Pyxis, Fenrir, lumbered out from the bed chamber in a relaxed manner and greeted Bry with drool on his pants legs.

Bry guessed the large creature would protect Stori, and he didn't need to worry as much, but he still did.

"Bry?"

Bry smiled at Stori, ready to answer, but a knock at the door interrupted. He recognized Shad's knocking before the wraith entered.

He nodded to Stori before turning to Bry.

"Lawr's fine. Klaas and Eleanora too," he stated as he fidgeted with the handles of both his sheathed Moro blades.

"Bry, what's happening?" Stori asked again, staring up at him.

Bry noticed he still had an arm wrapped in a protective hold around her. He relaxed enough to let her go as he spoke.

"Someone broke into the castle, the guards around the mainframe computer were disabled, and Chesler said someone was in his office."

He walked the length of the room again, double-checking that the windows were locked as he mumbled.

"He's so obsessively organized, you know."

"Oh, that's…" Stori trailed off as she, too, glanced around the room, a hand hovering protectively over her belly.

"Who do you think it was?" she asked.

Bry shook his head and noticed Shad frowning.

"Don't know what they got off the computer downstairs, but Chesler knows what is missing from his office." Shad held Bry's gaze. "The AaD that had all the info about Oracaede we found in Lucianca."

"Do we have another copy?"

Shad nodded.

"Lawr said he had one in his desk. I assume if anyone broke in, they would have woken you up."

Bry nodded but wanted to check anyway.

Shad already had his hand up to stop him.

"Lawr knows which AaD it was on, but he's still busy with the main computer right now."

Stori grabbed his hand, distracting him from checking his study again.

"Did anyone check on Caelyn?" she asked, glancing between him and Shad.

Shad grimaced and started to turn toward the door.

"No, I forgot, I'll go—"

"No," Bry interrupted, "I'll go check on her."

Bry headed for the door with a quick smile to Stori. He paused by Shad when his concern for his wife didn't dissipate.

Shad caught on to his worry at the same time Bry realized it himself.

Too much stress is bad for the baby.

"Stori, you want to wait in Bry's study and think of more baby names with me?" Shad asked, offering his arm to her. "Bry can join us when he's done."

Bry nodded his gratitude to Shad and gave Stori an encouraging smile before he quit the room and moved hastily through the hallways to Caelyn's section of the floor.

He pounded on the door, only considering after he did that he would likely be waking the younger girl up.

He waited for several moments in silence. His concern grew as the stillness from inside the room remained.

Bry knocked again and called her name as he debated if it was necessary to try and break the door down.

What if something happened because we forgot to check on her...

He banged on the door again before turning to the guard stationed at the end of the hall and motioning him over. The guard ran over and was about to try prying the door with his spear when the sound of the lock turning stopped them both.

Caelyn's sleepy face appeared at the creak in the door as she stared out.

"Bry? What are you—"

Bry interrupted by pushing the door open, turning on the Aequorian torch nearby, and wrapping an arm around the girl in a half hug. Caelyn's questions sputtered into confusion.

Bry released her just as she started pushing him away.

"What are you doing?" Caelyn's voice broke into a squeak as she was awake enough to glare.

Bry ignored the question as he dismissed the guard and walked the length of the room, checking every dark corner.

"Have you had any other disturbances tonight? Any noise nearby?"

Caelyn crossed her arms over her fluffy purple night robe.

"You're disturbing enough for one evening, don't you think?"

"Caelyn." Bry didn't snap, he hoped, but his voice was sharp enough that it surprised her.

"No. There's been no one and no noise, except for you," she stated with a frown that started looking worried. "What's going on?"

Bry walked a circle around the room again, peeking into the dark study before answering. "There was an intruder. They may have stolen something valuable."

"Good for them."

Caelyn stood glaring at him and fidgeting with her messy braids.

Bry growled but refrained from saying anything until he returned to the door.

"I'm glad you are all right. Sorry to disturb your sleep, go back to bed."

He stated before closing the door on her confused expression.

Bry grumbled to himself the whole way back to his study. Shad, ever dependable, already had Stori's complete focus directed toward sweet little Alina or Hazael.

"What? Jassmira was nixed already?" Bry questioned as he moved over to his desk for the list of names.

"Yeah," Shad sighed, "after some thought, the name remains me of someone we met traveling. You remember? I think her name was Jasmir actually. Bad memories."

"Jasmir? Lux Aequor maybe?" Bry grabbed his list and frowned at the blanket on the floor.

He remembered shrugging it off when the guards had barged into his study, but he certainly hadn't had it when he fell asleep. He glanced between Shad and Stori. Shad was regaling Stori with a tale of just how terrible the Jasmir he had met was.

Stori wasn't stealthy enough to have brought him a blanket without waking him, and while Shad was, he would have woken him up just to tell him to go to bed anyway.

The twist of anxiety shifted in his stomach as he glanced over the list to calm himself.

Ara.

A new name in a new style of handwriting.

Bry squeezed his eyes shut before glancing toward Lawr's desk. It was organized with a dozen AaDs neatly lined up, but he could guess one of them was missing.

Bry tried his best to smile as he sat next to Stori and pretended to listen to the name discussion.

Shad had immediately noticed Bry's stress and helpfully drew Stori's attention further to himself while slipping concerned glances at Bry.

Bry just shook his head and the discussion continued.

CHAPTER 28

Hid moved through the back of the crowd, always keeping half a watchful eye on Aike's performance, rousing the people's outrage.

He paused near anyone not looking particularly swayed and chatted quietly with them until they agreed with the general idea of Aike's speech.

Reb's unrealistic changes to their timetable forced them to take a more aggressive approach.

Hid didn't like it. He hated being rushed. Rushed was where mistakes happened. And where simple mistakes could become deadly. They weren't equipped to handle the city, or even the current crowd, if they turned against the Wolves.

Even with most of the Wolves circulating through the crowd, Hid wished they had more support. Xiulan, their team's only long-range fighter, had her bow in a building overlooking the crowd from behind, but shooting people was not her preferred method of operating nor the one she practiced often.

Hid was grateful Dain was providing overwatch too, but the city streets were too cramped and winding for the sniper to cover the whole crowd.

As for the Ghost, Hid could easily believe the man was an effective monster in any situation, but that did nothing to make the circumstances less threatening. Hid still could not reconcile that the man was even human with how quiet and phantom-like he was. He could easier believe the Ghost was really some kind of Shade in disguise.

Shade's like to play with their food.

He shuttered at the memory.

We just have to be near him/it until he's dead or at least away from us.

Hid could deal with the terrifying man that long. Not that they had any idea how they would follow Reb's orders to assassinate either of Oracaede's operatives.

One step at a time, and that is not step one.

A rising stir in the crowd snapped Hid's attention back to his surroundings.

Aike's gamed little presentation had reached the point of politely asking for a revolt.

Aike wasn't polite as he continued riling up the crowd while attempting to focus their anger toward the king, guards, the castle, or anything besides himself. The mood of the crowd was already sour, but Hid noted it seemed to be turning against Aike.

"Damn it, *hermano*," Hid grumbled to himself as he weaved to the edge of the crowd, checking and double-checking that Aike was still standing as he did.

Hid caught his breath as his skin crawled with an unparalleled urge to flee.

Damned Ghost.

Hid knew the man had appeared next to him without needing to look.

"Have Retha prepare a distraction in the back," the low voice commanded as Sverre scanned the crowd ahead of him with cool, indifferent eyes. "The rest of you should be shouting in support."

In the same breath, he was gone.

Hid would be in awe of his skills if the man wasn't so unnerving.

Gulping down his aversion, Hid moved to catch Retha's attention. The small dark girl was tucked away in the shadow of a few crates on the shady side of the crowd.

Hid only had to take a step in her direction before she caught sight of him, and he gestured a few short orders.

She rolled her eyes at his emphasis on a non-lethal distraction before acknowledging and disappearing into an alley.

Hid turned toward Xiulan next with a whistle, short and flute-like.

He watched her eyes search through the crowd until she found him. He made several hasty hand signals to her and waited for her nod of understanding.

Xiulan, in turn, loosed a loud shrieking whistle that bounced off the buildings without giving away her location. Every Wolf would know to look at her for instructions. Hid watched until he saw her start gesturing directions for what to do before he turned back to the scene around him.

Aike was still talking, though distracted by watching Xiulan as well.

Hid scanned the crowd nearest his friend for any threats. His stomach dropped as he spotted the Ghost's familiar cloak and mask standing beside Aike.

Hid's body jerked with an initial reaction to warn Aike and get him away from the man, but he stopped himself to observe.

Taking a breath to steady his fears, Hid noticed Sverre had taken up a defensive position to guard Aike. He gaped at the realization. Hid had assumed the Ghost would not have cared in the slightest if one of the Wolves was injured or killed.

He's just protecting assets.

Hid needed the assurance though he did not understand why he did.

He turned his attention to someone shouting from the crowd. Bary's familiar voice was easily heard over the din as he shouted support for Aike.

Sa'dia was next, shouting less open support and more general hate of the king and his rule.

Hid took his turn, shouting nonsense to sway the mob, followed in overlap by Idir. Aike shouted back, using the team's provocation for all it was worth.

Hid paused, holding his breath even, to listen a moment to the shouting. The moment stretched toward the end of his stressed patience. He was about to signal Retha for their exit distraction when a new voice caught his attention. A stranger shouting support for Aike. Then another.

He breathed in relief. The shouting caught on. Hid observed the moment the crowd changed into a mob with rising anger toward the king.

Aike wasted no time directing that anger toward acting against the king or the castle guards or any close target. The mob surged with a new bloodlust in the direction of the castle.

Aike led the party as Hid tried to get close enough to help him get away.

Hid watched carefully as Sverre remained by Aike's side and threw a cloak over his shoulders. In a moment, Aike was indistinguishable from anyone else, and the mob moved on without him.

Hid whistled to call the other Wolves to him as he moved to the alleyway he had seen Aike and Sverre duck into.

Xiulan and the others were at his side before he even reached the alley.

"I wanted to use my distraction," Retha complained, leisurely tossing a bottle of liquor with something inside and a fuse.

Caesar Apollo caught the bottle midair and held it out of the girl's reach.

"Aike made it out safe?" Xiulan said with only a slight inflection to make it a question rather than a statement.

Hid turned down the alley instead of answering to see for himself.

Aike was cheerfully thanking the Ghost for his help and Dain, equally cheerfully, accepted the praise in proxy for his silent partner.

Hid had no idea how the sniper had beat them to the alley, but he didn't question the man's skills as he moved next to Aike to thank Sverre too.

The Ghost shifted with what Hid might have called abashed uncertainty. Might. If he considered the man anything even approaching human. But the Ghost was so far into being a monster, Hid decided he was just too sure of himself to care about being praised.

They turned as a group to leave with Aike still talking in praise and cheer, though too loud for Hid's always uneasy comfort. But hid recognized his friend's attempts to draw Sverre into a useful conversation so chose to ignore it.

They continued moving down the alley until a loud, suspicious shuffling from behind a few crates stopped them. Sverre was the first to stop, knife in hand as he moved toward the noise.

The Wolves shifted instinctually to defensive positions centered around Caesar Apollo, who was closest.

Maybe a bit overkill. Even to me.

Hid frowned at their jumpy reaction, but standing next to the sniper, watching the Ghost approach the noise, it didn't seem too extreme in such dangerous company.

Sverre jerked the crate aside. The knife in his hand disappeared even faster than he had pulled it out.

"Stand down," he growled with a note of firm gentleness Hid had never heard from him before.

Hid blinked with surprise as he shifted back. He dropped out of his fighting stance with his dagger already half tucked away before hesitating. Should he really be blindly following the Ghost's order?

Aike's cheerful voice, hinting at panic, interrupted Hid's indecision.

"Hi-ya kid-o, what're ya doing 'round here?"

Hid moved to see around Sverre to a small child huddled in the corner. The child—Hid could not immediately tell if it was a boy or a girl under the dirty clothes and choppy haircut —stared up at them with big fearful eyes, focusing mainly on Sverre.

Hid turned his attention to the Ghost as well. The man was unreadable as ever with his vacant eyes, but the mask he still wore to hide his features made him even more so. Still, Hid could recognize the potential threat.

The kid must have heard Aike talking about our plans.

Panic crept unabated into Hid's mind as he shared a glance with Aike. Aike was already shifting to put himself between the assassins and the child.

Reasonably speaking, it was almost a non-issue. The kid likely would not have understood what they were talking about. Even if they did repeat it to someone, they could not provide enough details to be a threat.

But that was only a matter of being reasonable as someone valuing a child's life. Hid still had no idea if he could consider the two Oracaede assassins so reasonable.

After all, logically speaking, getting rid of the child is a solid idea.

Hid reminded himself as he glanced between Sverre and Dain without any luck guessing their thoughts.

Illogically speaking, of course, I would rather try killing these two right now than hurt the kid.

Dain's chipper, soothing voice spoke fast nonsense, half to the kid, half to Sa'dia and Bary, who had sidled over to position themselves as an extra barrier in front of Aike and the kid.

Sverre and Dain were exchanging glances of their own. Dain stepped to the side, sandwiching himself between Sa'dia and Bary and the rest of the Wolves. He stood directly before Hid as he spoke. "Now, you kids need to calm down. No one's going to hurt the child."

His voice remained an octave lower than the usual cheerful tone he used as he caught their gazes. "So, stand down."

"Why would we ever trust that?" Hid growled back. He watched Aike move directly behind the sniper. He held Aike's gaze.

There is no way we can fight both of them and win.

Aike looked like he was thinking the same, but they didn't back down.

Even if they could take Dain out, Sverre was the more dangerous one in close combat.

Sverre?

Hid glanced around to the spot the Ghost had just been standing to find it empty. His stomach dropped at the realization he had lost track of their most worrisome target.

Shit!

Hid scanned around his teammates and was relieved not to find the Ghost near any of them.

But that still leaves…

"Where are your parents, missy?"

Sverre's low voice spoke with a tone gentler than Hid would have thought possible for the assassin, and everyone's attention snapped to him. The man was kneeling in front of the child. Sverre had removed his mask and was motioning to coax the kid out of the corner.

"Don't worry about those fellows, they're not really all that scary."

Hid blinked when he realized Sverre was talking about them.

The child pouted, still with a look of terror as she—*Sverre had called her a girl, right?*—glanced toward the Wolves. The look melted to one approaching trust, however, when her gaze returned to Sverre.

"It's all right, luv." Dain smiled a genuine, kind smile as the kid testily crept out toward Sverre.

The Ghost picked her up and settled her on his hip with a comfortable ease only born from practice.

Hid gawked.

The most terrifying person he had ever met was talking easily to the child and smiling. Not a wide smile, like Dain or Aike's, but just enough of one to make him look friendly. And he did.

If Hid did not know who he really was, he would not have been able to guess how much the man could change his presence.

Sverre turned his attention toward Hid and Aike. He was no longer smiling, but his presence was still softer and much warmer than usual.

"We'll take her to a guard station."

"Her parents were likely in that crowd headed to the castle," Dain added as he rubbed his head staring in that direction.

Hid could only bob his head as he stared at the stranger in front of him.

Sverre returned to talking softly to the child as he carried her out toward the main road.

Dain spared a moment to scoff at them with a quiet, "You'd think so poorly of us?" And then he followed after Sverre with more smiles as he spoke, holding the girl's attention and pulling her out of her fears before they even reached the road.

"What...just happened there? Anyone know?" Bary asked, scratching his head as he glanced between Aike and where the two assassins had disappeared around the corner.

Aike shrugged as he held Hid's gaze.

"Think we just got shown up, fellas."

CHAPTER 29

Retha pouted all the way back to their inn that she had not had the chance to use her distraction.

Hid left the comforting of their youngest member to Xiulan as he and Aike discussed what had happened.

"Ya know, he coulda planned on killing the kid after—"

"Aike," Hid growled the interruption.

He had considered that already. He had considered every possibility that left Sverre to be the same cold-blooded psychopath they all thought he was. But nothing stuck. Every possibility ended with Hid remembering the gentle smile and voice. The memory was greatly unsettling.

"Yeah, I know," Aike conceded. He was frowning too.

The easiest part of trying to follow Reb's orders to assassinate the Ghost had been how easy it was to imagine the world would be better off without him. That he was too much of a monster.

Now though...

Hid trailed off from the thought. Now that didn't seem completely true.

"Now what?" he asked in a low voice, sneaking a glance at Aike.

His stomach turned at the extra pressure he was putting on Aike, but he needed to know if their plans should change.

Aike hummed as he walked, staring at the sky before answering. "Plan's the same," he stated. A small twang slipping into his accent was Hid's only clue into Aike's underline uncertainty. Aike's grin returned, not matching his words as usual.

"So he's not a *heartless* heartless monster. He's still a monster. Unless

Reb changes our mission, it remains the same."

Hid gridded his teeth.

It doesn't matter what I think of the Ghost, Reb will still have Aike killed for failing.

He grimaced at the reminder.

There is nothing to consider except how to get the job done.

"Sorry, *hermano*. I know nothing has changed." Hid ducked his head with the apology.

Aike blinked at him, his goofy grin shifting to confusion for a moment before latching on again.

"No need for that, I was shocked back there too." He shook his head, "Those two are full of surprises."

Hid nodded and let the topic drop as they neared their inn.

The team puttered around their rooms, waiting for the assassins to return.

Aike went along with the others in bouncing lighthearted ideas that Sverre might still be as heartless as they all assumed initially. None of the ideas stuck.

Hid mentally reviewed the fragments of what he deigned to call a plan to kill the pair. They had already decided to wait for whatever chaos Reb brought with her, but the plan still relied too much on luck for any of their comforts. Especially Hid's, but they still did not have anything better.

And most of the luck needed went to separating the two and keeping Dain from providing Sverre long-distance support. So far, this had been fruitless as the pair always looked out for each other.

A noise at the door snapped Hid from his dejected, spiraling thoughts.

The door opened as the assassins entered.

Sverre, as silent and stoic as always, and Dain with his normal, bubbly chatter. They acted as though nothing at all was different.

Aike will certainly be the first to call that out—

"So, you like kids, huh? Wouldn't have guessed it."

Let me think through being right before you prove it, hermano.

Hid shook his head at his curious friend as the man wasted no time in blocking the Ghost's path with a goofy grin.

Sverre's expression remained the same emotionless void as he glared through the line of freckles.

"They are not a problem," Sverre stated in his low, monotone voice as he stepped passed Aike, "when they are not standing in my way."

Was that a joke?

Hid's immediate reaction was 'no,' but now he paused to think about it.

"Well, I'd thought, being—" Aike's beginnings of a ramble was cut short as Sverre stepped back to stand in his personal space.

"Next time, keep your voice down in public."

Hid flinched at the sudden chill. From Aike's sudden silence and dropped grin, he could guess that he sensed a threat even more.

Finally, Aike jerked a quick nod with his eyes remaining locked on the floor.

"Good." Sverre stepped back and moved further into the room, leaving Aike blinking in clear relief.

Hid moved to stand next to his friend on the off chance the assassin was still angry.

"Don't let him bother you," a chipper voice said from behind them, making both Hid and Aike jump. More so when a dark hand clapped down on either of their shoulders.

"We just had a spot of trouble finding the girl's parents, so he's a little on edge."

Dain was grinning as he patted their shoulders again before moving to talk with Retha and Xiulan. Compliments Hid couldn't hear rolled off the sniper's tongue.

"Shit," Aike breathed, just loud enough for Hid to hear as he tracked both assassins' movements across the room.

"Any word from Reb?" Sverre asked in the same empty tone Hid already hated but now loathed even further. He could not determine at all if the man was still angry.

We messed up, of course he's angry. And anger is always dangerous.

Hid traded a quick glance with Aike before Aike forced a smile and answered.

"Nah, she hasn't said a peep. Though she probably won't until she is about to leave. Not good with communicating, that one. She may not even call 'til she's already here."

Aike paused his rambling for an uneasy laugh as he continued pacing around the living space and sputtering on as he could not quite be calm enough to sit.

Sverre's sharp eyes followed the erratic pacing in what Hid hoped he imagined to be growing impatience.

"Aike."

The Ghost's tone was surprisingly gentle, the same as he used for the child.

The surprising tone did nothing to relax Hid's worry as the man motioned Aike to come.

Every Wolf froze and stared. Hid broke his gaze to quickly catch each of the team's eyes and shake off their habitual, stealthy grab for their weapons.

Aike moved a couple of timid steps at a time before gathering himself enough to march the rest of the way to stand in front of the albino.

"Sverre, I apologize for my slip in conduct earlier. It won't happen again," Aike apologized with the careful choice of words and suppressing his accent the way he normally did for meetings with the chief and Reb.

Sverre stared at him with a confused look, and his head cocked sideways. His gaze shifted toward Dain a moment as an unreadable exchange passed between them before his attention snapped back to Aike.

Hid used the half-moment pause to again cross the room and stand just behind and beside Aike. He gave his friend a quick tap on the arm to ensure he knew Hid was there to back him up.

Aike's posture relaxed just the slightest, but Hid noticed. More than anything, Aike always hated to be alone for a reprimand.

Hate flared up and touched Hid's mind as he recalled Reb always separated them to yell at Aike alone.

A fresh degree of hatred for their boss filled his mind and slipped out toward the man in front of them.

"So long as you noticed, it is fine," Sverre stated, shifting his weight to stand.

Hid tried not to cringe as that brought the Ghost within striking distance.

"I am not mad, Aike."

Hid analyzed the Ghost's face for the truth of that statement.

He doesn't look like he's lying, but I can never tell with this damned man.

Sverre's gaze shifted between them as a faint smile, more subdued than he had used with the child but still warm, graced his lips.

The Ghost stepped around Aike and paused again next to Hid.

"You're a good friend."

Sverre moved toward the door where Dain already stood waiting.

"It's been a long day," Dain's cheerful voice called, "have a rest, and we'll be back tomorrow."

Hid and Aike exchanged another confused glance as the assassins closed the door behind themselves.

The rest of the Wolves stared expectantly at the door, half expecting the two to return.

CHAPTER 30

"You had to scare that kid so much? I thought they were going to attack us right there."

Dain shook his head and pinched the bridge of his nose as they walked.

"I didn't mean to." Sverre frowned as he spoke. He had not meant to scare the kid at all, just to tell him to be more careful in the future.

Didn't do any more than that, did I?

"Those kids were raised to see everything as some form of aggression, how'd ya think he'd take it?"

Sverre shuffled his feet as he walked, grumbling, "Not that badly."

A weight across his shoulders tipped Sverre forward a step before he adjusted his balance. Dain leaned his full body weight casually against Sverre and the arm he looped around his neck.

"Now you know how I feel. You used to do that to me all the time, and better pray to the Vis if I ever so much as brushed up against you. You'd have cut my hand off just for this."

Dain laughed and waved the hand he had around Sverre's shoulders.

"I wasn't that bad."

Sverre tried to defend, but he did remember how much he had distrusted Dain. The idea that someone would be kind to him without trying to get something in return was so foreign he assumed Atanas had paid Dain to backstab him.

The idea was silly in his mind now, but at the time, it was all he expected.

Sverre ignored Dain's ardent protests that he was indeed 'that bad' and tried to shrug out from under Dain instead. His friend's mass moved with him without deterrence.

"You still do, sometimes," Dain mumbled.

The soft tone made Sverre pause as he caught the forlorn look in Dain's eyes.

Dain withdrew his arm, and they walked in relative silence. The sniper was rarely silent and didn't remain so for long. Sverre ignored his chipper discussion about nothing while he thought.

I could've sworn I was getting better.

He lamented the idea. Sverre had always been sensitive to anger in others. He learned it from whenever Atanas had been angry with him as a child.

Angry is always dangerous.

Sverre shuttered at the memories that sprung forth uninvited.

"So, what are we gonna do now?"

Dain tapped Sverre's side before asking so Sverre knew he actually wanted an answer.

Sverre remained silent as he tried forcing down the memories to focus on the matter at hand.

"Atanas will be wanting the AaDs we took from the castle," Dain continued in a low voice when Sverre didn't immediately answer.

"Should expect Echo in the next week or so," Sverre stated the obvious just to focus his thoughts.

Dain hummed agreement, "Reb is moving fast. If she keeps moving up the time of her invasion, she may get here before he does."

Sverre nodded, still only half listening.

He stiffened as he sensed someone behind him. A small hand latched around his wrist. He was already fingering a knife when he spun around.

The Wolves' youngest member—Sverre had not learned all their names yet—stared at him with her wild look. She had jumped back when he turned, and now she waited in a half crouch for his reaction.

Sverre released his knife and remained still with his palms visibly empty, hoping she would not run away.

Don't be threatening, don't be threatening, don't be threatening…

She backed away another few steps.

Damn it, don't be threatening.

"Hey, Retha, what are you doing here?" Dain also maintained a nonthreatening pose as the girl still looked one vocal-tone shift away from disappearing.

Retha shifted as a small predator analyzing a larger one before she finally relaxed, just a little. Enough to talk.

"Aike and Xiulan were taken."

Sverre exchanged a glance with Dain.

"What? By who?" Dain asked, still keeping his voice light and easy.

Retha was already bouncing away in the direction of the inn.

"Guards. Come."

She disappeared into the crowd on the street.

Sverre and Dain hurried through the streets and alleys until they reached the inn again, where Retha was waiting out front. She led the way inside but always maintained an excessive distance from them.

All the Wolves feared him, but Retha definitely made Sverre feel the guiltiest about it. He wished he could show her he wasn't a monster. Or at least not as much of one as she thought.

Retha hurried through the door just when Sverre had reached the top of the stairs. He followed into the room to see Hid and Idir in the middle of the room, trying not to argue.

"We have to get them out. There is no way the king will release them," Hid stated, his voice hinting at panic while he skimmed an AaD for something.

"That will cost mission," Idir stated. "Can use for inspire crowd against king."

"We will, but first—"

"Why were they taken?" Sverre interrupted Hid to ask.

Hid's attention snapped around to them. He remained frozen except for a glance and nod to Retha before speaking again, his tone guarded and accent suppressed as always when he was talking to them.

"Someone reported them to the guards for inciting a mob. Aike was obvious, and someone noticed Xiulan signaling into the crowd."

Hid paused and gestured around to the rest of the Wolves. "They didn't have any reason to arrest the rest of us, but they'll be back if they decide we were involved."

Sverre nodded at the information as he paced the room, stopping at the window to scan for guards and pulling the curtains closed when he saw none. He moved back to the center of the room, standing in front of Hid.

He tried to ignore how the kid had tensed up at even the generously wide berth he had given him.

"We can make good use of this against the king," he addressed Idir, "but getting them back is the highest priority."

Both of the kids nodded.

"Do you know where they were taken? A local—"

"Castle dungeon," Retha chirped. "Heard it when I was following them."

Sverre nodded and glanced at Dain. His partner disappeared without a word.

"Dain will scout the security. Hid, your team needs to start playing this angle to the public now."

The tension in Hid's shoulders had relaxed the moment Sverre mentioned getting them back. The man was all focus now.

"Retha, Caesar Apollo, find anyone you can from that crowd, scour that neighborhood. They likely live around there. Bary, Sa'dia, go back around the pubs. Don't anyone go inciting violence, just swing it that the king is trying to silence people who disagree with him."

Hid paused and glanced back toward Sverre.

"Idir and I can go talk to some of the guards and folks we know in the castle, see what we can do there."

A sea of 'yes, sirs' followed as the others bolted from the room to complete their tasks.

"I will scout the castle for a way out of the dungeon," Sverre answered the unasked question flickering in Hid's eyes.

"Thank you, Sverre," Hid said hesitantly, "I didn't know if you would…"

He trailed off as Sverre held his gaze.

Sverre could not help the smile that curled his lip.

See, I'm not all a monster.

"Of course," he stated, "we have the same goals, after all. Well, most of them."

He remembered Reb probably had ordered the Wolves to execute him if given the opportunity.

If only you kids didn't have to try to kill me…

Hid blinked at him a moment.

"You should smile more, *amigo*. You almost look like a human being when you do. Might even trick Retha."

Sverre tried to keep his surprise from showing. Leon had said the same thing when he had first brought the child home.

Home...

Hid was nodding to himself as he hurried out of the room after Idir.

Hopefully, Leon and Ali are enjoying their new home.

Sverre mused to himself as he, too, left.

CHAPTER 31

A li watched with careful attentiveness to Erc's every move as the experienced woman demonstrated how to safely check and load the firearms strewn around them.

"What are the four rules?" Erc quizzed as she showed Ali the shotgun was cleared before setting it down.

"Treat every firearm like it's loaded, finger off the trigger until you're ready to shoot, be sure of your target and what's behind it, and …" Ali paused to remember the last one, "don't point a gun at anything you don't intend to kill?"

Ali flinched as she heard the questioning tone of the last rule.

Erc raised an expectant eyebrow.

"Don't point it at anything you don't want to destroy," Ali repeated in a firm voice.

Erc nodded as she turned to pick up a rifle, check it was as clear, and hand it to Ali.

"Dis and reassemble," she ordered, watching with a sharp eye as Ali checked the weapon for herself before taking it apart.

The last several days, Erc had started teaching Ali about guns in any spare moments to be found. They had not yet even fired the weapons. Instead, Erc spent the time teaching Ali how to disassemble, clean, and reassemble each of the several firearms Erc had available.

Erc said the shooting was the fun part, but no one got to put ammo in a weapon until they knew what they were doing. That was the rule for her house.

Ali did not even attempt to argue. Anytime she thought she knew what she was doing, she recalled any time the kids had come to join them. All three of the children were at least twice as fast as she was.

Handling firearms was one area Leon always beat Charlton, no matter what. Sverre had never been negligent in teaching Leon how to handle one.

"Done." Ali held her hands up with a smile as the rifle lay across the table, back in firing condition with the bolt open.

Erc frowned at the weapon, then back at Ali.

"Then what's this part?"

She pointed to a small spring near the edge of the table.

Ali's stomach did a quick flip as she stared dumbly at the piece.

She frowned.

"That's from the Glock."

She turned her confused gaze back to Erc.

The woman smirked as she picked up the spring and set it on the table. She gathered the rest of the disassembled handgun from its hiding place on her lap.

"Good catch."

Ali beamed as she watched Erc reassemble the handgun quicker than she could ever hope to match.

"After we fix lunch," Erc started, picking up two of the guns and waiting for Ali to collect the remaining ones before she continued, "and make sure the troublemakers are still alive, we can go out for some target practice.

Ali scrambled after the woman as she put the weapons back in the safe.

"Really?!"

Erc nodded.

"Sure, the vacant island we use for storage is also a firing range."

Ali tried to contain her giddy joy at the idea of finally using some of the knowledge Erc had been teaching and quizzing her on.

In the kitchen, Erc was still the teacher. She worked hard to improve Ali's cooking skills beyond the risk of burning everything to the ground.

Which was all well and good, but Ali lamented the loss of using it as a threat to motivate Leon.

She flinched from remembering the last time she had used that reasoning on Leon. Her heart twinged with sorrow at the last night they had been in their home.

Not our home anymore.

174

She tried reminding herself, but the idea just did not stick.

Ali instead tried ignoring all thoughts of it as she busied herself with making lunch up to Erc's high standards.

"Hey, Ma." Charlton's voice disturbed Ali's thoughts as a welcome distraction.

The boys were moving in sync as they sat at the counter and handed their fishing catches, cleaned and gutted, to Erc.

Erc examined the offerings with a passing examination.

"Looks good, thanks boys," Erc said, moving to the spice rack.

"Aunt Erc," Leon started after sharing a glance with Charlton, "was there anything important on the island with the shooting range?"

Erc gave the boys a pointed look.

"Of course there is. Why?"

More suspicious, worried glances were exchanged.

Erc narrowed wary eyes between the two.

"Did you boys take the boat out and do something foolish?"

"No." They were both quick to shake their heads in emphatic denial. Charlton paused. "We did take the boat out fishing, but we didn't do anything, honest, Ma. There was something out in the water."

Leon nodded.

"Yeah, we couldn't see it well, but it looked like it was rampaging around the island before it swam away."

Erc scowled and moved around the kitchen in a hurry to shut off every heat source and remove her apron.

"Rampaging around the island?" Ali blinked at Leon, hoping he would elaborate. "You couldn't see any of it?"

Leon shook his head.

"It was big, knocking over some trees."

"It had scales, but a lot of beasts around here do." Charlton added, "I've never seen anything that big before."

"Aunt Erc, the blocker Sverre brought wasn't on that island, right?"

Ali blinked.

What blocker? Was that something Sverre had?

At the question, Charlton froze and stared wide-eyed, "No, Pa was finally able to come here, it can't—"

"Incara!" Erc called up the stairs, "Come down here."

Erc spared the boys a glance.

"Yes, it is."

Ali frowned at whatever she was missing from the conversation and followed Erc to the table where they had left all the firearms. Erc had materialized several wooden boxes of ammo that she placed next to its corresponding weapon.

"What do you want me to do?" Ali asked in a whisper.

It must be important, whatever it is.

Erc pointed to the shotgun and its accompanying box of ammo as she started loading the clip for the rifle.

The shotgun's strap had slots to hold its ammo and was in desperate want of more.

"Shotgun's short range," Erc said in a low voice. "There's not much aiming, just point it in the right direction. If the creature is still there, aim for the soft spots, eyes, and nose."

Ali nodded as she stuffed round after round into the fittings on the shoulder strap. Her hands shook despite her best efforts to still them. She was grateful Erc did not mention it, though, even when it was clear to see her fear.

Hunting some kind of sea monster was not where she thought her life would end up, but...

Life is interesting like that.

"What's wrong, Ma?" Incara's voice startled Ali as she clenched the ammo she was holding.

"They're gonna go find a sea monster," Charlton answered with a nervous tone from where his position perched on a stool at the kitchen counter.

"What?" Incara turned to her mom with confusion clear in her features. She glanced over the table before her frown rested on Ali.

"I should be going with you, Ma." Incara spared another scowl at Ali. "I know how to shoot better."

The last word was added after a pause.

Ali ignored the dig the same way Incara had been ignoring her since she arrived.

Erc moved to her daughter and squeezed her shoulder.

"I know, hun, that's why I need you here to protect the boys."

Incara held her glare for a moment, but no one outstared Erc. The girl finally nodded.

"Yes, Ma."

"You know where the other shotgun is," Erc waited for Incara to nod again, "get it and stay inside."

She spared a glance toward the boys. "All of you, stay put 'til we get back."

The kids chorused agreement before Erc turned and lead the way outside.

Ali tried to stay calm as she followed, but it wasn't working as she found her fear taking hold.

"Erc, do you think we'll find it?"

"If we have to hunt it, we will," Erc stated with perfect self-assurance Ali could only envy. "First we need to see the damage and if it took anything."

"What it took?" Ali frowned, "You think it ate something important?"

Erc had a hard, unusually expressionless look as they reached the boat.

"We store everything at the range island," she answered as she untied the dingy, "Supplies for winter, Dain's stuff, the network array, everything."

Network array? Is that something to do with this 'blocker' thing?

Ali wanted to ask, but Erc's hard look stopped her. The woman was not in the mood for questions, so Ali kept hers to herself.

Ali took her position at the motor and steered in the direction Erc pointed. The dark woman remained at the bow with her rifle.

They stalked closer to the island in silence.

CHAPTER 32

"Sorry, Bry," Stori grumbled into her pillow. "I'll talk to Caelyn more later."

Bry had to lean close to hear the mumbling and needed a moment to work out what she had said.

"And I said don't worry about it."

He answered his best guess to what she said.

Stori had been feeling off for the last several days and remained in bed most of the time. Eleanora assured them, mostly Bry, that it was normal for pregnancy and that Stori just needed to rest and recover until her body was ready to move around again.

Stori was a most unwilling patient. Bry had to keep her from working. Any work seemed to be overworking in her now more fragile state. But she was nothing if not stubborn and tried sneaking work whenever someone was not watching over her.

Bry wished he could trust Stori's handmaid to help, but the girl was still upset and always avoided him. Klaas, Eleanora, and Lawr were usually busy with their own work, though they all took turns watching over Stori when they could.

Shad was the only other person Bry trusted to watch over her and keep Stori from overworking herself, but he had gone to the dungeon to interview the two riot starters they had arrested earlier.

Bry glanced out the window at the growing shadows cast across the buildings.

Really, Shad. How long does it take to get some answers out of a couple of kids?

Bry rolled his eyes and frowned. He could imagine Shad had probably made friends with the rebels and forgot to report back.

Of all the things I have time for, this is not one of them, Shad.

"Stori, I have to go check on Shad and the prisoners, you have to—"

"Oh, I'm sorry," gleaming silver eyes focused on Bry with starlight enough to melt the rest of this thought. "You don't have to stay, I'm all right."

Bry blinked before smiling and pulling the blankets tighter around his wife.

"You will be fine if you stay in bed and get some rest. Doctor's orders. And my orders, too. Rest."

He kissed her forehead before standing up from the bed.

Stori grumbled something incoherent and nestled further into the mountain of pillows and blankets that now adorned her bed.

Bry grimaced as he moved toward the front door. Shad had better have a good reason for not reporting back and thus taking him away from his darling wife, whom he was sure would not stay in bed more than a few moments after he was gone.

Leaving through the main door instead of the side passage connecting to his own room was the only reason he ran into Stori's maid as she was waiting outside in the hallway.

The girl tried to move passed Bry, but he caught her arm as gently as he could to stop her.

"Leah, right?"

"L*é*ha," she corrected with a snap.

"Leha," Bry ignored her rudeness, "can you watch over Stori and make sure she doesn't try to do any work."

"Of course I will." Leha yanked her arm out of his loose grip. "It's my job when you're too busy."

Bry ground his teeth and pinched the bridge of his nose.

One more thing I just do not have time for.

"Yeah, it is your job, and I have my own to do," He tried not to snap as he stepped further into the hallway, "Just make sure—"

She slammed the door.

Bry clenched his fists and wondered if he should reprimand the girl's complete lack of respect.

Oh, I do not have time for this.

He reasoned it was Stori's responsibility to discipline her maid. Though that seemed to just be putting one more task to his wife to do.

Either way, he had work of his own.

Bry continued down the castle halls and stairs until he arrived in the dungeon. He ignored the guard's flustered surprise at seeing him and waited, less than patiently, for the man to lead him to wherever Shad had been camped out all afternoon.

They wound through the ribcage layout of the cells. As usual, Bry heard Shad long before they reached him.

Bry tried listening to the conversation that was being carried through the maze of cells as they approached. It seemed to be without rhyme or reason as it continued between his friend and someone younger with an accent.

The guard led him around one last bend before Bry caught sight of his friend. Shad was indeed camped out in front of one of the cells with a chair and snack cart positioned so those inside the cells could eat too.

In the cell closest to Shad was a young man with a lopsided grin wide enough to rival Shad. In the next cell was a girl with inky black hair and porcelain skin with a tin just above pale. The girl was silent, watching the nonsensical conversation between Shad and the other fellow.

Bry first noticed just how young the two rioters were. They couldn't have even been twenty.

The conversation paused at Bry's approach as he dismissed the guard back to his station before coming up to Shad.

"Hey, Bry!" Shad chirped. "I didn't know you were planning on coming here."

Shad's grin held a small frown and his tone a question.

"I wasn't. It's evening Shad, you've been here for ages."

"Oh, really?" Shad smiled in full again as he motioned to the kid in the cell. "Aike here is great at not answering questions, so we just got to chatting about nothing."

"Hmm, it's a vastly interesting nothing too, I'll say." The man, Aike, said with a mischievous wink to Bry.

"Yeah, it was. And I don't remember what it was about now." Shad frowned.

Aike answered, "Nothin' at all."

"Right," Shad said before turning toward the girl with a wave of introductions. "Xiulan here isn't as chatty, but hopefully we've at least been entertaining for you."

The girl tucked a loose lock of hair behind her ear. "Very."

Her voice was sweet as honey, and she smiled seductively. Shad only frowned and turned to pretend he didn't see.

"So you see, Bry, we're very busy here." Shad turned his ear-to-ear grin back at Bry.

Bry grimaced and resisted the urge to pinch the bridge of his nose again. He already had a stress headache.

Don't make it worse.

"Shad, you were supposed to be getting answers, not gaming around."

The kid in the cell frowned. "I don't think 'gaming' is really the word for this."

Bry leveled a glare at his friend and ignored Aike's comment.

"Yeah, yeah, I know. It just sorta happened." Shad frowned and turned his attention back toward the cell. "Aike, I'm supposed to be asking you questions."

Aike shrugged. "I know. Just planned on not answering them."

The kid winked at Bry as the goofy grin never faded.

Bry gave in at pinching the bridge of his nose. He wondered if he could break that little bone with his fingers so he wouldn't have to deal with these kids anymore.

What a terrible idea.

"Aike, is it?" Bry dropped his hand as he held the kid's smirking gaze. "Why are you encouraging uprisings against me?"

Aike shrugged without a care in the worlds.

"Why does anyone do anything? To pass the time? Cause they want to? Maybe it's because—"

"No, why are *you* doing this?"

"Me?" Aike motioned toward himself with an innocent fluttering gaze. "I haven't done anything. What makes you think I did anything?"

Bry tried un-grimacing his expression as soon as he noticed the scowl.

"You were seen. At the square, inciting a crowd to attack guards. You both were."

He shifted his glare toward the girl.

Xiulan held his gaze with a soft smile that reminded him infinitely of Stori. He turned away.

"Someone was watching us?!" Aike's mock stare was almost funny; Shad laughed, and Bry might have if he had any patience left.

"Yes! Now, why were you there?"

The innocent look was replaced with a smirk. "Buying fruit?" Aike said it as a question as he glanced back to Shad. "It's a marketplace, no?"

Bry was back to crushing the little bone in his nose.

"I don't have time for this."

"Who has time for anything? Who even—"

"Shut up, kid. Don't start with me."

Bry growled as he leveled a finger at the grinning kid. He glanced at Shad for help, but Shad only shrugged.

"I've been talking to him for ages, haven't gotten anywhere."

Shad had an easy grin as he laced his hands behind his head.

I even tried to read his mind, but it was stubbornly all rubbish.

The voice invaded Bry's mind, but he just sighed and nodded.

Bry shook his head and watched Aike. The kid leaned with a casual air against the bars of his cell as though they were all out at a pub rather than in a dungeon.

He's a little too laid back, isn't he?

Bry glanced at the girl. Xiulan brushed a speck of dust off her skirt with the same air of nonchalance.

The youth of both of them was again apparent to By as he watched their behavior. They really were just kids, and yet kids didn't take being imprisoned on charges of treason and espionage so lightly.

Bry coughed and caught Shad's inquiring gaze. A glance was all that was needed before his friend's chipper voice returned to his head.

What's up? You gotta plan? Cause I'm out of ideas. Just trying to keep them talking has been my plan, but it's not working much—

Shad. Bry shook his head as he interrupted the chatter. He thought through the idea that they were both too young and asked Shad what he had thought of that.

Shad was silent a moment before his voice returned.

Yeah, I noticed that too. There was a pause and an increase to Bry's headache. *Was thinking about how the Nomads might retaliate. I'm still waiting for my contacts to tell me anything definite, but whatever they do, the Nomads would send in their Wolves first, right?*

Bry grimaced at the idea.

They're so young, though.

He watched Aike continue grinning at them, though his expression held a look of confusion at their prolonged silence.

The kids being Wolves would account for their conduct and inciting a riot. Bry knew the Nomads kept kids from slave trades and raised them to fight, but he thought they would be older. Wished they were older.

At least a little.

Me, too. Shad's thoughts echoed through Bry's head, reminding him Shad was still listening for some answer. *Sorry, Bry. I'll hum or something next time.*

With an apologetic grin from Shad, the headache subsided, and Bry was again alone with his thoughts.

"Let's go, Shad." Bry turned to leave so he could think of what to do in peace.

He heard Shad saying his goodbyes to the two before following, but he remained silent until they were out of earshot.

"What're we going to do with them, Bry? They're just kids, but if they are Wolves too…"

Shad frowned as he sunk into silence again.

Bry remained in his thoughts as Shad began rambling about everything he and Aike had discussed.

CHAPTER 33

Caelyn stared down at Stori as the queen lay in bed, sighing about not being able to work while she struggled to keep her eyes open.

"If you're so tired, just go to sleep. Stubborn woman." Caelyn tried an insulting tone to see if that would help.

Stori turned over to regard her with lidded eyes and a smile.

"I'm not tired," she insisted over a yawn.

Caelyn groaned, turning to Leha for backup. The handmaid only shrugged as she continued tucking blankets around Stori. The queen was already at the bottom of an impressive pile.

Caelyn had to admire the maid's scheme that left Stori having a hard time either insisting she wasn't tired or escaping from the bed without their help.

Leha muttered to herself, "If King Brynte weren't so slow to resolve these problems himself, you wouldn't have to work so hard."

Caelyn snapped a glare at the maid. Even if she agreed with the sentiment, she flinched at the timing.

She paused and hoped Stori hadn't heard. The queen grumbled and shifted in her pillow nest.

"Leha," Stori's voice was gentle, as it always was, but held a note of warning, "don't talk about Bry in that manner around me."

Leha held Stori's strong gaze with a defiant look for a moment.

She glanced away with a mumble, "Sorry, Stori."

The firmness of Stori's look softened as she held her hand out and clutched Leha's, giving it a forgiving squeeze.

"I am tired, actually," Stori finally conceded, "I will go to sleep for the night."

Caelyn nodded. "Good, we didn't want to dig you out anyway."

The queen's soft smile shifted to Caelyn.

"I'm sorry, Caelyn, I meant to have tea with you today."

Caelyn tensed at the sudden attention. "I know. It's fine. You have your own things to worry—"

"No."

Caelyn admired the single word, spoken in a gentle voice still with a smile, but with authority that silenced her protests immediately.

"I have desired to spend more time with you," Stori continued, "I do not want you to feel alone here or unwelcome. And I have so enjoyed our time together thus far."

"Okay. Thanks." Caelyn squirmed under the focused gaze. Stori smiled before pulling a blanket tighter around her shoulders.

"Now, since you both are so insistent, I will be turning in for the evening."

"Finally."

Caelyn exhaled with relief as she escaped the queen's gaze.

"Good night, Stori." Leha led the way out of the bedchamber, pausing at the door. "There's an AaD on the nightstand, call me if you need anything at all."

Caelyn turned off the Aequorian torch as she closed the door behind her.

In the hallway, Leha parted ways with a nod before trudging off toward her own room.

Caelyn milled around the hallways, spent a short moment in her rooms, despising the emptiness of it, and wandered out again to find Rhoeo.

She started heading to the guard's room, several floors down in a nearly abandoned section of the castle.

Caelyn puzzled over the vacantness of the floor as she found a posted listing of the guards' quarters. Rhoeo's room was the only one occupied in the entire wing.

She frowned at that. It seemed odd, but maybe everyone was moving out of the wing for construction and Rhoeo was just the last to move.

That's reasonable, right?

A headache took hold as she reached her bodyguard's room and knocked on the door.

A man's voice drifted to her ears, but she could not understand what he was saying. The voice drifted, moving and circling around her.

Caelyn glanced down the empty hallway.

Were other rooms occupied, but just not listed on the posting?

This is supposed to be the women's quarters though.

The hallway moved with her searching gaze, bending, and warping around her as she blinked.

"Wh-what?" Caelyn reached for the nearest wall to steady herself but found it out of reach.

"…Should have killed Loreda and the girl too."

Bry's distorted voice was right next to her ear.

Caelyn jumped and screeched. She turned but still couldn't see who was speaking. She staggered down the hall as it continued twisting around her. She couldn't tell if she was heading back the way she had come or not.

Bry's voice warped and mixed with another familiar one. Her mother's.

"My dear, why are you running? There's no need to be afraid."

Caelyn stopped.

"Mom?"

She turned around. The hallway was stable, and she was still standing in front of Rhoeo's door when her mother's voice came again.

"I'm in the room, go inside."

Multiple voices whispered in her ears, but her mother's was most predominant.

"Go in. I'm inside. The box in the corner. Open it."

Loreda's voice twisted mid-sentence into her father's.

"I'm inside. You want to see me again, don't you?"

"Dad?!" Caelyn lunged to grab the door handle.

Locked.

"Dad!"

She pounded on the door.

Clawed at it.

Beat on it.

The voice grew stronger, calling her name.

"Caelyn!"

A new, sharp voice behind her was accompanied by a hand on her shoulder, yanking her around.

Rhoeo stood with a calm expression that twitched at a grimace.

"Why are you trying to break into my room?"

"Rhoeo!" Caelyn latched onto the woman's arms, "My father! He's inside."

As she spoke, the absurdity of the words hit her.

My father's dead.

She blinked as the thought grounded her in reality.

Her father was dead, and her mother was exiled. Neither of them could possibly be behind the door.

"And what have you done to my door?" Rhoeo sighed an irritated sound. "Need a better lock on that box."

Caelyn turned to look at the door. Bloody scratch marks covered it. She stared in shock.

"I-I didn't d-do that."

"Oh, really?"

Rhoeo grabbed one of her hands and held it in front of her.

Caelyn's fingers were bloodied, with a fingernail missing and splinters embedded under the blood.

"I-I didn't..." Caelyn sputtered, staring at her hand. She looked at the other to find it in the same bloody state.

Pain shot up through her hands as she noticed the damage.

Caelyn cried and moaned at the agony her hands were in as she held them protectively against her chest.

"I don't know what happened. I didn't mean to—"

She sputtered out attempts at explanations between sobs.

A hand on her back was a small comfort as Rhoeo led her down the hallway.

"It'll be fine. Let's go see the healer, Caelyn. It's just a couple of little splinters, no need to cry."

Caelyn tried to bite her lip to keep from crying as she glanced back toward the door. Her parent's voices were faint, but she could still hear them calling to her.

She turned away, focusing on trying to match the guard's gait.

"Why were you down here anyway?"

Rhoeo asked with an irritated, suspicious glance that did not match her constant little smile.

The smile reminded Caelyn of the smile Rhoeo had for the man in the alley. Not for the first time, she was afraid of her friend, but she tried to answer anyway.

"I just wanted to talk with you. I haven't seen you all day."

Caelyn failed to keep her voice from trembling. She tried not to focus on the pain in her hands, but she was failing at that too.

Rhoeo sighed again, an annoyed sound.

"You think I might have a break from being with you all day every day since we arrived? A single day is just too much to ask then, is it?"

"No, Rhoeo. I'm sorry."

Caelyn's chest constricted in new pain at the admonishment.

"I don't mean to always pester you."

They weaved through hallways and stairways in silence. Caelyn bit her lip and focused her energy on not crying as the searing agony of her hands grew with each passing step.

Rhoeo will be mad if you start crying again.

She bit her lip harder at the thought. Caelyn did not want to make her friend even more upset at her than she already was for trying to break into her room.

Why did I do that?

Caelyn still could not find an answer to that question, and she frowned at the memory of it. Looking back, it was so stupid. Her mother would never say that, and her father…He was still dead.

New tears pinched at her eyes.

"What do you want to tell the healer?" Rhoeo asked, finally breaking the silence. "You know whatever you say will get back to Brynte and Istoria, right?"

That notion sparked even more tears in Caelyn. Of course, the healer was a personal friend to both her half-brother and Stori and would tell them.

She'll tell them I'm hearing voices.

They would start treating her as if she was crazy.

"If you want," Rhoeo's voice was close to her ear, "I could say you got stuck in some dark closet and panicked to get out."

Caelyn stared at her with wide-eyed relief.

"Really?!" Her voice was a sob." You would? I would be so happ—"

"But," Rhoeo interrupted with a sharp tone, "if you ever try to go to my room again, I may have to tell them what really happened. And you will have to explain this nervous break of yours. You don't want that, right?"

Caelyn shook her head with a frantic hum and cry. "No."

She managed to speak through her trembling lips.

"Good." Rhoeo's voice was gentle again, "Then I can help you explain this."

CHAPTER 34

"Bry," Lawr waited for the king's fragmented attention to return to frowning back at him, "you have an excellent chance here to attack the Nomads and end their retaliation before they even launch it."

"If there is any way to avoid a pitched battle, though, we should take it," Shad said to Lawr's infinite annoyance. "There aren't enough people here supporting Bry to fight an army of Nomads."

"Yes, 'dere are," Jair interjected, breaking into the argument that had been going on since breakfast.

"Actually, there are not that many." Chesler countered. He stood shifting in the corner of the study, clearly just as irritated at the standstill of the discussion of what to do with the Nomads as everyone else.

Lawr snuck a glance toward Klaas, hoping for support, but the man remained stubbornly silent.

"There is also the fact I'd be invading Glacius Tesca to attack them," Bry said, grasping at scraps of an objection the same as he had been doing all meeting.

"The Tescan Counsel has already given their preemptive blessing on our entering the sphaere for an ambush," Chesler growled out the clarification, "They want the Nomads gone as much, if not more than we do."

Bry glowered at the Castle Manager with new irritation from where he leaned against his desk with his arms crossed defensively. He had only broken that posture occasionally to pace or massage the scar on his face.

"Bry, why are you so against this?" Klaas finally said, asking the same question Lawr had been stonewalled many times prior.

"I just don't think it's the best option."

"Id's going 'o be da only option soon, Bryn'de."

Lawr nodded his agreement with Jair, but Bry was still glowering at the notion.

"I don't see how you," Shad nodded toward Jair, "believe we have anything close to enough men to launch this kind of assault."

"Depending on how the ambush was planned," Chesler jumped in to answer with a snarl and ever-present irritation, "we may have enough, wraith, but that is still dependent on—"

"You know, I have a name. And 'wraith' isn't it," Shad snapped, taking a step in the man's direction.

Lawr blinked at the sudden spike of pressure from a headache. He reached out to grab Shad's arm before the kid could get within striking range. Jair shifted too, standing at Chesler's side.

Chesler leveled an ugly glare at the kid.

"I didn't call you 'Shade,' at least, though, with this crushing headache, that would seem more appropriate."

"Bastard!"

Shad made a move to lunge at him, yanking his arm from Lawr's grasp.

"Shadric!" Bry snapped, stepping in between the two.

Chesler held his ground better than Lawr would have expected, but he looked as though he had not breathed since Shad had moved and was still waiting for a punch.

Shad turned angry eyes toward Bry.

"Bry, I don't—"

"Shad, you're giving us all headaches." Bry stated, "calm down."

Lawr glanced away to ignore the way Shad flinched and just how fast the headache disappeared.

The wraith mumbled an apology.

Bry nodded and turned to address the room.

"We can take a break now and discuss this again later."

Chesler and Jair left first, exiting the room as fast as they could with dirty looks back at Shad.

Klaas stayed, sitting as quietly on the sofa as before.

Shad also turned to leave, but Lawr stepped into his path at the same time Bry grabbed his arm.

"Sorry, Bry. I shouldn't have lost control like that."

Bry only shrugged and rubbed his head without having anything contrary to say.

The peace lasted only a moment before Lawr turned back toward Bry.

"We need to stop the Nomads before they attack on their own terms."

Bry glowered at Lawr.

"I can't. Another pitched battle will mean the loss of the few troops we have left."

"There's no avoiding that." Klaas spoke again, "You will either have a battle you choose or wait for them to come here."

Bry stood, clenching his fists.

Lawr frowned at the king. He could tell the reason he was so opposed was personal, and Bry's comment about a pitched battle reminded him of Oroitz, but the redhead just wasn't making any sense.

"I called for a break." Bry glared pikes through Lawr, "I need one, too."

Bry's glare shifted to include Klaas as well.

Klaas held the glare with the same unmoving, stoic gaze he always maintained before nodding.

"All right Bry. But you know the same as us, this is not a wise strategy."

Klaas stood and walked past Lawr to the door. Lawr remained a moment longer, trying to catch Shad's eye. He could see the kid was kicking himself, but he was also avoiding anyone's gaze.

Lawr decided Bry was the best person to help anyway and turned to leave as well.

Klaas waited for him in the hallway as Lawr closed the door. They walked together at a slow pace heading back to the healer's quarters.

"There is no reason not to complete this attack now."

Lawr stated. Or he hoped it sounded like a statement as he glanced to Klaas with a question, wondering if he had missed something about the strategy. Something that made Bry's stance make sense.

Klaas continued staring straight ahead as they turned around a bend and descended a flight of stairs before he answered.

"It does not have to be a reason. Bry's afraid of something."

"Afraid? Of what?"

Klaas shrugged and remained silent.

Lawr frowned as he thought. He remembered Brys' mention of a pitched battle again.

Did Oroitz affect him that much? To create a whole new fear?

"I've never seen Bry, so…"

Klaas trailed off with a concerned frown.

"Even Shad is being odd about it," Lawr said with a nod. He had not known the pair nearly as long, but they were certainly acting out of character about that issue.

The next few days passed with them all trying to talk to Bry and Shad, but the two remained stubbornly against the idea.

Finally, Chesler came stalking around to announce they had missed their chance. The Nomads were moving.

Chesler was as irritated as the rest. Even if he hadn't agreed with the plan, he agreed with taking action before the Nomads moved into Medius.

Lawr took breaks from the exhausting work of advising Bry to visit Stori as often as his tired conscience allowed.

He found he brought his issues to the young queen more frequently than he should just to be in her calming presence. Lawr noticed many times that Bry would do the same, and he was careful on to intrude.

Unfortunately, she was the only calm one, apart from Klaas, in their inner circle and was much more engaging to talk with than the older man.

"If I knew what his issue with the ambush was, I could have helped."

Lawr found himself complaining yet again to Stori.

He tapped his foot against the bedside table at the thought.

Bry had missed a second opportunity to attack the Nomads. Lawr still had no idea how to get through to the king that they absolutely needed to launch some offensive attack.

"He's doing as he sees best," Stori stated as she sipped a cup of tea with endless grace. "Even if you don't think it is the right choice, won't you still help him? The war is not going to leave us anytime soon."

Lawr frowned at the young woman. He did admire that she would not say a word about anything Bry may have told her in confidence, but he could still wish she would give him a hint.

Stori stared back at him with a gentle smile as she shifted through a few documents she had been working on.

Lawr and Bry had come up with a solution to her overworking that seemed to work so far. They would simply give her a few small tasks and hid the rest of the work and documents so she could not find them.

Even Lawr wasn't sure where Shad had hidden everything, but their strategy was working. The queen still pouted every morning when she received her small task load for the day.

"The Nomads will attack us here now," Lawr thought aloud. "Bry thinks those kids he has locked up are Wolves, but we don't know where the rest of them are. Causing trouble and unrest in the city, no doubt."

He huffed a breath as he stood and paced to the window. The bustling in the courtyard a few floors below was visible, but the rest of the city remained silent by virtue of the distance. Lawr could not see the discontented clamoring and occasional riots, but he read reports of their happening daily.

"It's good you fixed the AaD issue then," Stori said with the same absentminded vacancy and lack of intent that Lawr's statement had held.

Lawr hummed. He had talked through every problem he had come to talk to her about, they both noticed it, but he didn't want to leave yet. Time spent with Stori was as close to how he felt looking after Ali and he missed that.

His heart twinged at the thought. He could not rightly recall the last time he had seen his niece. Forever ago, it always seemed.

I could maybe go check up on her. Just to make sure she's okay...

Lawr sighed at the thought.

Leaving right as the Nomads are moving and there may be battles soon is just poor taste.

Then again, maybe he could get Shad talking if he dragged the wraith back with him.

Now that's an idea.

"Stori, would you...Or do you think Bry would mind if I borrowed Shad for a few days?"

Lawr turned back to the queen, unable to completely hide his smile at the thought of seeing Ali again.

Stori was regarding him with a startled look. He assumed his attempt to stomp out the smile had resulted in a grimace.

Get yourself squared away, old man.

The chide did make his grimace real.

Stori stared a moment longer before answering that he should ask Shad, then Bry instead of her.

"Have a good trip," she called lightly after him as he headed toward the door.

CHAPTER 35

"Move."

Hid wished he had brought Sa'dia to talk to the queen's maid instead of trying to deal with the cranky woman himself. He squeezed around the tiny space until he was out of her way.

"Why should I care that you fools got some of your people captured?" The girl glowered at him while bustling around the small linen room, collecting fresh cloth for her mistress.

"It's a matter that should concern anyone."

Hid grimaced to himself as he was already sounding like a televised announcement for a petty revolution. He continued despite his irritation.

"The king should not be throwing people—"

"Move."

Leha glared at him over a stack of linen with growing exasperation in her voice.

Hid sidestepped out of her way.

"Throwing people in the dungeon for nothing—"

"You were trying to incite a mob, weren't you?"

"That was not the goal."

Hid fought to keep his voice above a growl and from slipping into Spanish as he lied.

"I remember telling the gal you talked to me that I wouldn't be supporting anything that endangered my mistress."

Leha dropped her stack of linen on her cart and turned her angry scowl back to Hid.

"You can see how people attacking the castle might contradict that, right?"

Hid bit his tongue as he struggled to just ignore the condescension in her voice.

"We're just trying to get our friends out now."

She held his stare with a level glare.

Hid's brain spun for what more he could say. What else he might add to convince her to help. He came up empty, so he settled into the stare-down, hoping that silence was indeed his best response.

Leha's hostility remained as tangible as the Vis in the air for a moment longer. Then she sighed and pinched the bridge of her nose as she shook her head.

I win.

Hid straightened out the smirk that crossed his face before she could see it.

"So what is it you need from me then?"

Hid fought harder to stomp out his smile, but he settled for an appreciative one with a nod before answering.

"Do you know anyone else in the castle who might be sympathetic toward this injustice?"

Leha scoffed at the careful wording he used. She scrunched up her nose in thought. After a moment, she started rattling off a list of names.

Hid stood in shocked silence. Leha's list included the few guards Idir was talking to, plus several others. He overcame his shock to make note of the names she gave.

She reached an end with a quiet mumble, "That's all I can think of right now."

She turned back to her linen cart.

"How..?" Hid stopped her, looking over the long list of potential allies she had given him.

She glanced back, regarding him with cautious eyes before dropping her gaze and answering.

"Chess...he introduced me to all his friends and the guards he worked with." She wiped a quick hand across her eyes. "He was so happy and wanted to show off his fiancé."

Hid remained silent until Leha had dried the tears which sprung to her eyes. Based on what Sa'dia said, he knew she had lost someone, but he did not know any of the details.

"He must have been proud," Hid said in a quiet voice.

Comforting people made him nervous and uneasy about saying the wrong, insensitive thing. Aike was always the sensitive one, not him.

Leha sniffed and scoffed at once, mumbling something incoherent under her breath.

"Anything else?" she asked after she left off mumbling.

"No." Hid nodded with an attempt at a smile, "Thank you for the names you shared, they will be a great help."

Leha mumbled something to herself and withdrew from the room without another word to Hid.

Hid waited a moment before leaving to check over the list of names. He would have to get them to Idir since the man knew who all the guards in the castle were better than he did.

He snuck out of the room and through the halls, heading steadily lower as he ducked out of sight of the guards.

A chill danced along his spine, making him freeze as he tried to understand what it was. Hid recognized it when a shadow moved next to him.

"I found which guards take shifts in the dungeon," Sverre stated as he fell in step next to Hid.

Hid swallowed the same gut instinct that always told him to run whenever Sverre was around.

"There are a few more guards who may be helpful." Hid waved his notepad around just enough for Sverre to notice before tucking it away. "I'm going to meet up with Idir, then regroup at the inn."

Sverre grunted and nodded as he kept walking until they passed a side corridor. He nimbly hopped out the nearest window in the corridor.

Hid started and blinked after the man. He resisted the urge to check if the assassin had picked a window to jump from where the fall would not result in injury or death.

The lack of exclamations from below suggested that the Ghost did indeed know the castle well enough to pick the right windows to jump from. Another bit of knowledge Hid wondered about.

He continued his trek unimpeded to the armory and the guard's training area. Hid waited in the shadows along the edge of the training arena as he watched for Idir's hulking form.

Idir was easy to spot, though he did blend in better among the crowd of muscular men than on the streets of Sentre.

Idir caught Hid's gaze for a short moment, long enough he shook his head before he returned to arguing with another soldier.

Hid sank further into the shadows and watched. Idir was arguing with a lithe man with copper skin and sharp, hawkish features.

The man—Idir and others were calling him Ammon—was arguing vehemently in Brynte's favor, defending his character with first-hand knowledge and not backing down on a single point.

After a moment of watching the lost cause the argument was becoming, Hid caught Idir's attention again and jerked his head toward the door.

Idir nodded and immediately started making excuses to leave as he shifted away from the group.

Ammon continued his aggressive style of arguing until Idir was already halfway across the arena heading toward the door. Finally, the hawkish man relented and returned to the other soldiers and guards.

Hid grimaced after the man.

That wasn't a point in our favor. And those guards who were listening are also going to be lost causes now.

He ducked out the door a step ahead of Idir. The dark hulk of a man continued to grumble to himself —in very un-Idir fashion—Hid did not even have to wonder how irritated he was.

"Loudmouth hawk. Couldn't speak straight…Bastard undoing all our rumors…Said he knows Brynte, and he would never…Anything we said."

Idir growled out his frustrations, his voice occasionally dipping so low that even Hid could not hear him. His walking stick tapped against the floor in sharp notes, punctuating the words.

"It's all right, Idir." Hid loosely clapped the man on the back. "I had better luck, and the Ghost did too. We can use what the two of us gathered well enough, and you can talk to guards individually."

Hid's reassurance caused Idir to pause his grumblings, but only for a moment. He continued with the same irritation, but in a lower tone that Hid could not hear.

"As long as nothing else happens," Hid leaned in as he spoke, "we can get them out within the next day or so."

That quieted Idir's irritated mumbles.

The comfortable silence remained as they slipped out of the castle and made their way through cobbled streets toward their inn.

Hid stopped short in the hallway leading to their suite as he spotted

Retha, crouched in hiding behind an unused sofa. His anxiety spiked a the sight of her hiding.

"Retha?"

Hid whispered as he and Idir both dropped to a crouch and moved toward the girl. Hid had thought she was overcoming her fear or natural instincts about Sverre the same as he was. She had been able to bring the man back by herself when Aike was caught after all.

She cut a sharp gaze to Hid.

"There's another monster."

She whispered back.

Hid sucked in a nervous breath and frowned at their room door.

Another monster?

"Besides Sverre?"

He needed the clarification.

Retha nodded.

"A crazy one and a messenger. Messenger's not a monster, though."

Two more unknowns then.

Hid exchanged a glance with Idir.

"Retha, are the others inside?"

She nodded again.

His initial panic threatened to run away from him. He took a deep breath and focused to shove that panic into a box in his mind, to be ignored until the team was safe.

"We can't leave them alone then, *muchacha.*"

Hid straightened from his crouch and moved to the door. He waited until Idir and Retha were flanked behind him, already fidgeting with their weapons before proceeding.

He knocked their greeting code before entering. He found the gazes of all three of his teammates first and sighed internally that they were all safe. Frozen, with peaked looks between fear and anxiety, but safe.

Next, Hid took note of the newcomers. A man with dull, boring features and dead-fish eyes stood completely still near Caesar Apollo, but far enough away with open displayed palms clearly meant to show that he wasn't a threat.

The messenger?

Hid assumed since the man was not scary apart from his dead eyes. He certainly was not disturbing enough to upset Retha.

Hid turned and noted the one who was.

The man, if it could be called that, was of average height and build, with the blandest shade of hair and eyes imaginable.

Eye. Singular.

Hid forced himself to stay still and not to bolt from the room as the robotic eye wondered independently of the natural one until it was focused on him.

The man was standing toe to toe, much closer than Hid could ever imagine daring, with Sverre, babbling nonsense about a little pain being good for character and fun.

"If you so much as speak to any of these kids without Dain or myself present, I will rip your tongue out."

Sverre's cold gaze left no room for doubting his sincerity, even though Hid blinked as he realized the assassin was talking about protecting them.

The freak ignored all common sense as his grin widened, and he opened his mouth to speak.

Sverre cut him off.

"Through your throat."

The clown of a man tipped his head to the side in thought. It took him less than half a moment to start smirking again as he rocked up to his toes.

"Ata would be mad."

"Oh, you'd live," Sverre stated.

Hid had never heard a threat of life sound so dangerous.

The freak just hummed.

"Sverry, you're no fun," he stated with such a pained conviction, "But luckily, Ata's already gonna be mad. Gonna have me take you apart again. Are the modifications I added last time still holding up?"

The man tipped further forward to tap a finger against Sverre's chest.

"Such a lovely hole, watching your heart beat was fun."

Hid tried to swallow his horror and disgust for the newcomer. He couldn't understand most of what the man was babbling about, but he pitied Sverre for having to spend any time at all with the freak.

"Duqa."

Dain's voice was so flat and cold Hid did not even recognize it was the cheerful sniper speaking until he glanced at him. Dain was standing in front of Bary and Sa'dia, acting as their personal bodyguard.

"We're on a job." The sniper enunciated each word, "Sverre AND the kids are off limits."

Duqa sighed and whined a moment before Sverre caught his attention with a growl. No words, just a rumbling from the back of his throat, and the freak's attention settled back to the albino.

"Fine!" Duqa threw his hands up in an overly animated manner. "No kids, got it."

The freak wagged a clawed finger toward Sa'dia.

"But you have to admit, her hands would look much prettier inside out."

The robotic eye focused on Hid's hands, followed by Duqa's full attention.

"And his. My, my."

An over-wide grin stretched Duqa's face beyond the limits of human, revealing a row of sharp teeth. Hid was not sure if they were metal, plastic, or bone, only that the sharpened points weren't his natural ones.

Duqa started tip-toeing toward Hid with clawed hands poised to grab. It would have been comical if there was not such a threat in his approach.

Hid overcame his frozen fear to stumble back, but the clown had already stopped moving because of the pale hand wrapped around his neck.

"How short is your memory, fish?" Sverre asked as he used one hand to throw Duqa into the wall. The other pointed toward Hid.

"Off. Limits."

Hid flinched when the man hit the wall. For a one-handed throw, Sverre was too strong. The word from the freak, 'modifications' flitted through Hid's mind with new, uncomfortable weight.

He's not really human anymore...

At the moment, when Sverre was standing between the freak and Hid, that thought was a relief. Recalling their job, that relief melted into new stress.

Duqa stood up, snapping Hid's attention immediately back to him. The freak was groaning and sighing in an overdramatic show.

"I know, I know."

The thing's carefree smile returned as though the new hole in the wall had not just been made with his head.

He turned his sickening smile to Hid as he jerked a thumb toward Sverre.

"No sense of humor, this one."

Hid's heart jumped as he noticed the freak was now closer to Caesar

Apollo, but the messenger moved between them as soon as the clown had spoken.

"Report required."

Hid blinked at the messenger's short few words, but the change was all he needed to force his feet into motion. He led the way toward Sverre, both Idir and Retha kept within arm's reach of him, and Caesar Apollo too was able to attach to their little group.

Now this is almost funny.

Hid shook his head at the realization that Sverre, and Dain—he was trusting the sniper with the bickering pair after all—were the safest people in the room.

He blinked at the messenger. Hid didn't trust him, but the man had moved to help and was now attracting all of the freak's short attention.

"Can we talk about the plan?" Hid asked Sverre when the albino's attention finally turned away from Duqa toward him, "Or is that thing going to get in the way?"

"Duqa will remain out of the way." Sverre stated, "He is only here because he is bored and followed Echo."

Hid nodded as he watched the crazy one abandon tormenting the messenger—*Echo?*—to lean against the dented wall and twist himself into a shapeless, reminiscent attempt at an abstract statue.

CHAPTER 36

Aike shifted under the intense gaze of the pair of haggard older men. He tried a joke, a comment on the weather, a back-handed insult, a compliment.

Nothing worked.

The pair continued frowning at him.

Shifting again, Aike turned his attention to the bubbly, one-sided conversation happening next to him.

When Xiulan had developed a reaction to a hitherto unknown food allergy, Aike had asked in his sweetest 'we're just kids' voice if the guard could do anything for her. He had hoped for a change in diet and maybe some medicine. Instead, Xiulan was being fawned over and personally doctored by the court healer.

Aike had initially worried the king would be angry, perhaps even vindictive, about his doctor attending to a stranger, but Aike was told the king had encouraged the court healer along.

Aike twinged with guilt over what they were trying to do to the man when he heard that. That twinge of guilt only grew stronger listening to the healer, Eleanora, talk about Brynte as though he were her son as she treated Xiulan.

While Xiulan was under expert ministrations, Aike was left to hold a staring contest with the two older men who had accompanied the healer.

One, Aike understood, was the woman's husband. Designated bag holder and server of food.

The other, Lawr, was some kind of advisor, currently ill-tempered at being kept waiting for some trip, but he still helped the couple with minimal grumblings.

Xiulan's reaction to Eleanora's gentle chastisements caught Aike's attention. The girl was increasing in shades of red as she nodded along.

"You, young lady, have to pay more attention to what you put in your body."

The older woman continued to admonish as she juggled herbs, a mortar and pestle, and a small bowl of the finished product. Her husband reached forward, taking the unneeded items with ease.

Eleanora smiled at him and patted his arm affectionately before turning back to Xiulan.

"You must take good care of yourself, young lady. You only have one body. There is no excuse for just taking what you're given. If it's making you ill, speak up."

"Yes, ma'am." Xiulan nodded, taking the small bowl of medicine when Eleanora handed it to her.

"It's my fault, ma'am," Aike said and moved closer to the edge of his cell, closer to Xiulan, "I should have noticed and called for a healer sooner. It was my responsibility, I'm sorry."

Xiulan spared him a warm, grateful glance before ducking her head again to focus her attention on the bowl of reddish herb juice.

"Your responsibility?" The woman's shrewd eyes narrowed on Aike as she scoffed, "Why would this be your responsibility?"

"Well..." Aike sputtered.

Not Wolves, just kids. Not Wolves.

Aike repeated the statement like a mantra to himself as he tried to think of a reason other than the fact that he was the team's leader and thus responsible for Xiulan's safety.

"She's...like a sister to me."

That is true.

The woman stared at him with an eyebrow raised, searching his face for a lie in his statement.

Aike grinned on reflex and hid the expression just as fast. 'Shifty' was the word people used whenever he smiled. Even when he was being genuine.

Or almost genuine, at least.

His nerves grew as the woman continued to stare. The healer had an intensity he had only ever seen before in Reb. He didn't know if this woman had an angry, throw-everything-in-sight side too, but he did not want to find out while she was near one of his team members and he was unable to help.

"Humph." Eleanora turned back to Xiulan and motioned her to drink. "You're responsible for your own health too, you hear me, girl?"

Xiulan nodded. "I'll be more careful in the future, ma'am."

Aike breathed a little easier when the older woman smiled again as Xiulan took a sip of the medicine.

"I thought medicine was supposed to be bitter?" Xiulan asked the healer with a small smile, her charming one, not the manipulative one.

The older woman nodded sagely.

"It's sweet when it's warm. As soon as those herbs cool down, though, you will be gagging on them. And you'll still have to drink it."

Eleanora added the last sentence with a pointed look which Xiulan immediately made note of and obeyed by emptying the bowl before handing it back.

"There now." Eleanora had a sweet smile but a heavy look. "You'll be feeling better enough to hassle Bry more in no time."

"I do apologize for the trouble, ma'am."

Aike could not keep his guilty conscience from cropping up as he watched the woman gather her tools.

He was sorry. They had more damage to inflict to fulfill their orders, and the kindly older woman would be poorly affected by it.

"You kids…" Eleanora trailed off with a shake of her head.

When she finished her thought, it was more to herself than to them. "Children shouldn't be involved in such matters."

Her husband chuffed, "That's the truth."

Aike met the man's hard glare and was surprised to see pity and worry in the look.

Aike ducked his head away from the caring gaze and mumbled his thanks to the healer. He glanced at Xiulan to see she was receiving a similar, concerned look from the woman and was reacting just the same.

"You kids…If there is any way…" Eleanora spoke in halting bursts. "You'd be safe here, if you could come back. All of you."

Aike snapped in attention to her, realizing she knew exactly who they were.

"Thank you," Xiulan said in her calm, collected voice that told Aike she was nearing tears, "If we could, we would."

Eleanora turned to look at the two older men for help, but they only shrugged and frowned. Finally, she left the cell, and the guard locked it behind her.

The silent moment stretched out as the three adults seemed unwilling to leave but did not have anything further to say.

The healer looked as though she was still trying to grasp at any thought of how to convince them to stay.

A singsong voice, humming a tuneless melody, interrupted the somber moment to Aike's instant relief.

A glance at Xiulan was all he needed to know the sensitive girl was moments from tears.

The three older folks looked much less pleased with the interruption as Shad rounded the corner and made himself further known with cheerful greetings.

"Shad, have I mentioned that your timing is terrible." The man who had so far been silent spoke, "Because it's atrocious."

"Lawr, now don't be mean. I bring good news. I'm ready to go." Shad held his arms up in a triumphant gesture as though the news was the grandest the older man would ever hear.

The healer's husband spoke, "Shad, your timing is terrible."

"Ehh?" Shad glanced between the two before settling his gaze on Aike, "What's this? You'll talk to them, but not to me. I'm hurt."

Aike grinned back, grateful for the man's change of pace.

"What can I say, kid? They have a way with silence."

"I'm older than you, punk." Shad returned with a half frown but the same lively, dancing eyes.

Aike just grinned at him. He had a sense that the wraith could tell when he was genuine in his smile, regardless of the 'shifty' look.

Shad's beaming grin confirmed Aike's thoughts.

"You two need a moment in private?"

"Lawr, has anyone ever told you that you have a great sense of humor? 'Cause they'd have been lying."

Lawr just fixed the wraith with a dark glare.

"Wow, he's even better at that than Sverre." Aike glanced at Xiulan with a grin and a wink, glad that the attention was finally off of them.

Or not.

When he turned back, Shad was staring at him in shock and awe.

"You know the Ghost?" Shad blinked at him.

Oops. Should have kept my mouth shut.

"What?"

Aike decided to plead ignorance.

How do they even know the Ghost's name is Sverre? That's hardly common knowledge.

"You said, 'Sverre,' that isn't a very common name. Do you know Dain?" Shad asked.

Aike blinked at the wraith.

Are you kidding me? This has to be the only other living person who knows those two by name.

"You do know him, don't you?"

Aike balked as he realized he was showing his knowledge in his reactions.

Shad was still smiling, but it was no longer friendly and carefree. His smile was as dark and cold as Lawr's glare.

"You meet a lot of strange people in our line of work," Aike stated with a shrug.

They already know we're Wolves, this shouldn't be surprising, but I really need to learn about keeping my mouth shut.

Aike scoffed to himself as he remembered Sverre was the last person to tell him that.

He focused on the wraith again with a frown.

"How do you know them?"

"Oh, they've helped us out before." Shad frowned. "Kind of."

"Shad." Lawr's level glare returned to the wraith with a warning head shake.

"I probably shouldn't say anything more."

Aike smiled. "Me neither."

Shad grumbled with the others before they decided to leave.

Aike watched them go as he turned over what Shad had said in his mind.

They helped *them?*

As far as he knew, Oracaede was very much against Sentre and would not be helping anyone. Much less sending their best assassin and sniper to help the king's friend.

We don't follow all of Reb's orders either.

That idea sent a chill down his spine. He could only trust the two assassins when they were following their orders and helping, if they were off doing whatever they wanted…

Especially if they are helping the king…

"This is bad."

Aike only glanced at Xiulan to see her frowning too.

CHAPTER 37

Lawr hurried Shad along in his rush to depart. Goodbyes were said multiple times before Lawr realized Shad was intentionally messing with him.

Once they were underway, they were back to the endless walking that Lawr had forgotten how much he loathed.

Lawr did try using the time walking to draw out any information Shad could offer about why he and Bry were so against a direct attack on the Nomads.

Shad was still cagy about the topic, but Lawr heard the pain and fear beneath the kid's excuses as he mentioned Oroitz again in his reasoning.

PTSD maybe?

Lawr blinked at the thought as he stared sharply at his walking partner. He turned over both Shad and Bry's behavior since the Oroitz battle, and the idea fit more and more.

Bry wasn't even eating or sleeping after he returned. He's only just getting back to a healthy normal.

The realization was painful to Lawr as he thought of how he hadn't noticed. Bry and Shad had been so set against a pitched battle, and they always mentioned the one they had been in as a why.

"Lawr?"

Lawr glanced over to Shad, realizing he had been ignoring whatever the wraith had said.

"Sorry, Shad, I was thinking, not listening. What'd you say?"

Shad laughed a light sound, but not one with any happiness in it.

"I just asked what Ali is like. You haven't told me anything."

"Oh, right."

Lawr shook his head to try focusing again. He guessed Shad was trying to change the topic to get away from having to answer any more questions.

Oh well, can't push him too far to talk.

Lawr relented and started talking about Ali.

As they drew closer, Lawr realized he was rambling on and on about his niece. And Shad was humoring him with eager listening and questions as needed. Lawr had a feeling the kid was trying to get as much material as possible to tease him endlessly later.

As they opened a doorway into Terrae, Lawr let out a small sigh that it was at least night. Hiding Shad's shadowy, Shade form would be easier, and Ali would definitely be home.

Lawr was surprised at how close to his building the doorway had opened. He had assumed they would need a taxi ride at least, but they were only a block away.

"You live near a natural gaet," Shad explained with his usual lack of attention to the relevant details. "I bet a lot of weird stuff happens in this area because of it."

Lawr hummed. He couldn't remember what he had thought was weird before an oversized shadow had stepped into his living room, but Ali had always said the area was strange.

They entered the lobby of his building and headed for the elevators.

"Lawrence?!" A shrill woman's voice called from the entrance to the apartment complex.

Shad lurched and squeezed his large shadowy self between the vending machines and the lobby wall.

Lawr turned around to frown at the woman. A neighbor he hardly remembered other than that she had always been extremely nosy.

"Good evening." Lawr didn't even try guessing what her name might have been.

"Lawr, where have you been? There was a lot of confusion when you disappeared." The woman walked up to him with an expression of confusion and greedy curiosity. "Shouldn't you be at the police station?"

"The police station?" Lawr frowned again. "No, I'm fine. Just came by to check on Ali."

The woman had a hand over her heart in an instant. "Oh, you didn't know?"

Lawr cocked an eyebrow and waited.

He watched the sympathy in her eyes that could barely cover her sickly excitement at a chance to gossip and have information someone else did not.

Lawr was tempted to just walk away and leave her to gossip by herself. But if she had anything to say about Ali, it might be necessary to listen.

Lawr?

Shad's voice interrupted Lawr's irritation.

It's kind of tight back here. Really uncomfortable.

Lawr glanced toward the shadow pouring unnaturally out of the crevasses next to him. It shifted until glowing blue eyes appeared.

Think thin thoughts. Lawr offered, returning his attention to the rambling woman.

"...I always assumed you knew and that's why you left. Though the police thought you might..."

"Did you want to tell me anything useful, or can I go see Ali now?"

Lawr interrupted the woman's maunder about nothing as he shifted to hide Shad from her view.

The woman stared up at him for a moment. The first trace of genuine concern fluttered through her features.

"Those people took her. No one has seen her or them since and—"

"What?!" Lawr blinked, "What people? Took her where?"

"Well, it didn't make any sense. One of the neighbors spoke to them, actually. Said they were nice kids, but—"

"Who took her?" Lawr shook the woman's shoulders as he repeated his question.

"The police don't know. Your neighbor said the kids called themselves the Iiner or Diner Wolves or something. I don't know if that's a gang or a band or what."

Aynur Wolves, probably. Shad said to Lawr's mind as he moved to escape his small confine.

The woman gasped but soon settled with ignoring the shadow.

"That's all I know about it," Shad said with a frown, "your neighbor didn't see anything else, and the police still have no idea what happened or where that poor girl is."

The woman was still talking.

"They considered she may have run away with her boyfriend, one of those kids, but nothing—"

Lawr walked away from the woman's rambling since she didn't know anything else.

He turned to Shad as they headed toward the exit.

"You know who these guys are? Are they the ones we have in the dungeon?"

Lawr growled the questions while he pulled out an AaD and punched in commands to find the next doorway back.

"I don't know. We don't know which tribe those two belong to," Shad said with an unusually calm as he pulled the AaD away from Lawr and started searching for a different doorway. "Aynur inherited four Wolf packs after the Oroitz battle. They may be from one of those."

"How did they find her? And why would they take her?"

Lawr tried to keep from snapping, but his voice was hitching in panic already.

How long have they had her? Since I left? That's what the woman said, right…

All the questions terrified him with the idea of what he would find out.

Calm down.

The voice was not his. The unnatural sense of calm that forced its way over his mind certainly was not either.

"Shad. Get out of my head," Lawr ordered, grounding out each word with a glare to the shadow.

Blue eyes held his gaze before Shad sighed, and the presence in his mind dropped.

"We can find her," Shad started, still sounding too calm, "We can go check the Aynur marketplace. That's where they would have taken her anyway. But you need to keep your head, especially while we're there."

"We wouldn't need to find her if you had thought of the danger when we left…"

Lawr bit his tongue to physically cut off the sentence. It wasn't fair and, more importantly, it wasn't useful to blame Shad for this.

I am responsible for her, I promised my brother to keep her safe, I should have thought of the danger.

"I know." Shad's nebulous posture drooped. "This is my fault…And I should have thought of this happening. I'm sorry, Lawr…"

"No, this is on me. I shouldn't have snapped."

Lawr continued grounding out each word without unclenching his teeth.

Shad grumbled disagreements that Lawr ignored as he followed the direction the shadow moved.

Shad led the way to and through a doorway into the Empty, where they continued walking in near silence.

Occasionally, Lawr caught a whisper of Shad's voice in his head, either apologizing or blaming himself. He was not sure the wraith even meant to talk to him, but that some of his thoughts and powers were slipping out in his stress.

Either way, Lawr was too busy beating himself up and imagining the worst-case scenarios to note much of what Shad was doing.

In Glacius Tesca, Shad continued to lead the way toward the marketplace. Shad weaved through the maze setup of the market, getting turned around a few times before they entered a large tent with a ratio of people bound with rope or chain and people handling coins.

Lawr's stomach did flips before settling into nauseous disgust. The disgust multiplied at the thought of Ali alone in the crowd.

With a grimace at the thought and a new dull headache from Shad, Lawr pulled his attention back to his surroundings. Surroundings that seemed very interested in them too.

A quick scan of the room and Lawr noted they were the center of attention. He flinched at the idea of attracting the attention of the kind of people in that room.

Do we stand out that much as not being Nomads?

The headache subsided, only a noticeably small amount, as Shad started toward one particular table and began talking to the man behind in it their language.

Lawr stayed where he was and watched at the attention of the room stayed on Shad. The kid normally drew the attention of a space, usually with fear and discomfort from strangers, but this was different. The Nomads were not afraid of the traces of Shade dancing under Shad's skin. They were not afraid at all, it was something else.

I see why Shad dislikes them so...Of course, these people do trade in abnormal slaves, naturally, they wouldn't be afraid.

The thought flitted across Lawr's mind, ready to be ignored, but Lawr jerked instinctively at it.

Abnormal slaves. Shad would be abnormal...

Lawr's attention snapped back to Shad as he covered the distance between them in a few large steps. He couldn't think of anything else except getting Shad out of there.

He reached the wraith just as he wished the man at the table a good day with a stiff, hate-filled smile.

Lawr latched onto his arm and started dragging him toward the exit.

"We need to leave," Lawr growled after Shad stumbled and tried asking a question.

"Okay."

A sharp headache split Lawr's skull before dulling in an instant. The people around them all doubled over, grabbing at their heads.

Only once they were outside the tent did Shad release whatever he had been doing to cause the pain.

Lawr was still pulling Shad along as he ducked through side paths until they were safely out of sight.

"You all right?" Shad asked, panting and holding his head gingerly.

"Yeah, we need to get out of here, though. These people take way too much of an interest in you." Lawr grimaced. "I'll come back by myself to get the information."

Sorry, Ali. Wait a little longer for me, kid.

"No need." Shad forced a pained smile. "I got what we need, but you're not gonna like it."

Lawr regarded Shad with a quick appraisal. The kid was still holding his head and leaning against Lawr. He looked a moment away from either puking or having a seizure. Maybe both.

"Hold that thought, Shad. We should get out of this sphaere."

Lawr held Shad up as he took the AaD out of the kid's robes and plotted a careful course to the nearest doorway.

He half dragged Shad's teetering form along the path toward relative safety.

"I read his mind, saw images of who bought her," Shad said as they reached the edge of the market. "It's Sverre. Oracaede must have wanted her."

Lawr let out a shaky breath and closed his eyes.

Oh, Ali. I'm sorry.

CHAPTER 38

A li crept up on the island as Erc pointed out the dock. They tied the boat with a slip knot in case they needed to make a quick escape.

Erc led the way along a path over a gradually ascending hill. They passed small outbuildings and a firing range. All undisturbed.

"It doesn't look like—"

"Shh." Erc cut off Ali's hopeful remark as they ventured further into the island.

At the summit of the little hill, Erc froze.

Ali waited behind her for Erc to move, but the dark woman remained frozen. After a moment, Ali moved up next to her.

A small bunker or root cellar of a building had been dug into the hill with an array of satellite-looking dishes and instruments around.

Had.

The destruction was appalling. The root cellar was now a clawed-up hole in the ground. The door and roof were shredded and strewn across the jungle floor.

The satellite array, whatever it had been, was trampled, with a few dishes stuck up in trees where they had been flung.

The ground was littered with squash, fruit, and the remains of wooden and clay jars with other preserved vegetables oozing out all over the jungle floor.

Ali pulled her attention from the destruction to Erc. The woman stared with vapid focus at the disaster in front of her.

Erc stepped forward, walking through the mess with Ali trailing behind.

Ali made note of the upturned trees and torn-up earth where the creature had come and gone down the backside of the island.

"No! No, no, nonono."

The litany pulled Ali's attention back to Erc as the woman ran to a torn open metal box. She searched inside and on the ground, repeating the one word before dropping to her knees.

"Erc?"

Ali tiptoed through the razed area and dropped down next to Erc.

"What is it?"

"It took it. Why would it take this?"

Erc tipped the heavy box toward herself to peer inside again.

"Took what?"

"The blocker!" Erc snapped, leveling her enraged gaze at Ali.

Ali pulled back, but only for a moment.

"What blocker?" Ali asked, keeping her voice steady and resting a hand on Erc's shoulder.

Erc growled and grumbled to herself a moment before taking a breath. "Atanas. He tracks them. All of his operatives."

Ali blinked and stared.

"What?" she whispered, "I didn't know any—"

"You didn't need to, it didn't matter. Sverre would have told you eventually. But Sverre isn't tracked anyway."

Ali frowned. "But you just said he tracks all—"

"Sverre had cut out so many of them, Atanas just stopped bothering with tracking him. But Dain," Erc clapped a hand over her mouth as she stared out at the destruction. "they put it next to his heart. We haven't found a skilled healer we could trust to remove it."

Ali flinched at the thought.

She blinked, hoping she was understanding right. "And this blocker stops Oracaede from tracking him?"

Erc nodded and even chuckled though the humor died long before it reached her eyes.

"Through some degree of science and magic, Sverre has been working on having this blocker made for years. Anytime he's been on assignment in Terrae. He just finished it."

Erc cradled her head in her hands as she hunched forward in silent tears.

Ali frowned, trying to think of anything Sverre might have mentioned about it. She couldn't think of anything, but it did raise a curiosity.

"Sverre said you hadn't seen Dain in two years." Ali timidly broached the subject. "How did you see him before this?"

Erc continued holding her head.

"Painstakingly."

Ali waited for her to continue.

"Sverre would tell us a time to meet. Dain doesn't have a home, really, so he just moved around between jobs. Usually, he'd stay with Sverre; his house was in something of a blackout zone the tracker couldn't register the exact location. That was easiest, but it was season contingent. Dain couldn't always go there."

Erc stared at her hands with a faint smile of remembrance.

"Otherwise, Sverre would give a location, and I'd pack up the kids and travel to some nowhere for a few days. Before he had to move again."

"That's…" Ali swallowed, "I couldn't even imagine."

Erc nodded, the hard set of her jaw returned.

"We made it work. Sverre worked to get that blocker and test it was functional. They set it up here on their way out this last time."

Erc swatted a tear that escaped down her cheek.

"It was the first time Dain's seen our home."

Erc stood in a quick motion and grabbed Ali's hand to haul her up too. She examined the box one last time and the ground around it.

"It's not destroyed."

"What?" Ali glanced around at the ground for whatever Erc was looking for or had seen.

Erc pointed to the box.

"There aren't any pieces of the blocker," She gestured at the jungle floor, "I don't see any parts from it either. It didn't destroy it, it took it."

"Why would it do that?" Ali pondered aloud, wondering what kind of monster they were up against. Ali knew enough about Erc to know she would be going after the creature to get the blocker back.

Erc shrugged. "No idea, but the blocker emits a frequency that we can track."

Ali wandered over the destruction of the path the creature had left in its wake. She glanced at the shotgun she still gripped with white knuckles.

"So, we can find it then?"

How are we getting the blocker back from something that can uproot trees?

That was a better question, but she knew Erc didn't have an answer for that now either, so she didn't bother asking.

"You don't have to come." Erc offered.

Ali turned back to her, pretending the constant reminders of how little skills she had to be helpful didn't hurt.

"I'd do it for Sverre, and I know you would too. Dain's important to me also."

Erc smiled. An easy, relieved smile.

"Thank you."

CHAPTER 39

Ali and Erc returned to the house to an immediate barrage of questions from the kids.

"Did you see it?"

"Did you shoot it?"

"Did it destroy anything?"

Erc stopped next to her daughter at the question.

"Yes, and it took the blocker Uncle Sverre brought. Ali and I are going after it."

All the kids quieted at that.

"What?" Incara stared at her mother, "No, I should go with you, Ma."

"Incara." Erc's voice held a warning that this issue wasn't up for discussion, but Incara ignored it.

"She's useless. She can't even shoot a gun. How's she going to help you?"

Ali flinched as she wavered at the idea of intervening or letting Erc talk to her daughter alone. She did not have any argument that the girl was wrong.

Leon jumped in before she could decide, stepping in front of Incara.

"Don't say that about Ali. She can shoot and you're not that great a shot yourself anyways."

"Leon, it's all right." Ali rested a hand on his shoulder and pulled his stout body back away from Incara. "And Incara, I know you want to go with your mom. You are better at handling weapons than me, but Erc doesn't want you to be in danger."

"I don't care," Incara shouted, switching between glaring at Ali and sending imploring looks toward Erc.

"I do," Erc stated.

Her tone left no room for arguments or questions. Incara took a step back before Erc continued.

"Incara, you'll stay here and protect Charlton and Leon. The creature, whatever it is, made a mess of the satellite array the blocker needs to be effective. You three work on fixing it while we're gone. Clear."

"Yes, Ma." Incara hung her head and bit her lip.

"Boys?"

"Yes, ma'am," they said in unison.

Ali wished she could say something to Incara, but nothing seemed appropriate for the girl's turmoil of emotions.

Erc was already heading for the kitchen with a word to Charlton and Incara to help her pack supplies.

"Don't worry, Incara," Ali offered as the girl remained stationary, "I'll make sure your mom makes it back safe."

Incara's head snapped up to glare at Ali.

Ali steeled her features to remain pleasant against whatever stinging remark the twelve-year-old had to offer.

Incara scoffed and turned to follow her mother into the kitchen.

"Ma can do that herself, and now she has to protect you too..."

Incara continued grumbling to herself, but she was out of earshot, much to Ali's relief.

"You have to come back safe too."

Leon's voice was so uncharacteristically soft, Ali blinked when she realizes it was actually him that spoke.

Ali dropped her hand from his shoulder as she noted she was still holding him still. The boy didn't move.

"I will." Ali tried to sound more assured of that idea than she was, but Leon remained where he was. She guessed she had not been that convincing.

"I'll be mad. And Sverre will be mad too if you don't."

Leon sniffed and turned around so Ali could see his shaky panicked look. His fear stabbed at her heart as he continued.

"He'll be mad, and I'll have to go after you. Then Charlton and Aunt Erc will be mad, and even Incara too. Everyone will be upset, so you have to come back safe."

Leon swallowed as he looked up at Ali with a forced smile.

"'Kay?"

Ali squeezed him in a hug.

"I'll do my best." She promised when she drew back again.

The boy put on a brave, smiling face before darting off, past Erc, into the kitchen.

Erc walked over to Ali with a glance over her shoulder to the start of a ruckus in the pantry.

"These kids," she grumbled, shaking her head with a smile.

Erc turned back to Ali.

"Don't worry, kids adapt quicker than adults. They'll be fine once we get back."

She patted Ali's shoulder as she moved passed her to head up the stairs.

Ali still watched the kitchen though all the kids were out of sight.

"I don't know about that," she mumbled to herself.

Ali still remembered when her parents would leave on some peacekeeping adventure. She remembered when she had finally been allowed to come. The travel was fun and exciting, but overwhelming too. She had never complained about how scared she had been because the thought of being left behind was scarier.

She wondered how much of Leon's cheerful indifference to the circumstances was an act. How much he was hurting but wouldn't show it.

If anyone knew, it would be Charlton. The boys spent every waking minute together, pretending not to get into mischief.

Ali made a mental note to have an individual chat with both of the boys when she returned.

She turned and made her way up the stairs to her own room. She had no idea what to take since she had no idea how long they might be gone.

After walking around her room a couple of times, Ali decided on two changes of clothes and a dagger Sverre had given her.

She slung the small bag over her shoulder and went back downstairs. Erc was already waiting with her own small bag, plus a large basket separated between food and a couple weapons.

"Ready?" Erc asked.

Ali nodded as she glanced around at the kids. Leon stood next to Charlton at the base of the stairs, shifting his feet and trying not to look nervous as he stared with an imploring look up at her.

Charlton was calmer but was staring at his mother with the same look. Incara was still in the kitchen with her arms crossed, glaring at her feet with a trembling lip.

Ali swallowed hard and squeezed Leon's shoulder as she passed him, following Erc out of the house.

They walked in silence down the path while Ali tried thinking of a way to talk about the kids to Erc. A sniffle beside her snapped Ali's attention to it.

Erc roughly wiped her cheek as she noticed Ali watching.

"It's the same thing," she stated in a sharp tone, "The same as when Dain leaves, and I'm sure when Sverre leaves for his jobs too."

Ali mumbled in agreement. She recalled how hurt and scared Leon always was when Sverre left. She hated thinking he might be that scared for her now.

A tear pricked her eyes.

Erc coughed and cleared her throat.

"They'll be fine. We'll come back and they'll…" Her face twisted into a focused grimace as she seemed intent on not letting a single tear fall.

Ali blinked as she considered this may be one thing she may be better at than Erc.

"It's okay."

Ali rested on hand on her shoulder and grabbed one of the basket's handles to help Erc carry it.

"It's better to cry now, let it all out, than to store it up to burst out some random time later."

Erc blinked at Ali as she readjusted her grip on the basket.

Erc coughed out a word of appreciation as they continued in silence except for some sniffles and shaking breathing.

CHAPTER 40

"Y ou sure Dain and Caesar Apollo will be safe with that... thing?" Bary asked Sverre in a whisper.

Hid craned his neck and broke his gaze from the linen closet's door to hear the answer.

It had amazed him how quickly the team grouped around Sverre as being safe when the freak, Duqa, had shown up. Hid was glad the plan only had one of his teammates working with Duqa. And of all of them, Caesar Apollo would have the best fighting chance against him.

"Dain will keep Caesar Apollo safe," Sverre stated.

It also surprised Hid just how much he trusted the sniper and that statement.

Bary hummed, "Who's going to keep Dain safe, though?"

The question hung in the air as Sverre did not seem like he would bother answering, but Hid was worried about that too.

"Echo would report back to your boss if Duqa did anything."

Hid hoped it sounded like a statement, not a question, but that was the only thing that seemed to keep the clown in check.

Sverre held his gaze a moment before he nodded.

Hid could only hope that was enough to tame the freak's behavior, but there was nothing to be done about it at present.

Light footsteps announced Sa'dia's presence just before she knocked out their code on the door and opened it.

"Everyone cozy?" Sa'dia asked with an extra grin thrown in Sverre's direction.

The added bit of disguise he had to wear over his distinctive features could only leave him over-warm after the ages they had spent in the cramped supply closet.

"Sufficiently so," Sverre stated.

It did surprise Hid that the Ghost responded to the joke, but he had been making an apparent effort to be friendly and human around the Wolves. The effort was only for when Duqa was not around, though.

Sverre led their little group stealthily through the castle with expert knowledge of the building's layout.

At the entrance to the dungeon, Sverre incapacitated the guards and stole the keys quicker than Hid could even comprehend.

The actual dungeon had remarkably few guards since reaching that level deep within the castle was such an effort. They hurried through the maze to the cells Idir's guard contact had said there would be.

Hid breathed a small sigh. The guard had been telling the truth when they found their teammates, and Sverre opened the cells.

"Great to see you, and it's about time!" Aike slapped Hid's back in a friendly manner, but the smile did not reach his eyes as he watched Sverre with a cautious gaze.

"It's good, *hermano*," Hid stated with a small gesture and tap code toward Sverre.

Aike held his gaze a half moment too long and shook his head.

Hid dropped the topic. Aike would have to see Sverre was an oddly good sort of person in his own way. Especially when compared to the freak outside.

"We need to go." Sverre's quiet voice spurred the team into motion as they returned through the dungeon along the path they had just traversed.

They reached the exit in time to see the incapacitated guards being discovered by another squad.

"And that would be our cue to bolt, now, would it?" Aike whispered as a guard caught sight of their stealthy retreat.

"Correct," Sverre stated as they took to sprinting their route out.

They rounded the last corner to the courtyard and bounced to a quick stop. Half a platoon of guards, still waiting on orders, milled around the yard in front of the last gate, separating the team from freedom.

The guards stared at the intruders with the same shocked expression Hid wore.

"Don't kill them," Sverre whispered, shifting to the front of their group. "We don't need guards with personal vendettas chasing us around the city."

"You guys!" A voice from the balcony above caught everyone's attention.

Hid looked up to see the general they had tried conning glaring directly at him.

"Shit." Hid and Bary spat at once.

"Run," Sverre ordered, giving Hid a shove toward the gate as he launched himself into the midst of the guards.

Hid's pounding heart drowned out the shouting around him as the general gave orders to the guards.

A series of controlled explosions rocked the courtyard. Hid focused on the shadows until he caught sight of Retha and Idir as they snuck closer to the gate, lighting Retha's homemade flash bangs as they went.

The cackling laughter of the clown emitting from the tower with the gate controls was less of a comfort, but at least the sniper could keep the freak in place while they escaped.

The panicked confusion of the guards was a tangible scent as the gate started to open despite the constant shouts from the general and nearby guards to close it.

Hid ushered the team through the wake Sverre was carving passed the guards with renewed gratitude the assassin was on their side for this escape. By the time Aike and Xiulan met up with Retha and the gate closed behind them, trapping the guards inside, Hid was overjoyed at both the assassins' participation.

Outside the gate, Hid paused for a quick count of all his teammates as they darted away on their separate routes back to their new safe house.

All safe, thank the Vis.

Hid reached that conclusion just as he noticed Sverre standing next to him doing the same thing. He ended his count to include Hid before giving Hid a light shove in the direction of their own route back.

They weaved through the back alleyways, deserted buildings, and a rank sewage drain until the number of guards perusing them shrank to zero. At the lower levels of the city, where the nightlife was still well awake with petty crime, their group began reconvening as their paths started to cross.

Aike and Retha were the last pair to meet up with them at the dingy tavern Dain had rented rooms in.

Aike entered the room mid-complement of the explosions but Hid caught the slight look of confusion on Retha that gave away that Aike had jumped topics as soon as he saw noticed the others.

"That was quite the impressive escape plan there, Hid." Aike shifted to Hid's side with a friendly elbow to the gut. "That exit, though, that may need some work next time."

Hid scoffed. "That's usually your job, *hermano*, of course, our improvisation wasn't as great."

Aike mumbled some inconsequential comeback Hid ignored in favor of enjoying the relief that came from having all his teammates back together again.

"Oooh…this one's pretty."

The relief vanished.

Duqa bent forward to study Xiulan's hands while stroking his chin with his claw-encrusted hands, leaving little scratches across his face.

"Who…?" Aike half asked while he and Hid both automatically moved to stand between Xiulan and Duqa.

"Clown," Sverre growled out the warning while he removed his mask and hood, catching the freak's gaze with a cold glare.

"No, kids, no kids." Duqa let out a shriek, covered his ears, and turned toward Sverre. "I know, Sverry."

The two held a short glaring match before Dain interrupted.

"Duqa," his voice was filled with threat, "knives down."

Hid balked when he noticed the three throwing knives that had materialized in the clown's palm. Duqa loosely twirled them around his hands as he decided which assassin to glower at. He picked Dain and, with a quick flick of his wrist, loosed all three knives in the sniper's direction.

Dain shifted the smallest distance to avoid the weapons before they were embedded in the wall.

Hid shifted a glance at Sverre for direction if the clown was a threat. He hesitated a half moment again to respond to Sverre's negative before tapping a message for the team to stand down.

Aike stared in shock at Hid's decision but followed his lead in calming the others.

Sverre and Dain hardly reacted to Duqa's outburst, that at least assured Hid that this wasn't about to be a problem. Sverre had not even glanced at the knives to know they had missed his partner.

The air hung heavier than the Vis for a long moment before a playful smile from Duqa cut it.

"Sverry, you're the worst, and I swear to Ata, I will kill you for it."

Sverre nodded more with his eyes than his head.

Duqa made a dramatic show of sighing as he moved to collect his knives and head for the door.

"Echo, we have reports to make."

Echo stood waiting outside the door but stepped into the room rather than follow Duqa.

"Fine, I'll beat you back." Duqa hummed and skipped down the hall toward the stairs.

Echo closed the door behind him.

The room remained frozen as Hid watched Sverre for any sign they should be concerned about the clown's behavior or his leaving.

Sverre seemed to be in a silent conversation of stares with Dain and occasionally Echo before he caught Hid's look.

"It's good."

The team, minus Aike and Xiulan, collectively sighed at the two short words.

"Echo," Dain was grinning at the dead-eyed man, "suppose you might make a good report without details of this little rescue operation?"

The messenger shrugged, then rubbed a thumb and two fingers together in a sign for money or payment.

"Of course, of course." Dain nodded. "Insults or general conversation?"

Echo wobbled an outstretched hand.

"Both?"

Echo nodded and made a show of counting everyone in the room before holding up eight fingers—he was missing two on his left hand—and then flashed two more.

"What from everyone? Steep. Maybe your name is Avarice or some variant. Am I close?"

Echo shook his head. "Blundering blowfish."

"Hey, that's mine, you can't use that against me."

Dain continued a conversation Hid could not follow as he started listing names and waiting for a response from the mute one.

"Am I the only one out of the loop?" Aike asked with a smile, but Hid read his distrust and concern as he waved a hand toward Echo. "Who's that? And who was the freak show?"

"Oh, Echo's our messenger, he reports to our boss when AaDs aren't trusted," Dain answered. "I'm assuming he's really here to get Oracaede's other operative's late report."

"He's good." Sverre stated, "Can't talk unless relaying a message though, or…"

"Or by repeating what someone else says, so if he does us a favor, like smudging some details of this rescue, we repay him with phrases he can use freely. And someday, I'm going to get him to tell me his name."

Dain stated the last part with pride, but both Sverre and Echo were shaking their heads at the hopeless task that was.

The sniper clapped Echo on the back as he continued, "And this time, he's being greedy and wants a general phrase, something for everyday life, from everyone here."

Echo shrugged and gestured to Dain, "Weak."

"I'm insulted."

"And the freak show?" Aike interrupted the camaraderie with an edge still in his voice.

"Oracaede's resident sociopath," Sverre stated.

"I thought that was your title."

Aike's tone was light, but Hid could tell he was still serious.

"Nah," Hid interrupted Sverre's cold stare and Dain's quick retaliatory remark, "Sverre's a sweetheart in comparison to that thing."

Aike only seemed to accept that, though unwillingly, before they all turned to the task of 'paying' the messenger.

Sa'dia and Bary were the only ones who were able to give him phrases he didn't call 'weaker than a sunburned snowflake.'

A phrase Dain protested for being used unfairly against its original attributor.

CHAPTER 41

"No, they looked more like this, sir."

The frustration of the dungeon guard was evident as he took the piece of charcoal from Jair again to make corrections to the drawing.

Bry and Jair watched the man add a few different lines of detail and smudge out others to the increasingly distorted sketches of the two Wolves Jair had recognized had talked to him at the pub.

The guard was adamant his more recent experience of being knocked out and tied up had given him a better view of their looks.

"No," Jair snatched the charcoal back, "'dat pale kid had curly hair."

"Not that curly." The guard grabbed the writing tool back.

"Oh, for the love of Vis." Bry wrestled the charcoal away from both of them and handed it and the drawings back to the court-employed artist who had been watching with a floating hand, ready to pluck his art tools back at any moment of opportunity.

"Thank you, sir." The artist stashed all his tools safely away from the guard and the general. "I'll have these sketches cleaned up and mass-produced for your warrants, sir."

Bry nodded out of habit and relief that the endless night might soon be over.

The artist, smart man, took his cue to leave without further prompting. The guard had to be more formally dismissed, and he was still discontented with leaving.

"You're free to go too, Jair."

"'Da guards saw three opening 'da ga'de and one more ou'dside wai'ding." Jair paced the study, ignoring Bry's prompting. "And another 'dwo se'ding 'da fires."

Bry glowered at the general, willing him to leave so he could finally work on his hour of sleep for the night.

Jair turned in his pacing without regarding the look.

Bry groaned and stood from his desk to pace as well.

"So twelve Wolves total with the six you saw in the courtyard leaving the castle."

Bry rubbed his eyes as he struggled to drag his feet along.

Jair paused his pacing to stare through Bry. "I've never heard of a Wolf pack with more d'an 'den. Six 'o eigh'd is normal."

"Maybe they combined two of the leftover packs from the tribes in Oroitz," Bry offered. He cringed at how dumb the idea was as he said it.

Jair glared at him with a look to further cement its stupidity.

"I know, I know." Bry jumped to correct himself before Jair could. "Wolves raised together, to fight together, and die together don't just join other packs."

"Nomads wouldn't send a new or conjoined 'deam here," Jair added, chewing aggressively at his thumbnail.

"Must have had local help."

Bry tried again. That idea was only slightly more plausible. And any help would have to be from people they trusted. Wolves were notorious for only working with their own teams.

Jair ignored the suggestion entirely as he kept wearing a hole through the flooring.

Bry cast a glance around the room, wishing for the umpteenth time that Shad was back.

"Someone else working with 'dem." Jair stilled again to scowl at the thought, "'da fighd'er who d'ook oud' 'da guards was good. *Very* good."

"Jair, we'll have to continue this discussion in the morning," Bry paused to glance out the window to note the night sky was already beginning to lighten with the dawn, "the later morning."

Jair followed his gaze out the window. "Righ'd, I'll be back la'der."

Bry nodded and collapsed back into his chair the moment the door closed behind Jair. Resting his head atop his arms on the desk, he desperately tried catching any wisps of sleep he could before he would need to go back to work again.

The room stood still and quiet until someone knocked at the door.

Bry clapped his hands over his ears for a moment of bliss, pretending he could just ignore whoever it was.

"Come in," Bry finally called as he dragged his head up from the desk with the greatest of efforts.

Stori poked her head into the room.

"Stori, it's late…early." Bry frowned, "You need your rest."

"I was hungry," Stori said, stepping into the room and lifting a small tray of assorted fruits, nuts, and cured meats to help her point before she closed the door behind herself.

She set the tray on the arm of the sofa before padding over to Bry's desk with a look of increasing concern.

"Bry, have you slept at all the last few days?"

Bry tried to force a smile, but he was too exhausted to keep it up for long.

"Not really."

He reached a hand toward her midsection and the small bump that could still hide under her nightgown from most angles.

"You're just going to have to get enough sleep for the three of us."

Stori pouted at the joke and caught his hand, pulling it until Bry took the hint to stand up and follow her. She sat at one end of the sofa and waited for him to sit next to her. She awkwardly shuffled until Bry could lie down with his head on her lap.

Bry sighed against Stori's hand running through his hair comfortingly.

"I have to go back to work in an hour," Bry mumbled without an attempt to move.

"Shh," Stori gave his scarred cheek a reprimanding pat, "I want to eat in silence."

Bry smiled as the silence lasted long enough for unconsciousness to overtake him.

The bliss of darkness lasted only a short time to a sleeping mind before Bry woke up again. A glance as Stori, dozing about him, provided the most comforting sight he had seen in an age.

Bry stayed still in the restful moment, admiring his perfect image of his wife. He leaned closer to her belly, hoping to hear or feel something of the baby. Eleanora told him daily that it was still too soon, but he was impatient for the first day it would not be.

"One day, little one," Bry whispered, "when you're out here with us, you can keep us awake all night. You can take on your uncle's bad habits and be a troublemaker with him. Hopefully, some of Stori's good—"

"Bry!? You up?"

The voice of said troublemaker startled Bry to a sitting position as Stori woke with a start as well.

Shad poked his head through the door with a grin, though Bry thought it looked more strained than usual.

"Didn't want to interrupt anything spic—"

Bry flung a pillow at the offending head.

"Don't startle Stori, you oaf."

Lawr entered a moment later, glanced around the room, and rested on Stori before he landed a heavy hand atop Shad's head.

"Don't startle pregnant women." He reprimanded with a grave but amused tone.

"All right, all right." Shad offered a weak apologetic smile to Stori. "Sorry, didn't mean to startle you."

Stori waved off the apology, "I'm fine, Shad. You know these two, always worrying."

She gave Bry's arm a sympathetic pat before turning the same smile to Lawr.

Bry snorted at the sympathy before turning back to the two men. A glance at the door revealed no one else was outside.

He frowned.

"What's the news?" Bry asked, trying to smile as he shuffled to stand. "Do I get to meet your niece, Lawr?"

He glanced at the doorway again but said niece still did not appear.

The mood of the traveling pair instantly fell.

"We need to talk to those kids you have in the dungeon." Lawr stated, "Find out if they're from the Aynur tribe and what they know about Sverre, the Ghost. The boy, Aike, seemed to know him."

Lawr's glare was as cold as Bry had ever seen from him. Enough to send a chill up his spine.

"Yeah, Bry, they kidnapped her." Shad hung his head as he spoke, "they took her and sold her at their market in Glacius Tesca. To the Ghost."

"What?!" Bry stared, hoping for...anything else. This wasn't the kind of news he needed that morning.

"Why would the albino want her?"

"I don't know." Shad's voice was tight

"And how were they able to find her"

"I don't know, Bry. They did."

Shad glared, and Bry took it as a hint to drop the questions.

He did, but Shad spoke again without prompting.

"I don't know, but I should have thought of it. I should have brought her here with me when I picked up Lawr."

Bry was about to counter that, but Lawr beat him to it.

"It's not your fault." Lawr turned to Bry. "I need to talk to those kids, though."

Bry deflated as he reached again to try and break that small bone at the bridge of his nose.

"They're gone. Broke out last night."

The silence was sharp and painful before Lawr's quiet growl broke it.

"What?"

"They had help, a lot of it," Bry explained as he forced himself to meet Lawr's gaze. "We spent the whole night searching. I just finished getting warrants made to be distributed."

Lawr let out a rare swear.

The mood of the room followed him in quiet agitation as each person slipped deeper into their own morose thoughts.

CHAPTER 42

Stori left Bry's study in a more dejected mood as she thought of Lawr's poor niece. She had not even known of the girl's existence until recently but felt a connection with anyone who was forced from their homes.

Her situation is worse than anyone else I've talked to...

Stori tried distracting herself from worrying about Lawr. He had looked so completely miserable the entire time, and she felt a spike of concern for his wellbeing.

Stori continued wandering aimlessly through the halls. The comfort of her own rooms seemed to her to be a betrayal of all the pain and sorrow her friends and family were going through.

She finally decided to visit the other girl who had been torn away from her home. Stori stopped by her own room to collect Fenrir before wandering until she made her way to Caelyn's door and knocked.

The door remained closed and the room silent, long enough for Stori to turn to leave before she heard a rustling from inside.

"Caelyn?" Stori called out, unsure if she should stay or leave the girl in peace.

The door opened and the bodyguard, Rhoeo, stood blocking the entrance. Fenrir growled at the woman with his same, unusual dislike for her.

"Your Majesty, Caelyn is resting."

Stori frowned as irritation stirred within her. Both from the guard's dismissive and disrespectful tone, and because Stori could see Caelyn sitting at her desk, glancing between them with an expression of uncertainty.

Stori focused her attention on Rhoeo again.

"I have come to visit her anyway."

She took a half-step forward, holding Rhoeo's gaze as she waited for the woman to back up and let her in.

Fenrir stepped further, pushing his muzzle against the woman's midsection to physically push her back away from Stori.

Rhoeo's right eye twitched a moment with disgust. Her whole expression twisted into an ugly look before settling into an untrustworthy smile. She moved back with a quick gesture for Stori to enter.

Stori blinked at the ordering tone of the motion. She instead stepped aside, so she was no longer blocking the doorway. Fenrir was already in the room, still focused entirely on the guard.

"I wish to visit with her alone."

Stori smiled as Rhoeo's irritated facial twitch returned with a scowl. The ugly expression continued until the guard turned her sharp gaze to Caelyn.

"If you will excuse me, Caelyn," Rhoeo gave Stori a mocking bow as she spoke, "I'm afraid I have been dismissed against your wishes."

Rhoeo stepped outside, allowing Stori to enter before the guard closed the door.

"I like Rhoeo, why did you send her away?"

Caelyn glared at Stori without moving to stand and greet her.

Stori paused to try and stop her irritation with the guard from spilling over into her interaction with the girl.

She watched as Fenrir padded over to rest an enormous head on Caelyn's lap. Even if the girl was upset with Stori, she still doted on the overgrown puppy, ignoring the drool stains on her gold and arctic blue skirt.

"I just wished to speak with you alone as a change," Stori said instead of risking an argument about how she did not trust the guard.

"Fine, what do you want to talk about alone then?" Caelyn changed her attention away from the Pyxis for a moment to ask.

"Well," Stori rummaged through her thoughts to find something appropriate as she settled on the sofa across from the girl's chair. "There was some chaos last night in the courtyard, I wanted to make sure you were not too disturbed."

Caelyn scoffed with an angry grin that did not belong to her.

"You mean when the prisoners Brynte was holding without cause escaped? Yeah, I heard. Good for them."

Stori blinked at the girls' open defiance.

"Bry had a perfectly just cause for arresting riot start—"

"Yeah, right," Caelyn interrupted with a roll of her eyes, "Brynte can't stand people criticizing him. He's a coward."

Stori remained silent, wrestling against her first thought to slap the girl for calling Bry, of all people, a coward. Though, given Caelyn's other charge about not taking criticism, that was not her best move.

"Especially in the castle, Caelyn, it is important not to believe every rumor you hear," Stori stated instead of a more aggressive response.

"I don't listen to rumors, I have a direct source," Caelyn said with a degree of pride slipping into her voice.

Stori could guess the 'direct source' was Rhoeo since Caelyn did not seem to talk to anyone else. She bit her tongue against saying so and reminded herself that she was biased in her dislike of the guard.

"Taking all your information from one source, who received it second-hand, doesn't make it reliable or less rumor based." Stori struggled to keep her voice level and continued speaking before Caelyn could cut in. "And I know you have no direct information on the matter because that would come from Bry, who you refuse to talk to."

Caelyn grumbled in irritation, but her silence did not last long.

"I can't believe you could even be in the same room as him," she said flippantly. "The man's a monster."

Something dark curled in Stori's gut as the memory of Loreda calling Bry a monster replayed across her mind.

"You have no idea what you are talking about while you repeat things you've just heard from others," Stori stated in a tone that made Caelyn gap at her.

A tear pricked Stori's eye as she grew angry.

"I don't just repeat things," Caelyn snapped before continuing, "and I know he's—"

"No, you don't. You don't know anything about him," Stori repeated in a lower tone, "Again, you've believed each rumor you hear, but you never even try to speak to Bry directly. You know less about him than when you first arrived because you have clouded your opinion with every bit of gossip."

Caelyn glared with cold, steady rage. "You have to say that, you're his wife."

"Do you think there weren't awful rumors circulating when I first arrived here?" Stori asked, as her mind immediately turned back to Loreda, "If I had listened to every passing whisper of rubbish, do you think I could ever have formed an accurate idea of who he was?"

"If you had listened to my mother—" Caelyn cut herself off as she glared daggers.

"If I had listened to Loreda, I would likely have been involved in murdering my husband and usurping the crown."

The alternate possibility of reality made Stori's stomach turn in ways she hated as her thoughts went to her baby. Her hand fluttered in a protective motion over her midsection as Caelyn snarled in wordless anger.

"Would that have been better?" Stori asked in a gentler voice, hoping she was reaching the girl. "Would you have listened to every rumor circulating about Loreda?"

"Don't talk about my mother like that," Caelyn spat.

"Don't talk about my husband the same," Stori returned with the last ounce of cool-headedness she possessed.

Stori stood and smoothed her dress with deliberate, slow motions, hoping to calm down.

"There is no point in arguing while we are both upset. I will take my leave." She turned to the door, "Fenrir, come."

The beast was at her side before she finished the command.

"*I'm* not upset." Stori heard the stubborn girl grumble behind her as she left the room.

Immediately outside, she bumped into Rhoeo.

Fenrir was growling again as he forced his large mass of a body between them. Stori settled her hand on his back, but the creature never took his eyes off of the guard.

"You've upset Caelyn, I see," Rhoeo stated with a cool indifference that angered Stori further.

"Your gossiping is what upset her to start," Stori countered. She tried reigning in her anger since it was hardly fair.

"You should avoid talking with her then," Rhoeo continued as though she had not heard, "we wouldn't want the stress of your emotional instability to cause your baby any harm."

Stori's blood froze. She grasped a tight handful of Fenrir's fur as she heard the barest hint of a threat in the woman's voice and from her cold smile.

Fenrir barked a deep-throated noise as his low growl turned into bared teeth and a snarl. Stori had never been more grateful for the animal than when he angled himself into an attack position, forcing the guard woman to back away.

"Don't you dare threaten my child," Stori hissed, still holding a handful of Fenrir's scruff.

Rhoeo's cold smile was tense as she focused on the beast snarling at her. She turned an irritated gaze back to Stori.

"Of course not, Your Majesty. I wouldn't dream of it."

Stori pulled at Fenrir as she backed away and watched Rhoeo enter Caelyn's room before she could breathe easy.

The large animal was by her side, still with a growl in his throat as they walked away.

"Good boy," Stori whispered, stroking Fenrir's head. "You're going to come with me everywhere from now on."

Stori worked to steady her irritation as she changed directions to head for Klaas and Eleanora's chambers instead of her own.

A pair of guards rushed past her with hurried apologies. She smiled but ignored them. A second and third group hurrying in different directions made her pause though. She hailed the fourth group to pass her and inquired what the rush was.

"The Nomads," one of the guards said breathlessly. "We just received a report that the Nomads have entered Medius and are marching toward Sentre."

CHAPTER 43

A ike stared wide-eyed at a panting Retha as she stood in the doorway.
        "What?" he croaked in a whisper.
        He swallowed and tried again, "What do you mean the Avare are already here?"

"What I just said," Retha said in a balanced voice. She steadied her breathing before stepping into the room and closing the door.

She scanned the room in haste, taking note of who was there, and more importantly, who wasn't. The assassins were out with most of the Wolves.

Hid stood from the couch and approached Retha with a calmer air of stress about him than Aike could manage.

"Retha, where did you learn that?"

The small, dark girl hopped from one foot to the other as she shifted further into the room to meet Hid halfway.

"Merchants, castle staff, town guards. The city is in an uproar about it."

Aike heard Hid's sigh before he turned around to face him.

"We're going to have to speed up our timeframe again, *hermano*," Hid stated with a tired, nervous, and worn-out smile that disappeared in an instant of thought. "Gonna have to cut out as much of the unnecessary elements as possible and…"

He trailed off, rubbing his temple as though he could massage away this headache that was their life.

Aike dropped back to the couch and stared at the notepads and scrolls of plans that were all useless now.

Already cut out everything unnecessary the last time that bitch changed the timeline. Damn it, Reb.

He did not say anything aloud.

Aike switched between thinking through how they could possibly still pull off their schemes and watching Hid, hoping he was having better luck at thinking of a solution.

"We'll put off the *other* job until the end," Hid stated with a quick glance around to Aike.

Aike nodded.

They were planning on attempting the assassination at the end when the Avare attacked anyways. They still needed a solid plan for it, but Aike assumed Hid meant they would have to just improvise that when they finished everything else.

Not a great idea, but we don't have time for better.

He tried to ignore the growing sense of guilt the thought of killing the sniper and albino had started to arouse. There was still something about their motivations he did not trust, but...

They aren't bad people. Not any worse than us, anyhow.

"...minimum we need to do to create the circumstances Reb wants?" Hid had been talking while Aike wasn't listening. At that, he turned toward Aike for an answer to his question.

Aike perched his head atop his steepled hands and rested his elbows on his bouncing knees, attempting to look like his thoughts were all there in the room too.

"Minimum? The whole city, starting with the soldiers, need to mistrust the king and his judgments for battle."

Aike paused to consider if that was really all they needed to meet Reb's orders.

Hid used the pause to add on.

"We can focus entirely on the soldiers then. Idir has been working the closest with them, we need an immediate update."

Hid turned toward Retha, and the girl scampered out the door without another word needed to find Idir.

"What else?"

Hid returned to the couch.

"We are so buggered," Aike said now that it was just him and Hid. He continued bouncing as he closed his eyes to think.

"Doesn't matter," Hid was pragmatic as ever, "We need to figure it out."

"*Seo cac!*" Aike stilled his knees and rubbed his temple, "It doesn't have to be complete and utter disarray."

Aike could sense Hid's eyes burning holes into him without having to look.

"I mean." Aike thought through the ghost of an idea that had snuck through his mind a moment ago, "all the soldiers don't have to be fanatically against him, just mistrustful enough to be slow in following commands he gives in battle. If we focused more on the officers giving orders…"

"We haven't made use of the casualties from the Oroitz battle much either." Hid nodded as he thought. "Those men had friends. If we could convince them the death of their brothers in arms was unnecessary, that may be enough."

Aike groaned and returned to holding his head atop his hands, "I hate using people's lost friends like that."

"Me too," Hid patted his shoulder, "but I would hate losing a friend even more."

Aike squeezed his eyes closed as he thought of Reb's threat against his Wolves before nodding.

Footfalls from the hallway announced the return of some of their teammates. Aike recognized Idir's footsteps as well as Dain's. He knew Retha and Sverre had to be there as well, though he could never hear either of them coming.

A quick knock code at the door and Idir entered followed by the others Aike had guessed.

He let out a quick breath. The freak show had not shown up again. The assassins assured him it wasn't likely Duqa would come back, but he remained wary of the possibility.

Aike blinked and did a double take as he noticed Retha speaking quietly with Sverre. The albino's remarks were said even quieter, so Aike could not even guess their conversation topic.

Aike leaned over to Hid with a whisper.

"How long has Retha been…comfortable being in the same room as the Ghost?"

Hid shrugged and fidgeted.

"Recently. You missed a lot in jail."

Aike blinked at Hid as the man remained his own nervous version of stoic.

"Idir, how are the soldiers? What are they thinking about Brynte?"

Hid focused the conversation on the topic at hand while Aike continued to marvel at his team's newfound trust in the assassins.

Everyone in the room leaned close in anticipation of Idir's soft voice.

"Any which fought and know personally Brynte, loyal and committed."

Idir paused as he noticed everyone straining to hear him. He straightened up and attempted to speak louder, but his voice returned to a whisper before the end of the next sentence.

"Fought in Oroitz, any heard our stories, know false, but believe some. The rest, dubious. Trust Jair and follow. As long the general loyal, soldiers follow Brynte."

"Too bad we couldn't snare him," Hid lamented with an anxious head twitch and darkening features.

Idir nodded. "Would been useful."

"Focus on what we can still do." Sverre's quiet voice interrupted the dejected mood.

Hid glanced over to the Ghost and nodded.

"Yes," Hid continued on the thought, "Jair clarified in a statement that he was loyal to Bry, but there must be some that doubt that."

Idir nodded.

"Think Brynte ordered statement, not Jair's actual thoughts. Soldiers circulating rumors themselves."

"Excellent," Aike pointed to Idir, "we can use that. It may be just what we needed."

Hid hummed. "Anyone know how far the Avare are from reaching the city?"

"About two weeks of steady marching." Dain said, squinting as though he could read the answer in the ceiling boards, "That's what I heard around the castle, anyways."

"Brynte may launch an attack to slow them down." Sverre stated, "Especially now that his wraith friend, Shadric, is back in Medius."

Aike swung a sidelong glance toward the Ghost.

How did Shad know your name?

Aike groaned.

This distrust is the last thing I need when the rest of the team seems to trust him now. Even Hid.

The groan caught the attention of the room's occupants.

"Thoughts, Aike?" Sverre asked with his usual unreadable expression.

Damned stoic bastard.

Retha scoffed, catching Aike off guard, though he was grateful for any distraction he could use to gather his thoughts.

"Don't worry," Retha said, patting the albino's arm, "Aike's fine, just being dramatic."

There went all of Aike's attempts to focus.

"Worry?" Aike gaped at Retha before switching his focus to Sverre.

The man is worried?

He squinted as the assassin remained expressionless and shifted his weight.

How can ya tell?

Aike shook his head, whatever their newfound bond was, it did not matter as long as Retha remembered their secondary mission.

"Anyway." Aike caught Hid's gaze with a plea for help to refocus the discussion on more important topics.

"Anyways, assuming the king sends an offensive response immediately," Hid picked up the point without needing further prompting, "We don't have to worry about the first response unit. We should focus on the next units to be dispatched."

"We start by using any lingering misgivings about Jair's loyalties," Aike continued, finally able to think again. "Idir, keep a close eye on what the soldiers are thinking, that will be most important."

The room sounded in various degrees of agreement.

CHAPTER 44

Ali watched as Erc conversed with a villager who owned something of a tech shop. Some of the food in the basket sat on the counter as Erc continued haggling over the man's prices.

The store was a hodgepodge mess of Aequorian technology with a surprising about of Earth, Terranian, tech too.

Lawr would love this place.

She glanced around with a new fondness for the peculiar devices that lined the walls.

"That went well."

Erc startled Ali by appearing next to her and speaking at once.

Ali helped with the basket as Erc set some kind of Aequorian contraption in it with a satisfied look.

"Oh? That will track the blocker then?" Ali questioned, stealing a glance at the unassuming little device.

"That it will. Or else Haifon will be hearing from me again."

Erc waved to the man at the counter as they exited his store.

They made a quick pace back to their boat, but not without delays. Several villagers, friends of Erc's, came out to chat with her and were immediately concerned with what they were doing.

Erc tried answering their concerns, especially about why there were going, without mentioning the blocker. She gave Ali a few pointed glances not to mention anything about it or why Dain needed it.

Ali guessed it made sense that none of the villagers knew much about Dain or who he worked for since they had never met him.

I wonder what they know about Sverre?

She frowned at the thought.

Erc continued trying to explain away their situation as just the loss of food as they shifted closer and closer to their boat. That excuse turned out flawed as well as all Erc's friends readily offered to share their own food supplies.

"We have to find something precious of mine that was taken," Ali stated in a loud voice.

She held her breath at the lie.

It's not that much of a lie anyways. Dain is important to me and the blocker is precious to his life here.

Ali swallowed at the rationalization as she ducked her head and continued.

"Erc was trying to spare me the embarrassment, but it is important, and we have to get it back."

Ali focused on trying to look embarrassed. It wasn't difficult since she wanted to disappear away from the blank and confused stares of the villagers.

Erc stared at her with a similar look of confusion before she snapped into action.

"Yes, uhh, sorry for being evasive, but we have to go and go alone."

The small trips in the dark woman's voice were Ali's only clue to how uncomfortable Erc was at lying to her friends.

They escaped out of the receding circle of confused villagers and dashed to their boat. They only relaxed after they had pushed away from the dock.

"That was unexpected." Erc turned to Ali with a cocked eyebrow and a frown that did not last as the corner of her lips twitched into a smile. "What precious thing is it you were planning on saying you'd lost?"

"I wasn't." Ali held back her abashed grin as she worked to straighten her face out with more confidence. "Decent sorts of people don't like pushing someone who's already so embarrassed. They'll just come up with their own ideas, much worse than anything I could think up. Hopefully, they never ask again though."

Erc hummed a doubtful note.

"Yeah, we can have a bet about that."

Once they were out of the harbor, Ali switched places to command the engine as Erc started messing with the new contraption and worked to figure out how to track the blocker.

Ali steered them around in the direction of the range island.

She watched the water beneath them, hoping for a glimpse of a Merii or some other interesting sea creature.

When they were centered in the middle of nowhere, she spotted a large, dark shadow swimming beneath them.

Ali stopped watching the water and she hoped the shadow wasn't something that liked attacking boats.

"Think I've got this little devil box sorted," Erc stated, rousing Ali from her concern about sea creatures.

Ali shifted a little closer to hear Erc's findings over the puttering of the engine and the boat hitting the water's surface.

"I searched for the frequency Sverre said it was on. It's very specific, and now it's giving me a direction…There's no way of telling distance, though."

Erc looked up from where she was still hunched over the device and squinted at the horizon.

"Head that way." She pointed in a direction to the side of Ali's course.

Ali complied, turning the boat in the direction pointed.

Erc continued frowning at the device for a moment.

"Little more to the left."

Ali adjusted.

"No, my left."

Ali corrected the course again.

Erc frowned at the device.

"That looks good." She looked up at Ali with an unsure smile. "I'm hoping this little dot will get closer as we do, but it may take some trial and error."

Ali nodded as she watched the sun sink lower on the horizon.

After what seemed like hours, the sun touched the ocean, and Erc stated they needed to find an island to spend the night.

Ali continued on course until they saw an island in the distance and headed toward that instead. They reached it as the sun disappeared, but luckily, two moons were already out with light bright enough to work.

Erc growled at having to set up camp after sundown, but they were able to get a fire going with a small Aequorian lighter without much difficulty. Erc pulled blankets out from the bottom of the basket before starting on the food.

Ali left dinner to Erc as she wandered to gather more firewood from among the dead vines and trees in the jungle.

She returned to their little camp as Erc turned two small squashes set directly in the fire. Erc handed Ali some fruit and dried meat to complete the meal.

They ate in silence, listening to the noise of the jungle and the sound of the ocean.

"How much further do you think it is?" Ali finally asked, "Any guesses?"

Erc frowned toward the boat where the device still sat. She shrugged after a moment.

"Don't know. We're a little closer to it, but not much." She paused and thought before settling into her blanket for the night. "At least another few days of steady travel."

Ali tried not to grimace as she too settled in for the night. Camping wasn't her favorite activity, even in such a gorgeous beach setting. She wanted to get back to Leon as quickly as possible.

"'Night," she whispered.

She listened until she heard Erc mumble something similar back.

Ali watched the fire and tried not to think of how Leon must feel with both her and Sverre gone. She hoped Incara and Charlton were doing well without Erc around too.

Sleep overtook her before she could worry too long about the subject.

CHAPTER 45

Lawr watched from his small, corner desk as Bry planned a counter for the newly arrived Nomads. He watched but could not rouse himself to help at all.

How long has Ali been gone? My neighbor thought I went after her, so around the time I left.

He frowned at the idea.

So long…And she's by herself with…with…

He had tried asking Bry and Shad about Sverre, but they did not know much and considered it more likely the Ghost had turned her over to someone else in Oracaede. He spiraled into new miserable speculation at that idea.

You're not going to get anywhere thinking about it. We need the beat the Nomads before anything else can be attempted. And the Wolf kid knew about the Ghost too…

Lawr leaned forward to stare at the AaD in front of him. He did not have any particular task to complete, so focusing on 'work' seemed as useless as worrying about his niece.

"Bry," Lawr fixed his gaze on the redhead and waited a moment to gain his attention, "how do you want me to help?"

Bry blinked a moment, either surprised Lawr was even in the room or trying to remember where he himself was. Lawr could not tell which.

"Huh?"

Bry, ever the master of eloquence, expressed his confusion.

"What do you want me to do about the Nomads?" Lawr spoke in a slow, easy tone to give Bry time to blink through bloodshot eyes and think.

"Oh," Bry straightened the hunch out of his shoulders as he rubbed his neck and frowned at the contents of the top of his desk, "give me a sec to think."

Lawr nodded and watched the king's face shift through several expressive frowns. Finally, he settled into one and Lawr could guess Bry had settled on an idea.

"Well?" He queried, waiting expectantly.

Bry gave him an irritated look before returning to the thoughtful frown.

"Don't know if you'd be up for it?" Bry returned to rubbing his neck and tangled hair as he studied Lawr.

Lawr affixed the redhead with a glare he had dubbed are-you-kidding-me-punk.

Bry hunched his shoulder and focused on his desk again. "Sorry."

Lawr worked to keep his smirk under control. As usual, are-you-kidding-me-punk was a resounding success.

"We need to find those Wolf kids," Bry stated, back to full business planning mode. "I have a couple units of guards going around in every inn and campsite in the city, but there are a lot, and some people will try protecting them too."

Lawr nodded along, waiting to see if Bry had a more actionable idea than 'find them.'

"And I don't know if it's possible…"

Lawr tried not to flinch away from the phrase.

Usually, the answer to that phase is 'no, it's not possible,' but…

"Wherever they are in the city, they would surely be contacting the Nomads that just arrived. Is there any way you could use the AaDs to narrow down the location for my guards to search?"

Bry must have sensed Lawr's doubt as he quickly added, "Or maybe not?"

Lawr sighed, thinking through what he had done to reactivate the AaD network. He had not found any way to track individual calls at the time. The network seemed to have been designed precisely against such tracking or invasions of privacy.

"I don't know how we can find them quicker," Bry said.

Lawr paused in his thoughts to glance over at the man. Bry stood hunched over, leaning against his desk with a frustrated look that bordered on defeated.

Sorry, Ali. Lawr groaned at the thought of making his niece wait longer. *I'm gonna need Bry around to find you, kid. And he needs to get through this invasion first.*

"I can help with the current threat of the Nomads, too," Lawr reminded the king.

He ignored the gnawing pain in his gut that said he was abandoning Ali.

Bry watched him with a calculative look.

"I didn't want to assume," he tested.

Lawr nodded. "Thanks, but I'm good. I'll be assuming some help in finding Ali once your city isn't in immediate danger."

Bry smiled as relief slipped into his features. "Sounds fair."

The smile disappeared as the redhead returned to frowning at the mess of paperwork and AaDs on his desk.

"I'll give you some tasking once I come up with something," Bry assured without glancing up.

Lawr grunted when he noticed Bry could not see his nod.

"In the meantime," Lawr stood and took a moment to stretch and check Bry was actually listening, "I'll go check on the others, make sure Stori is good, and think on a way to find the Wolves."

Bry focused on him at the mention of Stori.

"I appreciate it."

Bry paused to smile again. The look morphed back to a frown just as quick as before.

"And make sure Shad isn't trying to sneak off and scout the Nomads himself."

Lawr scoffed at the real possibility there. "Will do."

He headed for the door and turned to head down to Stori's room first. He was not surprised that she was not there and headed to his next best guess, Klaas and Eleanora's chambers.

Lawr meandered through the halls and stairs, thinking about the Wolves and finding them until he arrived at the court healer's door. He knocked and waited.

Bustling and tell-tale fussing noises announced Eleanora's presents long before she opened the door.

"Oh, Lawr. It's so good to see you again. Stori told us about your niece, I'm so sorry. Come in, come in." She spoke with overwhelming sincerity and all at once, pulling him into a hug before ushering him inside.

"Is Stori here?" Lawr asked once her greetings had died down.

"Ahh, just came to visit to find her, huh?" Eleanora teased as she turned and lead the way back to the kitchen.

"Well, I'm here to see you, too. And to find Shad if he's around."

"Oh, are we having another one of your 'interventions' for Bry?" Eleanora cooed in amusement at the idea before snapping around to Lawr again, "Is he doing all right? Healthy? He hasn't come to visit and he's always so busy when I try to see him."

Lawr chuckled.

"Bry's Bry. His health is as much a priority to him as seeing to all the petty complains of the nobles is to you."

Eleanora looked affronted enough that Lawr remembered he still needed to watch for the lines in friendships that he wasn't supposed to cross.

How come I never improve in this area?

"My patients are a priority to me," Eleanora insisted, "I just have other things that are more important to do right now."

Lawr nodded as he moved passed her into the kitchen. "Yeah, exactly my point."

He was pleased to see Stori at the kitchen table with the giant wolfish beast she deigned to call a pet lounging by her feet. The creature cracked an eye open and lifted its head at Lawr's approach, but it relaxed back to the floor in a moment.

"Hello, Lawr. How are you?"

Stori's eyes fluctuated between concern and sorrow as she set her cup of tea down and focused her attention passed Klaas toward Lawr.

"I'm all right." Lawr smiled as her concern reminded him again of Ali.

"Trying to stay busy," he added hastily to distract from the sudden reminder of his niece.

Stori smiled. "Bry asked you to check on me," she said as a statement of fact rather than a question.

"I offered." Lawr shrugged. "Someone has a bad habit of overworking themselves."

A delicate eyebrow arched at that.

"You, me, or Bry?"

Lawr scoffed as Eleanora tutted her agreement.

"Touché."

A soft frown graced Stori's features at the unfamiliar word.

"It means 'good point,'" Lawr clarified.

Stori looked proud of herself for a moment before she returned to the conversation with a serious tone.

"Any news of Alisha? Or, Ali, is it?" She stumbled at the name, breaking her intense gaze for a moment.

"Ali. No, haven't heard anything new," Lawr answered.

He settled in the chair next to Stori and across from Klaas. The man nodded in acknowledgment before continuing to stare through Lawr.

"I can't believe those kids would take her, though," Eleanora chimed in, setting a cup of tea in front of Lawr and gesturing to the plate of cookies already set closest to Stori.

"We don't know if it was them or ones from a different tribe yet," Lawr corrected out of habit.

He grumbled to himself, "Would be good to ask them about it next time though."

"I know," Eleanora groaned to herself, "And if we could have just kept them around another day...I may have convinced them to join us too. What did they mean, 'if we could, we would?' Why couldn't they?"

Eleanora glanced around the table at her own question. Lawr had no more idea than she did.

Klaas hummed as he stroked his beard and reached for a cookie to gnaw on. Everyone turned to him and waited expectantly for him to speak.

"This might be well classified as an unsubstantiated rumor," Klaas started, glancing around the table to impart that he was not sure about the information.

Lawr and the others nodded.

"Each Wolf pack is raised together. They are put through hell together so that they'll bond. It's the same principle used in military special operation units. They just start much, much younger with these kids. The pack is the only family these kids have ever known. They're closer than siblings and would die for each other."

Klaas paused to brush crumbs out of this beard, but his frown darkened before he continued.

"Then that's used against them. Each team is created with at least one member suffering from some sort of terminal ailment. They are dependent on their Nomad tribe to survive. Once they bond with each other, they would prefer to all die in service to the Nomads than leave one member behind."

"That's cruel." Stori covered her mouth with one trembling hand and her belly with the other.

Klaas shrugged. "It's effective."

"Could…?" Stori cut herself off, glancing at Eleanora for an answer to the unasked question.

"If they came here, I would do everything I could to find a treatment, but we don't even know which one it is. We only met the two." Eleanora clenched her hands together, glaring at the table, "The Nomads using children like that. It's despicable."

Klaas and Lawr both grunted in agreement.

Lawr frowned as a small thread of guilt over the hatred he had let himself build against the Wolves manifested.

"We couldn't even find them to try and help," Stori lamented.

"They could come to us," Eleanora offered with a sigh, "not that they would."

Lawr shot up at the sudden idea. He grumbled to himself while heading for the door.

Couldn't trace a call from an AaD, but I can easily message every AaD in the city…Maybe…

He frowned. He had an idea for how to do that location-based messaging from fixing the network, but he was not sure if it would work the way he needed it to.

Lawr stopped as he reached the door of the chamber. He had one other task he needed to do before finding Bry again.

He returned and popped his head back into the kitchen.

"And if you see Shad, tell him to come find me. He's been avoiding me since we returned to Sentre."

Lawr heard the women call out an 'all right' but he was already back at the door and hurrying to find an AaD to test out his theory.

CHAPTER 46

Hid watched from the window as Aike traced a careful path down the alleyway. He hated that Aike was leaving again to meet with Reb alone. The woman was so unpredictable and violent at the slightest provocation.

If only Dain could go to watch his back.

It still surprised him how comfortable he had become in trusting the assassins. But he knew he could have trusted Dain's long-distance support to protect Aike.

However, Dain was scouting the castle, and Reb had ordered Aike to come alone.

Hid turned back to the room.

Idir was out with the soldiers gathering updates and Retha was out, being Retha. She was probably gathering ingredients for bombs.

The rest of the Wolves and Sverre were hunkered down in the inn room, keeping a low profile.

"Hidalgo?"

Hid started and snapped to attention at the sound of his name. Sverre was staring at him expectantly.

"Sorry, what?"

Sverre blinked slowly.

Amused.

Hid smiled. He was getting much better at reading the solemn one too.

Sverre refocused on the scattered pages of notes on the coffee table in front of him.

"I asked how you planned on convincing the soldiers Jair is actually working against Brynte. There is not much to work with here."

Hid frowned. He was still working the details of that out himself.

"Whoa. Slow down there, chatterbox." Sa'dia propped herself up from her position of napping on the floor. "That's the most words you've slung together in one go since you've been here. We need to celebrate or something."

"Sa'dia." Hid glared at her for the joke. All he needed was for Bary to pick an argument about—

"No, no. Remember when he threatens to rip Duqa's tongue out," Bary was already ready to argue, "that was more words."

Sverre scoffed but Hid noticed his ashen skin had reddened. Unfortunately, Sa'dia noticed too.

"Yeah, I remember." She cleared her throat and deepened her voice in mimicry, "'Through your throat.'"

"Sa'dia." Hid glared harder and shook his head. Even he was surprised at how well the team had warmed up to Sverre, enough to tease the Ghost.

Sa'dia laid back down with a smirk and winked at Sverre.

The albino remained silent, but turned to Hid, still expectant of an answer.

"Spreading rumors is fine, but we need something actionable to attribute to the general."

Hid nodded to himself, pulling at the shaggy ends of his hair. It had been too long since, Xiulan, their resident beautician, had been able to cut any of their hair.

"You can say that again," Bary said as he and Caesar Apollo had to writhe around each other in the tiny kitchen. They each successfully burned yet another element of lunch.

"This time we need to cause some major havoc and get the soldiers to believe it was tasked by Jair."

"Should be easy enough," Sa'dia grumbled without opening her eyes to distract from her nap.

Hid hummed with doubt. "I don't know about easy, but it might be doable."

He spent a moment frowning and stressing about it before turning to Sverre. "That sounds good, or do you have any other plans?"

"Reasonable plan," Sverre said in his low voice.

He glanced at Hid with what Hid recognized as an abashed smile, even if it was barely noticeable.

"I'm not much of a strategist, so—"

A spurt of flame from the kitchen interrupted Sverre.

Bary extinguished the fire quickly as he and Caesar Apollo were left staring at the charred remains of lunch.

"Anyone for charcoal?" Sa'dia jeered, wrinkling her nose at the smell. She sat up and glowered at the smokey kitchen.

Hid sighed and rubbed his head again. He did not know how it always happened, but no matter what rotations they took, at some point, the two Wolves who absolutely could not cook always ended up in the kitchen together.

Sverre stood from the couch and sauntered into the smoke-filled kitchen.

"Err, lunch might be a-a little late," Bary stated as he and Caesar Apollo took their chance to squeeze passed Sverre and out of the cramped space.

The assassin took a moment to examine the remains of the food before throwing it all into the trash.

Bary and Caesar Apollo grumbled at the act. Saying something about it still being somewhat edible.

Stone-cold, crimson eyes fixed a glare at each of them in turn.

The grumbling stopped.

"Bary," the assassin's quiet voice held the attention of every person in the room as usual, "wash the rice first. Caesar Apollo, chop the vegetables."

A practiced hand made quick work of roughly chopping the nearest carrot before handing the knife toward the musclebound reminiscence of Greek sculptures.

Hid stared, once again shocked and awed at the hidden skills the assassin possessed.

The Ghost continued with quiet, patient instructions to guide the two hapless cooks toward a meal that, even to Hid's lax standards, looked phenomenal.

Dain, Retha, and Idir returned as though drawn by the smell of an edible lunch.

"Hey, there was a message sent from the castle directed to you guys— Is Sverre cooking?" Dain glanced up from his AaD to ask.

"It seems like it," Hid answered hoping for a clue or information if that feat was normal.

"All right." The sniper danced over to the kitchen and slapped his friend on the back before he was immediately distracted by the food Bary and Caesar Apollo were just finishing.

Hid waited a spell for the man to continue what he had been saying, but he gave up and turned to Idir.

"A message? Did you see it too?"

Idir nodded and handed over one of the teams' AaD.

"Sent all AaDs we saw," Idir stated.

He glanced over the message with a frown.

"Xiulan." He looked over to the girl as he noticed Dain was showing the message to Sverre and the two in the kitchen.

Xiulan gracefully removed herself from the couch and sashayed to Hid's side. She read the message over, a small frown clouded her features as she did.

The message was short but no less confusing for it. It stated in a concise fashion that the court healer would be ready and willing to treat any member of the group associated with the two kids recently imprisoned in the castle. It stated explicitly the goal to find a cure for a member's long-term ailment.

Xiulan shook her head, still in thought.

"Neither Aike nor I mentioned anything of Bary or his condition. The court healer, Eleanora, did come to treat me when I was ill."

"You were ill?"

Hid tried to keep the exasperation out of his voice.

Aike, you should have mentioned that...

Xiulan still ducked her head a fraction. "A mild food allergy. The healer was very kind and already chastised me for ignoring it."

Hid fidgeted with this new concern. He watched Xiulan for honesty and was finally satisfied, though still worried. He decided to drop the point for the time being.

He leveled his anxious gaze toward the kitchen.

Bary was glancing with a frown between Dain's device and the rest of the group. He raised his hands in surrender.

"I have not told a soul here of my condition."

Hid never doubted that, but it did not lessen his concern that their current enemy knew about it.

"The methods the Avare use to keep their Wolves in check is not a tightly guarded secret," Sverre stated, reminding Hid of the Ghost's presence when he moved back to the living room.

Hid spared a moment's concern to consider if the assassins had known about Bary previously, but he scoffed over it.

Of course they did. Oracaede is informed about everything.

The lack of surprise from either assassin was as much of a confirmation as Hid could expect.

"Why would they send this though?" Sa'dia was up and pacing, consciously or not, she ended up in a protective position near Bary, "It's a trap, right? It's got to be."

Hid returned to frowning at the AaD in his hands at that fear. A trap seemed likely, but if there was *any* chance of curing Bary…He could not just ignore that.

No one has ever offered help like this before…

"You should take them up on it." Sverre's quiet voice nearby shocked Hid.

He agrees?

Dain had taken up residence behind Sverre, leaning against the couch. He too was nodding.

"It could still be a trap…" Sa'dia moved in front of Sverre with a glare and crossed arms, "What happens then?"

"You guys come break me out." Bary moved toward Hid, ignoring Sa'dia even as he was picking a fight, "We already proved it's not difficult to do."

Bary stood square in front of Hid, eyes pleading for the chance. Hid knew Bary would do anything, no matter how dangerous, if it meant no longer being the one tying them to Reb and the Avare.

"The rest of us will continue work as usual," Dain added, "if they can't help, then no harm done."

"If they can help Bary," Sverre picked up without missing a beat, "then you don't have to complete this job. Or any suicidal side missions."

Hid's stomach did a flip as he and every Wolf stared at Sverre.

He knows.

Hid gulped his suddenly dry throat.

Of course he knows, but damn…some element of surprise would have been useful.

The crimson eyes burned into Hid's as silence held the room.

Hid broke the stare. He dropped his gaze to his shaking hands and read the message again.

"Sa'dia," Hid squeezed his eyes shut, hoping this was not about to be a major mistake before he focused on the tanned girl. "You'll accompany Bary."

Sa'dia jerked a nod without a word of complaint.

Bary sighed in relief as he stepped back to stand next to his partner.

"I'll update Aike on the plan," Hid stated while the attention of the room was still on him.

He's going to need to be much more cautious of what Reb knows now.

CHAPTER 47

"The Nomads are already attacking my sphaere, and you want to invite them into the castle?" Bry squeezed the bridge of his nose as the little bone there still refused to break despite his best efforts.

"A calculated risk," Lawr stated with his usual indifference which, at that moment, made Bry want to punch him.

"I may not be great at math, but that seems like a miscalculation," Bry fumed.

He glanced at Shad but his friend was remaining stubbornly silent.

"No, it's not."

Irritation finally breached the facade of apathy as Lawr leaned forward against his desk and skewered Bry with an unyielding glare.

"You've already seen we can't beat the Wolves at their own game," Lawr continued for the first time, giving an explanation, "the only thing left to do is to take them out of the equation. And you're not going to kill a bunch of kids any more than I am. Leaving only this option."

"Fine," Bry ground out, "but that didn't need to involve Eleanora or inviting them to the castle."

"If you have a better idea that doesn't involve sacrificing whichever kid is terminally ill..." Lawr stretched his arms open, inviting any unheard ideas.

Bry growled, but his retort was interrupted by a knock at the door.

"Come in," Bry growled, still holding Lawr's glare.

A guard entered, took stock of the mood in the room, and was already backing out before he spoke.

"Two kids came to see the court healer in response to the message Mr. Lawrence put out. Mrs. Eleanora asked for you to visit her, Your Majesty."

Bry shared a quick look of surprise with both Shad and Lawr before they all darted out of the room after the long-escaped guard and headed toward Klaas and Eleanora's chambers.

They entered the rooms a breath after knocking without waiting for an answer.

Bry led the way through the mess of a living room and kitchen to one of the exam rooms, following the sound of voices.

Pushing open the door, Bry took stock of Klaas standing immediately inside the room and Eleanora, sitting in her chair in front of a curly-haired kid.

Bry recognized the boy from Jair's drawing for the warrant. He was struck by how young the kid was.

A girl of tanned complexion and hawkish features hovered at the boy's side with a glower of distrust for everyone in the room.

Eleanora nodded to Bry in acknowledgment before turning her attention back to her patient.

"Look, Barry—"

"Bār-REE," The girl corrected with a growl, "his name is pronounced Bar-ree."

"Cool it, Sa'dia, we're fine." The boy said, though his eyes did not have the same confidence as his voice as he studied Bry, Shad, and Lawr in turn.

Sa'dia scoffed and grumbled an insult Bry could not hear as she continued to shift her weight and clench her crossed arms tighter around herself.

"Right, Bary, why don't you tell me more about your condition?" Eleanora encouraged with a smile.

She waved a hand toward Bry when she noticed her patient was distracted.

"Give us a moment, would you Bry?"

Bry glanced at Klaas and relaxed when the man nodded it was fine. He turned back to the girl.

"Sa'dia, is it? Would you mind chatting with us for a moment?" Bry asked.

Shad and Lawr were quick to back out of the doorway and settle around the kitchen table with an inviting chair open for the girl.

The two kids shared a nervous glance before the girl moved out of the room.

"You'll be fine, I promise, I just want to talk," Bry added, though it did not alleviate either of their hesitancy.

Sa'dia sneered at him but remained silent as she moved passed him into the kitchen.

"Aike and Xiulan make it out safely? Guess they must have if you two are back." Shad was quick to offer the girl a seat as he rambled, "Want some cookies? I think Eleanora has some around here somewhere."

The girl took the offered seat, ostensibly growling at the wraith though her posture was already more relaxed.

"It's like Aike 2.0. You're never gonna shut up either, are you?" She griped as she snatched a cookie the moment one was within reach.

"Technically, Aike is a Shad 2.0 because I'm older," Shad stated with such pride even Bry had to scoff.

"Really? I couldn't tell." Sa'dia rolled her eyes though she still looked amused.

Lawr sat in the seat diagonally from the girl with the same observant gaze as usual.

Bry took a seat on Sa'dia's side of the table so she didn't feel she was being interrogated by a three-against-one inquisition. He made sure to give her a comfortable amount of space though.

"Anything you could tell us about why the Nomads sent you here?" Bry asked.

If he still had any skill in reading people, he could tell the young Wolf would not respond to subtlety.

"Well, no." Sa'dia frowned and focused on an intense study of the half of a cookie still in her hands.

"Which tribe are you from?" Lawr surprised both Bry and the girl with his sudden question.

"Aynur." She blinked.

Bry watched Lawr's expression darken.

"You kidnapped a young woman from Terrae, who did you sell her to?"

Sa'dia cocked her head to the side. "Recently?"

Lawr's jaw clenched tight, "Yes."

"We brought her back to the marketplace, don't know what happened to her after." She scrunched up her face in thought. "I think that job was for Oracaede, though."

Lawr clenched his fists as he continued glaring. "You don't even remember the job?"

Sa'dia shrugged, nonchalant at the older man's quiet rage.

"Not really, no."

"Lawr, take a breath," Bry ordered, holding out a hand to placate the man.

Lawr's gaze snapped to Bry for a short moment before returning to the girl.

"Look, she's important," Shad jumped in before Lawr could say anything. "We're trying to find her."

Sa'dia's features changed to a remorseful frown.

"Sorry, I have no idea what happened to her after we returned to the marketplace." She furrowed her brows. "She was supposed to be handed over to Oracaede, but I got the sense they were just going to sell her at the market. She was pretty."

She mumbled the last sentence while she returned to focusing on the cookie in her hands.

Bry leaned back, cautiously stealing glances toward Lawr. The man was glaring with the focus of trying to set the table on fire as he sporadically clenched his fists.

Bry looked away. He hated seeing the man he had come to rely on for his level-headedness fight to keep his composure.

"So, they weren't going to give her to Oracaede, but ended up selling her to the Ghost anyway." Shad shook his head at the idea.

"What?" Sa'dia's head snapped up as her hawkish eyes zeroed in on Shad. "They sold her to Sverre?"

Lawr snapped to attention at that while Shad smiled a sly look.

"You guys do know him personally then?" Lawr's tone held the hint of a question, but it was more of a statement searching for confirmation.

Sa'dia's eyes were wide as she stuttered at an answer.

"W-what? N-no I...I don't..."

Lawr leaned forward, holding her gaze.

"There aren't that many people who know of Oracaede's Ghost being still around and fewer who know his name is Sverre."

Panic overtook Sa'dia's features as she continued stuttering nonsensical excuses.

Shad reached out to grab her hands and attention.

"Hey, it's okay." He released her hands once she stopped trying to speak. "We're just trying to figure out what's going on and where the girl is."

The panic settled out of the girl's face, but a cold, impassive look took its place.

"I can't tell you anything about Sverre, I have no idea where the girl is, and I'm not talking about our job."

Bry frowned and pulled at his tangled hair.

There goes our chance of getting any intel.

"What if Eleanora is able to get Bary a treatment here?" Lawr's gaze remained sharp as he continued his focused stare.

Sa'dia looked thoughtful. When she met Lawr's eyes again, her gaze was doubtful but mixed with a smidge of hope.

"It would be up to our team leader, not me. But, if we didn't have to work for the Avare, we wouldn't. And I'd tell you…anything that doesn't endanger the rest of our team."

She paused before shrugging, "But I still don't know what happened to your girl, just…" She trailed off, shifting with uncertainty in her seat.

"Just…?" Shad pushed.

Sa'dia glanced between them all.

"He's not a creep," she finally stated, "Sverre, I mean. If he has her, I don't think he'd do anything to hurt her. With us, at least, he's protective a-and kind. He's way too decent for what he does for Oracaede."

Lawr stared a long moment as he seemed to be processing the information.

"I want to know about him, anything you know," he said finally, "when Bary's treatment is sorted."

"Do you…" Sa'dia frowned before she tried again, "Do you really think the healer woman will be able to help Bary?"

Shad laughed and Bry had to share a smile with him.

"Believe me, if there is anything that can possibly be done for your friend, Eleanora will do it."

Bry stated with a nod.

"She's still worried about Xiulan," Shad added, "Eleanora isn't going to help Bary because we need it, she'll do whatever she can just because she cares."

Sa'dia smiled at that.

"I don't understand you people."

CHAPTER 48

Bry left the healer's chambers with Lawr in tow and a more optimistic outlook on the current mess his sphaere was in. Shad remained behind to keep the girl company and tell Bry of any news once Eleanora was finished.

By the amount of time Eleanora was spending with the boy, Bry guessed whatever medical issue he had was severe.

Bry and Lawr had almost reached the study when Chesler ambushed them.

"Your Majesty," Chesler started, sparing Lawr a quick nod of greeting before launching into the purpose of speaking to them, "it has come to Jair's attention that several soldiers believe he is still rebelling against you."

Chesler turned and marched toward Bry's study, leaving Bry and Lawr to exchange confused glances before hurrying to catch up.

Chesler continued speaking without waiting for them.

"Jair immediately brought it to me, and he's currently in the training yard trying to find out how these rumors started."

"I'm betting on the Wolves," Bry chirped the thought with as much energy as he could manage.

He looked around and remembered Shad was not there to add choice words about the situation.

They entered his study and Bry immediately started pacing as Lawr sat at his small corner desk.

"How are the soldiers reacting?" Lawr asked, perching his head atop steepled hands.

"Unfortunately." Chesler scowled.

Bry waited for the man to continue until he realized he had meant the word as a sentence to itself.

"They believe Jair is against me? Why?"

Chesler exhaled heavily.

"Because they want to. It's easier for them to believe they were right in distrusting you than it is for them to see they've been deceived."

"So my going to Oroitz accomplished nothing. They still don't trust me." Bry could not stop the dejection from slipping into his tone.

"Not entirely," Chesler stated with a rare show of conscientiousness, pretending not to notice the change in tone, "the soldiers who worked with you directly in the battle are still supporting you."

Chesler shuffled around on his AaD a moment to find something.

"On that note, I am making a recommendation for a promotion for First Lieutenant Ammon Torvis. He earned many recommendations from his superiors in the battle, and he has been ardently defending you since returning to the castle training grounds."

Bry smiled. "Ammon, yeah, he's a friend."

Chesler arched an eyebrow.

"He was the one who brought Harailt's disloyalty to my attention in Oroitz, I worked with him before I became king."

"Well, it's good you have at least one person who knows you and will defend you."

Chesler stated in an off-hand manner, ignoring the glare Bry leveled at him.

"How can Bry convince the soldiers Jair is loyal to him?" Lawr asked, drawing Bry's attention away from how much he truly disliked Chesler and back to the real issue.

Chesler focused on Lawr a moment before changing to stare at his AaD with a frown.

"I don't know yet."

"Great." Bry huffed to himself as he interrupted his pacing to sit at his desk.

"What are the soldiers distrustful of Bry about?" Lawr asked, still in his problem-solving mode. "Any specific issues?"

Chesler remained focused on his AaD and glowering.

"It's more a culmination of all the rumors the Wolves have spread and what Brynte stated about Oracaede. The troops think you were doing something shady in Oroitz, but everyone has a different idea of what."

Some of Chesler's irritation was evident in his voice as he paused to massage his temple before continuing with a shake of his head.

"They trust Jair because he has a reputation for acting against the king. Vlasis, specifically, but they are extrapolating that against you."

"So the reason I trusted him in the first place is the same reason my soldiers think he must be against me? Fantastic."

Bry rolled his eyes. He was still at a loss for what he could do to fix that trust.

"You certainly won't be able to talk them into trusting you," Chesler stated, again agitating Bry's shot nerves.

"Thanks for stating the obvious, don't know what I would have thought without the clarification."

Chesler growled.

"I mean, you will have to think of something more actionable. I can't do *that* for you."

Bry turned his glower to the man, "Well, you are here to suggest plans, aren't you? No genius ideas then, huh?"

Chesler held his glare just as steady.

"Jumping into situations without thinking them through is more your forte."

Bry jerked up to stand and stocked toward the man.

"Hey, I think things through, I just do it faster than you."

"If that were the case, would we be—"

"Enough!"

Lawr stood from his desk and fixed his death glare on both of them in turn.

"Both of you need to cool it. We have problems to solve and plans to make."

Bry glared at Lawr with a comeback ready, but the man continued speaking first.

"The threat we should be concerned with are the Nomads. How are we going to deal with them given our current predicament?"

A huff pulled Bry's attention back to Chesler. He snarled, ready to snap if the man wanted to keep arguing.

Chesler had focused his glare at the AaD he held as his face contorted with all kinds of thoughts.

Bry dropped his glare just as quick, irritated that he was the only one still ready to fight.

Not kingly…

How those words still haunted him. He focused on controlling his irritation and emotions in the space of silence while the others were thinking.

"Planning and preparations can be done around the soldiers as a start." Chesler stated after a moment.

"What?" Bry frowned back.

He had focused so much on controlling himself that he was slow to catch what Chesler meant.

"You have work to do planning how to counter the Nomads still," Chesler started again without the previous condescension, "rather than doing it up here…"

"Interact with Jair and the other soldiers." Bry finally caught up to Chesler's idea, but he continued grimacing. "It's a good start."

He left out the 'I suppose' but continued thinking. He was not having any better luck with ideas for repairing trust than he had earlier.

"All right, I'll go find Jair."

Bry nodded and started gathering some of his plans from off the surface of his desk and the floor around it.

"He's down with the soldiers training," Chesler offered on his way out the door.

Bry grunted acknowledgment as he also exited the study to find the general.

CHAPTER 49

Ali watched the horizon as the sun sank into it. At the end of day three of their little trip, Erc said it looked like they were at least nearing their target.

Hopefully.

Ali turned the boat, steering it toward the nearest island where they could stay the night. She ran the boat up onto the sandy beach.

Erc jumped out, carrying the heavy rope to the nearest tree to secure the boat for the night.

Ali gathered the few supplies they would need immediately from the bottom of the boat and hobbled a few steps with them before setting them down on the beach.

"Those are fruit trees." Erc pointed through the jungle of the island.

Ali squinted at the expanse of the jungle, but she could not tell which ones Erc was pointing at. The dark woman was already heading into the jungle, shotgun in hand.

"I'll start the fire," Ali called after her.

She dug a small pit and gathered firewood from the jungle's edge. Night was already upon them as the fire roared to life from lots of small twig encouragements from Ali.

With step one completed, Ali moved on to preparing dinner. She glanced to the dark wilderness every other moment, waiting for Erc to reappear.

A growl caught her attention. Ali squinted into the darkness but could not discern anything.

"Erc?"

Ali stood and held the rifle close. Something rustled in the undergrowth. Ali clicked the safety off as she stared into the dark.

"Erc!?"

Bang!

Ali flinched at the gunshot from the depth of the jungle. She held her breath and listened.

Silence.

Ali raised her rifle to the undergrowth as she heard another rustling sound. She took a step back toward the boat as she did.

A muted shout caught her ears.

"Erc!" Ali moved closer to the tree line.

"Get in the boat!"

Ali raced to the line securing the boat to the tree and hastened to undo it. She heard Erc continue to shout about getting in the boat as the voice grew closer.

She finally freed the boat and shoved it back until it was free of the sandbar. She hopped in, still holding the rope tied to the tree to make sure she did not drift from the beach.

She focused on the beach again, watching for any sign of movement.

All was still.

Ali could not breathe normally as she waited, tense and gripping the rope.

Erc broke through the tree line in a dead run.

"Push off!" Erc shouted, waving the shotgun.

Ali dropped the rope and grabbed an oar, shoving it against the sand.

A snarl from the beach caught Ali's attention again. A large animal, like a panther, covered in thick scales with a long, whip-like tail, burst through the trees, bounding after Erc.

Erc reached the boat and pushed it further into the water before jumping in and diving for the motor.

Ali flung the oar back into the boat and grabbed her rifle. She pointed it as the creature leaped for the boat.

BANG!

Ali's head rang from the noise of the shot. A splash in front of her made her look at the creature.

It swam and darted from the water in great disgust.

The engine roared and the boat started moving backward.

Ali spared a glance at Erc. The woman was still panting. She focused her attention on the beach.

Looking back, Ali thought she had missed the animal altogether until she saw it was favoring its hind leg.

Three more scaled creatures emerged on the beach. All four started tearing into the food Ali had made for dinner.

Lucky the basket was on the boat.

Ali clenched the rifle in a white-knuckled grip as she sat back in the boat.

Behind her, she heard Erc take a shaky breath.

Ali turned and squinted in the dim light at the woman.

"Are you okay?"

Erc nodded and wiped the sweat from her face. She had the same white-knuckled grip on her shotgun that Ali had on the rifle, but she relaxed it sooner.

"Those were Pythers. They're nasty creatures but don't like the water," Erc stated with a strained chuckle as she set her gun down.

Ali looked back at the island as it faded from view.

"They sure picked the wrong sphaere to live."

Erc hummed in agreement.

"Looks like you get to try camping in an open dingy on this trip too," Erc mused with a grin as she cut the engine and shifted to drop the small anchor.

"Sounds better than stopping at another island."

Ali mumbled as she moved to the basket and took out what remained of their food supplies.

"We're going to have to find food tomorrow."

She handed Erc her portion as the woman sat down again.

Ali set a portion of her own aside for breakfast and saw Erc doing the same.

She settled in for what she imagined would be a long night of rocking. The night was long, but Ali surprised herself with how much of it she slept through.

When the morning light woke her, Ali took to scanning the horizon for an island other than the one from last night. She could only see one other, just barely visible in the distance.

Ali contemplated waking Erc up with the motor or just waiting. She munched on the last of her potion of dinner for breakfast as she thought.

The decision was moot when Erc woke up shortly after Ali had and stared around with a groggy irritation at the morning world.

"I was going to head to that island to look for supplies." Ali pointed toward the destination as she stood and carefully moved past Erc to the motor.

Erc grumbled something of an affirmative and shifted out of the way.

Ali drove them to the island and remained more cautious than before, keeping her gun close as they each moved off into the trees to relieve themselves and then find food.

Ali's search ended quickly and successfully as the island was not short on edible trees and plants she could recognize from what Erc served at her house.

She gathered what she could carry and returned to the boat. Erc was already there, sorting her haul into the basket.

They were underway again in short order, heading back the way they had come.

The morning faded to afternoon the same as it had the past three days.

"We're getting close," Erc finally said after they finished their lunch.

Erc remained frowning at the device in her hands, the same way she had been the entire trip.

Ali sat up straighter and scanned the islands on the horizon. There were a half dozen within view.

The idea of finding whatever monster took the blocker was less appealing after the encounter with the Pythers.

At least they didn't swim.

"A little to the left," Erc said with a gesture to clarify the direction.

Ali adjusted their course, heading directly for a large island with a mountain on it.

"This island, or around it?" Ali asked.

"Around."

Erc's voice sounded unsure as she watched the device while Ali steered them around it.

"No, this is it," Erc corrected, "It's on this back side of the island."

Ali nodded.

Around the back of the island was a large inlet. Ali directed the boat to and edged closer.

Erc hopped out and scouted the area, stopping when she found some vines to use in place of the rope they had lost.

Once they had the boat secured, Erc helped Ali out with a motion for her to stay behind Erc.

Ali tried in vain to swallow her nerves as she tightened her grip on the rifle and followed.

They crept around the rocky edge of the inlet toward the back. A half-flooded cave continued in from the inlet under the mountain.

"Give me the rifle," Erc ordered once they reached the mouth of the cave, holding the shotgun out to Ali.

Ali accepted the trade with relief that she would not need to aim, but a small twinge of regret that she still could not handle the rifle well enough to be of use.

Erc led the way, skirting the rocks along the edge of the cave with a nimbleness Ali could only envy. Ali followed without even attempting to be as graceful as Erc, only focusing on being quiet and keeping a strong grip on the gun.

Near an outcropping or boulders near the back of the cave, Erc held up her hand to stop. Erc crouched and motioned for silence as she tilted her head to listen.

Ali crouched next to her and strained to hear what Erc had. She caught the sound in a moment.

Breathing.

Deep and heavy breathing. From some large creature coming from the other side of the boulders.

CHAPTER 50

R eb glowered out at the world from the edge of her tent.
Our tent.
Erasyl's voice echoed around Reb's head as she snarled at it.
"My tent. You left." Reb growled, hoping to silence the voice.
In her mind, she could see her husband smirk at the correction.
"Uhh, Chief? Do you want me to leave?"
"No," Reb snapped, turning back to her third least favorite person in existence, after the two assassins, of course.
The useless Wolf knelt, watching her with a cautious gaze. A hint of his habitual smile made Reb want to punch it off his face.
"Shut up, unless reporting," Reb stated, pacing the space in the tent.
"Yes, Chief," Aike said, his voice not quite hiding his accent.
She hated his accent even more than his stupid smile. Something in it sounded like Erasyl.
"We were not expecting the arrival of the Avare so soon, there are still preparations we were unable to complete," Aike continued in a toneless droll. "We are working with the assassins to complete as much as possible while the king reacts to your—"
"You haven't killed them yet?!" Reb screeched.
If she had anything in her hands, she would have chucked it at him.
How could they not have avenged Erasyl?
Her mind screamed at the affront, drowning out Erasyl's voice asking why they would care.
"There has not been any opportunity to kill either of them," Aike replied.

Reb flew over to him, snatching him up by his jacket.

"You haven't made opportunity," she jeered.

Aike looked startled as he ducked his head. Reb could see thoughts, and fear flit across his face.

She smirked.

Fear is only look damned Wolf should have.

"They are the best Oracaede agents in all the worlds, Chief," Aike said finally, the fear changed to a quiet confidence Reb hated, "if killing them were easy, everyone else would have done so by now."

Reb snarled and backhanded him. One of her rings cut a line of blood in his cheek.

She smiled at any drawn blood, but the boy's expression shifted immediately into one of expectant apathy.

She released his jacket and shoved him away. It irritated her even more that he did not fall over, just pivoted on his knee.

Reb spun around so she did not have to look at him anymore.

"Finish report."

"Yes, Chief. The king hasn't reacted to your arrival yet, but we will be focusing on turning the soldiers that already distrust him.

Reb glowered at the wall of the tent before moving to pace again.

Wolves can't even turn soldiers yet? Useless.

She paused, hoping that if her husband's ghost was going to haunt her, he might at least offer useful suggestions.

In her mind, Erasyl remained stubbornly silent and smirking.

"Soldiers not even against king?!"

Reb stormed back to the kneeling man. She grabbed a handful of his jacket again and wrenched him up into a standing position.

"What have you been doing in city?!"

"We planned with anticipation of having more time," Aike stated in a slow, methodical voice.

Reb growled again and threw him back.

"My fault, then? Eh?"

Aike's face flashed with the fear and confusion Reb loved as he scrambled to his kneeling position again.

Erasyl's voice pitched in that she was being too irrational. The one thing she absolutely hated to hear from her husband.

Aike was still talking.

"N-no. I d-didn't mean that—"

"Shut up!"

Reb grabbed a clay jar and hurled it toward Aike's face. Luckily, Erasyl seemed to take the hint as well as his voice ceased, but he was still smirking.

Reb grumbled to herself as she went back to pacing. She spared a glance to Aike. One side of his face was a bloody mess, and a piece of the clay jar was still embedded in his cheek.

Good. Should learn stay quiet.

Reb paused at the entrance of the tent to glance out.

"Your report finished?"

"Yes." A hitch in his voice annoyed her with the knowledge that he was not done talking.

"Bary needs more medicine."

Reb scoffed and turned back to him.

"He should have enough," Reb said as a dismissal.

Aike remained where he was, his face pinched in pain as he kept one eye squeezed shut.

"He will run out before this battle is over. I could return then, but it would be more difficult and would interrupt your plans..."

Reb glared at him for the tentative threat of the further inconvenience he would cause in his voice.

She stomped over to the corner chest and pulled out a small vial.

"Useless Wolves," Reb growled as she chucked the vial at Aike. He snatched it out of the air without any trouble.

"Thank you, Chief."

"Dismissed!" Reb shouted.

He was gone in an instant, leaving her alone with a smirking Erasyl.

Touchy, touchy.

Reb ignored her husband's voice as he, too, faded in her mind.

CHAPTER 51

Aike trudged through the gate into Sentre. He took every back alley
he saw toward the inn his team would be staying in.

The blood on his face had dried to tacky, sealing his one eye
shut. He was not sure he wanted to try opening it anyway. He did not know
if he was blind in that eye now or if it had just been the blood, but he
dreaded finding out.

A passerby gave him a startled look, which he tried to return with a
smile, but it was not quite working.

The shard of clay still in his face hampered his facial movements, but it
was so close to his eye, he did not dare try to pull it out.

Aike settled for pulling his hood tighter to hide his injury.

Hid's going to lose it when he sees this.

The thought was comforting as Aike climbed the stairs to their rooms.
He paused outside the door, trying to make his appearance a little less
dramatic. The blood staining his shirt and jacket made that difficult never-
mind his face.

Aike knocked out the code and pushed the door open slowly. His heart
sank when he did not see anyone in the room.

"You're injured."

Aike jumped and yelped as the Ghost appeared from the other side of
the door.

"Aike? You back?" Hid's voice called from one of the back bedrooms.

Aike breathed a sigh of relief until Sverre was in his face again.

The assassin gently touched his face to examine the wound.

"What happened? Reb?" Hid appeared in the doorway, blanched at the sight of the blood, and immediately rushed to Aike's side.

"Yeah, 'course." Aike tried to smile, but it had the same null effect as the last time.

"Can you open your eye?" Sverre's voice startled Aike again.

The assassin had moved to his blind side.

"Hmm, no. Not really."

Aike reached into his pocket and pulled out Bary's vial of medicine. He only had a small hope of distracting the two away from his injuries, but he tried anyway.

"I got extra. Think the healer could replicate it?" Aike asked, waving the vial in front of Hid as distractingly as possible.

Hid frowned at him, only sparing a parting glance at the vial.

"I could bandage this up, but..." Hid trailed off, shifting his focus from the injury to Sverre.

"No."

Aike could see the assassin shaking his head before he moved again, back out of Aike's limited field of vision.

"I'll take him and the vial to the court healer," Sverre reappeared with his cloak and hood to hide his appearance.

"What? No." Aike turned to Hid for help, "You can patch this—"

"Aike."

The fear in Hid's voice, far beyond his normal level of anxiety, stopped Aike's complaint.

"I can't tell if your eye is injured or just your face, but..." Hid paused to swallow hard and glance toward Sverre, "but it doesn't look good."

Aike froze. His friend confirmed the idea already terrifying him, and it was too much. He had hoped worrywart Hid would say he was making a big deal out of nothing. He hoped it was just his fear and distrust of medical help that made it seem worse than it was.

But no...

"If a professional healer is willing to treat you, there is no reason not to go," Sverre said, resting a hand on Aike's shoulder.

Aike glanced at the concern reflected in crimson eyes.

You're supposed to be the enemy.

Aike swallowed and nodded.

"I'll call Sa'dia and let her know to expect you," Hid said, nodding to himself in an anxious, jerking fashion.

"Tell her to meet us in the courtyard by the stables," Sverre stated while he moved toward the door with a hand still on Aike's shoulder, directing him.

Aike let the Ghost lead the way toward the castle.

"How are you going to get inside?" Aike tried asking, "Aren't you public enemy number one?"

"I can sneak in," Sverre answered.

"'Course you can." Aike sighed. He had hoped for some comfort in conversation, but...

This is Sverre, after all. And Sverre just does not talk.

Sverre led the way, ducking in through one side door after another, none of which Aike had even guessed existed until they reached the stable.

Aike glanced around for Sa'dia and tried not to flinch when a pale hand wrapped around his arm. Sverre led the way to a door in the courtyard.

Aike did flinch when someone moved from the shadow of the doorway. He cursed his blind...

Temporarily blind.

...side that he could not see who it was.

"Aike?" Sa'dia's voice emanated from the person in the shadows as she stepped forward.

Her face and voice were filled with the same fear Hid had.

"Not as bad as it looks." Aike lied.

Sa'dia ignored him, instead exchanging a nod with Sverre as the assassin releases his grip on Aike's arm and Sa'dia took it up. She led him into the castle, speaking in a low voice as she did.

"I told Eleanora you're coming."

Aike just nodded as Sa'dia weaved through hallways that made Aike dizzy with the idea of trying to navigate.

"How's Bary? I got more medicine," Aike stated.

"That's good, Eleanora said it should help to have it on hand."

They stopped at a door, and Sa'dia knocked once before entering.

The room they entered was in such a state of mess, Aike instantly felt at home in it.

"Sa'dia? That you? You have my patient?" The familiar, high-pitched female voice called from around the divide.

The owner of the voice followed in a moment.

"Allo, ma'am. Eleanora, right? Remember me?" Aike greeted and tried to smile again, hoping the third time would be the charm.

It was not.

"Oh, my!" Eleanora rushed toward him, calling over her shoulder, "Klaas, my things! Now!"

Eleanora's gentle, wrinkled hands touched at his face while Sa'dia led him beyond the divide into one of the smaller side rooms.

The older man Aike recognized from his time in the dungeon as the healer's husband, Klaas, appeared with a bag of herbs and tools. He took one look at Aike and disappeared back to the kitchen.

He reappeared a moment later with a damp rag. The withered hand cautiously dabbed at the blood.

Eleanora never stopped talking. Anger toward whoever was responsible for the injury was intermingled with requests for different herbs and tools.

"You said having Bary's medicine could help you?" Aike tentatively interrupted the woman's tangent.

He took the vial from his pocket and handed it over to her.

"Oh, honey." Eleanora took the vial in firm hands, squeezing his in a reassuring gesture, "You're a good friend, aren't you?"

"I try."

Eleanora set the vial down on a table as she turned her attention toward combining herbs in a bowl. She accepted a hot kettle from Klaas and added the water to the herb mixture. She let it sit a short span before straining the tea and moving back to Aike.

"This is an anesthetic mix. It should knock you right out for this," she said as she set the bowl in his hands.

"It's all right," Aike stated in a quick reaction, trying to hand the bowl back, "I'd prefer to stay awake."

"Honey," Eleanora started with pain in her voice, "There is a shard very close to your eye. I'm not sure the damage it has already done, but I can't have you moving at all when I take it out."

Aike gulped as the fear he would be blind in that eye returned.

"Okay," he mumbled.

He swallowed the tea in a single hot gulp and handed the bowl back.

Sa'dia's voice came from somewhere beside him, but his vision was already darkening. "I'll be right here."

CHAPTER 52

Caelyn fidgeted. She twisted her hands together, twirled the pen on her desk, and tried doodling on a blank scroll in front of her, but she never focused on it long enough to create anything.

She had tried sewing new some of her new red feathers onto a scarf, but Rhoeo complained it was too loud and distracting. Caelyn had not tried sewing anything else, but she lamented the yellow scarf was still too boring without the feathers to consider wearing.

She stole a glance toward Rhoeo every other moment.

"It's a nice day out," she tried.

The guard woman grunted without looking up from the AaD she had been working on.

Caelyn paused her fidgeting to examine her bandaged fingers. Several nails had been torn off from her attempt...

She shook her head.

What was I even trying to do?

There was never an answer to that question. Caelyn had wondered if she was going crazy and if it would happen again, but so far nothing.

Her actions terrified her, but she was more afraid of what had driven her to try breaking into Rhoeo's room. The voices of her parents still haunted her mind when she let it wander.

"I thought maybe a ride in the countryside would be nice."

Caelyn tried again, hoping to rouse Rhoeo's attention.

The guard sighed and finally lifted her gaze to glare at Caelyn.

"M-maybe not."

Caelyn sunk further into her chair as Rhoeo grunted and returned her focus to the AaD.

Returning to twisting her fingers, Caelyn frowned. Rhoeo had been in a foul mood since the Nomads arrived in the sphaere.

Anyone would be upset about that.

Caelyn chided herself. She really did not know anything about the guard's past.

Maybe she has a personal grudge against them. Lots of people do, it's reasonable.

She nodded to herself about the rationalization. Rhoeo had mentioned having family near Oroitz, though the guard never visited them to make sure they were all right.

Maybe they were killed, and that's why she's upset.

Caelyn told herself that was perfectly reasonable and probably what was agitating the guard.

Still…

She glanced over to Rhoeo again. The guard had become so irritated about her talking to anyone after the last time Stori had come to visit. She had demanded to know everything that was said and chided Caelyn for not telling the queen to leave as soon as she arrived.

Caelyn was not sorry for that, even though she did apologize profusely for whatever Rhoeo had thought she had done wrong.

She missed talking to people, though. Even Stori, when they were arguing, was better than Rhoeo's irritated silence.

"Maybe I could go see Mygic." Caelyn hesitantly stood.

Even if Rhoeo did not want to go out for a ride, she at least should not begrudge Caelyn seeing her horse.

That's reasonable, right?

The guard's eyes were on Caelyn again.

"Is that really a good idea?" Rhoeo asked. "With all the soldiers trying to prepare for battle, you'd just be in the way."

Caelyn sank back into her seat.

"I could help, maybe?" she mumbled, unsure of what she would actually do.

Rhoeo continued, ignoring Caelyn's comment. "Besides, the king is down there. You don't want to bump into Brynte, do you?"

Caelyn ducked her head and mumbled. She almost would not mind talking to Brynte. It would be better than not talking with anyone as she had been the last many days. She missed people.

I don't know why Rhoeo's being so mean and antisocial. Just cause she doesn't want to talk to people, doesn't mean I can't.

Caelyn pulled at her bandages again while she ruminated on the frustrating thought.

Rhoeo sat back at a seeming thought. She tapped her fingers against her chair before finding some conclusion.

"Actually, maybe it would be a good idea for you to go see the mess that the castle is in. It'll be good for you to see how not to rule a kingdom."

Rhoeo nodded to herself, but Caelyn heard her continue to grumble about peace and quiet.

Caelyn's first thought was to jump up and fly out the door, but Rhoeo might think she was too excited and change her mind.

Instead, she took as much time as she could manage to stand, straighten her skirt and count her steps to the door. Once the door was closed behind her, she bolted down the hallway, running this direction and that until she was out of breath and sure Rhoeo won't be able to find her.

Caelyn skipped down a flight of stairs and tried holding a conversation with the first servant she found. The servant was busy though and just dropped a curtsy and gave her quick directions to the training courtyard.

Caelyn frowned, she didn't know why the servant thought that was what she was looking for, but she was too high on her new freedom to question. She headed in the direction the servant said, still skipping a few steps when she was too excited to walk.

In the lower levels of the castle, she followed the noise of clashing metal until she saw the training area. She stood in the shade near the doorway and watched soldiers swing weapons at each other in practice.

A familiar flash of red hair made her pause. She blinked when she spotted Brynte, apparently sparring with an older man in a general's uniform. She wasn't sure they were actually sparring with how much Brynte was just dancing around the older man's sword.

"Why don'd you jus' hold s'dill?" The general said as he lunged.

"Now's where's the fun in that?" Bry asked, just tapping the sword when he dodged away.

The general growled and spent another few moments lunging before he gave up.

Caelyn watched. She had never seen Brynte smile so easily.

The king sheathed his sword and swaggered back to a small table, strewn with papers. The general followed suit though he was still grumbling things Caelyn could not hear, but which made Brynte laugh.

The few soldiers who had been watching the match exchanged coins and returned to their own training.

Brynte and the general also turned to frowning at the papers on the table and exchanging a few remarks.

Caelyn shifted in the shadows, wondering if she should stay. She hadn't meant to find Brynte, but she guessed the servant thought that was who she was looking for. She did not want to talk to him, but the idea of going back to her room was worse.

She finally took a hesitant step into the training area, out of the way of the soldiers, and headed toward Brynte.

The general noted her approach and offered a smile before he nudged Brynte to turn around.

Brynte was beaming bright. He was expecting someone else, but the look stiffened when he saw her.

"Caelyn." He greeted with an unsure tone. His smile slipped several degrees until it was just a stiff twist in his lip.

"Scarface." Caelyn snapped back without thinking. She wanted to apologize for it, but her mouth refused to verbalize remorse, instead twisting to a grimace.

Brynte breathed a defeated noise and jerked a hand through his tangles. He continued to keep the twist in his lips, but he was tired.

"What can I do for you, Caelyn?" He asked in a kinder tone than she knew she deserved. "I almost didn't recognize you without something" — He gestured up and down at her person — "colorful and *extra* extra."

Caelyn patted down her plain emerald green dress and again lamented she did not have the yellow scarf with feathers that would have added the energy her look was missing. She decided to ignore his comment instead of try explaining.

"I'm sorry. I shouldn't have called you that." Caelyn finally forced the words out.

Brynte blinked at her and exchanged a glance with the general. The general just looked confused, but he took the moment of pause to move to the other side of the sparring arena, out of earshot.

This would be the time to escape.

Caelyn ignored the thought. There was nowhere to escape to except back to her room.

Maybe that's what Rhoeo was hoping for…

She didn't like that thought. She planted her feet, determined to have some conversation with her half-brother.

Brynte was still staring at her with his head cocked sideways and his ugly lopsided smirk.

"That's alright," Brynte tried again with an easy look though it was still stiff. He gestured loosely toward the scar, "Ugly, I know."

Caelyn did not know what to say so she just nodded.

Brynte shifted his weight and glanced around the courtyard as though searching for a topic of conversation.

"What are you trying to do here?" Caelyn asked, hoping to clutch at any conversation as she jerked her head toward the table of papers.

Brynte followed her gaze to it.

"Ah, we're just figuring out how to handle the Nomads. Nothing you need to worry about."

"I'd like to learn." Caelyn jumped at the potential experience. Rhoeo's words about learning how not to rule a kingdom echoed around her head, but she ignored them.

Brynte continued blinking at her with a confused, owlish look.

"Uh, sure." He said eventually. He moved back toward the table, still casting hopeful, but unsure glances her way.

Caelyn approached the mess. She picked up one piece of paper, glanced over the gibberish, and set it down to look at another.

Brynte took her silent interest as an invitation to explain what they were doing, the problems faced, and some of their ideas to solve them. The sheer volume of issues the king was handling at once was nauseating to Caelyn.

Rhoeo's wrong about him not doing good with all these problems.

"Too much?" Brynte's voice broke through her distress.

"No," Caelyn answered on instinct.

Brynte looked doubtful. He continued explaining some of what they were working on, but he talked slower and provided more details anytime she frowned at an explanation.

Caelyn took in the new information with curiosity and dread.

It was entirely different hearing about the specifics of the problems Brynte was facing from him, rather than listening to Rhoeo's jaded remarks. Different still being high up in the castle, above all the details, than being in a training arena, looking at the soldiers who would soon be fighting.

Caelyn looked around the courtyard at all the men training, laughing and endlessly jeering each other.

They all have faces.

It was an odd realization, but something she forgot. When she listened to Rhoeo talk about the battles she'd seen, or the one that was coming to them now, she didn't think of individual soldiers. In her mind, a battle was just a swath of shining armor moving and falling in time with the story.

"Do you think you'll get enough people ready to fight in time?" She asked.

Brynte twisted his face up cheerfully and opened his mouth to answer, but stopped. His expression settled back to one of irritation and thought.

"Maybe."

Caelyn blinked.

Honesty?

She was used to so many people just telling her nice things, the doubt in her brother's voice was surprisingly refreshing, even if the subject matter was not.

"You can do it if anyone can," Caelyn mumbled. She had never had to encourage someone else, but people always did that for her. "There's a lot more people counting on it now."

Brynte was staring at her with a surprised, but pleased expression.

"Thanks."

Caelyn nodded and shifted.

Now it's awkward…

Caelyn did not know what to say so she continued shifting her weight. Brynte on the other hand was glaring at the papers with a new, thoughtful look.

He must have found some solution or other.

Caelyn could guess as much, which made this as good a time to leave as any.

"Well," Caelyn latched her hands behind her back and rocked on her feet. "Bye."

Brynte was so focused he hardly seemed aware of what she said. He just nodded and muttered something unintelligible.

Caelyn headed back to the castle. She paused inside and glanced back toward Brynte. He had just noticed she was gone and was turning around, searching for her, and scratching his head. He gave up in a moment and waved the general over, talking something about his new idea.

Caelyn left the lower courtyard. She headed in the direction of Stori's rooms, hoping this would be a good day for a visit.

Stori'll be glad to hear I talked to Brynte too.

The thought gave her pride. She did not know why Stori's opinion of her mattered so much, just that the queen was so much closer to what Caelyn wanted to be.

"Caelyn."

Rhoeo's voice was immediately unsettling when it sounded from the shadows.

Caelyn spun toward her, an excuse already on her lips.

"I was just wandering around and—"

"You didn't go see Brynte?" Rhoeo had a knowing smile on her lips, but it was not a kind one.

"Yeah, I did. We talked a bit."

"And?" Rhoeo arched an expectant eyebrow when she spoke.

Caelyn stumbled over her words, unsure what Rhoeo was wanting to hear.

Just be honest.

Caelyn still squirmed away from that idea. She did not want to agitate Rhoeo, but the why was too fuzzy in her mind for reason.

"He was just explaining some of what he's been doing," Caelyn stated.

Rhoeo's eyebrow was still arched and waiting.

Caelyn clenched her jaw, a flame of her own irritation sprouting.

Why do I have to explain everything I do to her?

The thought rattled around the back of her mind before an answer was spat back.

You don't.

Caelyn shrugged at the raised brow.

"Yeah." She moved to pass Rhoeo on her way down the hall.

"Caelyn," Rhoeo's voice was sweet and kind, "Is something the matter?"

Her voice was so kind, Caelyn stopped. Rhoeo hadn't spoken that nicely to her in a long time. She glanced back to the guard's sweet expression.

"I'm well, there is nothing the matter," Caelyn answered, but her voice tipped up at the end in a question. She wanted to ask if Rhoeo was well, but her concern was not verbalized.

"Good," Rhoeo's expression was still a kind placidity, "I would not want you to be overstressed by seeing your half-brother."

Caelyn's gut tightened at the statement.

"I'm not that fragile, Rhoeo." She snapped.

"Well, I didn't want to assume." Rhoeo was still smiling, but Caelyn did not see any kindness in the look, "I shouldn't have pushed you to interact with him."

"I wanted to go," Caelyn said. Rhoeo's insistence that talking to Brynte had been a bad idea— *Her bad idea* — irritated Caelyn. As though she could not decide what to do with her time on her own.

"I understand how talking with him must upset you." Rhoeo said, "I should not have been so selfish to force you to learn from the mistakes he's making."

Caelyn balked.

"You didn't force me, I *wanted* to talk with him! And I'm not upset."

Caelyn stomped away, still growling insults under her breath.

"Your Highness," Rhoeo said in an apologetic tone. Caelyn did not turn around.

CHAPTER 53

S had shuffled out of Klaas and Eleanora's chambers with a dejected step. The Wolf kid, Aike, was still sedated as he had been since he arrived, and the other two were not talking until he woke up.

And it seems like he's the leader too...

Shad groaned as he trudged toward Bry's study, then, thinking better of it, headed to the courtyard where Bry and Jair had set up to work on strategizing.

Hopefully, Lawr isn't there.

Shad was immediately guilty at the thought, but he still wanted to find some way of helping the man's niece before talking to him again.

"Shad?"

Shad started at the sound of Lawr's voice.

How does he even do that? He's creepier than I am.

"Hey, Lawr! What're you going down here?"

Shad plastered his best smile on as he turned to the side hallway the man had materialized from.

"Was going to check if the Wolf kid's awake. I take it he's not?" Lawr answered and asked.

"Nope. And Eleanora is getting sick of people bugging her about it. Said she'll send a message when he wakes up and not do disturb her about it until then."

Shad paused and thought about the kid before continuing in a lower voice. "Her priority is making sure he's not blind in one eye, so..."

Lawr grunted in acknowledgment as he fell in step beside Shad.

"You've been avoiding me," Lawr stated.

"What? No. I've been working on preparing for the battle and getting…"

Lawr leveled his granite-piercing gaze that staunched the rest of Shad's excuses.

Shad dropped his head and frowned as he thought of how to explain.

"Ali being taken," Lawr started, his perpetual frown deepening as he focused straight ahead, "that wasn't your fault.'"

"Yeah, but I should have thought of it," Shad said, rubbing his head. "You're not angry at me about it, but I still am."

They walked in silence until Lawr broke it.

"I know. I'm angry at myself too."

Shad frowned, trying to find what he should say. A simple 'it's not your fault' was hollow since Lawr would not believe it any more than Shad had a moment ago.

Besides, it is my fault, and maybe a little of Lawr's, too. But I should have thought of family being targeted.

"I should have too." Lawr hummed.

"What?" Shad blinked.

Lawr tapped his head.

"I didn't mean to." Shad stared wide-eyed.

How long had his thoughts been slipping out? Shad held a hand to his temple and focused on keeping all the thoughts in his head silent.

"It's all right. And you are correct."

Lawr was as usual, unfazed by the intrusion.

"Why are you always so calm about this stuff? Shad asked, dropping his hand.

Lawr shrugged.

"There are very few people I actually trust, but you're one of them."

Shad blinked at the older man. That was more honesty than he had expected. Though with Lawr, there was always something unexpected.

Deflect, deflect, deflect.

Shad struggled to escape the honesty of emotions from Lawr. He clapped a hand over his heart and tried a joke instead of responding with honesty himself.

"Lawr, I had no idea you felt that way."

He could have kicked himself as soon as the words were spoken for messing up moments like these. He just needed more time to process than the few moments between breaths would allow.

Lawr ignored Shad's comment as they continued toward the courtyard.

The chatter in the courtyard reached Shad's ears long before he stepped through the doorway outside.

"Not only does the king suck, but he's a phenomenally terrible strategist and a worse friend."

Shad heard Lawr's jaw snap together in unison with his.

"What kind of lie is that? Everyone knows it isn't even a good one," Shad growled as he marched into the courtyard in search of the speaker.

"Indeed," Lawr said, standing next to Shad, "factually incorrect to an extreme."

Shad blinked at the familiar faces of Bry, Jair, and Ammon—*that 'ol devil!*—and immediately forgot his indignation as he moved to greet his old friend.

"Wow, it really works," Ammon stood in shock, blinking at Shad, "I did not expect that."

"Me nied'er." Jair shook his head, an amused frown beating out his usual dark one for a moment.

"What?" Shad glanced between the trio in confusion and sparing a glance to an equally confused Lawr, "what worked?"

"We were waiting for you two," Bry said as he shifted in front of a table strewn with maps.

Bry's own surprised look immediately changed to his cockeyed grin. "I didn't know it would work this well, but I bet Ammon I could summon you with petty insults."

Lawr scoffed at a laugh.

Shad blinked at the brief lack of tension around them at the small joke. It had been sorely missed. He jumped at the chance to keep the tension light for any moment longer.

"Bry, you can't give away my secrets like that." He complained and returned to his original plan of greeting Ammon, "You know Ammon will abuse it to no end."

"Oh, I know." Bry was still smirking.

"Hey-o punk, good to see you made it out of Oroitz alive." Ammon clapped his arm around Shad's neck in a strangling greeting, "Or whatever passes for alive with your kind."

"You too, Amm-off." Shad returned the side hug-strangle by punching the man playfully in the side.

Ammon shoved Shad away with a scoff.

"How are the Wolves? One of you check on them?" Bry sobered the discussion with the change of topic.

Shad waved his hand.

"The leader's still out, Eleanora's not taking any more visitors for him, and the other two are not talking. Apparently finding a treatment for that kid's medical issue isn't going to be easy. Something to do with his heart and lungs."

Bry nodded. The near-permanent frown he so often sported had retaken residence across his features again.

Shad had a joke about that, but he sensed the mood and saved it for later.

Bry returned his attention to the mess on the table, and both militants followed his cue. Ammon shoved Shad one last jovial time as he passed him.

"How's the plan coming?" Lawr asked distracting Bry from the table with a pointed look.

Shad frowned as he watched Bry glance around at the soldiers milling around the courtyard.

"Better than nothing, but we'll still need a plan B, C, D, and maybe E," Bry answered with a stiff, humorless smile.

Shad caught Lawr's eye and motioned briefly to his own head. Lawr nodded, and Shad was quickly lost in the maelstrom of thoughts and ideas that characterized the older man's mind.

Shad asked about whatever plan Bry and him had discussed and then listened until he found something like a response.

He groaned.

Great. The soldiers don't even believe Jair.

Shad rolled his eyes as he heard the older man say 'nope' in his mind.

"So, what's the plan?" Shad turned his attention back to Bry and gestured toward the table covered in a Bry-level mess.

Bry rubbed his head and glared doubtfully at some of the papers atop the pile.

"We were going to look for you to ask for your assistance in carrying out a diversion."

Shad clapped his hands together to distract himself from how worn out Bry looked.

Please be something that takes a load off his shoulders...

"I love diversions. I'm very diverting."

"That doesn't even mean the same thing, and it's still accurate." Lawr was shaking his head. "Somewhat."

Bry ignored the antics as he continued focusing on the pile of papers and AaDs.

"We need you to keep the Nomads busy and slow their progress toward the city. Ambushes, sneak attacks, whatever works. You'll have a small team."

"Will do. Who's my team."

Ammon laughed and threw his arm around Shad's shoulder.

"Me, plus a couple of chumps, whoever we can find. We'll gonna be working together, just like old times."

Shad raised his hand jokingly to Bry, still holding Ammon's smirk.

"Change partners?"

Ammon gave him a stiff punch in the gut.

"No two steppin' out on me now, wraith-head." Ammon grinned like a shark, creepy as he always was, and he unhooked himself from around Shad.

Wouldn't dream of it.

Shad returned the smirk before turning again to Bry.

"When do you want us—"

"Now, actually." Bry interrupted with an apologetic smile, "We are so short on army personnel, I'll need all the time you can give me to gather fighting men."

"Okay then."

Shad gave Bry a sharp, two-finger salute before pivoting. He caught Ammon by the neck and dragged the man after him as he walked back to the castle entrance.

"Right, let's find some chumps then, huh."

Shad released his captive just as Ammon was geared to forcefully extricate himself.

"So angry." Shad laughed.

Just like old times all right.

CHAPTER 54

Sverre sagged on the couch of the inn room he and Dain shared. Dain would return from his daily scouting work soon, but Sverre wanted more time to decide what to say.

Directly stated is your best option here.

The change in plans would entail a visit to Atanas on top of everything else. A visit to him would mean seeing Duqa again, which never ended well for him.

What has to be done, has to be done. No need for hesitation.

Familiar footfalls near the door were the only warning Dain gave before he entered.

Sverre straightened out of his slouch and waited expectantly for Dain to give his report of the day before they could talk about anything else.

"Thacea is sure something, you know," Dain started as soon as he had closed the door behind him, "And I don't mean that in a good way."

Sverre nodded, though Dain was not paying attention to him as he paced up and down their room.

"She really is. I think she's doing some of this just to mess with us."

"Doing what?" Sverre frowned.

He had not heard of the woman doing anything out of sorts, but he had not been paying close attention to what she had been doing in the castle anyway.

"She's just..." Dain waved his hands in a wild gesticulation that meant nothing to Sverre.

Dain stilled in a moment, and Sverre could see him thinking harder than before.

"I think she's leading up to a coup."

Sverre jerked.

"What?"

He worked to keep his voice steady, but he was glad only Dain was around to notice how much he failed.

"Yeah, from what I've seen…"

Dain trailed off again as he nodded along to his own thoughts. He turned a pointed look back to Sverre.

"What do you want to do about it?"

Sverre had not found a better way of telling Dain his change of plan, so he decided to jump straight into it.

"We're going to back the king and the Sentrians in the coming battle. The Nomads have enough support."

Dain blinked at him a moment before he shook his head.

"You came to that decision fast. Been thinking on this a while?"

Sverre nodded and shifted in his seat as he thought again about explaining such a rash change of plan.

"Because of him? You think he'll need the support that much?"

Sverre nodded again. He was always glad Dain was so fast on the uptake and could guess his thoughts without much help.

But this is a risk…An unnecessary one.

"You do not have to—"

Dain scoffed.

"Who do you take me for? Someone who abandons friends at the first onset of a crisis? Sverre, I'm hurt."

Sverre smiled.

"Besides," Dain shrugged as he spoke, "what can you do, he's family, right? Even if you're the only one who knows that."

"Thank you, Dain." Sverre stood and moved to the small kitchen to showcase the food he had prepared as a last meal if necessary.

Dain sat to eat. They had dinner before any more discussion of the next obvious steps.

"I'll leave tonight to tell Atanas," Sverre stated.

Dain groaned as though that task was somehow a surprise.

"Can't we just call?"

Sverre did not bother to state the obvious, which Dain knew just as well. Atanas would never accept an AaD call for a decision of the magnitude of changing sides right before battle.

"I will be the one to go through," Dain added.

"No, changing sides is my deci—"

"Do me a favor, think. Who will Duqa have more fun tormenting over this? You or me?"

Sverre clenched his jaw tight together instead of answering.

"Exactly," Dain leaned back in his seat, "I may even get a pardon and be able to make it back here in time to do anything."

"I can't ask for you to—"

"You didn't, I'm volunteering, and you're being voluntold to stay here."

"Dain..."

"No," Dain held his pleading gaze with an unmoving one, "I'm going, Sverre, not you. The end."

Sverre shook his head. Of every aspect he had considered would be difficult to convince Dain about, which one of them would have the unfortunate task of relaying the change to Atanas was not one of them.

I should expect Dain to surprise me by now.

"Thank you, Dain," Sverre repeated.

He still had a lingering hope he might be able to convince Dain to let him take the difficult task, but he would let it rest until later.

"Well," Dain stood from the table and checked his AaD, "no time like the present."

Sverre blinked as he realized Dain was already going to cut short his plan to convince him later.

"Wait, I can go, it is my plan, and Erc will not forgive you for putting yourself at risk like this."

Dain had already started bouncing toward the door.

"Nope." Dain closed the door behind himself without listening to Sverre's renewed attempts to persuade him.

Sverre stared at the door in blank surprise for a moment with a vague hope his partner would return through it any moment.

After several moments passed in stillness, Sverre gave up on that hope.

Thank you, Dain.

Sverre turned his full attention toward how he could help the Sentrian army have a chance against the Nomads. He scorned himself for not being a better strategist, but no matter how hard he thought on the subject, he did not have any useful solutions.

Better leave that to Brynte, then.

He took his cloak and headed out toward the Wolves' inn. Even if he could not directly tell them he would not be able to support them any longer, he could give Hid a hint in case they had any dangerous plans to change last minute.

If there was any chance the court healer had been able to help their terminal team member, he would see to convincing the kids to back out of the fight.

Sverre walked the busy streets with a keen interest in how the city's people reacted to the threat marching toward their walls. He was encouraged at the sight of so many people now brandishing arms and seemingly ready to defend their homes.

The longer he walked, the more people there seemed to be. He stopped at a street corner and listened in to the conversations around him.

"...Think a few merchants and farmers will really matter against the Nomads."

"I'd rather be a'fightin' than a'waitin.' You could wait with da women and children if ya scared."

The first man scoffed and grumbled something Sverre could not understand. Another man joined the discussion.

"The king doesn't have any more soldiers anyway, this would be the best time to..."

The third man leaned closer to the other two and whispered the rest of his sentence. The first two started glancing around with a sudden case of nerves.

"I don't think there's reason for that to be necessary now."

"Doesn't matter anyway, we're all gonna be out fighting the Nomads in the next few days."

"Fightin' and dyin' to protect our own, that's what's right."

The third man shrugged, "The king won't be able to keep his crown after this crisis, with all the hell he raised in Oroitz. Would just be wrong, and any of us could have done better."

Sverre raised an eyebrow at the statement but moved away from the corner without a word since he had the information he wanted.

He was glad Brynte had already implemented some ideas for how to counter the overwhelming numbers the Nomads always brought to a fight.

Sverre stopped a couple more times to listen in on conversations that repeated most of the same sentiments.

He was relieved by the news as he reached the Wolves' inn. Though he did pity all the work they had lost.

At their door, he knocked their code and entered into the midst of complete panic.

Hid was on an AaD call with someone. Someone Sverre guessed he did not like or trust from how much he was hiding his accent and trying to speak properly. Hid was so stressed though that his attempt at proper speech was broken into stutters every other few words.

Xiulan was the only other Wolf in the room, and she was in tears.

Sverre approached the girl. He knew his presence was not a comfort to any of them, but he still hoped he might be able to get the girl to stop crying and possibly tell him what had happened.

Xiulan surprised him by leaning against his side as soon as he sat down.

"You'll help, won't you?" Xiulan stared at him with huge eyes.

"I will do whatever I can," Sverre stated and meant it, "What happened?"

"Reb kidnapped Retha. We came back and she was gone."

Xiulan gestured toward Hid, who looked to be quietly panicking his own way. His voice on the call remained steady, however.

"I a-apologize, Chief." Hid bowed his head even over the call at the apology, "We are... we are w-working our task as-as-as fast as we can to keep up with your—"

"Why would your chief take Retha?" Sverre turned his attention back to Xiulan.

She sniffled and shrugged. "She did not think we were completing our job in time for her approach."

"Yes, Chief, we-we will." Hid hung up the call and immediately threw the AaD across the room.

Hid held his head in his hands and spewed Spanish swears. He was starting to hyperventilate between curses.

"Hid," Sverre waited for the young man to look at him, "what can I do to help?"

More swearing in Spanish.

Hid sat up straight with a bitter laugh as he held Sverre's gaze.

Except die. I can't do that yet, though that is probably the only thing Reb wants in exchange for the girl.

Sverre swallowed at the thought.

"We have to find her," Hid stated, standing up in a quick motion. At least his breathing had slowed toward normal.

Xiulan was on her feet in the same instant, already heading toward the door.

"I will help you look," Sverre offered as he too moved closer to the exit.

Hid nodded. "Could…could Dain scope the Nomad camp to look for her?"

Sverre clenched his jaw at the terrible timing before shaking his head.

"Dain's away for a time on another job."

Sverre wondered if that statement was wise given the Wolves' secondary mission, but it was too late to take it back.

Hid frowned at him but nodded.

They left for the long trek to find the Nomad camp.

CHAPTER 55

Aike awoke with a groggy start.

"Where am I?" Is what he meant to say, but all that came from his unused vocals was an incoherent series of groans.

"It's okay, Aike," a voice that was as familiar as breathing said somewhere to his left, "The healer had you drugged so you could heal, but we need to leave the castle."

"Sa'dia, what's going on?" Aike tried to ask, but more groans sounded instead, "Water."

"Way to bedside-manner." Another familiar voice, "Guy just woke up from days of being comatose and you want him to start running immediately."

Aike worked to pry his eyes open. The chore took more effort than he had imagined was possible before a blurry picture of two faces, already arguing, filtered into his brain.

He spied a hand within grabbing distance and latched onto it.

Sa'dia turned to him with a blurry face of surprise, "Aike?"

"Water."

Aike ground the word out with as careful enunciation as possible. Relief swept over him as the voice coming from his throat was finally intelligible.

"Oh, right." Sa'dia pried Aike's hand from her wrist before turning to find the requested item.

Aike turned his head to the fuzzy, blacked-out area of his vision where Bary had just been.

"What's going on?" he repeated his earlier question, careful to try and make it clear as he worked at sitting up.

"Easy." Bary's hand on his back guided Aike upright but remained as he struggled through dizziness for balance.

Aike blinked at the room they were in. It was familiar, but only just. He recognized it as the healer's room in the castle.

The memory of why he had come there hit Aike as he instantly felt at his face. Bandages covered half of his head and one eye.

A glass of water appeared from his good side. Aike took it with an attempt at a grateful smile to Sa'dia. He gulped the entire glass in one breath.

"Feelin' okay?" Sa'dia asked, taking the glass back, "'Cause we gotta go."

"I'll live," Aike said, hoping his legs would support that statement as he swung them over the edge of the table and stood up.

"Good," Bary was at his side again, out of view, "'Cause you may not see out of that eye again."

"What?" Aike turned to affix his gaze on Bary as the trio slowly made their way toward the door.

"The healer said we would have to wait and see if it healed properly, but that if you start moving before it's healed, you will be blind in it."

"Oh." Aike nodded.

"We're sorry, Aike," Sa'dia said, "We tried letting you rest as long as possible, but the Avare and the king have started moving, and we can't stay here any longer."

Aike nodded again. He focused on trying to remember everything that had been going on when he first arrived at the castle.

"Bary's medicine?" Aike turned back to Bary, "Was the healer able to..."

Bary shook his head.

"She said she would be able to, given time. We don't have that anymore."

Sa'dia left his side to move through the healer's front room and open the door. She peeked outside before waving them over.

"Reb took Retha," Bary stated.

"What?!" Aike stopped and stared at Bary.

"As motivation. She thinks we're not going to complete our mission with Sverre."

"Damn it," Aike growled.

He recalled every detail of his last conversation with their chief, searching his memory for how he could have worded his report better.

"I wasn't convincing enough," he grumbled to himself.

"Hey," Bary shook his shoulder as they walked, "this isn't your fault. Reb's crazier than usual. She's talking to herself, or Erasyl, or something. We don't know, but Hid said she's lost it."

They continued making their way down hallway after hallway, with Sa'dia leading the way, avoiding guards. Bary helped Aike until his feet were stable enough to carry him.

"Where's Hid? And the assassins?" Aike asked as they all gathered around a door to the outer courtyard.

They watched and waited as a group of soldiers moved passed.

"At this very moment? I don't know," Sa'dia said, "We're here with you."

"Hid switched inns a couple of days ago and sent us a message. We're heading there now." Bary answered. "As for Sverre and Dain, I don't know."

"Yeah, Sverre was upset Retha was taken, but they have their orders too," Sa'dia added.

"Upset?" Aike stared at his teammates.

The idea of the assassin caring about any of them still seemed too foreign to consider. He recalled the concern in the Ghost's eyes as he brought him to the healers', but it still troubled him.

"Yeah, that's what Hid said," Bary reaffirmed as they took their chance to sprint across the courtyard.

"We have to get Retha back," Aike stated.

Sa'dia and Bary exchanged glances, one between themselves and one looking at the bandaged side of Aike's head.

"We know," they said in rare agreement.

"And we are sorry," Bary said, "But we don't have a way to get her back yet."

"That's why Hid needs you out," Sa'dia added.

Aike nodded. "I know, and I need to talk to Hid."

The pair nodded as they returned to weaving a path through the city.

CHAPTER 56

Hid watched from the street corner, all the passersby. Caesar Apollo appeared among the crowd and made his way over.

"Idir says the soldiers are unsure who to trust and follow," Caesar Apollo's high-pitched voice stated in a whisper as he stood next to Hid, ostensibly examining the wares at the far corner of the street shop.

"Can he persuade them who not to follow?" Hid mumbled back, keeping his focus steady on the flow of the crowd in the street.

"Given a month's time, otherwise no."

Hid rubbed his temple as he thought.

"Have him pull back. And find Xiulan too. We'll leave the city as soon as Aike and everyone are back together."

The bronze giant nodded and turned, leaving the corner to weave his way back to his targets.

Hid stared out at the street for several moments before he also moved to return to the inn.

The same tavern and inn they had poached accomplices for the cause from was now their hideout. The older woman barkeep, who still thought he was too young to be in such trouble, scowled at Hid as he passed by on his way to his room.

Though, Hid reminded himself, *she may just be salty her tavern had become the stronghold for the resistance against the monarch. That's reasonable too.*

Hid could laugh at that if their own situation was not so bad. Egged on by the Wolves, the unrest in the city populous had grown from next to nothing. And had grown organized. Now leaders of the 'resistance' gathered and met on regular occasions to discuss matters Hid could care less about.

How life turns.

He supposed there had been enough hostility toward the king that the people would lead an uprising on their own at some point. He would consider his teams' particular involvement in the turn of events as some of their best work.

Unfortunate work though, but…

Hid trailed off as he reached the team's room. He knocked out the code even though he was sure there was no one there to hear or attack him either way and entered.

He cleared the one-room apartment carefully, as he did every time he returned. Partially for security, mostly in the hope Retha had escaped and somehow returned.

That's just stupid, amigo.

Hid chided himself. They had moved immediately after Reb's messengers had shown up unannounced at their inn and taken Retha while the other Wolves were away. Retha would not know where they had moved, though he had no doubt she could find out.

The sweep of the room turned up empty, as Hid expected. No sign of Retha, Aike, or any of the people he desperately wished to see. Even Sverre or Dain would have been welcome.

The empty room remained despite his wishes.

Hid growled at that as he moved to sit. He snatched up the AaD and stared at it a moment.

If Reb won't give Retha back when you go in person, she's certainly not going to from another call.

Hid exhaled a frustrated breath and set the AaD down. He remained seated on the couch, sporadically bouncing his knees and watching the door.

He took a break from the door watching to pack the few belongings each of the team members possessed. This task was interrupted anytime there was noise in the hallway or coming through the window from the streets below.

Hid checked around at each interruption for his team, and each time he returned to his packing task disappointed.

Nothing is so wrong yet that we can't fix.

He had to convince himself that was true. Even if it was, the sense of dread that had been pooling in his gut the last several days still threatened to swallow him whole.

A knock-code sounded at the door without Hid having noticed any noise from the hallway. He ran out to the main room as the door opened on Aike. Sa'dia and Bary, odd in their silence, trailed in behind.

"Aike, *hermano*, I'm glad you're back."

Hid crossed the room in three steps and wrapped Aike in a tight hug. He released his grip a moment later and pulled back to frown at the bandages still hiding half of Aike's face.

"Your eye?"

Aike attempted his goofy grin, but the effect was dampened under the bandages.

"Probably wouldn't heal right," Aike stated, contrary to the smile, "but ignoring that…"

The smile withered, replaced by serious focus.

"We need to get Retha back. Tell me what happened."

Hid growled, rubbing a hand across his face as he started.

"We were all out in groups, except her. She was at the inn sleeping. She had been out all night before scouting. I received a call from the AaD. It was one of the Wolf teams Reb inherited from the Oroitz battle. They said Reb was concerned with our 'motivation' to complete our orders. They took Retha."

Hid watched a pacing Aike as a flurry of emotions and thoughts flitted across his face before the man turned back to Hid, waiting for him to continue.

Hid nodded.

"I went to meet Reb right away. She said no. Sverre and Xiulan searched the camp but couldn't find her."

Aike snorted and leveled a doubtful gaze at Hid, "And you trust he would tell you if he did?"

Hid blinked and reminded himself that Aike had not spent as much time with the Ghost and the sniper. Especially in times of crunch situations.

"Aike," Hid held his friend's gaze, "Sverre tried."

"I'd vouch for him too," Sa'dia said.

She and Bary remained off to the side, watching the conversation.

Bary nodded. "Same. Sverre was close with Retha, and he did well to help calm her."

Aike's expression remained doubtful, but he relented his point with a quick, "If you trust him…"

"On this, I do," Hid responded immediately.

Aike looked ready to fight it for a moment but stopped and let it go.

"All right." Aike conceded, "But they are both still part of the job."

Hid ducked his head in agreement, "And they know it."

Aike squeezed his eyes shut and breathed a moment, "For how long?"

"Don't know. They commented on it while we were deciding whether or not to send Bary to the castle."

Aike slammed his fist against the nearest wall.

"Guess we couldn't expect to surprise them." Aike paused to shake out his newly bruising fist and rock onto his toes, "But they have been helping since then? You're sure?"

Hid nodded.

Aike mused aloud, "Why would Oracaede have them do that?"

"It doesn't have anything to do with what Oracaede wants."

Aike turned to frown at Hid, "What?"

"Oracaede may hold their leash," Hid said, not completely positive of what he was saying, but he was sure of the two assassin's loyalties, "the same as Reb holds ours, but..."

"But they don't do everything for their master," Bary picked up quickly, "any more than we do."

Aike glanced between the two of them with a raised eyebrow.

"You're sure?"

"Positive."

Hid glanced at Bary and Sa'dia, they had spoken the same in perfect unison.

"The three of you in agreement like that, wow," Aike raised his hands in surrender, sparing a smile for each of them.

"They're not our enemy," Hid stated, "if possible, we need to stop being theirs."

"Bary," Aike turned to the curly-haired man, but included Sa'dia in his glance as well, "how close was the healer to finding you a treatment?"

The pair shook their heads in a disappointing sight.

"Eleanora was working on it furiously and was really trying but—"

"Even having a sample of his treatment," Sa'dia pitched in, "it seemed to confuse her about what would work. The Avare medical healers make the medicine so that it can't be reverse engineered."

"She will likely get something worked out," Bary picked up again.

"Yeah, she's damned tenacious and seemed to be taking this as a personal affront," Sa'dia added.

"But not in the next couple of days," Bary concluded, "Reb will bring the Avare down on this city and be halfway back to Glacius Tesca before there is anything remotely available for me to take."

Hid shook his head before glancing toward Aike. "This might be something to stay on top of after this battle. We should keep the connection in case there is any way the healer could figure something out in the future."

Aike nodded. "This could be our one way out."

"You guys can leave me here this—"

"Shut up!" Everyone shouted at once.

"That's not an option, and you know it," Aike stated as he reached out to pat Bary on the shoulder. "And if you so much as think of doing something stupid, I will kick the shit out of you."

"Followed by me." Sa'dia glowered at her bickering partner.

Bary held up his hands in surrender.

"Back to Retha." Aike refocused the conversation on their most immediate problem.

Hid watched the man chew on his thumb and pace. He winced when Aike walked into the couch once when he could not see it on his blind side.

"Can we get her back before the Avare reach the city?" Hid asked the room, "We need to leave the city before then, anyway."

Aike was nodding as he paced, but Hid could see he was not actually listening while he thought.

"What's the king's response been?" Aike asked finally.

Sa'dia pursed her lips and frowned before answering, "He sent out his wraith friend a couple of days ago to slow them down."

"Shad?" Aike smiled at that, "Yeah, he's a good guy."

"He's making a mess," Hid stated.

Aike nodded with an appreciative smile.

Hid sighed and continued to answer the prior question.

"The king is stalling to gather troops. Our ploys worked, and he doesn't have enough in Sentre to withstand the attack of a united Avare threat, but he's making good progress undoing all our work and getting soldiers to like him again. And he's making use of the refugees in the city to bolster his forces."

Aike stopped his pacing to turn and examine Hid with a pinched look.

"Using the refugees and making use of his troops? But if the Avare attack him now, ignoring Shad's attempts to slow them down...?"

Hid thought for a moment before he nodded.

"The King wouldn't be able to stop their attack, not without losing most of his troops."

Aike nodded. He was not smiling at the prospect, but he continued nodding as he started pacing again.

"That's half our mission right there." Bary stepped forward, looking uncharacteristically optimistic.

"We'd just have to handle Sverre and Dain somewhere along in the mess of the battle, right?" Sa'dia glance between Hid and Aike.

"That was always part of the plan and never the easy part." Bary rolled his eyes.

"Sa'dia," Aike interrupted the tanned girls' comeback remark, "go find the others and get them back here. We should leave now."

"I told Caesar Apollo to do the same," Hid stated with a quick nod for Bary to go with her. "He's starting with Idir, so find Xiulan first and make sure you meet up with him."

Once the pair left the room, Hid turned his attention back to Aike.

"We still have no real plan for taking out the assassins."

Aike nodded as he fidgeted with his bandages without looking at Hid.

"I know. We'll just have to wait for an opportunity in battle or create one."

Aike grinned at Hid. "I think we'll just have to get lucky with them."

"I hate this plan, *hermano*."

Aike forced a laugh. "Me too."

CHAPTER 57

Ali and Erc remained crouched in the cave entrance listening to the rhythmic breathing.

"Is it asleep?" Ali whispered, hoping Erc could see more than she could around the corner.

Erc shrugged and crept forward to check around the rocky outcropping. Ali followed a step behind, leaning above Erc to see.

A massive, scaled paw came into view first. It was an interesting shade of pale gold and as long as Ali was tall.

Ali exchanged a terrified glance with Erc before turning back to the thing on the other side of the rocks.

Erc adjusted her grip on her rifle, keeping it low and ready to fire as she crept further forward, a few cautious inches at a time.

Ali fought against her survival instincts telling her to run. She moved after Erc, careful not to disturb even a pebble, lest the creature wake.

They continued at the slow pace of absolute silence until they cleared the rocks. The creature lay sprawled across the floor of the cave on its back. One paw limply curled in the air, twitching every so often as the creature dreamed.

The beast's entire body was covered in scales that ranged from the palest golden to a burn earth tone with occasional blue and green highlights reflected in the dim light.

Ali could not even tell how large it was since it was curled into a snake-like pile of twists and scales. She could not help but gawk at it anyway. It looked like a Chinese dragon from old drawings.

She pulled on Erc's jacket to get her attention before pointing to the creature.

"Is that a dragon!?" she whispered.

Erc was scowling as she returned her gaze to the animal with a nod.

"Dragons are trouble."

"Who's there?" a resonant feminine voice purred, bouncing endlessly off the walls of the cave.

Ali exchanged another wide-eyed look with Erc as the pile of scales shifted and slithered until it was upright.

A giant head swung around from the depth of the cave. Cat-like, crystal eyes, clear as glass, stared at Ali and Erc.

"Who are you?" the dragon said with a new excitement in its voice.

Ali gapped at speech as she stared at the enormous creature before her. The dragon stared back with its head cocked to the side.

"I'm Ercilia, this is Ali," Erc answered, gesturing between herself and Ali.

"I'm Adalheidis. You may call me Heidis. I'm a water dragon and a goddess!"

The dragon raised her massive head in triumph as far as she could until she knocked it against the ceiling of the cave. She remained puffed up for a moment before she started cackling.

"No, I'm not a goddess. Did you believe me?"

At the question, the large head and crystal eyes snaked back down until it was at Ali's height and hovering a few feet away. The eyes snaked back and forth with the motion of its head to glance between Erc and Ali.

"Umm," Ali stumbled over what to say before she tried, "no?"

The dragon tsk-ed at that and raised her head.

"I thought I was believable," she chided.

"Heidis," Erc dared a step forward, "we came here for—"

"Did you believe me?" The dragon was back in their faces with her chin grazing the ground so she would be at eye level.

Erc froze before answering, "No, you're a dragon."

Heidis continued staring at Erc.

She heaved a heavy sigh, "Oh, you're so specific. I could be a dragon and a goddess, couldn't I?"

Ali nodded without listening as the dragon's sigh had focused all her attention on the rows of jagged teeth that were within arm's reach of her face.

The dragon dragged her head on the ground as she turned around in an overdramatic show of sorrow.

Erc glanced at Ali with a small questioning shrug. Ali shrugged back.

Of all the ideas she ever had of what a dragon was, Heidis was not it.

"So," Erc tried again, "we came here to retrieve something you took. It's important—"

"Want to play a game?!" Heidis interrupted again, whipping her large head back in front of them in an instant.

Ali balked at the speed the dragon could move at. Erc too had taken a step back before answering.

"No, we only came—"

"What?" Heidis interrupted again with a pitiful whine, "but I want to play."

Ali sighed.

Of course reasoning with a dragon wouldn't be an easy thing.

"Okay, Heidis, we'll play with you," Ali said, stepping forward.

Erc shot her a look, but Ali waved it off.

"Yay!" The dragon spun around in a circle, shaking the cave with her giant, energetic steps. "Great, great, great! I want to play—"

"Hold up," Ali interrupted.

The dragons' attention snapped to her.

"If we play with you, you have to give us back what you took. Deal?"

"Sure, sure, yeah. You can have it."

Heidis nodded while wagging her tail and most of her body along with it. She straightened up, looking around the cave as she continued.

"Now, we can play— Wait! What stuff do you want back?"

Ali exchanged another nervous glance with Erc.

"All of it?" she tried.

Erc nodded. "Yep, all of it would be good."

The dragon hummed a sad note as she sank back to resting her head on the ground.

"Well, that may be difficult…I mean, I ate the food. I didn't take it just to decorate, you know."

The dragon was dragging her head across the ground as she whined.

"You took a device too," Erc stated, shaking her head at the creature's antics, "It would have been emitting a frequency. You took it a couple of days ago."

Heidis raised her head as her toothy grin distracted Ali from their purpose for being there again.

"Oh, that thing is pretty, and it sounds so nice. That I did take to decorate."

Heidis wagged her tail as she spoke. The motion stirred up all the dust and small rocks in the back of the cave.

Ali coughed a moment before she tried reasoning again.

"We need it back. It's important."

"But I like it." The dragon's tail stilled as she whined in a dramatic display of sorrow.

"But we *need* it," Ali stressed, hoping the dragon would listen.

"No! I want it."

Heidis shook her head, still dragging her scales across the rock floor.

"Heidis," Erc tried speaking over the dragon's despair, "how about we make a trade then? Heidis, we'll give you something else instead of the blocker."

The dragon's head popped up at that idea.

"Like what?!"

"Well," Erc drew out the word with a glance at Ali for suggestions.

"The tracker?" Ali hesitantly offered, "does that emit nice frequencies?"

Erc thought a moment before nodding as she turned to backtrack out of the cave to retrieve it.

"Where's she going?"

Heidis snaked her neck to peer around the rocks after Erc's receding form.

"She's going to get something; you may like it better than the device you took."

Ali explained as she sidestepped further into the cave to escape being caught between the rocks and the dragon's neck.

"Is it nice?"

Heidis's head snapped around to stare at Ali.

Ali nodded and tried to ignore the fact she was now trapped away from the cave entrance.

"Why are you decorating in here anyway?" Ali asked with a glance around and a vain hope of distracting the creature so she could move back to the cave's entrance.

Heidis set her head down instead of moving.

"'Cause, it's so boring."

Ali frowned and looked around again. The cave was empty and devoid of features except for the rocks and occasional messy remains of what Ali assumed were Erc's food supplies.

She caught a glimpse of a metal box on one side of the cave that she guessed was the blocker.

"The top of the island, outside the cave is nice."Ali glanced back at the dragon's bright coloring. "And you would blend in better up there."

"I want to," Heidis cried, lifting her head a few feet, then dropping it back down to emphasize her point, "I do, but I can't. I'm supposed to guard down here."

"Guard? Guard what?"

"Shhhh," Heidis hushed as she moved forward until her sharp teeth were in front of Ali's face again, "I'm not supposed to say."

"Oh, okay." Ali tried backing a step away from the dragon's jaws, but the wall was already at her back.

"Fine, it's a door," Heidis pulled back and lifted her head to look toward the back of the cave, "but you made me tell you."

Ali took the moment to breathe while the dragon was distracted. She regarded Heidis with a look of doubt and amusement before she decided it might be best to play along.

"Uh-ha, sure I did," she glanced in the direction Heidis was looking, "a door to what?"

"Shush." Heidis was back in her face, though Ali was a little less concerned this time.

Ali waited as Heidis continued to stare at her. She quietly counted the seconds until the dragon would end up either telling her or changing the topic.

"Fine, it's pirates," Heidis said, dropping her chin to the ground again for emphasis.

"Pirates?" Ali raised an eyebrow.

Maybe staying here talking wasn't sure a good idea.

"Do you believe me?"

Heidis was in her face with a toothy smile again.

Ali sighed in relief at the dragon's tell.

"No," Ali stated.

"Aww, why not?"

The dragon was back to whining as she pulled her head back, unblocking the way back to the entrance of the cave for the first time.

"Just cause," Ali said, taking her chance to walk toward the opening.

She checked around the corner to see Erc was carefully picking her way back toward them.

"Fine, not pirates," Heidis lamented, "but I can't tell you who it is."

Ali nodded. She was excited to have the blocker back, but less so about leaving now. Heidis was fun to talk to and she wanted to talk to a dragon as long as possible.

When would I ever even have a chance at this again?

"It's a big organization," Heidis stated, obviously deciding the new game would be to guess what she was doing there.

"A big organization?" Ali mirrored the statement.

The only organization she knew of was Oracaede, and she did not want to think of them being nearby.

"It starts with 'O,'" Heidis added.

Ali froze. "Oracaede?"

"Yep!" The dragon chirped, "But I didn't tell you."

"Wait, Heidis, are you…"

Ali stopped herself and watched the dragon, willing her to ask Ali if she believed her.

Heidis stared back with the same big innocent eyes and curious head cock sideways.

"Am I what?"

"Joking. Are you joking with me, like with the pirates?" Ali tried keeping herself calm.

"No. They said I had to guard the door, but I'm not supposed to tell anyone. Not supposed to leave either, so don't tell them that."

Heidis finished by holding her paw up to her mouth in a shushing motion.

"Ali, are you all right?" Erc asked as she finally made it around the last corner.

She turned to Heidis without waiting for an answer.

"Here's the tracker, Heidis. Will you trade it for the blocker you took?"

"Ohh, that's pretty nice."

Heidis leaned down to examine the tracker, apparently forgetting about the conversation she had been having with Ali a moment ago.

Ali rushed to Erc and clutched her arm.

"We need to get out of here."

Erc and Heidis both stared at her.

"Ali, what happened? What's wrong?"

Erc shot a suspicious glance toward the dragon.

"Did I say something?" Heidis leaned her head toward them, "Don't go, please. I'm sorry."

"It's Oracaede," Ali answered Erc's questions, shooting Heidis an apologetic look.

"What?!" Erc stared at Ali.

"Aww, it's cause I said they're here."

Heidis lamented, dragging her head across the ground with a pitched whining cry.

"They're what?" Erc snapped her gaze back to the dragon.

"Yes, here," Ali stated. "She's supposed to be guarding a door that leads to them. We need to go."

CHAPTER 58

Ali primed Heidis to explain what she was there for to Erc while Ali investigated the back of the cave for a door.

The back of the cave looked the same as the front except without the watery inlet. Dark, brown, and a lot of rocks.

Ali frowned, walking around the back wall without finding any sign of a door. And nothing that looked or said anything about Oracaede.

Was she joking again?

Ali glanced over the slithering pile of scales toward the front of the cave and the dragon's head. Heidis stood with her head hung low as Erc reamed the creature about life choices and a few other things Ali could imagine.

The dragon was not joking around any longer and did not seem likely that she would listen to any kind of reprimand if she had only been joking in the first place.

Ali continued walking along the back edge of the cave, running her hand along the wall.

Still nothing.

"A door, a door," Ali mumbled to herself, scuffing her shoes against the ground.

She frowned at an idea, "A trapped door?"

Ali walked the length of the cave again, this time watching the ground. On the far side, the ground smoothed out suspiciously.

She tried wiping the dust and small rocks off the smooth patch with little success. The area was just dirt.

Ali crossed her arms and glanced around again. It was still the only spot that could hide a door.

A plume of dust suddenly engulfed the cave around her. Ali coughed and squinted to see.

Heidis's tail wagged gently back and forth. The soft tuft of fur at the end whipped dust and rocks into a vortex.

"Heidis!" Ali choked on dust.

"Ali, did you call?"

Ali squinted her eyes open to see the dragon's large face right in front of hers. She jumped back with a yelp.

Heidis cocked her head to the side with curious confusion, and her tail wagged in a happier exuberance.

"Ali?"

"Could you keep your tail still," Ali coughed on the dust, "you're kicking up all the dust."

"Oh." The dragon's posture drooped. "Sorry."

Ali waved her hand at the dust until she could breathe again.

"It's all right." She rested her hand on the creature's face and gave it a comforting rub.

Heidis purred and leaned into the touch.

"You shouldn't pet dragons," Heidis chimed, still enjoying the contact. "We're fierce and scary."

She snorted, disturbing the dust as though it proved her point.

"Very scary." Ali laughed as she returned her attention to the ground.

"Well, I didn't mean stop." Heidis chided while nuzzling Ali with her nose.

"Heidis, I'm still trying to find the door," Ali said, though she rested her hand on top of the dragon's nose anyway and rubbed it.

"You already did, it's right here." Heidis pointed to the smooth area of the ground.

Ali frowned, "I thought so, but there's a lot of dirt on top of it."

"Ali, you okay?" Erc's voice carried over from the twists of Heidis's body.

"Fine," Ali called back, "found the door, it's covered with dirt."

"Heidis, stay still. I'm going to climb over you," Erc called back.

"I'm a dragon! A terrifying creature of destruction," Heidis returned, though she did not bother moving her head away from where Ali was petting her.

"Yeah, yeah," Erc called back as she appeared over the top of the creature.

"Heidis, without moving the rest of your body," Ali prefaced as Erc started to descend, "could you bring your tail over here?"

The scaly mass shifted ever so slightly until the furry end popped out next to Ali. The feathered end of the tail flicked across Ali, disheveling a coat of dust.

Ali coughed. "Thanks, could you dust this spot."

She pointed to the door.

"Fine, but only if you keep petting me."

"Ali?" Erc appeared next to Ali, trying to dust herself off.

"Don't bother, it's going to get worse." Ali waved her free hand before pinching her nose. "Maybe hold your breath."

Heidis flicked her tail again, raising plumes of dust into the air.

Ali squeezed her eyes closed and waited a moment before squinting to see. The dust was still thick. She heard Erc coughing next to her.

"There, that good?" Heidis purred next to her, shifting her giant head to remind Ali to keep petting her.

Ali waved the dust away as she dared to breathe again.

Breathing was a mistake. Ali joined Erc in a fit of couching before the air cleared enough for comfort.

"That's it?" Erc was the first to speak.

Ali squinted again before she dared to open her eyes. A door melded seamlessly with the ground around it in a show of clever craftsmanship.

"Can we tell if it's Oracaede's or not?" Ali asked, glancing from the door to Erc.

The dark woman stood, frowning while examining the door. She shrugged and shook her head.

"Heidis, when was the last time this was opened?" Erc asked.

The dragon hummed as she pulled up from Ali and loosely scratched at her chin.

"The last new moon and a half moon, I think it was. Around then."

Erc squeezed her eyes closed.

"That would have been two months ago. They're still actively using it." Erc looked over to Ali, "You're right, we should go."

Heidis dropped her head back to their height, "What, you're leaving? Don't go. I miss you. There's no one here and it's lonely. Please…"

The dragon continued to whine as they walked back to the entrance.

"Sorry, Heidis," Ali raised her hand as the dragon immediately lowered her head to be petted, "but it's dangerous for us here."

Erc stopped walking next to the blocker.

"Heidis," Erc started, "we need this. Will you trade it for the tracker?"

Erc was already messing with the tracker, changing the frequency so it would not lead right back to them.

"No!" Heidis yelled.

She wrapped her tail around Ali, "I'll let you take it if Ali stays."

"Heidis." Ali unwrapped the dragon's tail.

"But," the big creature was verging on tears, "I don't want to be alone. I hate it! Please stay."

Ali exchanged a look with Erc.

We can't just leave her.

Erc sighed.

"Heidis, does Oracaede know you sneak out?"

"Hmm, yeah. They said I shouldn't, but they can't stop me. They stopped bringing me food since I get it myself when I'm out. I think that means they must be okay with it."

"All right," Erc granted, "we might be able to—"

"Yay!" Heidis did a bouncing wave of a jump as her body rolled through the air.

"But there are conditions."

The dragon still wasn't listening as she continued jumping around in excitement.

"Heidis!" Ali called.

The dragon's attention snapped to her.

"There are conditions," Ali repeated, pointing the dragon's attention back to Erc.

"Conditions?" Heidis groaned, dropping her head to the ground.

"First, you can only visit and only on the same regularity you go out for food now."

"But that's only every couple of days," the dragon whined, "Can't I just stay with you?"

"Heidis, if Oracaede found out you were visiting us at all, they would hurt us." Ali reasoned, "You don't want that, do you?"

"Of course not." Heidis purred, rubbing her head against Ali, "That would be too sad."

"On that note, condition number two." Erc held up two fingers, "You can't let anyone know you're visiting us. Especially Oracaede."

"That includes," Ali quickly picked up, "playing guessing games and offering hints. You can't let anyone know about this."

"That's easy, no one ever talks to me here." Heidis nodded. "Anything else?"

"Yes," Ali said as Erc started shaking her head, "You can't be stealing food from people anymore."

"Aww, but that's so much easier than finding it." Heidis pouted.

"The people you steal it from have to find and collect it for themselves too." Erc pointed out.

"Yeah, there are several islands between here and our island, you can eat what's on those islands, but don't steal anymore."

Ali waited for the big head to nod. "Those are all the conditions then."

"Then, can I come visit?" Heidis chirped with her tail already wagging furiously. "Right now?"

"When was the last time you were out?" Erc asked, "Condition number one."

Heidis frowned in thought a moment before smiling, "It was when I took your stuff, I was going out today or tomorrow anyway."

Erc sighed again. "Fine, you can come back with us now."

"You owe us a winter supply of food, you know," Ali added as she picked up the blocker and started heaving it toward the entrance of the cave.

"I'll bring you food. I will, I will!" Heidis was bouncing around the cave again before she dove into the water. "Come on!"

Erc balanced the tracker on top of the blocker as she helped Ali carry it on the precarious water passage.

"When something goes wrong and that dragon makes a mess, you're cleaning it up. Hear me, Ali?" Erc cocked an eyebrow in Ali's direction.

"I hear you."

CHAPTER 59

S had watched the unorganized line of Nomads march, if their uneven steps and pace could be called such.

A few more paces and they would be in position. He flashed a quick smile to Ammon before focusing on shifting his form.

He had initially hated Ammon's idea to use Shad's Shade form to scare the Nomads, but he couldn't deny that it was working. And working fantastically. He even found it fun to watch the Nomads run away from him in terror.

Shad could only keep his form shifted for a moment or two. Shifting combined with using his mental powers cut that time in half and he was losing more time each time he shifted. Half a moment was all he could manage before collapsing.

A half a moment of a Shade and unintelligible mumblings in the minds of every Nomad in sight was enough, however. The Nomads, surprisingly acting like sensible people, bolted at the first sight of a Shade.

Shad took a moment to steady himself from shifting before he stood from the undergrowth he and Ammon had been hiding and started moving toward the nearest Nomad. Said Nomad continued acting sensibly and screamed a warning for those around him before the unorganized march became a chaotic retreat.

Behind Shad, Ammon, and the few soldiers, they had brought along loosed arrows on the fleeing Nomads. Most of the ones they shot weren't killed, but the screams of pain were worth so much more in instilling terror.

Shad dropped behind some bushes and fell back into his wraith form, panting though he could not manage to catch his breath. He tried shaking the dizziness out of his head, but that only made it worst.

Don't pass out, don't pass out, don't pass out...

Shad repeated his mantra as he swayed on all fours, fighting to stay upright. He lost the battle and toppled onto his side where he lay still with a vain hope he might be able to catch his breath.

"Shad?" Ammon's voice was a whispered shout as the rustle of the undergrowth announce his approach.

Shad held up his hand and waved to let the man know his position before he returned his full attention to not passing out.

"Hey, that was great, pal. You had 'em runnin' like rabbits," Ammon said, taking a seat next to Shad and handing him a canteen of water.

Shad accepted the water and drank greedily.

"How you managin'? That the last time?" Ammon asked with a serious note in his tone.

Shad shook his head as he struggled to prop himself up on his elbows. The action was half to answer Ammon's question and half to clear his head.

"You sure?" Ammon's hawkish eyes bore through Shad, looking for a lie in the answer.

Shad did not even bother trying to hide his doubt with a smile.

"No, but we still have to try."

"You're an idiot," Ammon offered back in earnest.

"Thanks."

Shad rolled his eyes and pushed up to a sitting position. He was glad the change in posture did not arouse a dizzy spell.

Ammon noticed too as he stood and pulled Shad up with him.

"Good, dragging you back would be a hassle." Ammon was talking more to himself than Shad.

"Sirs," One of the soldiers sauntered over to them with a gesture toward the hill the Nomads had disappeared over, "they're regrouping."

"What? Already?" Shad moaned.

He was being honest when Ammon asked if he could go again, but not so soon.

Ammon patted his shoulder and offered a grin that was just barred teeth.

"Ready for another go-round?"

Shad shoved his hand away with a rude gesture.

Ammon cussed at Shad in the Glasic tongue as he turned to address his soldiers.

"Men, we're gonna need a new tactic, this one ain't keepin' 'em runnin' scared long enough anymore. Be knockin' your heads together thinkin' of somethin' while we go again."

"Let's fall back to that ridge," Shad added with a point to the next hill closer to the city.

"Move it!" Ammon ordered, still grinning like a shark as he spoke, "Get your tutus in order and march."

Shad fell in step next to the tanned man as they headed out.

"Man, you have such a way with people. How do you manage to survive?"

"Bite me, wraith-face."

Shad scoffed as they settled into silence for a moment.

"What else could we use to scare them or at least slow their approach?" Shad thought aloud as they approached the next hill.

"Hell, I don't know. Waitin' for you to think of something." Ammon yawned.

"Such a model of leadership you are." Shad shook his head.

"Delegation is a wonderful thing."

"I so only have one or two more shifts in me, then I'll be down for the day." Shad pivoted topics.

"I figured. That rouse was only going to be effective so long anyway."

The silence returned when they reached the top of the hill and hunkered down to wait.

"Sir," The same soldier as before approached them, "I had a thought for what we could try next."

Ammon nodded. "Spit it forth then, man."

Shad rolled his eyes.

"Yes, sir," The soldier smiled at the lieutenant's remark, "We have enough explosives and the like to lay some traps here. We could spread them out from here to the next ridge and start setting them off whensoever they be on them."

"That's a terrible idea," Ammon growled as he pinched his face to think about it.

He finally smirked. "I like it."

The soldier remained impassive and nodded.

Ammon gave Shad a sidelong glance.

"Sounds good to me." Shad pitched in.

"'Course it does, Sergeant Belfist here always has hideous ideas."

"Thank you, sir." Sgt. Belfist acknowledged before returning to the rest of the soldiers who were milling around.

"Here we are men, compliments of Belfist," Ammon started. "Take your packs and set whatever 'splosives you got between here and the far hill. Make sure to connect them to your AaDs for remote detonation and remember where you put 'em."

Shad moved back up the hill to grab his pouch where he had left it. He glanced over the top of the hill as he reached it.

The Nomads had already started over the last hill.

"Shi—Ammon!" Shad crouched and waved the man over.

Ammon crept to Shad's position and peered over the hilltop. He scowled.

"They're tryin' to set some records here."

"Sure looks like it," Shad grumbled to himself.

Ammon gave him a sharp look with a clear question.

"Yeah, I can go again." Shad answered, chewing at his lip, "But I can't promise I won't pass out, so be ready to drag me back."

Ammon scoffed, "You think I'm gonna let you sleep, you're crazy."

Shad rolled his eyes while he crept through the bushes over the hill. He continued along an uninterrupted line of underbrush tall enough to conceal him as long as possible. Small noises behind him let him know Ammon was right there to watch his back.

He paused and waited a moment for the Nomads to move closer to his position. He waited and breathed, collecting any reserves of strength he could.

Shad shifted forms and stood. He released a wave of mental energy forwards and swayed as the effort nearly knocked him out.

The screaming started and chaos erupted, but Shad was disappointed at how quickly it seemed to quiet. As soon as he saw most of the Nomads were facing away from him, he ducked back into the underbrush and collapsed.

Shad drifted through consciousness with little awareness of what was about him. Ammon's disembodied voice floated above him and a hand, gripping at his shoulders, shook him.

Shad tried to smack the hand away but could not quite manage to move his arm. The shaking stopped and Shad felt himself being dragged.

Blinking at the sky, Shad noticed it was coming back into focus and the voices around him became clearer. He fought on instinct against the hands pulling him along through the undergrowth.

"Shad?" Ammon whispered from behind his head. "You back with me?"

"Yeah," Shad mumbled as he focused his strength on the task of sitting upright.

"Shush," Ammon held him down, "they're onto us, Shad. They were shouting about it being a trick as soon as you dropped out."

Shad growled and forced himself onto his elbows. Through the bushes, he could see the Nomads steadily moving forward, weapons drawn and stabbing spears through any suspicious-looking undergrowth they passed.

"Can you move?" Ammon whispered.

"Yeah," Shad answered, hoping it was not a lie.

"Good," Ammon pushed Shad in front of him, "take point, then. We need to get over that hill and run to the next one before they reach this one and our boys start poppin' tops off."

Shad grunted but saved his talking energy to crawl. He kept up the fastest, quiet pace he could, but they were still only a step or two ahead of the Nomads.

Shad suspected they had moved faster when Ammon was dragging him, but he pushed himself onwards the best he could anyway.

Finally, they started putting distance between themselves and the enemy as Shad's head cleared enough for him to quicken his pace.

They cleared the hill before the Nomads reached the base of it.

Ammon pulled Shad up and pushed him forward.

Run," he growled.

Shad did as he was told, focusing all his energy on placing one foot in front of the other in quick succession without toppling over.

Ammon, running beside him, kept him upright several times he would have otherwise fallen over.

They reached the base of the next hill their soldiers stood at the top of, waving them up, just as shouts in multiple languages sounded from behind them. The Nomads cleared the last hill and were running to catch them.

"Get this party started, boys," Ammon shouted as they reached the hilltop.

Belfist waved the men to action with a call, "Furthest first."

The skyline behind them erupted as Shad collapsed. He could hear screams and shouts from the Nomads' many languages, but it was all out of focus to him.

He pulled out his AaD and dialed Bry's number. His friend answered on the second ring.

"Shad, how are—"

"They're not listening to our distractions much anymore!" Shad shouted as another charge went off, "Won't be buying you as much time as we hoped. We're about out of explosives and ideas here."

"Right, fall back." Bry ordered, "I'll send out what troops I have, meet up with them, and hold ground."

"Righto!" Shad shouted back and hung up the call.

He stood and pointed his men toward the next hill, snapping orders to retreat once they set off their charges.

"Shad," Ammon was at his elbow, pulling him away to the next ridge.

"Bry's sending out troops, we gotta meet up with them," Shad relayed as he started running after the soldiers.

"Great," Ammon, shouted next to him, bringing up the rear of their retreat.

CHAPTER 60

S had waited, crouched along the ridge top, checking over one side then the other as his group waited for either Bry's army or the Nomads to come into view first.

The hill they rested on was the last one before the city. Their army might have a small advantage they desperately needed if they could reach the high ground first.

"There!" Belfist shouted, pointing over the hill as the Nomads came into view.

"Damn," Ammon said at the same time Shad did.

They exchanged a glance before turning to scan the other side. A small, wooded area beyond the fields obscured the view of the city gate.

Movement among the trees had Shad leaning forwards and straining his eyes. A glint of metal helmets brought him immediate relief.

"There they are." Shad clapped his hands together and smiled at Ammon.

Ammon stared, with an ever-sharp gaze, at the Sentrian army before pivoting his stance to look back toward the Nomads.

"Not fast enough, they're not."

Ammon growled and rubbed at the stubble on his jaw.

"Belfist," Shad called the sergeant to him, "run over there, find the commander, and tell him to send his cavalry over here. We need to create a line on this ridge that the Nomads won't cross while the rest of the army gets here."

The sergeant nodded and took off running toward the wooded area.

"Gonna create an illusion of numbers up here, eh." Ammon nodded along to the idea.

"If you've got actual numbers hiding in that mustache, I'd take those too." Shad grinned.

Ammon snorted as he stroked the offending piece of facial hair.

They sat motionless on the hilltop, alternating between watching each side approach.

Belfist reached the soldiers, and Shad watched the short conversation take place before horsemen started galloping in their direction.

On the other side, the Nomads had reached the base of their hill, and a few optimistic fighters were running toward them.

The calvary reached the top first and the optimistic fighters about-faced to race back down.

Jair swung off his horse and walked toward Shad though he never took his eyes off the expanse of Nomads stretched out on the plane below them.

"Well, there's our little problem. A few too many Nomads for us." Shad tried to keep his smile cheerful, but he was still keen on passing out at any sudden movement.

Jair glowered at him. "A few, eh?"

"Yep."

Jair glared at him with a softer look, "Are you okay?"

Shad forced his smile wider, "Yep, just tired of these guys in my backyard."

Jair watched him for a few slow moments before he shrugged and returned to his horse. He rode down the line of horses and soldiers, shouting something, but Shad completely tuned him out to focus on steadying his breathing.

Shad clenched his fists to keep them from shaking from all the energy he had already used shifting so many times.

The front lines of the Nomads remained stationary at the base of the hill, shouting up insults and jeering at Jair.

Shad hoped they might remain so preoccupied until the rest of the soldiers on foot arrived, but the Nomads were too impatient and started running up the hill.

"Ready 'o fight, boys?" Ammon shouted, throwing a glance over the soldiers of their small team before settling his gaze on Shad's trembling fists.

Ammon flashed Shad a concerned look and nodded back toward the castle.

I'm fine, just tired, and no, I'm not going to sit this one out.

Shad spoke to Ammon's mind on reflex, forgetting in the moment that he had never done that with Ammon before.

The hawkish eyes widened and blinked before he nodded and turned back to the Nomads.

"Hold 'dis line!"

Shad heard Jair's orders as the Nomads clashed against them. Shad sliced with his Moro blades. He remained in constant motion as the battle dragged on.

Out of the corner of his eye, Shad saw Belfist drop with a spear in his side. Another of the soldiers he had just been working with fell a moment later.

A shout behind him sounded the arrival of the rest of the Sentrian army. The new troops brought more blood as they started pushing the Nomads back.

As the afternoon dragged on, Shad ducked behind a small cluster of trees to catch his breath. He surveyed the battle raging around him. The better-trained Sentrian army was holding its own for being so outnumbered.

After a moment of watching, Shad realized the Sentrian army seemed to be made up mostly of non-soldiers. Tradesmen, farmers, and castle guards all mixed together with spears and swords and some little armor.

Shad scanned the field in front of him, hoping to find Ammon at least, upright, and not injured.

A flash of white caught his attention and held it. Shad gaped at the Ghost. He was in the troughs of a gaggle of Nomads, cutting them to pieces.

"Since when was he on our side?" Shad mumbled as he pushed away from his resting place and steadily cut his way toward the assassin.

Shad neared the Ghost as a fanciful idea popped into his head.

If I can keep him around after the battle, Lawr might be able to find out about his niece.

An arrow flew past Shad and hit its target with a wet smack.

Shad scanned the direction it had come from and spotted the quiet girl they had arrested with Aike.

A Wolf?

Shad turned around to see the arrow firmly lodged in Sverre's back, near his shoulder blade.

The Ghost turned and scanned the trees as well before his gaze settled on Shad with a look approaching surprised.

"Hey," Shad started.

He watched the assassin shift his stance, unsure whether he should attack or not.

"You're gonna stay alive," Shad shouted over the din of battle, "Lawr has some questions for you about his niece."

Shad held his breath a moment until he saw the assassin nod and turn back to the fighting around them. He would count that as a tremendous triumph that the Ghost was not going to try fighting him.

Just wait, Lawr, I'll fix what I messed up.

Shad grinned and turned back to the battle. A voice behind him again distracted him from his own fight.

"Sorry, Sverre. It's nothing personal, but you're still our mission."

Shad turned in time to see a young Hispanic man launch at Sverre. The assassin dodged without striking back, but he was slow. The man's blade caught at the shaft of the arrow in his back. The motion pulled the arrowhead, tearing it through his shoulder before the shaft snapped.

Sverre yelped, dropping to his knees as he held his freely bleeding shoulder.

"Shit!" Shad jumped between the two.

A flick of his wrist sliced the young man deep across the chest, catching a piece of his neck.

Shad flinched at the gash. He had only meant to cut the kid, but the man had stepped forward to attack at the same moment.

The man gurgled as blood poured from his wound. He stared at Shad for a moment with wide blank eyes before he collapsed.

"Hid!"

The shout came from close behind Shad. He spun but was forced to stop short. He stared into the familiar freckled face of a bright-eyed young man that was somehow right in front of him.

Aike. A Wolf. Good kid.

His brain was slow to supply him with the information.

Aike had a wild, enraged look about him, but Shad could not focus. His chest hurt, and he glanced down to see Aike's sword buried hilt deep in it.

The world tilted and froze but started moving again before Shad could gain his balance.

Aike ripped his sword out, knocking Shad aside as he scrambled toward Shad's fallen opponent.

The world spun around Shad until he was staring straight up at the sky. His sight was fuzzy, but he could see Aike cradling his fallen comrade in his arms.

Bry...

He could not think straight, but Shad knew he needed Bry there.

Bry!

His power snapped out painfully before fading around him.

Shad was vaguely aware of a group forming near him and his last opponent being carried away. The world in his view was left still and void of movement as it darkened.

"Bry..." Shad called hopelessly.

In the darkness above him, a shadow moved and pulled itself to sit beside him.

Bry?

Shad reached out with his mind and hand, hoping to grasp any human contact he could.

"No, Shad." The voice was familiar, but not the one Shad hoped for.

The shadow above leaned closer. Through the darkness, Shad could make out white locks of hair and brilliant crimson eyes.

"It's okay," the voice continued speaking, "You're not alone, it's okay. Relax."

He clung with his powers to the man's mind who, while Shad knew he was familiar, could not place why. The world around him was completely dark.

He could sense the murmurings in the man's mind more than he could hear what was being said.

The voice soon joined the dark world as his mind fell into blackness.

CHAPTER 61

B ry doubled over with a yelp, interrupting Chesler's update as a splitting headache distracted him from all else.

It was the same kind of headache he had had once before when Shad first tried to use his powers.

"Bry."

Lawr's voice sounded like metal grinding together in his head.

Bry glanced up at the man. Lawr was at his desk, holding his head with his eyes screwed shut.

"Brynte, Lawrence, what's the matter?" Chesler glanced between them with a look of concern.

Bry ignored the man as he tried thinking through the immense pain.

"Is this Shad?" Lawr growled out, cracking an eye in Bry's direction.

"I don't know. Maybe a Shade attack," Bry managed to speak.

The sound of his own voice sent spikes of agony piercing through his head.

"I'll call the healer." Chesler was at his side with an AaD in his hand and an unusual, concerned look.

The AaD suddenly chirped to life as someone was calling him.

Bry yelped at the noise and clapped his hands over his ears.

"Make it stop," Lawr groaned from his desk.

Chesler answered, "It's the healer. Hello ma'am, we have a—"

"Bry, what is this?" Eleanora's pained voice said from the AaD, ignoring Chesler's greeting.

"El?" Bry growled into the device.

"Your Majesty, this is Leha." Another voice sounded from the AaD,

"Stori and both Klaas and Eleanora are in pain. What is happening?"

"Same with us," Bry ground out, "You're not hurting?"

"No, I'm fine," Leha answered.

"I'm not affected either." Chesler frowned.

Bry blinked at him.

Not a Shade attack, then.

"It must be Shad," Bry waved to Chesler, "call him."

The headache was subsiding by a minuscule amount, but he used the change to take the AaD from Chesler and dial Shad.

Bry clapped his hands back over his ears rather than listen to the device ring. Bry's heart constricted the longer the device rang without being answered.

Something's wrong.

A growing panic crept into Bry's mind that he could not shake. He thought through a hundred reasons why Shad would not answer, namely the battle, but his panic only grew.

"Lawr, I need to find Shad," Bry stated, pushing himself up from the desk and using Chesler as a crutch as he made his way to the door.

"I'll call him again," Lawr returned, taking one hand from his head to maneuver his AaD closer.

Bry did not wait as he exited the room. Turning to the guard posed at his door, Bry's heart sunk that the man was not affected.

Only us who are close to Shad.

The thought tightened the dread already knotting in his stomach.

"Your Majesty, are you all right?" The guard glanced between Bry and Chesler with eyes mixed with concern and confusion.

"I need to get to the battle," Bry growled.

The headache was growing fainter, enough that he did not need to lean against Chesler anymore, but it was still miserable.

"Your Majesty, that may not be—"

Bry glowered at Chesler until the man closed his mouth.

"Help him to the stable and prepare a horse and guards to accompany him."

Chesler turned to ordering the guard instead of debating Bry. Bry was more grateful to the man than he had ever been as he followed the guard.

They moved through the courtyards and to the stables without other interruptions. The guard spat orders with authority no one questioned, and

Bry was able to relax for a small moment before they mounted their horses and rode out.

Bry kept one hand on the reigns and one on his head. The rhythm of riding horseback continued rattling his brain painfully against his skull at each step.

Outside the gate, Bry galloped until the sounds of battle drowned his head with fresh agony. The headache was duller though, enough for Bry to think.

He remained on his horse and scanned the battlefield. The Sentrian army, mostly made up of refugees and people from the city desperate not to lose their homes, had pushed the Nomads back across the plane and over the next ridge.

Bry urged his horse forward. The animal nimbly picked its way through the field of bodies.

A soldier near the rear of the fighting started running toward Bry. When he reached him, he stopped with a breathless greeting.

"I need to find Shadric. Have you seen him?" Bry interrupted whatever the man intended to say.

The soldier paused to draw breath.

"Your Majesty...I haven't seen the wraith, but...there is something." The man paused again to catch his breath. "It's the Ghost, he's injured and unconscious. Looks like he was attacked by a Shade."

Bry jerked at the news.

"There aren't any Shades here, just Shad. Where's the Ghost?"

The soldier pointed to a huddle of soldiers back away from the main battle.

Bry turned his horse and galloped the short distance. He leaped from his horse and pushed his way through the crowd.

At the center, the albino assassin lay on his side, unconscious with half an arrow stabbed through his shoulder.

Blood streaked across his face. His eyes, nose, mouth, and ears all leaked the crimson fluid. A classic sign of someone whose mind had been overwhelmed by a Shade.

Bry scanned the area around him. Next to the assassin, a human-shaped pile of soot. The same soot of a disintegrated Shade when it died. Amiss the soot were black bands and ties Shad always had on him and an AaD.

Bry fell to his knees without taking his eyes from the soot.

"Shad?" he whispered, reaching out to stroke one of the black ties.

The AaD chirped with an incoming call. The ID of the caller read *weirdo genius*.

Bry reached a numb hand out to answer the call.

"Shad?" Lawr's voice sighed in relief as he spoke, "Are you okay? You're giving us all headaches."

"Lawr," Bry's voice was distant in his ears, "Shad isn't here."

"Bry? Where is he?"

"He's not *h-here* anymore," Bry repeated in a whisper.

His eyes drifted to the Ghost's prone body.

"Bastard killed him."

Bry lunged and wrapped his hands around the still man's throat. "You bastard!"

"Bry?! Bry?"

He ignored Lawr's voice as he growled every threat in an incoherent stream as he alternated between strangling and shaking the man to wake him up.

"Bry!" A pair of hands yanked Bry back.

Bry snarled at the familiar face in front of him.

Ammon was crouched next to him with a confused look glancing between Bry and the Ghost and holding a hand between them.

"Bry, he's out. You're going to kill him."

"Yes, I am."

Bry tried lunging back at the assassin's throat, but Ammon stopped him again.

"He killed Shad!" Bry screamed, gesturing to the soot.

Ammon froze and looked down for the first time.

Some of the soldiers in the circle stated something about someone else stabbing Shad, but Bry ignored them, glaring at Ammon.

Bry tried strangling the assassin again, but Ammon was there to pull him back in an instant.

"Bry, calm down."

There was a hitch in Ammon's voice as he dragged Bry back, out of the growing circle of soldiers.

"Take the Ghost prisoner. He needs medical treatment, but tie him up. And the soot on the ground there," Ammon swallowed hard, "that soot was an important member of the king's family. Gather it up carefully."

Ammon continued to push Bry back to the castle.

CHAPTER 62

Aike sat gazing off into space without a thought.

The small village they had run to was empty of inhabitants. The men had joined the fight, and the rest sought refuge in the city.

Aike's gaze turned down to where he cradled Hid's head in his lap. He stroked a hand over soft hair while Hid's body remained as limp and lifeless as it had when they took him from the battlefield.

Around him, the Wolves sat in various stages of grief. Xiulan sat by Hid's side, holding his hand and crying in complete silence. The others were louder, huddled nearby.

Aike returned his gaze to the empty face of his closest friend. He leaned down and kissed Hid's forehead. He shifted carefully to get out from under the man and gently set his head on the ground.

Aike stood and turned toward the receding battle.

The Sentrians are winning, Hid. Imagine that. We forgot about the refugees. They are fighting like hell not to lose their homes twice.

Aike glanced back toward the city, his mind still boarding on the edge of a decision.

We failed. Reb will kill Retha and me at least...

"Idir, Bary," Aike addressed the two teammates who were holding themselves together the best.

They did not look well either, but they had made themselves the shoulder others could cry on, and that was the best they had.

"W-we..." Aike's voice faltered before he tried again to wrangle his thoughts. "We need to get Retha back. We failed, and Reb won't keep her alive."

Aike watched the others gaze at him with tearful eyes. Idir stood from where he was comforting Caesar Apollo and Xiulan. Bary released Sa'dia and stood as well.

"Xiulan," Aike waited for the soulful eyes to focus on him, "get Hid…"

Again, his voice failed and he fought to continue, "Get him and everyone else into the city. We'll need to lay low. Go back to an inn we know, and we'll meet you there with Retha."

Xiulan trembled but nodded. She continued holding Hid's hand without any appearance of completing the task soon.

Aike spared a glance to the two teammates waiting at his side before nodding and moving off in the direction of the battle.

They picked their way around, skirting the battlefield until they ended up behind the Avare camp.

They crouched low in the bushes, watching the quiet campsite. The camp was mostly empty except for a few of the most skittish clan leaders and their aides.

"Idir, take left," Aike ordered, "Bary, right. I'll go talk to Reb, and I'll call your AaDs if I find anything."

"Yes, sir," the two said in unison before disappearing into the camp.

Aike continued straight, weaving through the tent maze until he reached Reb's. He steeled himself outside, wiping his eye, adjusting the bandage over the other, and clearing his face of any emotion.

He stepped inside and blinked to adjust to the low light.

"Wolf!" Reb's voice snapped from a back corner.

The woman marched over to him. Her eyes were still wild, but now held a haze of drunken stupor.

"What you doing here?" she snapped despite the slur in her voice.

"We completed our mission," Aike lied.

He had not bothered to kneel either as he stared forward with a vacant gaze, "The Ghost is dead, probably. I came to get Retha back."

"I'll return the brat when I decide…" Reb's slurring cut off as she looked Aike up and down, "why're you up here? Kneel."

Aike remained stationary.

You're gonna be in trouble, hermano.

Aike jerked at Hid's voice echoing in his head.

"Where is Retha?" Aike asked, ignoring the voice since listening would threaten more tears.

Reb stumbled backward, swearing in every language possible.

"Brat'll stay in my tent 'til I decide..." Reb still slurred.

Aike did not listen to the rest. He pulled out his AaD and called Idir.

"Idir, she's on your side, in Reb's tent. Call Bary back when you have her and meet outside camp, I'll be along in a moment."

Aike hung up, and Reb was snarling in his face.

"You can't ignore me, Wolf. Lying bastard," Reb growled, searching for anything in her immediate vicinity to throw at him.

Aike breathed in and out.

"Hid's dead."

"Who cares," Reb snapped back.

Aike nodded to himself. He took a knife from his belt and buried it in Reb's chest.

The woman stared at him with eyes frozen wide as she sputtered on breath.

"I care," Aike whispered.

He ripped the knife out and let her body drop.

Nice going, hermano.

Aike stepped over the body and walked to the cabinet in the back corner. He rifled through the draws until he found three vials marked 'Bary.' He took the medicine and left the tent, operating in a daze until he reached the edge of the camp where the others waited.

"What do you mean?" Retha was snarling, "Hid's fine. Hid's always fine."

She turned to Aike as he approached.

"Aike, tell them to stop lying. Hid is fine."

She repeated the statement until it started to turn into a question then a plea.

Aike wrapped an arm around the girl as soon as he reached her. Retha remained frozen and silent in his grip for only a moment before her body shook with silent sobs.

Aike handed the vials of medicine to Bary.

"How'd you get them?" Bary blinked at the vials as he took them before turning to stare at Aike.

"I took them," Aike stated.

"Reb let you?" Bary questioned.

Aike held his gaze until realization lit Bary's eyes.

"Bloody hell."

Idir caught on quickly too.

"We need run," Idir stated, pulling Retha away and pushing Bary forward, aimed toward the city, in one smooth motion.

Aike nodded and followed behind the others. Now that the immediate mission had been completed, tears started flowing down his face again.

Really, Hid's voice was back, *Good job, hermano. You keep them safe.*

CHAPTER 63

A li watched the boys use Heidis's back as a diving board. Splashing about in the water, Heidis was having a hard time containing her excitement enough to hold still.

"Leon, Leon, Leon! Great jump!" Heidis bubbled, twirling her body in circles before diving underwater and coming up again under Charlton.

"Want to jump?! Higher?" Heidis made an excited purr while she arched her back and extended her body up as high as she could. Some fifty feet above the water's surface, Charlton was peering down over the scaly surface he stood on.

Ali was about to say that was too high when Heidis realized the same thing.

"Too high." She purred and she snaked her body around itself until she had lowered her back by half the distance. She continued to lower her body, but Charlton, deciding it was low enough, leaped toward the water below with an energetic shout.

Ali clapped and laughed as Leon did the same, motioning to the dragon that he wanted to go again.

"These kids," Erc tutted as she and Incara carried their picnic items to set them beside Ali.

"Your son's a daredevil." Ali smiled as she stood and helped set up the picnic space.

"He's just crazy," Incara chimed as she hurried out of her hat and shoes, ready to jump in the water, "They both are."

She ran off the edge of the rock outcropping and dove into the clear blue water.

"Yep," Erc shook her head, "All three of them. Crazy."

Ali laughed again as she watched the children play and Leon jump from the dragon's back again.

We'll have to do this again when Sverre and Dain get back.

She smiled at the thought. She wondered what Sverre would say about their new friend. Surely Heidis could win over the two men as easily as she had done with everyone else. Even Incara had not been able to stay mad around the dragon.

Ali and Erc took turns watching the kids as they prepared sandwiches and set aside a massive pile of fruit and vegetables that Heidis had brought for her own lunch.

When they had everything set up, Erc called the kids over. The boys both complained, hoping for longer in the water before they each seemed to realize how hungry they were. The complaints turned into a race to the picnic space and in eating.

Incara bounced to the area in her own time and plopped down next to her mother.

"Oh, lunch? What is that? Can I have some?" Heidis twisted her body over to sniff the sandwiches.

"Heidis, no." Ali batted the nose away. "Your food is right there."

She patted the pile of vegetables and fruit next to her.

"For me!" Heidis lit up with such excitement, Ali wondered if the dragon had forgotten that she was the one who brought all the food.

"Yes, yes."

Ali stroked the dragon's head before the creature dove to devour her meal with such ferocity to make Ali thankful the dragon was a vegetarian.

As the meal ended, the boys impatiently tried to convince Erc that they could get back into the water immediately and not risk getting a cramp.

"Boys, why don't you show Heidis around the island?" Ali suggested an alternate. "On land, of course."

She added the last quickly before the kids or the dragon had any dangerous ideas.

A chirp of an AaD interrupted the boy's excitement. Erc picked up the AaD she had tucked away with the picnic supplies.

"It's Dain!" Erc clutched the AaD as the kids and Ali immediately gathered around her.

"Maybe they're coming back!" Leon said, excitedly leaning as close to the AaD as possible.

"Who's Dain?" Heidis asked, cocking her head to the side as she still seemed as excited as everyone else in the group and snuggled a little closer.

"My husband," Erc stated with pride as she answered, "The best man in all the worlds."

"That would be Sverre," Leon countered, turning to the dragon, "But Dain is the best too."

"Honey, how are you? Are you safe?" Erc asked into the device.

Her question was quickly drowned out as they all busily talked over each other with growing excitement.

"Sverre's gone," Dain said, silencing every one of them.

"What?" Ali sputtered. She and Leon leaned closer to each other and the device.

"Honey," Erc stared at the AaD with wide eyes, "what do you mean 'gone?'"

There was a heavy, hitching sigh from the other end of the call.

"Missing. Maybe dead." A pause, "Probably...Probably dead."

"What?" Ali choked, tears springing to her eyes.

Leon stared wide-eyed at the AaD as though he would not understand what was being said. Ali wrapped an arm tightly around the boy on instinct as she too stared at the device.

"We were separated before the battle," Dain continued, "I haven't seen him since, but I overheard some soldiers talking. They found the Ghost in critical condition. Attacked by a Shade. He's at the castle."

"A Shade?" Erc barely gave the words voice, "People don't live..."

Another sigh from the device, "People don't often live through Shade attacks. I know. I'm still trying to figure out what...how...I don't know."

"Dain, how can...when will...Please," Leon sputtered out fragments of questions before settling on the begging 'please' as he remained wide-eyed with tears finding their hold.

"I'll bring him back. Whatever I find..." Dain's voice trailed off before he started again, "I'm staying here until I can. Stay safe."

With that, the call dropped as Dain hung up.

Silence clung to the group, heavier that the Vis.

"That can't be...Sverre has to come back." Leon broke the silence with a voice that pitched with the falling tears.

CHAPTER 64

C aelyn stared out the window, taking in the bustle of the city even when most of the streets were empty of all men who were able to fight the Nomads.

Rhoeo had disappeared for the afternoon, and Caelyn was ashamed that the space brought her so much relief.

She had apologized profusely for yelling at the guard. Rhoeo had apologized stiffly for overstepping. She continued with sad news about her family. Rhoeo had said she was upset about the news and overacted to Caelyn being away.

Something in Caelyn's gut distrusted that, but she could not tell why so she ignored it. The news of Rhoeo's misfortune made Caelyn feel worse for pushing her away. She had promised the guard not to do so again, but she already regretted that commitment.

Now that Rhoeo was out of the room, Caelyn was thinking of breaking that promise. Even the thought made her twinge with guilt.

She's your friend. The only one you have too.

Caelyn repeated the line to convince herself it was true.

Stori could have been a friend.

Her lip quivered at the thought. She turned to the window, hoping to ignore it.

Immediately, a memory of Rhoeo's voice echoed in her mind.

She's not trying to be your friend. It's the queen's duty to interact with others such as yourself. You're not special. And with her being pregnant and everything, you don't want to be an inconvenience to her, do you?

Caelyn's shoulders dropped at the memory of what Rhoeo repeatedly told her. She did not want to inconvenience the queen, but…

But nothing.

Rhoeo had ignored any of her attempts at rebuttals with the same words.

There was nothing else to it, Caelyn should stop attempting to talk to Stori and let the woman be.

But maybe since Rhoeo isn't around…

Caelyn glanced around the empty room with new hope. She walked to the door and poked her head out.

She did not want to bother Stori, but maybe she could just stop by quickly to say 'hi.' Rhoeo wouldn't have to know.

"Caelyn?"

Caelyn jumped at Rhoeo's voice from behind her in the hallway.

"I was just going to dinner." Caelyn jumped at the first excuse she could think of. It fell limp on her tongue as she saw Rhoeo carrying a tray of food.

"I told you I would bring you your food," Rhoeo chastised, gesturing with her head for Caelyn to open the door.

Caelyn hung her head as she complied and moved back into the room.

"Besides, there's a huge fuss in the castle," Rhoeo continued as she followed, setting the tray down on the desk, "The king's wraith pet was killed."

"What!?" Caelyn stared at the guard woman for a moment. "That's terrible."

Brynte must be miserable. And Shad was the nicest one here…

"Maybe I should go see Bry? Or Stori, they must be upset."

Caelyn wondered aloud. She still did not like Bry, but she had enjoyed their last conversation. Besides, the idea of not being there to give any help or support he may need was too childish for her to even consider.

"Why should you go? He hates you."

Caelyn flinched.

Does he? I've been so rude to him, but the last time we talked…

"But when we talked—" Caelyn tried to reason.

"That was before. I heard him yelling that people who distracted him are to blame. I'm sure he blames you."

Caelyn's mouth dropped open. "He does? He said that?"

Rhoeo shrugged.

"And I could not imagine the queen wants anything to do with you, either. Not since your last fight."

Rhoeo guided Caelyn toward the desk chair and the tray of food.

"Maybe I should apologize to her—"

"For what?" Rhoeo interrupted. "You don't have to apologize for being right."

"But I was rude in how I said—"

Rhoeo cut her off with a scoff as she gave Caelyn a less-than-gentle push into the chair.

"Who cares? No one ever apologizes for rudeness when they're right. Your mother, Loreda, certainly would not."

Caelyn frowned. Her mother never did express sorrow for being rude or even cruel, but that was not a trait she ever wanted to emulate.

"Besides," Rhoeo continued, "if the queen held your rude behavior against you, she won't be much appeased with an apology, will she? Not since you have been rude every time she has seen you."

But I don't want Stori to hate me...

"I don't know," Caelyn tried to ignore the hurtful comment and glanced up at the woman standing over her, "maybe I could try and see?"

Rhoeo crossed her arms and glared.

Caelyn shrank into herself at the disappointed and irritated look on the woman's face.

"Or maybe not," she mumbled.

"Or maybe not," Rhoeo repeated with a nod, "they don't want you around anyway."

Caelyn flinched again at the statement and pulled her arms tight around herself in a hug.

"But you don't have to want them around either," Rhoeo added in a quiet voice.

"What?" Caelyn looked up at her.

"If they weren't here, you could do whatever you wanted, couldn't you?"

Caelyn blinked, not sure of what the guard was saying.

"I d-don't," she started with a stutter, "don't want them gone. I like Stori."

"Well," Rhoeo tossed her hair and strutted a couple of steps away to lean against the wall, "Stori could stay. You don't want Brynte around though, do you?"

"I-I don't know." Caelyn focused on her hands again, "How would you even—"

"If Brynte and his friends weren't here," Rhoeo started, taking a moment to pause and examine a lock of her thick black hair, "then Loreda could return, couldn't she?"

Caelyn's eyes widened as she stared, "Mom? I could see her again?"

Rhoeo shrugged, "Only if Brynte weren't around and you were the one ruling."

Caelyn swallowed, "But Stori would be—"

"Stori is sick," Rhoeo continued without waiting for Caelyn to finish, "She is pregnant with her first child. She should not have the strain of ruling an entire sphaere while so encumbered."

Caelyn thought it over in silence. She was convinced by Rhoeo's argument, but...

Mom! I could see you again.

She bit her lip as her thoughts always circled back to that idea.

But Brynte...?

"Brynte is still ruling. How would...?"

She trailed off with a glance at Rhoeo for an answer.

The one time she doesn't jump in to interrupt me.

Caelyn frowned as the thought reminded her how much she hated it when Rhoeo did.

Rhoeo shrugged at the question.

"The king is not taking the loss of his friend well. He hardly needs the added trouble of ruling any more than Stori does."

Caelyn bit her lip at the suggestion.

"I don't think he would want that."

"You know what he wants?" Rhoeo asked, the sharp note in her tone telling Caelyn she was tired of the conversation, "He wants his friend back. Can you give him that?"

Caelyn shook her head without daring to meet the guard's eyes.

"Thought not. But you could the second best thing." Rhoeo paused to return to stand in front of Caelyn and lean down to her level. "You could let him grieve in peace without worrying about the kingdom."

Caelyn nodded. She still was not convinced that would be best for Brynte, but the thought of having her mother back dulled the concern.

"Good girl," Rhoeo patted her shoulder, "now why don't you have your dinner? It's cold already."

Chapter 65

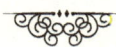

"**G**et out! Now!"

Bry gave Lawr a rough shove through the door and slammed it closed after him.

"Bry!" Lawr called through the door, his voice echoing in the still dull headache that had not dissipated since…

Damn it, Shad…

Lawr swallowed hard and turned away from the door as he heard Bry stomping away inside. He sniffed and wiped his already red-rimmed eyes as he trudged on.

He fought to keep his shoulders from slouching as he walked, even if it was only around the castle staff.

Lawr headed toward Klaas and Eleanora's chambers. He was losing the battle of keeping his shoulders from shaking and tears from flowing as he reached their door.

He knocked and entered without waiting for an answer.

On the couch of the main room, Klaas held a sobbing Eleanora and sniffling Stori.

Lawr studied the man's pinched face. Klaas looked as stoic as always at first glance. After a moment of study though, Lawr could tell the older man was using every facial muscle to keep his own tears from escaping.

Lawr exchanged a glance with the man and moved to sit beside Stori and let her lean on him.

"How's Bry?" Stori asked through sniffles, "He wouldn't talk to me when I tried."

Lawr nodded and swallowed, hoping to gain control of his voice.

"He wouldn't talk to me, either."

His voice cracked at the end and Lawr swallowed again.

He wished he did not have to be in the room.

Why did I think it was a good idea to come here?

He wanted to be in a far-off part of the castle. Somewhere he had never visited with Shad. Maybe then the kid's sweet laughter would stop bouncing off the walls in his mind.

"He shouldn't be alone," Klaas said. His wet voice did not break but still resonated with pain.

Lawr blinked a moment before realizing that Klaas was talking about Bry, not Shad.

The kid shouldn't have been alone, either...

"Eleanora." Klaas waited for the woman to collect herself.

Eleanora stood and wiped at the tears that continued uninterrupted.

"I'll make lunch," she said with a quivering voice, "I'd wager no one has eaten since..."

She did not finish the sentence, but everyone hung their heads at the unsaid.

"Well," she tried again with her focus on Stori, "Stori, you particularly can't be skipping so many meals."

Lawr hugged Stori closer as her lip trembled and her hand went to her belly. She nodded to Eleanora and hesitantly stood.

"I can help," Stori said, reaching for Eleanora's arm for the comfort of contact.

"I'll make lunch then, if you two," Eleanora trailed sorrowful eyes between Lawr and Klaas, "could bring Bry."

Lawr nodded, to himself more than to answer, as he stood and moved to the door without checking if Klaas was behind him.

Back in the corridor, Lawr retraced the path he had just taken without a thought. Instead, his mind focused on memories of Shad.

I should have gone with him...Or made him come back sooner.

Lawr frowned at the thoughts. He was of no use in battle and Shad rarely listened to him anyway. Distracting Shad on the battlefield could have had even worse results.

What's worse than this?

The question lingered in his mind. He could not think of anything.

"Lawr." Klaas's voice pulled Lawr from his thoughts.

Klaas stood at Bry's door as Lawr had continued walking passed it.

Klaas knocked and turned the handle. It was locked.

"Bry?" Lawr called.

Silence.

"Brynte Orian Godric, open the door. Now," Klaas ordered without a flutter of sorrow reaching his stern voice.

Shuffling from inside.

Lawr heard the lock click, and Klaas pushed the door open.

Bry glared at them with a puffy red face and ire drowning out the tears in his eyes.

Klaas entered and walked the short couple steps to rest a strong hand on Bry's shoulder.

Lawr hung back by the door as he watched and waited.

Klaas held Bry's gaze until the younger man dropped his head with a shudder.

"Everyone's downstairs," Lawr offered, "we're having lunch."

Bry's sharp eyes shot up and drilled into Lawr.

"I'm not hungry."

"Neither am I," Klaas stated, "Neither is Stori, but she has to eat for two anyway."

Bry's look softened at the mention of two, but it quickly returned to irritation.

"Either you come down willingly, or we drag you." Klaas beat Bry to speaking.

The redhead scoffed but did not move away from Klaas's grip on his shoulder.

"Like you could."

"We'd find a way," Lawr stated.

Bry held his gaze for a moment longer before relenting. He shrugged out from under Klaas's hand and moved to the door, pausing next to Lawr.

"Shad had to drag me before. He cheated you out of your coin."

Lawr's stomach tightened painfully at the mention of Shad.

"I know," he whispered, "he teased me about it later."

Bry kept moving until they reached the healer's chambers. He stopped outside the door and did not budge.

"How are they?" he finally asked.

Lawr sighed as he listened and could hear bustling and crying from the women inside. He struggled with what to say.

"Not good," Klaas answered instead, moving forward to push the door open.

Inside, they moved immediately to the kitchen. Eleanora stood at the stove, attempting to boil stock, but she was spending more time and attention trying to stop her tears. Stori was at the counter, chopping vegetables, but with the same trouble as Eleanora.

"Bry!"

Both women leaped to wrap their arms around the king as soon as they saw him.

Bry returned the hugs in mute silence.

Lawr could see Eleanora whispering in his ear but could not hear what was said. Bry just nodded.

Klaas moved to the stove to take over Eleanora's job. Lawr followed suit in chopping all the vegetables as the women steered Bry toward the table.

Lawr moved to add the vegetables to the stock. Klaas nodded the smallest motion. Lawr could see the stoic facade was threatening to crumble as the man tried to focus on the work.

Both continued to work in silence as Lawr too had to focus all his energy on maintaining his composure and not further distressing the rest of the room.

Finally, lunch was finished and Klaas and Lawr carried it to the table.

Compared to Eleanora's normal food, theirs was a sorrowful, overcooked mess. Only Stori made an effort to eat while the rest of the group contented to push the stew around in their bowls.

"Eat, Bry," Eleanora ordered in a soft, wet voice.

She pushed a slice of bread in front of both Bry and Stori.

Lawr watched Bry nibble on a small piece of the crust before they both returned to pushing the soup around.

Of course, Shad would be the one to know exactly what to say right now.

Lawr blinked at the thought as it threatened to bring the tears back.

Of all the people to lose…

He squeezed his eyes closed and clenched his fist under the table. He focused on the pain of his fingernails driving into his hand instead of the painful thoughts.

"Going to kill that damned assassin," Bry growled to himself as he continued glaring into his bowl.

Lawr watched the younger man.

"The soldiers there said it was someone else who…" Lawr trailed off, unable to complete his sentence, but still watching for Bry's reaction.

Bry sneered at him.

"They said 'maybe.' They can't tell what happened with all the confusion. He's an assassin, of course, he killed him. That's what he does."

Lawr doubted every word of that sentence. The soldiers had been certain the Ghost wasn't the one to kill Shad, but Bry was just not processing that yet.

Instead of arguing that point then, Lawr focused on keeping the assassin alive.

"You can't do anything to him yet."

Wild, angry green eyes flashed to him.

Lawr quickly finished, "I need to find out where Ali is first."

"That assassin had her, she's dead," Bry snapped.

"You don't know that any more than I do," Lawr growled back.

Don't get angry, he's just upset.

Lawr repeated the line to himself while willing Bry to leave the topic alone.

"We both know it!" Bry shouted.

Stori and Eleanora both jumped at the sudden shout.

"Bry," Stori reached to rest a hand on her husband's forearm, "that's not true."

Bry pulled his arm away.

"She's dead, and so is that assassin."

"No, she isn't." Lawr growled, holding Bry's gaze, "and you aren't going to do anything with that man until I talk to him."

"Both of you," Eleanora snapped, interrupting a growled retort from Bry, "calm down. The man hasn't even woken up yet. There's no telling if he ever will."

Lawr slumped at the thought.

Oh, Ali, how am I going to get you back, kid?

He spared a glance toward Bry to see the man lost in his own thoughts.

A knock at the door further interrupted the tension as everyone settled into silence and their own minds.

"I'll get it," Klaas grumbled when no one else moved.

Lawr watched the older man move passed the divider to answer the door, with further admiration.

I should be that put together in the future.

The rest of the table remained still with no one daring to broach any topic.

Klaas returned in a moment with a tanned young man in tow. Lawr thought the man looked vaguely familiar but could not place him.

"Ammon," Eleanora stood and wrapped the man in a hug, "oh, come in, sit down, honey. It's been so long."

"Thank you, ma'am."

Ammon took an empty seat across from Bry.

Lawr observed the token red-rimmed eyes on the man that adorned everyone else at the table and decided he must be a friend.

"Why are you here?" Bry growled.

Ammon held his glare for a moment.

"Figured anyone with sense would come to see Eleanora and Klaas," he answered as he accepted a bowl of soup from Eleanora but made no move to eat.

"You should have been with him." Bry leveled the accusation with poison in his voice.

Ammon returned the glare in silence a moment before speaking.

"Don't give me that shit. Shad was a damned good fighter and didn't need babysitting."

Bry slammed his fist against the table again.

"He needed someone to watch his back!"

Ammon continued to glare before he stood up and turned to leave.

"Stay," Klaas ordered, reaching out a hand to grab the man's arm.

"Bry," Klaas turned to Bry as some of the emotion held behind a crumbling mask slipped into his voice, "don't."

Bry hung his head and held it in his hands. Ammon returned to his seat and the lunch continued to not be eaten in silence.

CHAPTER 66

Atanas tried to hide his mirth as he pretended to listen to Duqa prattle on for the umpteenth time about his troubles in Sentre and how much the Sverre and Dain duo had stanched his fun with the Wolf kids.

"You know they were only doing their jobs, and I would not have approved of your hindering the Wolves unnecessarily."

Atanas stated with a vague hope he could mask his amusement with the reprimand.

"But, their hands, that one boy and girl, they *needed* their hands broken. Nothing unnecessary about it," Duqa continued, undeterred.

Atanas sighed and returned to filling out a form detailing the need for the assassination of one of the Tescan Counsel who had been a particular hindrance.

I should have told Dain this was his next mission while he was here.

Atanas tapped his chin with annoyance at the thought. He was as irritated with himself for not thinking of it at the time. But he had been mad at Dain for deciding to switch sides in the battle.

He grimaced at the memory. The reason Dain had provided was as weak as Terranian Vis, but he had kept to his story and stated Sverre was already acting on the change.

Nothing for it now, but when Sverre gets back…

Atanas smiled at the thought.

Duqa will be happy at least.

Duqa continued rattling on about the Wolves and his dislike of the assassins. He only paused when Echo entered to relay a message about the

Nomads being defeated in Medius.

Atanas clenched his fists, snapping his pen, at the news.

"Those useless slobs. And Sverre."

Atanas growled. He did not doubt that his operative's actions had played a significant part in the Nomads' defeat.

He dismissed Echo with a wave as he took in the mess his broken pen had made.

Duqa had quit his ranting to block the silent man's exit as he continued pestering one of his favorite people to torment.

"Duqa, let him go."

Atanas finally interrupted when Duqa's noisy antics of tormenting the man started to grow on his nerves.

"Oh, but can't I just—"

"Duqa." Atanas cut off the plea with a sharp look.

Echo took the opening to slip quietly out of the room.

The half-cyborg pouted in rare silence in the back of the room, only grumbling a few complaints every so often.

A low trill filled the room and Atanas moved quickly to grab the ringing AaD before Duqa could pounce on it.

"Off."

Atanas ordered Duqa, who was leaning across the desk while trying to grab the device.

"Aww," Duqa whined a pathetic sound before he fell to sprawl dramatically across the floor with a semblance halfway between a child throwing a tantrum and a kicked dog.

"Not a word."

Atanas ignored the antics as he looked at who was calling. A smile twisted the corner of his mouth.

"Ah, Thacea."

He answered the call with a curt 'what' that did not match his smile.

"Atanas, I have good news from Sentre," Thacea started.

"Really?" Atanas questioned before the sultry voice could continue, "Because I have just had news that the Nomads failed."

"Oh, they did. Magnificently," Thacea returned, her accent nestling each word spoken, "But they managed to accomplish the objective anyway. The city is divided."

"That is decent news, but not—"

"That isn't all," Thacea interrupted.

Atanas fought against his smile. The woman was the only person who would dare interrupt him and get away with it. Duqa would too, but never intentionally and certainly not with such a teasing tone.

"Go on," Atanas said.

"The Nomads or the Wolves, one of them managed to kill the king's best friend. The crown is vulnerable, to say the least. All of the king's inner circle is in mourning."

"And the girl?"

"The princess?" Thacea's voice held a mirthful laugh. "A silly little girl. She'll do as I tell her."

"Rhoeo Thacea, you are a wonder to behold."

"I am." Thacea's voice held a smile as she continued, "Everything here is in position as you wanted it and ready for the next steps…Except Sverre."

"Sverre!?"

Duqa jumped to latch his hands on the top of the desk and rest his chin on them with an expression of pure glee.

Atanas frowned. "What of Sverre? He missed a check-in. Dain as well."

Atanas continued to frown. Sverre missed check-ins all the time, but Dain did not.

Thacea purred a hum.

"He's out of commission. Perhaps permanently."

"NO!" Duqa wailed, "I'm the one who gets to take him out of commission! You promised."

"Duqa, quiet," Atanas snapped before turning back to the AaD, "What happened?"

"I'm not sure."

Thacea's voice betrayed how much it irritated her not to have an answer.

"It appears as though he was attacked by a Shade. And it wasn't the one I have before you ask. The king is under the impression Sverre is responsible for his Shade-wraith friend's death."

"That could be problematic." Atanas glared into space.

This will be a major problem…

"It won't halt the plan, but it will be an issue," Thacea offered.

Atanas growled at the inconvenience. He did not have any other operatives who could easily complete Sverre's mission. But Sverre had always been in a league of his own compared to others.

"What of Dain?" Atanas asked.

He pulled out his tracking system. Dain's chip was still moving.

"Don't know," Thacea answered, "Could be dead, I haven't seen him."

"He's still moving, Or at least his body is."

Thacea hummed again, "Until the plan is complete, I'm tied to the bratty little princess here. I'm afraid if you want him found, you'll have to rely on someone else."

Atanas glared at the device that showed the general location of the sniper. Still in Sentre, but he could not tell exactly where.

"Stay on your mission," Atanas decided after a moment, "I'll send someone else for Dain. And as much as you can without sacrificing your cover, keep Sverre alive. I'll want him back."

"Yes, sir. That shouldn't be a problem."

"Anything else to report?" Atanas waited.

"That's all here."

Atanas nodded to himself and hung up.

"You promised I could have him," Duqa whined from his spot at the edge of the desk.

"Get your paws off my desk," Atanas said as he set the AaD down, "We'll see what is left for you when we get our assassins back."

To Be Continued...

If you enjoyed this book, please leave a brief Amazon review
Thanks